Thomas Wetherald, Marcus T. C. Gould

Sermons Delivered

at Washington, Baltimore, Annapolis, Philadelphia, Wilmington, New York

Thomas Wetherald, Marcus T. C. Gould

Sermons Delivered
at Washington, Baltimore, Annapolis, Philadelphia, Wilmington, New York

ISBN/EAN: 9783337291853

Printed in Europe, USA, Canada, Australia, Japan

Cover: Foto ©Andreas Hilbeck / pixelio.de

More available books at **www.hansebooks.com**

SERMONS

THOMAS WETHERALD,

DELIVERED AT

WASHINGTON, BALTIMORE, ANNAPOLIS, PHILADELPHIA
WILMINGTON, NEW YORK;

TAKEN IN SHORT HAND BY T. C. GOULD.

REPUBLISHED BY HIS NEPHEWS,

THOMAS BAYNES, Baltimore; **WM. FERRIS**, Wilmington, Del.

————◦●◦————

Baltimore:
PRINTED BY JAMES YOUNG,
President First Branch City Council
1864.

SERMON I.

DELIVERED AT THE STATE HOUSE AT ANNAPOLIS, 8th OF FIRST MONTH, 182-

The most popular institutions of human wisdom have carried in themselves, the seeds of their own destruction, and the emblems of their own imbecility and consequent ruin. The glory of Rome is fallen—Greece is ruined, and thou whole Palestina, art dissolved. The continent of Europe is in confusion; and what reason have we to conclude, that the seeds of our own destruction are not sown also. The human body has been in all ages subject to variation and change; and in all ages, mankind having fulfilled their course have returned to their native dust. It is an examination not unworthy a rational being to see what causes have produced these effects. I apprehend that under all these circumstances, and in all these cases, it has been a total dereliction of the principles which brought those nations into eminence, that has produced their ruin: And hence the necessity of referring to first principles. I am not about to direct any of you in matters of religion, but to the experience of ages that have past, and to our own individual experience.

When luxury and pride were introduced into Rome, that power which had brought her into eminence became enervated; discords and dissentions were introduced, and hence was produced a separation from the source of purity, and also from the source of power. It was this which caused whole Palestina to be dissolved. And this may become a lesson to us, not only as individuals, but as members of civil society, and as members of religious associations; for in any of these, where purity gives way to impurity, where any of

4

those passions which corrode the human heart, gain the ascendency over the soul and relative virtues, here the seeds of corruption that mar domestic, social, civil and everlasting happiness, are brought into action, generate and ripen ; and this renders it necessary for us, in a subject of so much consequence as that in which the salvation of our souls is allowed to be involved, to become thinking beings ; and not to place our dependence upon the dogmas of men—upon systems built up and imbibed by education and tradition. The religion of forms and education is not the religion of our own experience ; it is not the religion of conviction ; but it is a religion imbibed while our minds are weak—it is a religion which we receive as imitative creatures, and not as reflecting ones. But if we ever come to experience the power of that religion which leads unto salvation, it must be the religion of conviction, by a revelation immediately from heaven. I am aware that this is a ground which has long been disputed —I am aware also, that the generality of professors, of the christian name, have denied the idea of immediate revelation to man in the present day ; and they have concluded that all the revelation which we are to receive is contained in the Scriptures of truth, which have been accordingly, though corruptly, dignified with the title of the word of God ; and the rule of faith and practice.

Now the Scriptures are not the word of God, neither are they the rule of faith and practice ; for the Scriptures declare, that the Word was in the beginning, but the Scriptures were not till Moses. "In the beginning was the word and the word was with God and the word was God. The same was in the beginning with God. And the word was made flesh and dwelt among us (said the Apostle) and we beheld his glory as of the only begotten of the Father, full of grace and truth." Now that which was word in the beginning, remains to be word in the present day, and also the rule of faith and practice.

Religion, I apprehend, may be divided into two kinds, viz : That religion which proceeds from an emanation, or revelation of the power of God, immediately upon the mind of each individual of the human family; and secondly, the religion of the Bible. The latter has been generally adopted —and what have been the fruits which it has produced? They are obvious to every reflecting mind. We see that out of the religions now extant there have arisen contention, confusion, hatred, envy and a variety of evil passions, among all the different classes and denominations, who are professors of the christian name. Yet all these professors have been governed by the Scriptures as their rule of faith and practice. Their doctrines have been supported by inferences therefrom; and they all justify their various discordant proceedings from this source: and in the high profession of religion, with which the world abounds, it is equally obvious that wickedness has increased in proportion to the increase of this religion in the land. There has been a great increase of religious profession within my recollection; and we must acknowledge, that instead of a decrease of wickedness, it has been found to increase in regular proportion—and there is no effect without a cause. It will therefore be well to examine a little into the causes which have produced these effects.

It has been considered as an essential of the christian religion that mankind should fulfil a variety of rites and ceremonies, better adapted to the legal dispensation than to that which is spiritual. Baptism, by water, has been imposed upon us; and with it there has been another symbol, another type; that of partaking the bread and wine as an emblem of Christ's death till he come. We have been led into a great variety of performances, which have been called public worship; and there has been a great deal of preaching, praying and singing: And to what do these things lead? To a nominal belief in those things which are declared to be mysterious and cannot be understood; but certain opinions, and doctrines, and dogmas of men, have been proposed; and it is required that we should subscribe to things unbecoming rational beings.

I want it to be impressed on each of our minds, that opinions are not religion, and that declamation is not gospel.

These dogmas which we cannot understand, we can never believe I have never been able to believe any thing of which I could not form an idea. We may have opinions and prejudices, and may adopt this or that position in which we have been educated; but this cannot give to a being, saving, operative faith—a faith which will overcome the world, or any one evil propensity or any one proposition which we cannot understand—this is an absurdity, it is an impossibility.

I believe that baptism is essential to the soul's salvation—I believe it is necessary to partake of the body of Christ—I believe there are three who bear record in heaven, and that these three are one—I believe that none are saved out of the pale of the holy Catholic Church. I believe with another society in God the Father, Almighty, Maker of heaven and earth, and in Jesus Christ his only son, our Lord; who was conceived of the Holy Ghost, born of the Virgin Mary, suffered under Pontius Pilate, was crucified, dead, and buried. But that He descended into Hell I dare not believe, because he declared unto the thief on the cross, this day wilt thou be with me in Paradise. I believe in the communion of saints, the forgiveness of sins, and the life everlasting. And I apprehend that I could subscribe to almost all that is called doctrine by the Christian churches: but this has been subscribed to by drunkards, thieves, whoremongers, and the worst of men; hence there is nothing in it of a saving nature—the greatest infidel may declare that he believes all these things, and still remain an alien from the commonwealth of Israel, having no hope, and he living without God in the world. Therefore, it is necessary for us to take another view of the subject, beside that of giving our assent to the popular doctrine of men being saved by this nominal belief. Now baptism, whereby many gain admission, and are initiated into those churches of which they are members, is the baptism of John; this was not only a type of the Gospel, but a preparatory dispensation. The design was to lead the minds to something more spiritual than that which came by Moses—that law which had made nothing perfect.

The law made nothing perfect, but the bringing in of a better hope did, by which we draw nigh unto God. And John, who was the minister of that baptism—that preparatory operation, declared that it should not continue; for when speaking of Christ, he said, he shall increase, but I shall decrease; and he also made a perfect declaration of his mission and office when he said, I am the voice of one crying in the wilderness, prepare the way of the Lord, as said the prophet Esaias. It was a preparatory work, to break down the partition walls of prejudice, and to enable the Jews to advance to a more spiritual dispensation. I am the voice of one crying in the wilderness, prepare ye the way; and when this way is prepared and the paths made straight, the inevitable consequence is, that every valley shall be exalted, and every mountain and hill shall be brought low: the crooked made straight, and the rough smooth. Now what are we to understand by this regulation of the hills and valleys, by which all are to be brought to their proper level. It has an unequivocal allusion to the inequality of the human mind, which is as various as the faces which we wear. Each disposition requires a different kind of baptism. Each power of the human mind requires to be regulated and brought into consonance with the spirit of divine truth. The mountains here spoken of, the rough and crooked places, have allusion to those passions and dispositions, which are distinguished by pride, highmindedness, ambition, fierceness, cruelty, revenge, &c. These soar above the witness for God in the soul, above the word of God and the rule of faith and practice. These must come under the baptism testified of by the forerunner of Christ, who also said, "I baptise with water: but there standeth one among you, whom ye know not. He it is who coming after me, is preferred before me, whose shoes latchet I am not worthy to unloose, he shall baptise you with the Holy Ghost and with fire: whose fan is in his hand, and he will thoroughly purge his floor and gather his wheat into the garner: but he will burn up the chaff with unquenchable fire." There are none of us, who have not experienced the operation of this very baptism.

Some of us may be compared to mountains, who have lifted our spirits up over the witness for God ; these have oftentimes felt distress, trouble and confusion, because they have given way and submitted to the feeling and ebulitions of their temper, and have thereby brought themselves under the baptism of the Holy Ghost. Are there not many of us who have been brought under feelings of sorrow, confusion, trouble, despair, horror and every feeling of torment? And this is symbolical of that place of punishment, commonly described as a lake burning with fire and brimstone, into which the wicked are turned, and punished with the devil and his angels. This will do to frighten children ; but we are not afraid of their consuming one immortal soul. It may be an instructive allegory, of a spiritual punishment adapted to the nature of the spirit. Such feelings as are of a spiritual nature, must consist in joy, sorrow, peace or woe ; and the punishment for wickedness being of a spiritual and intellectual nature, is often experienced while clothed upon with mortality. Not being willing to submit to this baptism, we bring trouble, sorrow and confusion upon us for evil, and abide there till unfeigned repentance not to be repented of, work our forgiveness ; then shall we experience the joy and consolation, and know that there is no joy equal to the joy of God's salvation in the soul. Many of us, who have experienced the power of this salvation, have, in some proportion, been redeemed from our evil propensities, and restored to the state in which we were first created, and into which we must eventually return, because in this way only can we be renewed up into the divine likeness of God, by the spirit of Christ and the operation of the Holy Ghost brought forth ; and thus we shall know a birth of Christ—we shall know that he is come in our flesh—we shall experience this birth, and know that he has appeared, not only in Jerusalem, and among the Jews, but that he has appeared, and remains to be Christ manifested in your flesh, which is the power of God unto salvation, to every one who believe, whether Jew or Gentile. There are others who are desponding, and ready to despair, and who have adopted the language, "a Saviour or I die, a Redeemer or I perish." The passions of these are weak ; they have more need of a cup of consolation, than of a reproof for evil—the minds of these are comforted—there is a stay, and this power becomes a stay and a staff: And thus it is that the valleys are exalted to a proper level ; the rough, the haughty, and the fierce, are reduced ; and those who are despairing, are raised into firmness—the crooked and perverse dispositions become straight, and the rough places smooth. And hence the necessary and irrevocable effect of all this purifying operation, will be that these well regulated minds will be filled with the knowledge of the Lord, as the waters cover the sea. Now this is a baptism which cleanses the affections, rectifies the passions, and crucifies the lusts. This baptism is of a spiritual nature, and there is none other essential to our salvation. It is written, "there is one Lord, one faith, one baptism, one God and Father of all, who is above all, and through all, and in you all." And it is this baptism alone which can introduce you into the one true, saving and living faith ; for without this experience of the power of God operating upon the mind, we never can come into possession of that faith which overcometh the world. For it is written, "And this is the victory that overcometh the world, even our faith. Who is it that overcometh the world, but he that believeth that Jesus is the son of God? This is he that came by water and blood, even Jesus Christ ; not by water only, but by water and blood : and it is the spirit that beareth witness, because the spirit is truth."

That faith which overcometh the world is of a spiritual nature, but that faith which is overcome by the world is that spurious faith received by education and tradition, and stands in opinions, and leads to the performance of external rituals ; but never regulates the passions or lusts : And hence, notwithstanding the high professions of this religion, it may be no better than that of the Jews who betrayed Christ in his outward manifestations, and which crucifies him in his inward and spiritual appearance, in which he comes a second time without sin unto salvation, and puts him to open shame. Therefore, the first step in religion is baptism ; and as we attend to this, which is the ministration of condemnation, glorious in its season, it leads not to believe that which we cannot understand, or to attend to those matters which are daily preached unto us. We are often informed that there are matters in religion which we cannot understand ; but still we must believe it ; this is a palpable absurdity. But when we come under the influence of this faith, though it be small as a grain of mustard seed, if we say unto any mountain of opposition between us and our God—any difficulty which may interfere, if we say unto them, be ye removed and cast into the sea, they will obey.

Now this faith that works by love, proceeds immediately from the operation of the spirit of God upon our spirits ; and here is communion between God and man—here is a link formed which unites man with the divinity. We are not mere animals—we are not placed here to eat and drink, and to pass away as the dreams of a night vision. There awaits us a more noble and dignified destiny, even to be united to our God, and when unclothed of mortality, to be received, and become partakers of the joys of heaven, and the glories of eternity in all their fulness. Here we can enjoy but a foretaste—there, all will be full and complete.

Now this faith has a progressive growth ; therefore, we must first become babes—we must be willing to become fools —we must be willing to attend to small manifestations of the Kingdom of Heaven, which may be compared to a grain of mustard seed. Are we to look at a great distance and beyond the grave? Christ told his followers, "the Kingdom of Heaven is within you ;" and there only ought we to look for his appearing ; and there experience his power, and there know that beautiful and prophetic declaration fulfilled. "For unto us a child is born, unto us a son is given, and the government shall be upon his shoulders ; and his name shall be called wonderful, counsellor, the Mighty God, the everlasting Father, the Prince of Peace. Of the increase of his government and peace there shall be no end; upon the throne of David, and upon the Kingdom to order it, and to estab-

lish it with Judgment and with Justice, from henceforth
even for ever."

This Kingdom of Heaven has been likened to a grain of
mustard seed, which a man took and sowed in the field—
which if it is cultivated will grow, and though the smallest
of seeds, will produce one of the greatest of herbs, so that
the fowls of the air may lodge in its branches—and these
fowls may be compared to the vain imaginations of the human mind.

Again, the Kingdom of Heaven has been likened to a little
leaven which was put into meal till the whole was leavened.
We all know the nature of meal, and many of us know the
nature of leaven. In meal there is no opposition—it is passive under the operation ; and therefore the leaven, though
small in quantity, finding no opposition to overcome, soon
brings the whole into its own likeness. Such is the operation of the spirit of God, the grace of God, the baptism of
the holy Ghost (or by whatever name you may call it) though
weak in its first appearance, if attended to, the power of
opposition will be directed from the mind ; and it will grow
stronger and stronger in the divine life till God shall be all
in all. And this is the very extent, to bring us into a heavenly state, and beget a new heart and a new mind, through
the operation of a living faith, which will overcome this corrupt influence into which nations and men have fallen. And
when we come under the influence of this faith, then we shall
come to know what it is to eat the flesh of the son of man
and to drink his blood ; not to take the bread and wine as
symbolical of that which is to come, for in so doing we deny
the coming of Christ in the flesh, and content ourselves in
the use of those things which perish in the using.

Baptism, with water, may cleanse from the filth of the
flesh ; and bread and wine may nourish the body ; but all
the waters of the sea can never cleanse the soul of one sin,
and all the bread and wine can never nourish up the soul to
eternal life. We now need none of these types and figures
and carnal rites and ceremonies. We do not want to go
back to former dispensations, but to come more fully to that

of which we make a profession, and to experience its regenerative effects. And what is the blood of Christ? It is the life. I have a hope in Christ, and a hope in salvation through him, but not in the unparalleled act of malevolence in the Jews; I have no hope of salvation in any act of wickedness—it is in his life, and in the power of his resurrection. His death being a legal offering under the law, by which they fulfilled and finished their charter, which had been broken and abrogated, it is a beautiful type of the substance into which we should come. The blood is the life, the circulating medium which gives vitality to the whole system. When the life of Christ, of holiness and obedience to our heavenly Father, comes to rule and reign in us, we shall be supported by the life of Christ. Then we shall know what it is to drink his blood, and to have our souls nourished thereby into eternal life. Now, in what does the blood circulate? Does it circulate in the body? So the life of Christ as it circulates in the soul, brings all our angry passions and perverse dispositions into accordance with its own nature. There is one kind of flesh of men, another of beasts, another of fishes, said the Apostle. Now as we come under the influence of any of these particular propensities, we may be considered as partakers of their flesh or nature, for this is equally emblematical and symbolical as that of Christ. Though I lead the life of a beast under the influence of beastial passions, and debase myself, yet I partake not of their flesh—I have still the form, nature and flesh of a man; if I partake of the nature of Christ, though I continue in this mortal body, yet being regenerated and born again I am not ashamed to call such brethren, for he was begotten of God and born of the virgin; and the same power brought forth in us in the same virgin purity, we shall become partakers of the same nature, because we are of the same seed, and hence grow from strength to strength, from stature to stature, and we shall be brought out of the bondage of sin and corruption, into the glorious liberty of the sons and daughters of God. The fundamental power of these operations, baptism, brings living faith and holy confidence, unshaken love. Now this faith, which works by love to the purifying of the heart, has nothing which is not essential to salvation : no dogmas which are incomprehensible ; neither are we called on to believe in the dogmas of any sect or society of the various divisions which we meet with in the world ; which, instead of giving an united appearance, has caused us to split and divide, so that even in the present day, christendom, so called, is more like the beasts with many heads and horns smiting against one another, than like the Lamb's wife, as the church is represented to be, clothed in pure and white linen, which is the righteousness of the saints. Is it the design, or was it ever the design, that mankind should be thus split and divided ? No, it never has arisen from the gospel dispensation, but from a dereliction of those first principles which lead to obedience to its manifestations. If we cast our eyes on this christian world, thus divided and separated from the first cause of all wisdom and knowledge, we may discover that we have assumed unto ourselves the power of studying, and lastly have delegated that power to others. We have appointed unto ourselves ministers and professors of the Gospel, and preachers of righteousness. These must preach in accordance with our own views. Here a door is opened which has produced incalculable mischief among men ; for having chosen our own dogmas, opinions and ceremonies, and having determined to have these preach-ed, we have imbued their minds with the dogmas which we have chosen, and have not only called them, but have remu-nerated them for their labors, contrary to every part of the Gospel, which says, "freely ye receive, freely give." Here is introduced the very worst of passions, the love of money, which the Apostle Paul calls the root of all evil ; corrupting that ministry which ought to be pure as emanating from God. Now while this wordly interest prevails among those who are called ministers of the Gospel, the consequent cor-ruption immediately tends to our ruin. The numbers of jarring religious sects will grow, and the seeds of discord will generate, till pure religion, and undefiled before God and the Father, is lost among us. For as this religion has increased wickedness has increased in the same ratio. This is a mournful view of the subject; but it is a view which we must necessarily take if we reflect upon it.

By thus encouraging a mercenary priesthood, we never need expect them to preach the gospel other than in accordance with our own views, or the views of the particular society for whom they are chosen to preach. While these individuals are receiving their one, two, or three thousand dollars a year, will they speak the truth plainly and explicitly? I fear many of them would not. And what is the religion preached by these? Is it to bring to the teaching of him who is minister of the sanctuary and true tabernacle? No verily. They deny the very existence of revelation—they tell us that revelation has ceased, and that all revelation is contained in the scriptures of truth, called the Bible. They declare themselves to be the vicegerants of God, and that unto them is committed the explanation of that word which is essential to salvation. Thus they become mediators between God and man; but I know of no mediator between God and man, save Christ Jesus—neither do I believe that there is any other mediatorial power by which we can be brought into communion and union with God. This mediatorial office is carried on in each of us by faith and baptism; for these are the ground-work of all true religion, and there is one Lord, one faith, and one baptism; and when baptised into one true and living faith, we are brought into the nature of our Lord, our God and "Father of all, who is above all, and through all, and in you all." But now instead of this, spurious religion is causing divisions and dissensions—splitting mankind into a thousand sects and parties, instead of regulating the affections, and crucifying the passions and lusts, and bringing down the vain mind, as lofty mountains to their true level, thus binding us together in a bundle of love. There is no interested motive, but man becomes united to his fellow man, so that God is above all, and through all, and in you all. We shall then have known what it is to experience that declaration fulfilled, "There was war in heaven: Michael and his angels fought against the dragon; and the dragon fought and his angels, and prevailed not; neither was their place found any more in heaven."

Now I want it to be remembered that the Kingdom of heaven is within you. Then righteousness must become predominant, and rule and reign in us, and govern by its own laws. There was never any one individual prince who governed by the laws of another nation; but each one has laws of his own, adapted to the circumstances of those whom he governs. And should he in whom dwells all knowledge and wisdom—from whom emanates all good and all power, be governed by laws dictated by man, or by wisdom which is corrupt. Now "there was war in heaven: Michael and his angels fought against the dragon; and the dragon fought and his angels, and prevailed not, neither was their place found any more in heaven."

And what are these angels? They are all formed on the platform of Homer and Milton. We have been led to look upon them as certain external beings: as women with wings have passed for angels. What are these angels? They are the heavenly dispositions—they are all ministering spirits, sent forth to minister unto those who shall become heirs of salvation by a life of obedience and adherence to those dispositions; cherish them, and they become the angels of God, ministering to them who are heirs of salvation. "He maketh his angels spirits: his ministers a flaming fire." But on the contrary if we pervert this disposition, the opposite will take possession of the mind and become our governors. These are the angels which will torment us as certainly; every virtuous disposition and practice will become a comfort to the mind, and every evil disposition a curse.

Now if the angel of love takes possession of the mind, and even under the former dispensation this was essential. Here O Israel, love the Lord your God, and serve him with all your heart, and with all your soul, and mind, and strength. This saith Jesus Christ, is the first and great commandment—"thou shalt love the Lord thy God with all thy heart, thou shalt love thy neighbor as thyself. On these two commandments, hang all the law and the prophets." God has said I will dwell in them : and here is a near unity and communion ; and when the angel of love takes posses- sion of the mind and casts out its opposite, and though this enemy may struggle severely, and may desire to indulge in hatred and malevolence, and enmity of the mind, yet if the spirit of love be obeyed steadily, it will cast out its opposite and adversary. The mind being under the influence of love, will cast out a number of evils, and put an end to all wars and fightings among nations, dissentions in neighborhoods, and squabbles in families. No man ever fought from love ; no nation ever fought from love ; no man in his own family ever encouraged squabbles from a principle of love. When love becomes predominant in the mind, hatred must be cast out, for they are as opposite as light and darkness, heaven and hell. And thus, when the angel of love casts out the devil of hatred ; and the angel of mercy, the devil of cruelty ; the angel of temperance, the devil of intemper- ance ; and the angel of hope, the devil of despair ; and the angel of faith, the devil of infidelity—when every heavenly disposition comes to take possession of the mind, darkness and all its angels every thing impure and un- holy will be no more found in heaven. This is the end of true religion ; and when the mind is brought under the influence of this regulating principle, where is the ne- cessity of ministers of man's ordination ; seeing that all those who submit to this baptism of the spirit, come under the faith to the purifying of the soul, a witness for Christ, a minister of Christ. All that a minister can do for his breth- ren, is, to call them to this self-same gospel, which will en- able them to testify what their ears have heard, their eyes seen, and their hands handled, of the good word of life and power of the world to come.

Election is not a foreordination from the foundation of the world. It is an absurdity to believe, that some of the hu- man family are doomed from eternity to misery, and others to sing praises in endless bliss. It is an absurdity and almost amounts to blasphemy. All men are placed in a situation, and endowed with a capability of arising into the state of the elect, or of descending into a state of reprobation.

Now as we attend to the little leaven it will leaven the whole lump, and the spirit will grow stronger and stronger by cultivation: and as we attend to this, we shall come more and more under its influence, and these heavenly dispositions will become more and more our governors. And by attending thereunto we shall become elected, for the election stands not in any thing but in our own obedience. All souls are mine, saith the Lord. As the soul of the master, so is the soul of the servant, as the soul of the mistress so is the soul of the hand maid.

And therefore we have reason to believe from this, that the gift is universally bestowed. But we have other evidences in the Scriptures, that election is not a foreordination of God. This would make him unjust, which is contrary to all the attributes of divinity with which we are acquainted. But as we attend to this manifestation, though small at first, it will grow in us and increase: And as has been observed, it will grow till it overcome all opposition, and becomes the greatest of herbs, so that every opposite disposition will lodge in the branches; and we shall become heirs of God, and joint heirs with Christ, through obedience to the manifestation wherewith we have been favored from God. But on the contrary, if we disregard the law written in the heart, and run counter to the intimations of Divine love, we shall involve ourselves in the guilt and misery of reprobation. I want this to be impressed upon all our minds, that if we do not come under the influence of this divine principle, and if we "will not have this man to rule over us," but remain under the influence of our own passions and unsubdued lusts—this little leaven, this divine manifestation, this baptism of the Holy Ghost, will gradually become weaker and weaker, and our hearts more and more hardened, till we experience a loss of its power, and we shall become ready to wound and inflict injury, with impunity, upon our brother without cause, and we shall thus

2

become reprobates in every thought, word and action. This is the true ground of election and reprobation ; and it is not from a foreordination from the foundation of the world. Those therefore who attend to this manifestation, will be-become holy, apostolic and catholic—they will be catholic in spirit, catholic in principle, and holy in practice ; and these can say, "I believe in God the Father Almighty, maker of heaven and earth : and in Jesus Christ his only Son, our Lord ; who was conceived by the Holy Ghost, born of the Virgin Mary," &c., because they have experienced that it took place not only formerly, but believe that he is con-ceived of the Holy Ghost, and born and brought forth in virgin purity, and that it is he that yet suffers under Pon-tius Pilate, as we become willing to resign the heavenly dis-positions by yielding to the domination of opposite passions.

Therefore I want us to be individually careful lest we bring ourselves under the punishment due unto sin, for I presume that, many things proscribed by men are not unlaw-ful.; nay, are not many things prescribed by man, sinful ? There is a great variety of things, which are considered commendable among men which are atrociously sinful. Has not this been the case within the times which many of us can recollect ? Has it not exalted the greatest enemies of mankind to worldly honor and glory, even the blood thirsty warrior, and a variety of others under the influence of the infernal passions, their pride and ambition ? There have been hosts of these devils who have been enemies of the human mind. In that quarter of the world from which I came, they have spread ruin and destruction ; nay, every evil of which we can conceive. Women have been made widows, and children fatherless, the ruin of civil societies, and the downfall of nations have been produced by the same, and yet these have been stamped with the name of glorious ; but in the eye of that wisdom which is pure and holy, that which is above the wisdom of man, and which is easily recognized without outward preaching, and confers that blessing which will unite us under the government of divine wisdom, and lead us certainly into the gospel dispensation, this is exceedingly wicked.

These heavenly virtues emanate from God: whereas, every thought of the imagination of the worldly minded, the *literal* believer, if suffered to be engendered in their minds, prompts to join in religious society. It becomes almost necessary for an individual to become a member of some religious society, that he may have a fair character in the world. Religion, notwithstanding all its corruption, is considered honorable. If a man be not a partaker in the rites and ceremonies of the day, he will scarcely pass for a Christian. But if he fulfill the rituals of any one of these various churches of the present day ; if he be zealous in the performance of public and family worship, so called ; if he gives liberally to the ministers, missionaries, bible societies, and other institutions which are characteristic, I hope, only of this age, he passes for a good Christian ; and in the view of thousands, he passes for a saint ; when perhaps his mind is under the influence of those vile passions which separate from the source of all purity, and from the enjoyment of heaven.

It is not a profession of religion, but the enjoyment of the peace of God, which constitutes Christians. This it is that has constituted Christians in all ages of the world, not only before Christ came in the flesh, but through all time ; for we have never been under any other dispensation—we were never Jews—we were always Gentiles, and we still remain to be Gentiles, and the law by which we always were, and always must be governed, is the law of God in the heart. And yet many are brought under these particular associations, under the influence of a religion which is part Jewish, part Christian, and part Pagan, a kind of heterogeneous commixture, which never leads any to the knowledge of God ; and we shall never come out of these prejudices and opinions till we begin for ourselves ; till we begin to be governed by our own experience ; till we read for ourselves the work of nature and of nature's. God. We remember that the Apostle wept much on a certain occasion, when he saw a book sealed with seven seals. But was it a bible? No, it was the hidden mystery of the kingdom of heaven, hid from the wise and prudent, and revealed unto babes.

And he wept much because no man was found able to open and read the book, neither to look therein. It is a truth that no man can open the book unto his fellow man, "for the things of God knoweth no man but the spirit of God." The rational man, can understand rational things; but it is the influence of the spirit of God, which alone can enable him to discern spiritual truths. "And one of the elders saith unto me, weep not: behold the lion of the tribe of Juda, the root of David, hath prevailed to open the book, and to loose the seals thereof:" and I rejoiced much; and the same lion of the tribe of Juda, the same manifestation of the power of God will open the mysteries of the Kingdom of heaven in our own souls, thus giving us to distinguish between truth and error. It is the word of a king, and where the word of the king is, there is power to overcome those things standing in opposition to his government.

Now there is one thing that spurious religion has introduced: I mean the observance of the Sabbath. Now what is the Sabbath? Is it to keep one day in seven in idleness? No; for I verily believe, that according to the present institution of the Sabbath, there is on this day more sin committed, than in all the other six, in which we labor for our support. This is obvious: there must therefore, be something else to constitute the Sabbath besides spending one day of the week in idleness. It is a state in which we must come to be like that which the Almighty experienced when he had finished the creation and found that all the works were good—He hallowed the seventh day and sanctified it. But there is no command for us to keep the Sabbath; there is no precept in the Scriptures, nor nothing which has been handed down to us that can be called a command, to keep the Sabbath. Neither is there any injunction in the Scriptures to keep the Sabbath. It was typical of that which was to come; but it is not till our works are finished that we are in this situation, regulated by the power of God, that we can keep the Sabbath and sanctify it. " Blow the trumpet Zion, sanctify a fast, call a solemn assembly: gather the people—let the bridgroom go forth of his chamber, and the bride out of her closet: let the priests, the ministers of the Lord, stand between the porch and the altar, and let them say, spare thy people, O Lord, and give not their heritage to reproach, that the heathen should rule over them: wherefore should they say among the people, where is their God."

What is a Sabbath? It is a state of rest in our minds; and in order to experience this state of rest, we must give up our own workings and prostrate all our affections—we must wait with resignation the power and will of the Lord, in whom is the fulness of all wisdom and knowledge. When we come to this state, we shall be prepared for that rest which remains for the people of God. It is not to keep one day in seven; for every day is a sabbath. It will not constitute every day devils and Sunday saints, whether we be engaged in our daily avocations, whether we walk by the way, whether we lie down or rise up, there will be a living concern in our minds to fulfill his righteousness—his righteous law, the law of Christ inwardly revealed; this is the daily and the interminable Sabbath which shall never end. And it is unto this state that all are called; and it was unto this state, it was designed that all should come. The election is within ourselves—we may choose or refuse. " Why will ye die, O house of Israel," said the prophet—life and death, good and evil are before you, therefore choose life and live ye.

When our minds are under the influence of this regulating principle, we come to the enjoyment of heaven—we come to experience a foretaste of immortality and eternal life. There is begotten in the soul through the operation of this light, an holy confidence, which all the powers of death, hell, and the grave can never prevail against. There will be no more doubting, fear, anxiety and despair in our souls—Our situation will be similar to that of the Apostle, when he was about to be offered up—at the time of his departure, when his time was near at hand, he said, "I have fought the good

fight, I have finished my course, I have kept the faith:
Henceforth there is laid up for me a crown of righteousness,
which the Lord, the righteous Judge, shall give me at that
day; and not to me only, but unto them also, that love the
appearing of our Lord and Saviour, Jesus Christ." When
the mind is brought under this regulating influence, under
that powerful baptising, which is the spirit of Christ, the
power of God unto salvation—they have not only this holy
confidence, but their life and conduct are regulated by it.
Preachers are led by it to be preachers in life and conversation, as well as in word and doctrine—setting a worthy example in all things; not as men making a high profession
of religion, and acting inconsistent with their profession;
but as faithful disciples laboring by example as well as precept to lead us into universal confidence and bonds of brother-
hood—thus all discussions would come to an end, and differences would no more abound among men ; but we should all
be united in one great family. This brings in a millennial
state, which has long been looked for by the Jews, very im-
properly to be brought about by some great miracle. But if
we ever come into that millennial state, we must know it by
obedience to this manifestation, which brings us into union
and communion with God, under the influence of those
angelic dispositions. This millennial state is now in the
world; and blessed be the name of Israel's God, there are
those who have experienced the enjoyment of it, and know
what it is to reign with Christ on earth : having come unto
God through the liberty of the Gospel ; not vainly expecting
to attain it by submitting to the priestly tyranny exercised
by man over his fellow men, for this results from a disposition at enmity with God, and stands as a wall of partition
between us and the life of Christ : And therefore seeing that
all men are capable of salvation, and that all men may come
equally under the influence of this divine principle, let us
be encourged to come unto that Teacher which can never be
removed into a corner. "Though the Lord shall give us the
bread of adversity and the waters of affliction, yet surely
our teacher shall not be removed into a corner, but our eyes

shall see our teacher, and we shall hear a voice saying, this is the way walk in it, when we turn to the right or left."

But my mind has been often grieved in seeing those who are well disposed, and who are endeavoring to come into a state in which their minds are brought under these convictions, and under condemnation; instead of abiding under them, and following their influence, which leadeth to a repentance that needeth not to be repented of; and instead of attending to that which passes in their own minds, they have gone and united themselves with some religious society; and instead of waiting for the finger of the divine instructor, to give direction, they have, under the feelings of those excitements, joined themselves to sects; and become very zealous in the performance of supposed religious duties, by which they have been led into various absurdities. In the land of my nativity strange extravagancies have appeared, jumping, dancing, and shouting, as though the God of heaven and earth could not hear the sighing of the poor and needy soul, without all this tumult and confusion. These absurdities have been a disgrace, and will continue to be a disgrace, in whatever society they may be practiced. God dwells with man, and he needs not all this outward show to cause him to hear us. He looks not to the position of the body, or to the form of words; but he searcheth the hearts, and trieth the reins of the children of men—he knows the inmost recesses of our thoughts before they are brought forth.

I have been instructed in the remembrance, and perhaps it may be instructive to you, to remember the situation of an eminent prophet, who was once placed alone, after he fled from the king, and had wandered in the wilderness for forty days and nights, he came to Mount Horeb, the mount of God. And he came thither and lodged there: And, behold the word of the Lord came to him, and said unto him, what doest thou here Elijah? And he said, I have been very jealous for the Lord God of Hosts: for the children of Israel have forsaken thy covenant, thrown down thine altars, and slain thy prophets with the sword; and I, even I only, am left; and they seek my life to take it away. And he said, go forth, and stand upon the mount before the Lord. And behold the Lord passed by, and a great and strong wind rent the mountains, and break in pieces the rocks, before the Lord ; but the Lord was not in the wind: And after the wind an earthquake ; but the Lord was not in the earth-quake : And after the earthquake a fire ; and the Lord was not in the fire : And after the fire a still small voice. And it was so, when Elijah heard it, that he wrapped his face in his mantle, and went out, and stood in the entering in of the cave : and behold, there came a voice unto him, and said what dost thou here Elijah ? Here was a calm—a quiet, and he had an opportunity to cast all his cares, and sorrows, and afflictions before his Almighty friend, and to receive as-surances of protection and comfort. They had thrown down the altars and slain the prophets with the sword, and he was the only one left, and they sought his life to take it away, but instead of being alone, he received the comfortable as-surance that there were yet seven thousand in Israel, all the knees which had not bowed unto Baal, and every mouth which hath not kissed him.

Now if we would wait till the whirlwind has passed by, till our minds, which are under condemnation have become calm, the light of God would bring life into our souls ; and we should experience a state of quietude, and a state of peace in which we could look as did Elijah formerly. We could cast all our cares, all our troubles and affections upon the bosom of our Almighty friend ; and then we should be able to receive a solemn assurance, that there are "seven thousand yet in Israel, all the knees which had not bowed unto Baal, and every mouth which hath not kissed him." Again, many of those who have been convicted for sin, have rushed into religious performances, like the horse into battle, and have not only been zealous in their families and in pub-lic, but have listened to the cry of those daughters of the horse leech, which are never satisfied with their abundance, but continue to cry give, give to support benevolent institutions, bible societies, missionary societies, and a variety of associa-tions of this kind, the object of which is stated to be the conversion of the heathen. But unto what are they converted—into the power of God which saveth the soul? No, these poor heathens are converted to the dogmas, opinions and ceremonies of those missionaries, or the societies to which they belong; and often into absurdities not inferior to their own. The missionaries who have been sent, have gone with great pomp and parade; and have endeavored to bring the heathen of a foreign land, into their particular views, dogmas, and doctrines. And I am verily afraid, that in so doing, they have been building, both for themselves and the heathen, upon a false foundation—making them two fold more the children of hell than they were before. For many of these beings are fully partakers of the divine blessing, that salvation which will really and substantially save. They have very just ideas of God—He is considered by them as a being who knows all things. He is all eye, and ear, and mind, and he understands all things. This was a description given by a native of your own forests, an Indian not long ago. Can there be a more definite idea given of the Deity, than that he sees all things, hears all things, knows all our minds, thoughts, words and actions? They not only believe all this, but they believe in the operation of the spirit upon the mind of man. When the good Indian dies, he will be happy, according to their views; and their views are many of them, not more absurd than ours—they are even less absurd in some respects, for they have not a fixed place for the souls of the wicked; neither have they a heaven filled like Mahomet's, with sensual enjoyments. Neither are they so far separated from the ideas of rectitude as we have been. And again; it is said, that one of these savages who visited a library in one of your cities, discovered a copy of the Scriptures in very elegant binding. He was told that it was the word of God. He saw another book, which was one of those commentaries, which have long darkened council, by words without knowledge. He was informed that it was an explanation of the word of God. The poor Indian said, white man's God, poor God, need so much explanation—Indian's God speak here, laying his hand on his heart. This shews that the Indians are not altogether ignorant of God. Yet we send missionaries to convert them from their superstitions, to our variety of dogmas, which are many of them, more superstitious than any thing which they have before known.

But with respect to these Bible societies, which are making such great exertion to send the scriptures to the heathen, as they pretend, without note or comment—whom do they commission to this office? They are missionaries who are like daughters of the horse leech, crying give, give. There are three things that are never satisfied; yea four things say not, it is enough: The grave, and the barren womb; the earth that is not filled with water; and the fire that saith not, it is enough. I have never heard of any of these societies being satisfied with gifts and donations. And can we believe that the gospel of Christ can be built on any thing which is so corrupt as the love of money, which is declared to be the root of all evil? And from whom is this money obtained? Is it from the righteous—from those who are willing to build up the Lord's house above the tops of the mountains, and above the hills, that all nations may flee unto it? Are not their subscriptions and donations received from the blood thirsty warrior, the oppressor of his brother, the drunkard, the whoremonger, the adulterer, and from those engaged in every species of evil? It is not virtue they are asking from them, it is money. And can we believe that the Lord's house is to be built up with materials so corruptible as these? No, verily; for the scriptures declare, that the vessels of the Lord's house are holy; and surely they are all holy, for "there shall in no wise enter into it whatsoever is impure or unholy, or worketh abomination, or maketh a lie." Therefore I want us all, individually, let our name and our profession be what they may, to examine these things for ourselves. I want you not to take my word with respect to any of these things, but I want you to bring this testimony, to the witness for God in your own consciences, that you may know whether these things are so or not; for the witness for God is placed there—I want you to come into obedience to it, and to experience the joy of God's salvation. If they are not so let them pass for what they are worth. I desire to Lord it over no man's conscience. I have no interested views or motives—I only seek your everlasting happiness; and therefore, I have spoken unto you with freedom, but I hope no more than becometh the gospel.

The root and ground of the ministry of the gospel, I apprehend, stands not in a legal knowledge of tongues and languages; but if we ever become members of the church of Christ; and if ever we become members of the gospel, it will not be by study; it will not be by human learning; for the natural man, can only understand the things of a man. All the knowledge that we can obtain, by the aid of the arts, sciences, and philosophy, with a knowledge of rhetoric, elocution and the elements of theology, so called, can never prepare, can never form or instruct one single solitary minister of the gospel. And there, if we ever come to be ministers of the gospel, in faith and unity, it must not be through literary knowledge, but by an education in the school of Christ. Knowing therefore, the terror of the Lord, for sin and disobedience, we persuade men to be reconciled to God. I well remember when my soul was in the depths of his judgments, and when I was willing to be, to do, and to suffer, any thing that was required at my hands; when I was even willing to give up my natural life, if I might have an assurance of peace with God.

I have not had a theological education, nor a classical education—I am not a prophet, neither a prophet's son; neither was I trained up in the school of war, to enable me to make merchandize of the souls of the people. I was trained up to labor, and I yet labor for the support of myself and those dependent on me. But when my soul was thus brought into the depths of judgment, so that I was willing to submit to any thing, there was begotten in me a love for the whole human family; and I earnestly desired their preservation from evil, and that they might enter into the city of our God. And under the influence of this love, my mind was enabled, as I believed it was right, to speak a word of caution unto my brethren and sisters where I resided. It was well accepted, and this was my first beginning. These were the motives which led me forth ; and these are the motives at the present, which have brought me from an affectionate wife and family, and led me, though an alien and a foreigner in a strange land, to this place, that we may be edified together, and, and God be glorified ; and that by the mutual faith of both, instructed together in wisdom, and come fully under the influence of those principles, which I am not ashamed to acknowledge, have brought peace to my mind. I would by no means teach you any dogmas, or prescribe any forms of doctrine ; but desire you as you desire your soul's salvation, to come under the influence of that principle which brings sorrow for disobedience, but which will make you wiser than all your teachers ; for it will instruct you in the wisdom of Godliness, to worship God in spirit and in truth.

For what is worship ? Is it to preach, to pray, or to sing outwardly ? No. They form no part of worship. And what is preaching ? The preaching of the gospel is experienced in every creature—it is that which baptisingly instructs us to determine between good and evil. It is preached in us baptisingly, that evil brings sorrow, and that what is right brings peace. This is a principle which we all recognize. There is something in man which operates immediately on the heart—this is the preaching of the gospel. When men neglect this operation, they will come to undervalue it, and call it a natural light ; something given to us as our natural conscience. We undervalue this principle—we despise this light, and necessarily crucify unto ourselves, the son of God afresh, and put him to an open shame. But if preaching the gospel opens the understanding, we must remember and attend to its manifestations. If we do not attend to it in its manifestations, I am convinced that we shall build up a partition wall between ourselves and our God. And what is prayer ? Is it the repetition of a certain form of words, upon the knees ? Does God see any particular position of the body, with acceptance ; or any form of words ? No, verily : And I am afraid that we often com-

mit grievous sins by our hypocrisy, when, whether we are
prepared or not, we, at stated times, fall down and make use
of the words of Christ, the words of our own contrivance,
or of others; and when we preach from books or extempore.
Let us look a little at the prayer of Christ to his disciples—
"Our Father which art in heaven." We never can call God
father, till we are begotten into his nature, and into the likeness of his person and image, his power of holiness, righteousness and truth. Till we come to experience this operation in our own minds, he is not our Father, we are not
begotten of him. And how can we say "hallowed be thy
name," when we perform and practice the absurdity of
swearing by his name? "But I say unto you, swear not at
all; neither by heaven, for it is God's throne; nor by the
earth, for it is his footstool: Neither by Jerusalem; for it
is the city of the great King. Neither shall thou swear by
thy head, because thou canst not make one hair white or
black." We are not to swear at all, because the law under
which we profess to live, leads into that truth and unity of
conduct in possession of these virtues which cannot make a
lie, because the spirit of God dwelleth in him. Hence it is
an absurdity, for any of us who are under the influence of
this principle, to swear by God. "But let your communication be yea, yea; nay, nay: for whatsoever is more than
these, cometh of evil, and must necessarily have the same
tendency. But if the spirit of God be not operating in us,
we shall not learn to speak the truth by all the tests and
oaths that were ever invented—they never can do it. "Our
Father, which art in heaven, hallowed be thy name; thy
kingdom come, thy will be done in earth as it is done in
heaven." How can we say this, when we are opposing his
will even in our own minds, and of course are not come into
his kingdom. We never can experience it while we are in a
a state of rebellion, and while we are adverse to his laws:
And yet we hypocritically adopt the language, "thy will be
done in earth as it is done in heaven." We pray God to
"give us this day our daily bread;" but instead of wanting spiritual nourishment, we have clothed ourselves with

opinions and dogmas, and will not receive it at his hands. We are righteous and wise in our own eyes; and will not attend to his manifestations; and yet we beg on our bended knees, that he will give us our daily bread, when we have formed a system, and are endeavoring to live under its requirements, instead of receiving daily wisdom from that unalterable, that almighty and eternal source of life and light. "Forgive us our trespasses as we forgive those who trespass against us." We never can forgive those who trespass against us, while in this spirit. We talk about forgiving, but we can never forgive; neither are we forgiven; and therefore I want us to examine our rule of prayer, for we must alter all these things before we can ascribe "the kingdom and the power and the glory forever, Amen."

What is prayer? It is not a particular form of words; but it is every aspiration of the soul of man, devoted to God, with a desire to do his will. As every aspiration is a prayer, there is nothing easier than to pray to God, for he is in every devoted soul—"I dwell in the high and holy place, with him also that is of a contrite and humble spirit, that trembles at my word, which will receive the spirit of the humble and the contrite." Hence, however deep our contrition may be, however remote from the comforts of our own minds, if we draw near unto him in a spirit of supplication, our prayer will be acceptable in his sight, and precious as the evening sacrifice. What an unspeakable blessing is it, that we can have this access to God the Father, through the spirit of our Lord Jesus Christ.

With respect to singing. How can we sing, till we have experienced a deliverance from the influence of those dispositions which separate us from God? How can our singing avail us? I appeal to yourselves, whether there is a single psalm to be found in the whole collection, which a company like this could sing and not lie unto God? Can we for instance, begin and sing "rivers of tears ran down my cheeks, because they keep not thy law?" When we keep not the laws of God, and when many of us have never bewailed our own backslidings: or can we even say "as the heart panteth after the water brooks, so panteth my soul after thee, O God"—when our minds are more intent on the gratification of our animal propensities, than in serving God. In singing praises to his name I am renewedly convinced that Israel could not sing until they were delivered from bondage: when Pharaoh and the Egyptian host were pursuing them behind, and the Red Sea before them, this was not a time for rejoicing; for they were afflicted and distressed, and therefore commanded to be still, and see the salvation of God. But when they had experienced a deliverance, and had passed over the Red Sea, and their enemies had been destroyed—there was a time for rejoicing—they sung Psalms; they felt "the mountains to skip like rams, and the little hills like lambs. What ailed thee, O thou Sea, that though fleddest? thou Jordan, that thou wast driven back? Ye mountains, that ye skipped like rams; and ye little hills, like lambs? Tremble, thou earth, at the presence of the Lord, at the presence of the God of Jacob; which turned the rock into a standing water, the flint into a fountain of waters," The same power which was gracious to Isreal, and which placed him in a land flowing with milk and honey, is still able to do for us spiritually, as he did for them outwardly. His arm is not shortened that he cannot save, nor his ears heavy that he cannot hear; but it is our iniquity, that has separated between us and our peace: and it must be by a removal of this obstruction, that we can enjoy the light of his countenance, and that when this mortality shall put on immortality, and this corruptible shall put on corruption, we shall yet flourish unhurt, amid the war of elements, the wreck of matter, and the crush of worlds.

.

SERMON II.

DELIVERED BY THOMAS WETHERALD, IN LOMBARD STREET MEETING, BALTI-
MORE, ON THE MORNING OF THE FIRST OF FIRST MONTH, 1826.

" To what purpose is the multitude of your sacrifices unto
me? saith the Lord: I am full of the burnt offering of rams,
and the fat of fed beasts; and I delight not in the blood of
bullocks, or of lambs, or of he-goats: bring no more vain
oblations; incense is an abomination unto me; the new
moons and Sabbaths, the calling of assemblies, I cannot,
away with; it is iniquity, even the solemn meeting; wash
you, make you clean; put away the evil of your doings
from before mine eyes; cease to do evil; learn to do well;
seek judgment, relieve the oppressed, judge the fatherless,
plead for the widow. Come now, and let us reason together,
saith the Lord; though your sins be as scarlet, they shall
be as white as snow; though they be red like crimson, they
shall be as wool."

Here is a plain and unequivocal distinction between form-
ality and religion. One leads to a strict observance of external rites and ceremonies; and that not only under the
legal dispensation, but under every dispensation of God to
man; whether it leads to an observance of the law, or to
the fulfilment of the rituals of that cloudy dispensation, the
law of Moses—which made not the observers thereof perfect. This we discover by the command "wash you, make
you clean; put away the evil of your doings from before
mine eyes; cease to do evil; learn to do well; seek judgment, relieve the oppressed, judge the fatherless, plead for
the widow;" and the effect which this was to produce, is
described in these words, "Come now, and let us reason

together, saith the Lord: though your sins be as scarlet, they shall be as white as snow, though they be red like crimson, they shall be as wool."

And I apprehend there is as great necessity for this cleansing operation, in the present day, as ever there was under the Jewish dispensation: And there is a medium appointed, whereby these effects can be produced, on every individual of the human family. We are all objects of this provision, for as the soul of the servant, so is the soul of the master; as the soul of the handmaid, so with her mistress. Now the medium whereby these effects are produced, is within ourselves; and none of us need say, who shall ascend into heaven to bring Christ down from above; or who shall descend into the depths to bring him up; and this is the word which the Gospel has preached unto you.

And what is the Gospel? Is it mere declamation? Is it the mere acknowledgment of certain abstract propositions, concerning the truth; or is it the teaching the dogmas and opinions of this or that society? Is this Gospel? No, my brethren, it is that which can never make perfect—it is that which stands in the wisdom of man, and is without the word or power of God. But the Gospel of the Lord Jesus Christ is the power of God unto salvation, to every one that believeth; but not the Scriptures, or historical account of his outward appearance in that prepared body of flesh. It consists in love and communion of our heavenly Father, whether they have received the Scriptures or not; for in these days men have made them the foundation of much spurious religion. God is the same unto all; and all are equally subjects of his regard, and all may equally receive his salvation in that manner, who look unto him. "For the word of God is quick, and powerful, and sharper than any two edged sword, piercing even to the dividing asunder of the soul and spirit, and of the joints and marrow, and is a discerner of the thoughts and intents of the heart." The reason why this is not more felt is, because of our disobedience—it is because we have crucified into ourselves the son of God afresh, and now, in his new and spiritual appear-

3

ance, have put him to an open shame, by offering unto him
the blood of bullocks, burnt offerings of rams, and the fat
of fed beasts, and of he-goats: And because we have neglected to wash and cleanse, and to put away the evil of our
doings, to rectify our passions, and to crucify those passions
which separate us from the source of all purity; so that
darkness covers the earth, and gross darkness the people.
And from this cause it is, that when we are thus assembled,
instead of being prepared to hear the word, and worship in
spirit and in truth, we are prepared to hear what this, that
or another individual may have to say upon abstract propositions relative to the truth.

Now, what are these abstract propositions? Abstract propositions may be applied to truth; but they can never form
a part of its essence. They are in truth but human speculations; and by these abstract propositions, we may understand what is generally considered the doctrines of various
religious societies of the present day; and although they
may be considered by many as essential in religion, I want
it to be understood, and I desire to be your companion in the
belief, that these abstract propositions never can form a part
of the vitality of the true system. They may have a tendency to disguise it; but we have a strong consolation, that
truth needs no cover. It never appears more amiable, than
when it appears in its own simplicity, as received from the
great fountain of all truth and wisdom.

"Therefore, leaving the principles of the doctrine of Christ,
let us go on unto perfection; not laying again the foundation of repentance, from dead work, and of faith towards
God, of the doctrine of baptism, and of laying on of hands,
and of the resurrection of the dead, and of eternal judgment.
And this will we do if God permit." From this we find,
that these principles, doctrines and views, into which some
have been led, are not a sufficient rule of faith and conduct:
And wherefore? Because the same divine illimitable power
which led the apostles, and other righteous men, in former
times, is still extended to the human family; and none need
say to his neighbor or brother, know ye the Lord, for we

may all know him, from the least to the greatest; and may experience the declaration fulfilled in our own selves. I will forgive them their sins and iniquities, and remember them no more. How vain it is, then, to be perplexed about these abstract propositions about truth, used in obscuring and preventing the gracious purposes of Omnipotence, not only at the coming of our Lord Jesus Christ in the body of flesh, but denying him in his new and spiritual appearance, when he shall come a second time, without sin; as a teacher, preserver, minister, sanctifier in the true tabernacle which God has pitched, and not man—a tabernacle not made with hands, but by God. "Know ye not that ye are the temple of God, and that the spirit of God dwelleth in you? If any man defile the temple of God, him shall God destroy: for the temple of God is holy, which temple ye are." Let no man deceive himself. "If any man among you seemeth to be wise in this world, let him become a fool that he may be wise." If we come not to enter within the veil, which is the holiest of all, we can have no communication between God and our souls; we can never go further than to be worshippers in the outward courts: if we offer the blood of bullocks, and the burnt offerings of rams and he-goats, and are strict in the performance of all the outward rituals of the various professions or names in the christian world. Although we may be bowing our heads like a bulrush, and may lift up our voice like a trumpet; yet if it does not emanate from the spirit of Christ, it is nothing better, while wanting this, than a sounding brass a tinkling cymbal.

And, I am renewedly convinced, while I stand among you, that a great part of the religion of the present day, is better calculated to condemn mankind than to save their souls. It leads us to place our dependence on those abstract propositions, doctrines and dogmas, taught by the commandment of men, who are persuading us on one side, that we must go into the water and be baptised, and on another, that we must become partakers of the bread and wine, as symbolical of the second coming of Christ; and by which, I apprehend, we deny him in his first and second coming. For if we be-

lieve in the baptism of the Holy Ghost and fire, as declared
by John: "I indeed baptise you with water unto repentance:
but he that cometh after me is mightier than I; he shall
baptise you with the Holy Ghost and with fire." If we believe this baptism, with these weak and beggarly elements,
and that not merely as preparatory to his coming, we thereby
virtually deny his coming in the flesh, under the gospel dispensation; and if we are partaking of bread and wine as
emblematical of his second coming, in his new and spiritual
appearance, do we not virtually deny him in these two particulars. Others have adopted abstract views, and dignified
them with the name of religion, while the life, power, and
vitality thereof, is wanting. These things ought not so to
be. It is the operation of the power of God upon the spirit;
it is the revelation of Jesus Christ, the immutable rock, on
which the true Church is, and ever has been, and will be
built.

I lay in Zion a foundation, a stone, a tried stone, a precious corner stone, a sure foundation. He that believeth on
this stone, shall not be confounded; for there is no other
name given under heaven, whereby we can experience salva-
vation, only the name of Jesus Christ, which is the power
of God unto salvation, I verily believe, whether Jew or Gentile. But I apprehend, that many people have indulged in
these abstract propositions, which have extended wide over
Christendom, and taken place of experimental truth. They
have taken the name of Jesus Christ, his outward name and
outward body, and professed to believe in his miracles, and
those things which he performed when in his prepared body,
in which he did his heavenly Father's will. We must believe in all these things, and I sincerely hope there are none
disposed to disbelieve them, not that this is essential that
they believe in all these historical accounts. And wherefore? Because these were under the former dispensation;
and in some of these acts was that dispensation fulfilled.
And I apprehend, that lessons of deep instruction are to be
found in the miracles of our Saviour Jesus Christ. But it
is not by a mere historical knowledge of them—it is not by

reading them as they are recorded, and by bringing them down to our own natural powers and faculties, that we are to be profited. But I have been ready to believe, that when we read them under the influence of the divine spirit, by the revelation of Christ, which is the only name by which salvation can be experienced, there is scarcely an act of his recorded, which may not become a lesson of instruction to the mind.

. I want us to remember that it is not enough to look to the Scriptures; but that it is essential for us to look inward, and come to a knowledge of God. A knowledge of the Scriptures may be an excellent handmaid—an excellent servant : as they are undoubtedly given for our comfort, reproof, correction and instruction in righteousness ; but they never can bring us to a knowledge of God, because he is inwardly revealed.

Now when we come under the influence of this principle, when our understanding becomes opened, by its manifestations, then, we know every miracle which he did, renewedly opened and performed within our own souls ; then those which were outward, now become inward and spiritual ; and thus opens the blind eyes and unstops the deaf ears, even at the present day—he heals us of every sickness and malady, and raises us from death unto life. These are the operations of his power; and this is a baptism of the Holy Ghost : which can speak, not in words, but in power.

And I am renewedly convinced, and I am not afraid to declare it among you, that opinions are not religion, neither is declamation Gospel. It is the washing which makes us clean. "Wash you ; make you clean ; put away the evil of your doings from before mine eyes ; cease to do evil ; learn to do well ; seek judgment, relieve the oppressed, judge the fatherless, plead for the widow." And in order to do this, I am convinced, we must obey the Apostolic injunction. "Therefore, leaving the principle of the doctrine of Christ. let us go on unto perfection ; not laying again the foundation of repentance, from dead works, and of faith toward God, of the doctrine of baptism, and of laying on of hands.

and of the resurrection of the dead, and of eternal judgment. And this will we do if God permit." And I apprehend there is no other medium than that of baptism; but this is not a baptism with water; for you may wash from youth to old age, and not cleanse the soul of one sin or of one lust. You may eat bread and wine from youth to old age; this may serve to sustain the body, but it will not support the soul—it will not give life to the spirit—it will not unite us to God. And I apprehend it is so of every other abstract proposition with which we attempt to clothe the truth. It has a tendency to cover it, and obscure its manifestations, and to bring us into that gross darkness which covers the minds of the people.

Now let us look a little at this baptism, which is necessary to salvation. It is to be found in every mind wherever there is a human being or a living soul. It is a medium of communication between the souls of other beings; for as our bodies have intercourse together, so have souls and spirits: And God is a spirit; and it is said that, they who worship him, must worship him in spirit and in truth. We are not to build up Babels in our own will and wisdom; for none of this is the worship that I want us all to come into. And we never can worship till we have experienced this manifestation—till it has cleansed our hearts and rectified our passions—for God will not dwell in impure or unholy vessels. And what is it that produces these effects? I can remember when my soul was brought into a concern for its everlasting well being; I can remember when I mourned for a Saviour, almost in my infancy, and when my soul was cast down in deep humility within me, in solitary places, when young in years; and this was not because I had been educated in a formal observance of these things, for I never had been thus educated. It was from a concern originating in my own mind; and I feel no hesitation in believing, that every concern on your minds has been impressed upon it by the finger of God. This is a baptism of the Holy Ghost; and it is a baptism essential unto salvation.

Now if we attend to these things as they pass in our own

minds, they will bring us into a knowledge of ourselves. We shall come to know that which is livingly written in every heart that is born of God; and here we get instruction. Now if we continue under the operation of these principles, we cannot commit an evil action, think an evil thought, or speak an evil word, without feeling sorrow, trouble, and confusion; and this trouble and confusion arise from a kind of despair and of horror; nay, from every feeling in which there is torment, and thus bringing ourselves into a hell even on this side the grave, and while clothed with mortality. There will be no joy, no hope, no consolation while in time, for we have crucified unto ourselves the son of God, and put him to open shame; but must continue in a place of torment, and if we have denied these manifestations, we shall grow stronger in evil propensities, and hence our testimony will grow weaker and weaker. When fully come under this divine influence, the more fully shall we be united to the gospel of Christ, which is the power of God unto salvation—this is Christ in you the hope of glory. There are many corroborative scripture testimonies, which go to prove, that there is a portion of this manifestation given to every man to profit with all—a manifestation sufficient unto salvation. Here the gospel is preached baptisingly in every creature. Go ye, therefore, and teach all nations, baptising them into the name of the Father, and of the Son, and of the Holy Ghost. This is presented to you under the influence of this power, and thus we come into a knowledge of God, as many of you can bear testimony. And when you have been reading the scriptures, and when your minds have been brought into solemnity and quietude, you have had your understandings opened—perhaps passages of scriptures may have appeared to you in a more beautiful garb. Perhaps from other writings, and not from the scriptures only, have you been instructed, and impressions made upon your minds, furnishing evidence of the mercy, wisdom, power and other attributes of God. Now when this kind of instruction is sealed upon the mind, we never can be moved, we cannot be led into doubts and fears;

for it does not lead into, but out of perplexities. It builds on a foundation, against which all the powers of death, hell and the grave can never prevail. And it has an unequivocal effect to produce, in our minds, the state of which John testified. "I am the voice of one crying in the wilderness, make straight the way of the Lord;" and when this is done, "every valley shall be exalted, and every mountain and hill shall be made low : And the crooked shall be made straight, and the rough plain : And the glory of the Lord shall cover the whole earth, even as the waters cover the sea." Now, I. cannot conceive that the roughness and undulating surface of this globe is understood to be brought under the influence of this operative principle ; every valley shall be exalted, and every mountain and hill shall be made low, and the crooked and perverse dispositions shall be made straight, and the rough places smooth. And I apprehend, that according to our various dispositions will be these operations. The minds may be compared to the mountains, lofty, high, cruel, fierce, &c. If there are any of these mountains in the mind, which have not been brought low, this operation will have a tendency to bring them to a proper level ; for all of these will have to come low, and be brought under this regulating power ; as many, very many, have had to mourn over the inequality of their own temper and dispositions ; because they have given way to the ebullition of anger, cruelty, passion and lust ; and where these have been predominating feelings in their minds, and if willing to submit, feelings of sorrow, distress, judgment, then come into that Godly sorrow, which worketh repentance not to be repented of. This is the ministration of condemnation, and it is glorious in its season, because it makes way unto the ministration of life.

When our minds become alienated from our darling lusts, then this divine principle reproves for evil, and speaks peace to the soul, and then we become partakers of the divine consolation, and bear testimony to the joy of God's salvation. And this knowledge of God—this experimental knowledge, will grow with our growth, and increase with our strength, and we shall thus be brought first to be babes and children in Christ, and our ideas will be few, and confined to our immediate observation ; but as we grow up through faith, we shall experience a growth of our ideas. in experimental things, and as the opening buds of reason, and the powers of the child are more fully developed, we shall become as young men, strong, but wanting experience. Here it is that we are apt to be rash and headstrong—here it is that we are liable to give way to vain imaginations, which lead to open rebellion. We are apt to imagine, that now we have attained to a knowledge of God, we may take our rest. Many have gone thus far, and praised God on the banks of deliverance, but have set down with the knowledge obtained, and instead of going on from stature to stature, and to give unto babes meat in due season, we have set down content with what we have experienced, and have finally become proud, high minded and Pharisaical, instead of being leaders of others. They have been in a degree partakers of the gospel of the Lord Jesus Christ, having been educated, nominally, in the school of Christ, and according to the forms of this or that religious society ; and their habits have led them into a kind of morality, consistent with the views of the world ; and they have become members of these churches, and from that to be denominated ministers. of the gospel. This has been a cause and source of incalculable evil to the churches of the present day ; for it is from them that the younger members look up to them for examples and advice—they look up to them for instruction, when they have yet hardly learned the principles of the first oracles of God. For it is not that which we have learned in this, that, or the other way, that can avail us, for we cannot live except we abide in the vine, "I am the vine, ye are the branches: he that abideth in me, and I in him, the same bringeth forth much fruit: for without me ye can do nothing." We must continue in his power, for if we separate ourselves from him, death is the inevitable consequence. But however high and lofty—however overbearing our dispositions may be, if we will submit to this instruction, it will bring us to a proper level. There are others who are ready to adopt the language of the Psalmist: "Hath God forgotten to be gracious? Hath he in anger shut up his tender mercies? Is his mercy clean gone forever?" Now, this man needs not to be reproved. with severity, nor the baptism of fire, but has become partaker of his consolation. These are the valleys that shall be exalted—these are the perverse dispositions that shall be made straight—and then it is that the glory of the Lord shall cover the earth, and all flesh shall see it. In this it is that we experience the power of God unto salvation; and know that power revealed in man against all unrighteousness and ungodliness of man. And if we come under the influence of this principle, how insignificant will appear, all the principles, doctrines, and dogmas of men. For all the abstract propositions which have been applied to truth and religion, have never formed any part of its essence; but they have led the minds of thousands off, to substitute self-righteousness; for that humility which leads to the peaceable practice of heavenly virtue, which can never be obtained but by an obedience to the manifestations of the power of God; that manifestation of the power of God, or operation of his spirit, spirit of Christ; and it is thus that some of us have not depended on these things which are external, believing that all these miracles are performed spiritually upon every well regulated mind, bringing us to see the things which are to be known by experience.

It is not merely the blood of Christ, shed without the gates of Jerusalem, that can save us; but when we come to know his blood to be a circulating medium within us, giving vitality to our whole system; when we become partakers of its nature, and experience its crucifying influence in and through our whole soul, then we shall come to know that the blood of Jesus Christ cleanses us from all sin. Then we shall become partakers of his nature, and be governed by the same power, by which he was governed; which was the power of God, enabling him to do all these mighty works, to perform so many miracles, and to leave all those valuable records and precepts; and in short, to work out man's salvation. But the salvation of man, and I am not afraid to repeat it, was never wrought out by any outward act of the outward body; but by the spirit which communes with spirit—which operates upon the spirit of man and "leads him out of sin and corruption into the glorious liberty of the children of God." Here, there is neither Jew nor Greek, Barbarian nor Scythian, bond nor free; neither Baptist, Presbyterian, Episcopalian, nor Quaker; who, if they come under the influence of this principle, and are guided by its power, let their names be what they may, will not be equally objects of Divine favor. And I apprehend that these divisions, which have arisen among the gathered churches, so called, must cease to prevail among us; or they will entitle us to the name of antichrist: For they have arisen, not from union, but from separating themselves, by making nice philosophical distinctions and abstract propositions, instead of attending to the revealed truth. And I apprehend, that these differences in names and forms, if those who countenance them come to that state in which they experience the glory of the Lord, to cover their minds as the waters cover the sea, will sink into their native insignificance: And that power being substituted for the forms which now prevail, our righteousness will be complete in Christ.

O my friends, if you ever experience these things—if ever you come under this divine power, it will not proceed from what your Fathers have taught you—not from reading the scriptures; notwithstanding they were written, no doubt by inspiration from God. But as the same arm is stretched forth for our deliverance, and for our support, we must individually experience its operation—we must individually come under its invigorating power, under those manifestations which open our understanding for the reception of those truths which are essential to our salvation. And until we experience these, worship in the outward courts must continue; and this is what my soul dreads, least these worshippers in the outward courts be trodden down with the gentile nations. And whilst these worshippers in the outward courts are under the government of these affections, depending on the efficacy of the outward blood of Christ and the Scriptures of truth, to lead them day by day; they may institute family worship if they choose, but it will rather produce darkness than light. We may pray with our families, we may use forms of words and call it prayer, we may read the Scriptures once, twice, or three times a day, and what will be its tendency upon the minds of our families? The tendency will be, that they will gain a name for fulfilling all the righteousness of the outward law; but, renewedly convinced I am (and I know it from experience) that if we adopt the practice of reading the Scriptures at particular hours, it will have a tendency to harden the young minds of children; because thus adhering to outward and sectarian forms, they will not receive these divine truths; and this adherence will beget a spirit of enmity; and perhaps I may appeal to others, who have noticed the very same thing, whether they have not found, that it has increased the reluctance of children to attend to such instruction. If we are ever made serviceable to our children (and I consider the responsibility of parents as peculiarly awful) if we are ever made the instruments of instructing them in divine things, it must not be by imposing peculiar restrictions, nor by forcing them into a performance of duties which they cannot comprehend; neither must it be by giving precept upon precept, and line upon line, day by day: For these things will have a tendency to harden every tender feeling. I remember the injunction of a beloved parent, when I had children that were young: he told me to be careful and tell them what was right, and to see that they did it. And I well remember when a child of mine, very young, asked me the meaning of some text in Scripture, not being able to answer the plain question of a little girl, I said you are too young to understand such matters; it was an important lesson to me, which I pray I may never forget, as it serves to show how incapable we are of fulfilling the awful duty of parents. I apprehend there are others in the same situation in which I then was; and are we to find a remedy by searching the Scriptures, ourselves? No: we must come to a knowledge of God, in order to get to a knowledge of the

Scriptures. Remember that all wisdom is founded on a knowledge of God. It is not a mere profession or belief, or any abstract proposition respecting his attributes, that will answer the purpose. But all the knowledge of God is predicated on knowledge, and that knowledge which is right and essential to salvation, must be obtained through that baptism which I have endeavored to open to your view.

I remember when our Lord and Saviour Jesus Christ, had performed a miracle on the blind man, he said, "Dost thou believe on the son of God?" He replied, "who is he, Lord, that I might believe on him?" He experienced that power which we all must experience, in order to believe. Jesus said unto him, thou hast both seen him, and it is he that talketh with thee. It was the same power which had relieved him of his outward malady: and he said, yea Lord, I believe; and he worshipped him. "And Jesus said, for Judgment I am come into this world, that they which see not might see, and that they which see might be made blind." Now, my friends, here is instruction in this account. For if judgment come into the world, which they saw not, must see, and they who are depending on the blood of bullocks, must be made conscious of the state of darkness in which they are placed. "And Jesus said, for Judgment I am come into the world, that they which see not, might see, and that they which see, might be made blind." Then said the Pharisees unto him, "Are we blind also? Jesus said unto them, if ye were blind, ye should have no sin : and now ye say, we see; therefore your sin remaineth." When they are willing to become blind, and poor, and lame, and miserable; and to be taught of God, and to experience his operative power in them, then they will come into a state to experience consolation, and to know that declaration fulfilled, that though the Lord shall give you the bread of adversity, and the water of affliction to drink, yet shall not thy teacher be removed into a corner any more, but thee shall see thy teacher, and thine ears will hear a voice behind thee, saying, this is the way, walk ye in it, when ye turn to the right hand, and when ye turn to the left ; and I apprehend that it is only as we come to experience these things, these operations in our own minds, that we shall ever come to a right knowledge of the scriptures: for it is here that we can know that Michael and his angels fought, and the dragon fought with his angels, and prevailed not, neither was there place to be found any more in heaven. It is here that religion will not find a hope of *future* reward or a dread of future punishment. A great part of our religion is founded on a hope of reward as the acting motive; the spring of action is self-gratification; being founded on a dread of hell for punishment, the motive is self-love; but this can never work righteousness; neither can it teach us to worship. This righteousness of the heart, must be brought under the divine influence, before we can worship in spirit and in truth. Many look for a reward; which, I believe, is their predominating motive and rule of action. But I apprehend, that that which is the most distinguishing attribute of God, will become a prevailing power, and will regulate our minds; and when we come into it, we shall know that there is war in heaven. And where is heaven? There are those who are looking away to a heaven of self-gratification, and even placing it at a great distance beyond the grave. And to escape from the pains of hell, they have placed it at a great distance beyond the grave. But it is a declaration of him in whom ye say ye believe—"the kingdom of heaven is within you," and it is there that the judgment is set, and the books are opened; and it is there that we must know, that there was war in heaven. "Michael and his angels fought, and the dragon and his angels." And when we come to know the angel of love to have dominion over the devil of hatred; and the angel of mercy, to predominate over the demon of cruelty; and the angel of temperance, to war with and overcome the demon of intemperance; when we come to know the angel of hope to cast out the angel of despair; and every heavenly disposition, and every ministering angel of God to rule in us; then we shall not only know war in heaven, Michael and his angels overcoming the dragon and his angels; the power of God contending in us, and thus, blessed be the name of Israel's God, the captain of our salvation is unconquered and unconquerable. The dragon was cast out with his angels, neither was there place found any more in heaven. When these results are produced, and we come under the government of that power in which we can know all the opposing demons cast out of the mind, then we can fulfill every injunction of Christ; love our enemies: we can bless them that curse us, pray for them that despitefully use us, and persecute us. And here one mountain is removed; for when the very root and ground of enmity is cast out; when the principle of love predominates, then we can love our neighbor as ourselves. And who is our neighbor? We shall then come to know the neighborship which is spoken of in these words: And Jesus, answering, said, a certain man went down from Jerusalem to Jericho, and fell among thieves, which stripped him of his raiment, and wounded him, and departed leaving him half dead. And, by chance, there came down a certain priest that way; and when he saw him, he passed by on the other side. And likewise a Levite, when he was at the place, came and looked at him, and passed by on the other side. But a certain Samaritan, as he journeyed, came where he was; and when he saw him, he had compassion on him, and went to him, and bound up his wounds, pouring in oil and wine, and set him on his own beast and brought him to an inn, and took care of him. And on the morrow, when he departed, he took out two pence, and gave them unto the host, and said unto him, Take care of him: and whatsoever thou spendest more, when I come again, I will repay thee. Which now of these three, thinkest thou, was neighbor unto him, that fell among thieves? And he said, he that showed mercy on him. Then said Jesus unto him, go and do likewise.

Now I apprehend this may apply to us. The one who showed mercy was the neighbor. Those christians who fulfil these works of love and mercy, in accordance with the mind that was in Christ, which was a mind of purity, with a single eye to the advancement of his Father's glory, will

be instrumental in making christians of others, and doubt-
less enable us to fulfil his word—for he declared, greater
works shall ye do. Therefore I want every one of us to be
encouraged, to persevere in the good way cast up for the redeemed of God to walk in; a way which the vulture's eye
hath not seen; and it shall be called the way of holiness;
the unclean shall not pass over it; but it shall be for those;
the wayfaring men, though fools, shall not err therein. No
lion shall be there, nor any rancorous beast shall go up
therein; it shall not be found there; but the redeemed shall
walk there; and the ransomed of the Lord shall return, and
come to Zion with songs and everlasting joy upon their
heads: they shall obtain joy and gladness, and sorrow and
sighing shall flee away. When we come under the influence of these heavenly dispositions, then there will be no
more war or outrage; there is not only an end put to these,
but unto all those perverted affections of mankind in the
present day, and no man will oppress his brother—the bones
and sinews of man will not be sold by their brother, but we
shall endeavor in all things to fulfil another injunction of
Christ: Do unto all men as you would have them do unto
you, for this is the law and the prophets.

Now, my friends, look at the effects of that religion, which
stands in external forms and rituals, and which leads the
affections of carnal minds, in their unconverted state, to indulge the passions, to rove at large without a governor, and
into the bondage of corruption, thus bringing ourselves into
a state of darkness, horror and despair.

Now, what are evil and darkness? Darkness is the absence of light; for we can none of us see the sun, but by its
own light; neither can any of us come to God, but by the
light which he has given us; and if darkness is the absence
of light, so in the same way, evil is the absence of good; in
which state we are separated from the source of all good,
and purity, and peace. But if we are under the influence
of this heavenly principle, the light of Christ, the consequence will be, that we shall experience the joys of his consolation—that this heavenly principle will govern us, and

also bear us up, lest we dash our foot against a stone; we shall experience mountains of opposition, to "skip like rams and the little hills like lambs;" and we shall be ready to say, "What ailed thee, O thou sea, that thou fleddest? Thou Jordan, that thou wast driven back? Ye mountains, that ye skipped like rams, and ye little hills like lambs? Tremble, thou earth, at the presence of the Lord, at the presence of the God of Jacob; which turned the rock into a standing water, the flint into a fountain of waters." When this is the case, we shall not only be delivered from wars and dissentions, but we shall be delivered from the oppression of man by his fellow man, and from every species of oppression. And it is only this principle that can make those become righteous, who unite in this manifestation; while, if we pursue the opposite, it will bring us into darkness, horror and despair, and every feeling in which there is torment; surely, then, our interest lies in pursuing that which will bring us into the kingdom of heaven here, while clothed with mortality, and in which we shall become partakers of those joys and consolations; and when we shall be unclothed of this flesh, we shall

> Flourish unhurt, amidst the war of elements,
> The wreck of matter, and the crush of worlds.

And when our conversation is in heaven, do whatsoever we may, we shall do all to the honor and glory of God; and when our affections are regulated, our passions subjected, and our lusts subdued, and brought into obedience to him—then, when we assemble ourselves together, our minds will be prepared for the reception of those divine truths which I apprehend are often communicative and instructive. But if we come here once, twice or three times a week, and remain listless while here, and return again and become wholly engrossed by our pursuits, our merchandise, our farms, filthy gains, &c.—worshippers like these, are not to expect consolation, neither to be benefited by assembling themselves together. For God looks not to outward appearances; he searches the hearts and tries the veins—he knows the inmost recesses of our thoughts and imaginations. And, therefore, I want us, my friends and fellow professors of the Christian name, (for I know no distinction) to have our conversation in heaven. And whether our hands are engaged in labor, whether we set in the house, walk by the way, lie down or rise up, I want us to endeavor to have our minds fixed on him; and thus every act of our lives will be an act of mercy. For worship stands not in words—it stands not in assembling ourselves together; but it stands in the disposition of our hearts. And if our hearts are right toward God, I apprehend that the fruits which we bring forth will be in accordance; fruits of the spirit of love, meekness, temperance, brotherly kindness, and a great variety of others, which the apostle enumerates; and against these there is no law; for if these bring forth such fruits under the law of the spirit of life in Christ, and the law of the spirit of Christ sets us free from the law of sin and death, I know of no other medium whereby freedom and liberty are to be obtained, but by coming under the influence of this law, which is riches and peace to every individual. Let us strive to come, then, into this law, and manifestation of this power, which is written in our hearts and minds. And I desire once more to recommend you to remember the declaration of the apostle. Finally, brethren, farewell: be perfect, be of good comfort, be of one mind, live in peace; and the God of love and peace shall be with you.

SERMON III.

DELIVERED BY THOMAS WETHERALD AT FRIENDS' MEETING, OLD TOWN, BAL-
TIMORE, ON THE FIRST OF FIRST MONTH, 1826.

It must be obvious to every reflecting mind, I apprehend,
that for a number of years past, there has been a great increase of what is termed religion in the land. We hear
of revivals in many places; and of additions to various
churches, so called, in many places; but it is equally ob-
servable, that with the increase of this religion, wickedness
has also increased.

Now, if I have formed a correct idea of religion, the design of it was to make men better; and to correct those
evils which are, perhaps, intimately connected with our nature.   Then, if wickedness increases in the same ratio with
religion, at the time that there is a great increase of religion,
there must necessarily be a radical defect some where.   And
I apprehend it is the duty of every individual, (for we all
are, or ought to be, fellow heirs of salvation) to endeavor to
examine into and investigate these causes, in order, if possible, to apply the proper remedy: For I apprehend there
is not, and never has been, an effect, without a producing or
corresponding cause.   And I have been led to look a little,
into the causes which have produced such effects in our land,
as the increase of religion and wickedness in the same ratio.

Now we know, that the religion which has been inculcated
and believed, and whose precepts, doctrines and principles
have been obeyed, is professedly the religion of the Bible.
And I apprehend, that professors generally have agreed in
the belief, that the Scriptures were written by inspiration
from God; and therefore they have been considered, in some

degree, as of divine origin. But we have also evidence that these Scriptures are not able, of themselves, to cause our salvation, without a faith in Christ. If this be wanting—this faith in Christ, which emanates from him, who is the Father of the whole family of mankind, our reading the Bible and our faith in doctrines and precepts are vain ; because in all the precepts of the Bible there is not power contained by which we can gain a victory over one solitary sin. For we have had precept upon precept, and line upon line, here a little and there a little, from our infancy to the present day, but we have found that these precepts, valuable as they have been, have not, in themselves, power to give us the victory over those things which rise in opposition to the justice, wisdom, mercy, and every attribute of God which ought to govern us. There is nothing in words, which can convert the human mind, and bring it into obedience to God. We find from accounts recorded in the Scriptures, that in the outward manifestation of Jesus Christ, in that prepared body of flesh, in which he came to do his heavenly Father's will, he gave to the obdurate Jews many pre-eminently valuable precepts, and these precepts were confirmed by miracles and sealed with his own blood. But, notwithstanding, many of the truths which he taught, and the precepts which he left, were self-evident in themselves—notwithstanding their high confirmation, and their irrevocable seal ; yet the Jews remained in the same state of obduracy, in the same state of alienation from God, and the wisdom of God: Crucifying unto themselves the son of God in the outward manifestation ; and crucifying him in his spiritual appearance, and in his body—and they even gloried in that act of pre-eminent wickedness, by which his blood has been upon them and their children. They even gloried, that they had made void the law of God, with their traditions. They put their own construction upon the legal dispensation, which came by Moses. And what was the consequence? It gave rise to a variety of sects and opinions, which were the Pharisees and Saddusees, and a variety of other names. Now from whence arose these divisions and distractions? They arose not from

the Mosaic law, but from the different descriptions of those
who were appointed Scribes, Doctors, Elders and Teachers.
They must have imposed their own views of the law upon
the minds of the people. And it is very obvious, that the
Pharisees stood pre-eminent in their adherence to what they
viewed to be the precepts of the external law. They believed in the coming of the Messiah; and in this respect
their belief was firm; and yet when he came, they were the
first to persecute him and deny him. And many of the first
were the rulers who would not believe on him, and also those
who laid violent hands on him at their instigation, and crucified him. Of this sort of religion there is a striking ex-
emplification in the account of the Pharisee and Publican.
who went up to pray; and the Pharisee gave thanks to God
that he was not as other men, and enumerated a number of
evils of which he was not guilty. "God, I thank thee, that
I am not as other men are, extortioners, unjust, adulterers,
or even as this publican. I fast twice in the week, I give
tithes of all I possess. And the publican standing afar off,
would not lift up so much as his eyes to heaven, but smote
upon his breast, saying, God be merciful to me a sinner. I
tell you this man went down to his house justified, rather
than the other." And like causes produce like effects; and
they were split and divided, by putting their own views, and
estimates, and opinions, or what may be called a traditional
construction upon the laws of Moses. They were split and
divided, and hence arose a spirit of opposition; they soon
became enemies, and of course despised and hated each other.
And the Pharisees came under such self-righteousness, that
they should say to others, "stand by thyself, come not near
to me; for I am holier than thou." Now arose the religion
of the Bible among men—and the religion of the Bible has
led to all these sects; and I have no doubt they can all prove,
as many did from strained views of the Mosaical law, that
their opinions are founded thereon. And this is not all—
these societies of professing christians, who profess that they
can prove their doctrines by the Scriptures, are as opposite
as any of the different doctrines of the Jews were. We

profess, as a society, to know no sectarian difference. But there are others who say, that none can be saved except those who come within the pale of a certain church; and others say, and they are perhaps about as liberal, that they believe in God the Father, and Jesus Christ our Lord, who was conceived of the Holy Ghost, born of the Virgin Mary, was crucified, dead and buried. And even those who have doubted the correctness and liberality of those views, which are considered essential, if they would be saved in the Catholic faith: and after that, there is a kind of creed which is incomprehensible in itself—a creed which I have never been able to comprehend or understand, and which is founded on a prediction, attributed to Athanasius; and this is the foundation of the Roman Catholic faith, and it is creed, which, as I before said, is incomprehensible; for to say that we can believe what we cannot understand, I never rightly believed, for I never yet learned to believe anything that I could not comprehend. There are others who say, that it is necessary to be baptised with water; but I am renewedly convinced, that all the waters of the sea, if poured upon one body, would never cleanse the soul from one stain, or spot, or sin, or lust. It may be said that baptism is used as a type or figure; but are we still under the legal dispensation? Are we under the legal dispensation, when we acknowledge that the spiritual power is come, which was designed to be, and which substantially is, the resurrection and the life? The legal dispensation was declared to be at an end, when Christ had finished all the rituals; and whenever the Jews were called into the gospel dispensation, if they would attend to those manifestations, which are the means of bringing us to a knowledge of God. They are all called into this spiritual dispensation, but cannot enter without the sacrifice of an honest and lowly heart; for even under the dispensation which came by Moses, it is declared, "to this man will I look, even to him that is poor, and of a contrite spirit, and who trembleth at my word. Wherewith shall I come before the Lord, and bow myself before the high God? Shall I come before him with burnt offerings, with calves of a year old? Will the Lord be pleased with thousands of rams, or with ten thousands rivers of oil? Shall I give my first born for my transgressions, the fruit of my body for the sin of my soul? He hath showed thee, O man, what is good; and what doth the Lord require of thee, but to do justly, and to love mercy, and to walk humbly with thy God."

Now we see that even under the outward dispensation this was a necessary qualification, "to do justly, to love mercy, and to walk humbly before God;" yea, this was better than all the burnt offerings of calves, of rams, and the thousands of rivers of oil, or any such sacrifice.

There are others who say, that a certain number were ordained from the foundation of the world, to salvation; and others to everlasting perdition. These doctrines I have ever believed to be little short of blasphemy, as it would be making God unjust. And can God recommend us to do justly, to love mercy, and to walk humbly before him, while He is himself treading under foot the precepts which He has given, and trampling upon those attributes which we are all willing to ascribe to Him? No, verily, my friends, and while I stand among you, I am renewedly convinced, that all souls are equal, as they are all the works of his creating hands. And I believe that all are in a state, that they may attain unto salvation; and experience the joys of his consolation; of which it has been said, there is no joy equal to the joy of God's salvation. Others have been willing to declare that all men will be saved: And some believe that God is one in three, and three in one. But I cannot reconcile myself to this; for I was never yet able to comprehend God, so as to worship him in trinity and unity.

Now, where there is any thing which admits of division, it admits of locality; and I cannot form this idea of the divinity—I cannot place him in any particular location, because he fills all flesh and all space. And the Psalmist appeared to have this in view, when he declared, "If I ascend up into heaven, thou art there; if I make my bed in hell, behold, thou art there. If I take the wings of the morning, and dwell in the uttermost parts of the sea, even there

shall thy hand lead me, and thy right hand shall hold me."
And seeing therefore, that he fills all space, he admits not
of locality; and certainly admits not of a division.

I am fully convinced that there have been various dispensations of providence to man. I am aware that he appeared
at sundry times, and in divers manners unto the fathers and
prophets; and I am also aware, that he appeared in the external manifestation of Jesus Christ in the flesh; and I am
also aware, that he appears in the present day in his inward
spiritual operation upon the minds of the children of men,
by which thousands are led out of every evil, into every
heavenly, manly, civil, social, and every relative virtue.
And seeing that he admits not of a division, that he is not
unjust, or cruel; and notwithstanding the declaration of
some, that all will be saved; yet is it required in these same
scriptures, called the bible, and which is the foundation of
most of the religions of the present day, that nothing impure,
or unholy, nothing which worketh an abomination; and
whoever loveth and maketh a lie, can never enter into the
kingdom, but all these doctrines, and sentiments, if you
please to call them so, are only the opinions of men. It is
necessary to come to something efficient, something more
powerful, than any thing recorded in the scriptures, or spoken by human tongues. It is necessary, in order that religion may increase, and wickedness decrease in the same ratio,
that we should come under the teachings of a power that is
superior to all the powers of man—a power which can preserve us from all the powers of evil; and when we have
gained this—this living, this operative principle, which is
not founded in the scriptures, and which depends not on the
notions and doctrines of the religious societies of the present
day, we shall see that mankind have mistaken the root and
ground of the whole matter. And it is necessary, as these
evils have been produced by depending on the words, writings
and opinions of others, that as we all have the same privileges, the same rational faculties, and actual ability to become
acquainted with it, to depend on his grace assisting us; and
we ought individually to depend on the operative power of

his spirit, which, instead of bringing us into a religion founded on the bible, or on any external things, it would bring us into a dependence on the only name given under heaven among men, by which all may be saved. For there is no other name under heaven, whereby we can be saved, but by the name of Jesus Christ. But it is not merely by a belief in his name—and that he had an existence in a body of flesh. It is not merely by a belief, that he was conceived by the Holy Ghost, born of the Virgin Mary, crucified, dead and buried. Neither is it by a belief in the miracles which he wrought at Jerusalem, nor by the precepts which he left, sealing them with his blood. There is great dependence placed on something which was done without the gates of Jerusalem, where his blood was shed. But, my friends and fellow professors, I cannot hope for salvation through the *death* of Christ, but through his *life*, and the power of his resurrection. He has appeared unto us in his outward body, to put an end to the legal dispensation. He has now come in his inward and spiritual manifestation, without sin, and to him we must look for salvation. This stone was testified of, "Behold, I lay in Zion a foundation stone, a tried stone, a precious corner stone, a sure foundation." This is not merely the name of Christ, but the power of God unto salvation, to every one who believes, whether Jew or Gentile—It is an operative power, which leads unto salvation. We must become first babes, then young men, then strong men, then Elders in the church. Now, the reason why this kind of religion is so odious, is, because it strikes at the root of all our inclinations—at the root of all our vain imaginations; at "pride, fulness of bread, and an abundance of idleness." These abound among us at the present day. But if our foundation is in Christ, if his power comes among us, as we are all willing to attend to it, I am renewedly convinced, that he would help our infirmities; for there is no evil in the world, that must not be counteracted. What shall we say then? Shall we continue in sin, that grace may abound? God forbid. It is like those who said, "let us do evil, that good may come;" but the determination of those, was just

like those nowadays, who are depending on the outward
sacrifice of Christ. But unto what is the mercy of God extended? Is it extended unto our proud hypocrisy, and to
our injustice? Is it extended to our cruelties? Is it extended to our evil thoughts and dispositions, which separate
man from man? Is it extended to a spirit of warfare, to a
spirit of oppression, or to any of these predominating influ-
ences? No. These must go to judgment. The mercy of
God is over all his works. It is these works which are not
of God—these are the works which man delights in. He
wants his own will, in opposition to the divine will; but for
this he must be brought into judgment, even at the present
day. There is a judgment, I am convinced, even in this
life; and we may, if we are disposed to come under its influence, experience a victory while clothed with mortality.
I am renewedly convinced that we may have a well grounded
hope of an habitation which is the building of God, an house
not made with hands, eternal in the heavens: Because, if
the declaration be true, which I before quoted, that nothing
impure or unholy, or which worketh an abomination, can
enter the kingdom; and seeing that we are placed here only
for a season, this is the only time to prepare ourselves; and
it is essential that we have our accounts ready, as we know
not how soon we shall be called on to account for the deeds
done in the body. Now, the religion of Christ is the power
of God unto salvation; and if the gospel is preached any
where, where is it preached? It is preached in every creature, according to the declaration of Christ—The Gospel
shall be preached in every creature. When he was about to
be taken away from this probationary state, he said, "it is
expedient for you that I go away, for if I go not away the
Comforter will not come; but if I go I will pray the Father,
and he will send you another Comforter, even the spirit of
Truth, which the world cannot receive; and which will lead
all who receive it into all Truth; for it dwelleth in us."

Here is the true place, where I want us to look for this
Comforter which the world cannot receive, any more than
they could when he came in his outward manifestation; but

if we come under the influence of his spirit, we shall know the declaration fulfilled, and shall know that he dwelleth with us—he shall be in you, Christ manifest in you, the hope of glory. This corroborates another testimony, "I will put my law in their inward parts, and write it in their hearts; and will be their God and they shall be my people." It is also written, "Ye are the temple of the living God; as God hath said, I will dwell in them; and walk in them; and I will be their God, and they shall be my people. Know ye not that ye are the temple of the living God, and that the spirit of God dwelleth in you? If any man defile the temple of God, him shall God destroy: For the temple of God is holy; which temple ye are."

Now, my friends, and fellow professors of the christian name, if we come under the influence of this principle, we shall be willing to become fools, that we may be made wise.

I have known what it was day by day, and month by month, to go mourning over my lost estate; when I was often times ready to faint by the way; I even could have adopted the language uttered formerly, a Saviour or I die, a Redeemer or I perish for ever; and O whither shall I go? It was in one of these seasons, when I was mourning over my lost estate and sorrowful condition, that this language arose, "Whither shall I go?" I fainted in the anguish of my oppressed soul; and when these words had escaped my lips, there was a calm. We should know this, many of us, if we were willing to mourn over our sins, and to be brought into a state of quietude. When the fleeting passions of the world and the vanities of life had passed away, my mind was in a state of quietude and stillness; and it was in one of these seasons, which succeeded the whirlwind and the storm, that I uttered the language, whither wilt thou go? and I believed in the manifestation and the power of the spirit.

Still, my imagination was not in a state to breathe such language as this. Now many have committed great evil, when they have been brought under judgment, and when sorrow, trouble, and confusion covered their minds; and when they have been ready to adopt the language, hath the Lord forgot to be gracious; and though many exceedingly anxious for the welfare of their immortal souls, instead of patiently waiting, they have gone and joined themselves to this or that society—they have adopted the peculiar views, and attended to the dogmas of this or that sect, and have become very zealous, and found peace to their troubled minds. But, if we ever come into this dispensation which is glorious; for it is the ministration of condemnation—and so if we ever rightly come through this, it will lead us in the ministration of love. Now, if instead of joining themselves to these societies, they would endeavor to be still, and to know that God is good, they might experience deeper instruction, than men or books could give—they might experience truths sealed unto them, which would render them stable and firm under all afflictions. All the dogmatical reasoning of men would never move them, or turn them aside; because, this being the result of our own experimental knowledge of the power of God, we should feel that we were built on a rock, immutable, immovable.

I have been often instructed, when I have looked at the situation of Elijah, when he had fled from Ahab, "and when he was in mount Horeb, the mount of God; he stood in the mouth of a cave, and there passed by a great and a strong wind, and it rent the mountains, and brake in pieces the rocks before the Lord; but the Lord was not in the wind: And after the wind an earthquake; but the Lord was not in the earthquake: And after the earthquake a fire; but the Lord was not in the fire: And after the fire a still small voice. And the voice said unto him, what doest thou here, Elijah? And he said, I have been very jealous for the Lord God of hosts, because the children of Israel have forsaken thy covenant, thrown down thine altars, and slain thy Prophets with the sword; and I, even I only, am left; and they seek my life to take it away." And it remains to be a truth at the present day, that when this calm comes over the mind we can pour forth unto the Lord our sorrows, our afflictions, and our troubles, (if I may use the expression) into the bosom of the Almighty Parent. · It was here in this state of quietude and calm, that Elijah received that encouraging assurance, that there were yet "seven thousand in Israel, all the knees which have not bowed unto Baal, and every mouth which hath not kissed him."

Thus it is that we receive instruction, immediately from the source of wisdom and power; and when it is sealed upon our minds, this is the preaching of the Gospel in faith and verity: For opinions are not religion, neither is declamation Gospel. This is the Gospel which is preached baptisingly— it is not the same as John's baptism, which only cleanses the earthly tabernacle. It is the blood which is the spiritual life of Christ, life of purity, holiness and self-denial, recommended immediately from God. It becomes our light, and we are governed by the same power, led by the same precepts, influenced by the same principles, and become partakers of the same nature, thus growing from a state of negative innocency into a state of positive virtue, and communion with God. And as we thus become willing to be taught, we become babes in Christ, willing to learn of him, and to sit like Mary of old to understand the words of his mouth, and to experience daily growth in wisdom and knowledge; and according to the Scripture expression, we shall "grow in stature and in favor with God and men." Now will fruits be brought forth. And what are the fruits brought forth by these two kinds of religion—the religion of Jesus Christ and the religion of the Bible?

It is a great incontrovertable truth, that like begets its like throughout the creation. Suppose then we adopt it, and say, this is the word of God, and the only rule of faith and practice, as many do; what must be the effects which are produced by this kind of religion? There are many anxiously engaged to circulate the Bible; and in their zeal for the formation of Bible societies and missionary associations, they have descended so low as to form mite societies, and cent societies. They have become as the daughters of the horse leech, crying give, give, which were represented as being insatiable. And hence every manly feeling has ceased to distinguish this religion. And in the present day, instead of the gospel of Christ being freely given, it has become an object of trade and barter, and of profitable gain to the dealers therein.

Many of you know as well as I do, that there are individuals who pretend to teach, who are themselves denying the doctrines of the Gospel, by preaching for hire, and divining for money, and "whose God is their belly, and whose glory is in their shame, who mind earthly things." But there are many of those, who if they had no pay, would do very little preaching—were it not for the gain in loaves and fishes. Many of these are anxious for the spread of these bible societies and missionary societies; but remember that like assimilates with like throughout the creation; and what proceeds from the scriptures gathers into them; and thus gives not a knowledge of God. There has been great anxiety to send bibles and missionaries to the heathen, while those who are so zealous, are themselves wallowing in wickedness, like the dog who returns to his vomit, and the sow to her wallowing in the mire. They had better reform themselves at home.

Let us carry the examination a little further. The vessels of the Lord's house are all holy; nothing impure can ever have admission there. Then can we believe that any will ever be converted by these efforts? If so, it must be a conversion to their absurdities, if not into their actual wickedness, fulfilling the declaration of Christ, who said, woe unto you, Scribes and Pharisees, for ye compass sea and land, to make one proselyte; and when he is made, he is two-fold more the child of hell than yourselves, because they are in a situation to sin with confidence and spiritual pride.

Let us look a little and see whence these funds are drawn, to support these associations. Are they drawn from the pious? Are they drawn from those who are desirous that the stakes of Jerusalem should be lengthened and straightened, and that it should become a quiet habitation? No. For we see among the most popular members, the bloodthirsty warrior, the slave-holding oppressor; those who have taken the advantage of their honest creditors, all uniting in these popular associations. And we see another class even worse than these, who are converting the choicest temporal blessings into distilled ardent spirits; and the dealers in this poison, down to the lowest retailers, casting into "the Lord's treasury." Now can any man for a moment believe that religion can be built on such a foundation as this? It may be likened unto the building of the "foolish man, which was founded on the sand, and the rains descended, and the floods came, and the winds blew, and beat upon the house, and it fell, and great was the fall of it." And this must fall; every thing which stands not in the power of God must fall, before we can come into unity of spirit, and the bonds of peace. Let us look a little in addition to this; for we see a great many rites and ceremonies, and ordinances; we witness a great deal of preaching, praying and singing. But I believe it is impossible for man, and for all the arts and sciences, and philosophy, and all the knowledge that can be procured from them, to qualify a single individual for a preacher of the gospel of the Lord Jesus Christ. And wherefore: Because no man taketh this office, but he who is called of God, as Aaron was called; and if he is not called as Aaron was—if he is not baptised under the influence of Christ's spirit, if he is not taught in the school of Christ, he cannot be a minister of the gospel. He may be a minister of another gospel through the delusions of a disordered brain. Neither do I apprehend it is essential, that there should always be preaching. For what is worship? It is a disposition of the mind, in which we can draw nigh to God, and pour forth all our wants, all our desires, all our afflictions, into the bosom of our almighty friend, in whom is all wisdom, all power, and all knowledge in heaven and in earth. To this power all have access. The word is within us, that we may hear it and do it, "for the grace of God that bringeth salvation hath appeared unto all men, teaching us, that denying ungodliness, and worldly lusts, we should live soberly, righteously and Godly, in this present world, looking for that blessed hope, and the glorious ap-

pearing of the great God and our Saviour Jesus Christ."
If there is anything in verbal communication, it must spring
from a source different from that of a salary of one, two or
three thousand dollars a year. The qualifications must be
something different from rhetoric, elocution, or the elements
of theology ; or any of those arts and sciences which are depended on to qualify preachers of the gospel, at the present
day. As said the Apostle: "Yet in the church I had rather
speak five words with my understanding, that by my voice
I might teach others also, than ten thousand words in an
unknown tongue." To what purpose is preaching? Is it
to tickle the ears of men ; or is it by well turned periods and
flowing speech to amuse the imagination or reason of men?
No. If the gospel is properly preached, it answers to the
spirit and power of God, in the conscience of men, what
is necessary between God and man ; for spirits, as well as
bodies, have intercourse with each other. So if the gospel
is rightly preached, whether immediately or instrumentally,
it answers the witness for God in the souls, individually for
which it was intended, as face answers face in a glass. But
till this kind of preaching prevails more than it has done—
the preaching of the present day, will only darken counsel
by words without knowledge, whether in these assemblies,
or when separated.

What is prayer? Is it a particular position of the body ;
or a particular form of words addressed to the most high ?
No, verily ; and I apprehend we have mistaken this whole
subject, more than any other. We have even adopted the
language which Jesus taught his disciples ; and we even lie
to God, on our bended knees, when we utter this language :
"Our Father which art in heaven ;" when at the same time
we love him not, we reverence him not, as our Father, because we are not begotten into his nature, life and image.
His spirit rules not in us, therefore he is not our Father
which is in heaven. "Hallowed be thy name ;" when perhaps we swear by his name falsely, and take his name in
vain. And yet we can bow our knees and adopt the language "hallowed be thy name," and add, "thy kingdom

come, thy will be done in earth as it is done in heaven."
But where is the kingdom of heaven? Are we to look for
it at a great distance beyond the grave? What said Jesus
Christ when in that prepared body? Did he not declare to
the Jews, "the kingdom of heaven is within you." It is
there we must experience him to come and rule and reign in
our hearts. It is there we must know the declaration fulfilled, "a sceptre of righteousness is the sceptre of the kingdom; thou hast loved righteousness and hated iniquity:
therefore God, even thy God, hath anointed thee with the
oil of gladness above thy fellows." And now it is that we
can rightly pray, "thy kingdom come, thy will be done, in
earth as it is in heaven;" because our will is made subject
to his divine will, and the manifestation of his spirit; and
as he must rule and govern, then will be another declaration
fulfilled, in which may be viewed these things: "For unto
us a child is born, unto us a son is given: And the government shall be upon his shoulder: And his name shall be
called wonderful, counsellor, the mighty God, the everlasting Father, the Prince of Peace. Of the increase of his
government and peace there shall be no end; upon the throne
of David, and upon his kingdom, to order it, and to establish it with judgment and with justice, from henceforth even
forever." And of this peace there is no end; for if we attend to it, it will grow, and his dominion will be more ad-
vanced, and it will spread and become so comprehensive in
us, that every thing opposed to him will be brought under
the divine influence, and be regulated by his righteous spirit.
Then we can pray, because we shall know his will done in
us as in heaven; and then we shall not be depending on the
precepts and dogmas of men—we shall not be looking to
others, for we can rightly pray: "Give us this day our daily
bread, and forgive us our trespasses as we forgive those
who trespass against us," because we are willing to forgive
others: Then, and not till then, can we with propriety say,
"lead us not into temptation, but deliver us from evil; for
thine is the kingdom, and the power, and the glory forever,
amen."

5

What then is prayer? It is the aspiration of a devoted soul to God; and, whether clothed in language upon the bended knees, whether our hands are engaged in labor, whether we walk by the way, lie down or rise up, he, whose power is over all, and who is not only omnipotent but omnipresent, will hear the petitions of his needy servants. "To this man will I look, even to him that is poor, and of a contrite spirit, and trembleth at my word. For I will not contend forever, neither will I be always wrath: for the spirit should fail before me, and the soul which I have made." And said the Apostle, and "likewise the spirit helpeth our infirmities: for we know not what we should pray for as we ought; but the spirit maketh intercession for us, with groanings which cannot be uttered. And he that searcheth the heart knoweth what is the mind of the spirit, because he maketh intercession for the saints according to the will of God." Here we know what it is to have a mediator with the Father, even Jesus Christ. We know that he inspires us to pray for those things which are needful and convenient for us; and these prayers ascend to his holy habitation, even in heaven—Yea; they ascend as an acceptable sacrifice. And thus it is, that we may draw nigh unto God, and fulfill the declaration of the inspired penman— "Morning, noon and evening will I pray and cry aloud, and he shall hear my voice." And whatever our situation may be, we have access to this fountain of light and life. I know this, for I have experienced it in my own native land; and I have known it in a land of strangers; and I have experienced it upon the sea, when the billows rolled around us, and the mariners trembled; and I can testify that we were not deserted, neither was my mind left without comfort at that awful moment. There was an evidence in me that the foaming billows were held in the hollow of the Almighty's hand; and after they had foamed and lashed their waves there was a calm; there was a quiet. And when I reflect on these things, I am renewedly convinced, that all the human family may have access to the same fountain of goodness; that they may all draw near to the same source.

God looks not unto forms of words from those who supplicate him. I crave it for you and for my own soul's sake, that when you draw nigh unto God, you do it with singleness of heart; and if your knees are bowed, and you have been brought into a state of willingness to be humbled and humiliated, and ask not for this or that, which you may imagine to be best for you, but cast your cares upon him; then shall you know that he is a Father that careth for you, and you will come to know that he is your God. And being begotten into his likeness, you will daily increase in a knowledge of his attributes, and in the joys of his salvation.

Neither do I believe, that when we are thus assembled together we can rightly sing any of those psalms and hymns which are selected for the purpose. Can an assembly like this sing—"rivers of tears run down mine eyes," when we have perhaps never known what it was to sufficiently bewail our own deplorable condition. Can we say "as the hart panteth after the water brooks, so panteth my soul after thee, O God," when we never knew what it was to draw nigh to God, and to feel that hungering and thirsting after righteousness, which would enable us to sing with propriety unto him. If we sing, let us sing with the spirit and understanding; and also, if we pray let us pray with the spirit and with the understanding, that God may in all things be glorified. But I am renewedly convinced, that we cannot rightly sing till we have experienced a deliverance from sin, and a state of consolation in our minds; because as our sufferings abound, so will our consolation abound.

I am well convinced that when the children of Israel were encamped between the mountain and the sea; and they saw Pharaoh and the Egyptians behind them, and the Red Sea before them, they were not in a situation to sing; but when the Lord had commanded that the waters of the Red Sea should be divided, so that they passed through the midst of the sea on dry ground; and when they saw that their pursuers and enemies were scattered and destroyed, then they could rejoice and sing upon the banks of deliverance. "I will sing unto the Lord, for he hath triumphed gloriously:

the horse and his rider hath he thrown into the sea. The Lord is my strength and my song, and he is become my salvation—and he is my God, and I will exalt him."

It is only when we have experienced the dispersion of our enemies, and a deliverance from them, that we can sing suitably to the occasion. I apprehend that none of those spiritual songs were ever designed to be placed in measured words; but every soul, as he hath received so let him occupy. But I apprehend, that in this company, there have been many suitably engaged in mental supplication; and in the quietude of their passions they have received impressions from on high, and have had deep instruction sealed unto them. And who could sing upon the banks of deliverance, and declare "The sea saw it, and fled: Jordan was driven back. The mountains skipped like rams, and the little hills like lambs—before the power of God." And, my friends, the effects brought forth by the spiritual operation of this divine power will regulate every passion—pride will be brought into humility. Every passion and every propensity; nay, every disposition of the human mind will be brought under the control of this principle; for man is a free agent. We are created with an animal body and a spiritual body—we have animal or instinctive propensities. as other animals have—we are subject to the effects of heat, cold, hunger and thirst; and we have other animal faculties. Now, I apprehend the efficacy of the holy religion is. in bringing our animal faculties into obedience to those which are spiritual.

If Adam and Eve had been willing to suffer the law of the spirit to govern their animal faculties, they would have grown from a state of negative innocency into a state of positive virtue. But choosing to become wise in their own way, by suffering their own affections and passions to have the pre-eminence, they lost that wisdom at which they were aiming; for those evil propensities gained the pre-eminence over them. And so it is with each individual of the present day. Those who have attended to the inward manifestation of the spirit, have grown in grace, and in the knowledge of

God ; but those who have suffered their animal propensities to govern them, have sunk deeper and deeper into the gulf of iniquity.

Now, with respect to this grace of God, this baptism of the Holy Ghost : Let us look a little at the effects which it produces in religion. It is a teacher of righteousness and doctrine, which preaches not according to the dogmas of men ; but it is that which is preached in all men, yea, in every creature ; and has been most beautifully described in an account recorded of the wars in heaven, and probably adopted with views similar to those of Homer and Milton.

Jesus Christ tells us the kingdom of heaven is within us, of course, then he must govern. "And there was war in heaven ; Michael and his angels fought against the dragon ; and the dragon fought and his angels, and prevailed not ; neither was there place found any more in heaven." Now what were these angels that fought with Michael? Were they any thing more than heavenly dispositions, which ought to govern the human mind? I apprehend that God maketh his angels spirits, and his ministers a flame of fire, and are they not all ministering spirits sent forth to minister, for those who shall be heirs of salvation? What are the fruits of the spirit? They are heavenly dispositions ; such as love, joy, peace, long-suffering, gentleness, goodness, together with a whole host of heavenly virtues ; against which there is no law : And when we come to find the angel of love to cast out the devil of hatred, and the angel of mercy, to war against the devil of cruelty ; and the angel of temperance, against the devil of intemperance ; and the angel of hope, to cast out the devil of despair, and every heavenly minister of God to cast out its opposite, or its enemy ; then we shall come into a state in which we can testify that there was war in heaven—In which "Michael and his angels fought against the dragon ; and the dragon fought and his angels, and prevailed not ; neither was there place found any more in heaven." This brings us as the Apostle spake, "I knew a man in Christ about fourteen years ago (whether in the body I cannot tell ; or whether out of the body I cannot tell: God knoweth,) such an one caught up to the third heaven. And I knew such a man, (whether in the body, or out of the body, I cannot tell : God knoweth,) how that he was caught up into Paradise, and heard unspeakable words which it is not lawful for a man to utter." And those who thus experience this warfare, will hear those things which are not lawful to be uttered. "To him that overcometh will I give to eat of the hidden manna, and will give him a white stone, and in the stone a new name written, which no man knoweth, saving he that receiveth it."

Now, I apprehend that heaven is a state and not a place : And if our affections are fixed on things of a low groveling nature ; and if our animal passions are permitted to govern, there is our heaven ; for there is a first and a last heaven ; and whatever our affections are placed in, there is our heaven, there is our hope of enjoyment. If then we are under the influence of our numerous passions, we are in the first or lowest heaven. But Paul was trained up at the feet of Gamalies, and taught according to the perfect manner of the law of the fathers, and was zealous towards God—he had advantages above many of us ; but he actually went so far in attempting to persecute those called by the name by which we are called, that he came into a state, in which he believed he was verily doing God service—here was a second heaven. But when he attained to that heavenly vision which appeared unto him, then he heard things which were not lawful to be uttered ; because thus the mysteries of heaven were revealed to him through the immediate communion with the author of his existence. And thus it is that we must advance from the lowest heaven to the highest—we must experience this war between the angels of God and the angels of the devil. And when we have experienced these operations—these effects—then when we stand on mount Zion, we can "sing the song of Moses the servant of God ; and the song of the lamb, saying, great and marvelous are thy works, Lord God Almighty ; just and true are thy ways, thou king of saints."

And this I apprehend constitutes the true ground of the doctrine of election and reprobation ; for reprobation I ap-

prehend has been from the foundation of the world, a disobedience to the manifestations of the spirit—but if we
attend to them, and obey them, we come under the influence
of the holy spirit, and know him to be a teacher, a preserver,
and a guide; and as we grow in grace and strength, we become more and more likened unto our divine pattern—we
become wedded together, and are heirs of God, and joint
heirs with Christ; for which cause he is not ashamed to call
them brethren, because they are begotten into the same
power. But if, on the contrary, we neglect these manifestations, and disobey him, we shall not have his power to
rule over us; and these manifestations will become weaker
and weaker, till we are brought into a state, that we are not
sensible of any good thought, word or work. This is not in
consequence of any foreordination of God; but because we
have hardened our hearts, and cast his law from us, "for it
is baptism that doth also now save us (not putting away the
filth of the flesh, but) the answer of a good conscience before God." It is my desire that we may all attain unto
this, let our name be what it may. Names are but the distinction of things; but Christ is one, religion is one; and
if we are not under the influence, and have not the mind of
Christ, and have none of his light, let our names be what
they may, it will avail us nothing. Therefore I have desired
that all may experience this, to become a growing principle
over our minds, conduct, and actions; for it will crucify
every passion. For the Lord shall comfort Zion, he will
comfort all her waste places; and he will make her wilderness like Eden, and her desert like the garden of the Lord:
joy and gladness shall be found therein, thanksgiving and
the voice of melody. And that you may individually experience a foretaste of this, here below, and enjoy its full consummation in a future state, is the earnest desire of your poor
brother, who was induced from these motives, to request this
opportunity. Feeling thankful for your attentive and quiet
deportment, I affectionately bid you all farewell. And may
the grace of the Lord Jesus Christ, and the love of God,
and the communion of the Holy Ghost, be with you all
henceforth.

SERMON IV.

DELIVERED BY THOMAS WETHERALD, IN LOMBARD STREET MEETING, BALTI-
MORE, ON THE MORNING OF THE SIXTH OF FIRST MONTH, 1826.

Our opinions of what some term religion, and religious
truth, are, in a great degree, formed by the circumstances
with which we are surrounded; and I apprehend, that a
great part of the religion of the present day, is founded in
tradition and education. Now, we find that causes which
are essentially different and opposite, may produce results
which, to the casual observer, are very similar.

There is a variety of causes which produce a great appearance of religious zeal, and of great religious knowledge;
and to instance one: I am convinced, that all the powers of
eloquence combined have never begotten in the soul of man
one single, actual, real, devotional feeling. It may have
caused ebullitions of the imagination, and an excitement of
the feelings; and under this excitement, from these external
causes, the powers of eloquence, (instead of the spirit of
God) have operated on the feelings and imagination: and
thence has arisen a great appearance of zeal; and many
have kindled a fire, and warmed themselves with the sparks
thereof, and brought upon themselves all the denunciation
of the Lord. "Behold, all ye that kindle a fire, that compass yourselves about with sparks; walk in the light of
your fire, and in the sparks that ye have kindled. This
shall ye have of mine hand; ye shall lie down in sorrow."

There is a great variety of other causes which have produced this kind of superficial religion in the world, which
stands in opinions, principles and doctrines, so called, which
never gained the victory over one solitary appetite, passion,

or lust. And from these causes, these traditional and external causes, have arisen those divisions, which even at the present day, are a disgrace to the christian name.

Was this ever the design of Omnipotence ; or is there any thing in the gospel dispensation that causes these divisions? No. For as God is one, his name one ; so is his design one : that mankind should become united in him, be brought into his own nature, created anew in Christ Jesus, begotten in the image of the Father. Hence it is evident, from truth positive, that the religion of the present day, is not the religion of the Lord Jesus Christ ; but it results from another, an inferior, an opposing source.

Now, if we place mankind at points which diverge from each other, the Papists, Episcopalians, Presbyterians, Baptists, Methodists and Quakers, each at the distance which they stand from the grand truth, and place them in the world around it, each at the distance at which they stand one from another, under the prejudice of education, and those things created by surrounding circumstances, all under the influence of passion, opposition, and a propensity to rule among us, we will find these sects all governed, more or less, by these circumstances, notwithstanding the divided state into which we have brought ourselves, by disobedience and forgetfulness of God, and the ebullitions of the imagination and passions. But notwithstanding all this, if we were willing in our own minds, to be led and guided by this principle, inherent in all men, and which remains a witness for God, set to be a light of the Gentiles ; and for salvation unto the ends of the earth. These sectarian feelings, these prejudices of education, and these traditional views, which we have imbibed, would be gradually decomposed ; our minds would come under the illimitable power of divine light ; and instead of diverging farther from each other, we should gradually draw into the same focus ; into the same power, the same light ; and that which was made to Israel formerly a pillar of cloud by day, and a pillar of fire by night, to guide them in their way, would be a guide unto us, and it would continue to lead us all, under the immediate influence of the spirit of truth.

And every opposing spirit would fall under its influence and power; and every opposing disposition, passion and propensity, would be overcome, crucified and slain. This becomes the root and ground of all true religion ; for it always has been and always will be, and it is in vain for these societies, or any society to boast of purity or holiness; unless they are led by the spirit of truth, the light of Christ, the grace of God, or call it by what name you may ;—while our minds are under the influence of opinions imbibed by education and traditional views, the ebullitions of the imagination, the excitement of feelings or passions. If we ever come to worship God aright, we shall know him to be the rule of our conduct and the gaide of our actions. We must be in a state opposed to and contrary to all those things—it must be by a quiet crucifixion of every passion, and by relinquishing every such tradition and doctrine, and we can become acquainted with our God, and experience the exercise into which this will lead us, though at times it may seem small, yet if faithfully submitted to, will assuredly lead into an acknowledgment of "one Lord, one faith, one baptism, one God and Father of all, who is above all, and through all, and in you all." And though the effect may be small to the view of the casual observer, between these and them, yet they are produced by different effects, and are essentially different. For one proceeding from the immediate power and influence of the operation of the spirit of God, leads the heart into subjection and obedience, and thus produces devotional feelings in the mind ; and under the influence of these feelings we draw nigh to God, with fervent hearts, with pure lips and holy affections. We draw nigh to him with a full purpose of heart and spirit of prayer to the Father of lights ; and thus we shall be led out of bondage, sin and corruption, into the glorious liberty of the sons and daughters of God. Others, under the influence of excitement, whether caused by this, or any other natural feeling, may be led to the same devotional exercise, but may be influenced by very different motives and feelings. Some may be actuated by a desire to appear popular and honorable among men; and others may be influenced by feelings of an interested nature, thinking that it is honorable to be religious; and there have been instances wherein the profession of the religion of Jesus Christ has been so disgraced; as individuals have been induced to embrace certain doctrines from corrupt and avaricious motives—they have taken the name of religion, and worshipped God; but these things ought not so to be. And to the casual observer, the careless, the inexperienced observer, the difference between these classes may appear very small; but God sees not as man sees. While man views the outward actions, God searcheth the hearts and trieth the reins of all men, and rewards us according to the works or deeds done in the body. If our affections are pure; if our passions are regulated; if our lusts are crucified, and we come immediately under the regenerating effects of light and life, designed by our God, to lead us through every trial and tribulation, into the heavenly wisdom, it will bring us into this principle of worship acceptably unto him. Every ebullition of a sincere heart will be accepted, if our affections are purely spiritual. Thus it will bring the whole human family into one point, the light of Christ which is the light of man in the conscience, soul, and spirit. Then where will be the room for these divisions which disgrace the christian name? Where will there be room for dissention, and for these wars and fightings? They would vanish, they would be cast out, they would be taken away; and every earthly propensity would become purified, and all the malignant passions would return to the regions of their native darkness. And I know of no other name under heaven among men, which can produce these results; neither do I know of any other religion, or doctrine, which will call off your attention from your grovelling habits, but the light of Christ, which operates upon your souls, and enables you to gain a victory over every opposing spirit and disposition. And it is inherent in all. There is not an individual of the whole human family, who has not a sufficiency of the light to lead him out of all the perplexities into which he has been drawn by disobedience and forgetfulness of God. And however widely we may have differed, and however we may have been opposed to the light of truth; however we may have surrounded it, at an immense distance; still if we come immediately under its influence, every traditional opinion would be removed, our prejudices would fall beneath its increasing light; and every passion being subdued, we should give way to conviction; and thus we should first become babes, and even at this point of divergance, we should be favored with so much light, as would overcome a little, of the many obstructions, by which we have been enveloped.

The more fully we attend to these manifestatinns, the stronger they will become, and the greater advances we shall make, till from this point, we shall draw nearer and our strength will increase; our knowledge of God will be strengthened; and our faith will be daily renewed; and through the daily operative power of the same spirit, a continued watchfulness of disposition would be recommended to us, as an essential of christianity, to watch and pray, lest ye enter into temptation.

I am renewedly convinced; and I am not ashamed to acknowledge it, that I know of no higher state of attainment, than that of watchfulness and prayer. For if we ever have this ground of safety, I know what will be the effect, for I have experienced it. We are apt to reason thus, I will take a little more latitutde now, I know the way, I can return to it at pleasure, and at leisure. I will take a little swing in the indulgence of imaginary gratifications—I will take a little swing in the pleasures of the world—I will stop a little in my religious career; but I shall know where I stopped, and of course return to my post. But thou fool, canst thou say to the troubled sea, thus far shalt thou go and no farther? This disposition, which may have prevailed in many of our minds, is evil in its nature, and evil in its tendency; as we thus choose our own ways, to walk under the influence of our own evil devices; and if we are ever able to return to the

point from which we diverged, we may rest assured, that it
must be through the depths of affliction—it must be through
the power of that baptism, which regulates every affection,
which crucifies every passion and lust, which our imagination and our visionary views may have suggested. And I
know not of a more dangerous state than that of those who
thus attempt to limit the Holy One of Israel; as many of
those who leave the path of rectitude, promising themselves
to return, will be more and more entangled in the twisting
and twining of the subtle enemy; and thus they will find to
their soul's loss and affliction, that they are not masters of
themselves; and when they give way to their passions and
inclinations, they cannot recall them to their proper subjection, to the light and power of God. But, by operating in
true obedience thereto, these passions are subjected, and thus
every disorderly emotion is regulated, every unruly appetite
subdued, and every lust crucified and staid. But when we
pollute this power, and diverge abroad, our evil propensities
will grow strong and powerful, and so in proportion as these
grow and increase, the power of light, of knowledge, and of
religious experience will daily decrease; and our spiritual
vision will become dim; and we shall go farther and farther
from the path of rectitude; and though at times, we may
attempt to return, yet mountains of opposition will interpose
to hide, from our view, the object of our desire; and hills of
difficulty will present, which we cannot surmount; and
oceans of imaginary troubles, which we can never pass without another marvellous interposition of that power, who has
in all ages commanded the winds and the waves; and who
has caused the mountains to skip like rams, and the little
hills like lambs.

O, my friends, and fellow professors of the christian name,
and fellow heirs of salvation, I know this ground; I have
trodden in these desolate and thorny paths; I have known
what it was to taste the mercy of God, in Christ Jesus—I
have known what it was to come to this consolation. But I
reasoned thus—I know the way to that power which passeth
all understanding, I need not to be so very cautious of every

thought—I will give loose a little to my imagination, I will quickly return—I will therefore give loose to conversation, contrary to the nature of this Gospel of Christ; and indulge in things, which, in the view of the world, are neither good nor evil—I can go thus far, and no man can say that I am inconsistent. I have tried this, my friends, and I found that it led my mind into a state of misery, and awful apostacy, and into greater degeneracy from the power of God, than I was ever placed in before I knew him, or was aware of his operations upon my spirit: In consequence of which a deeper baptism was necessary. I had to return through a more awful dispensation of the Almighty's judgment, in order to be replaced; and "day unto day uttereth speech, and night unto night sheweth knowledge." And if it may afford encouragement to my fellow travelers and heirs of eternity, I am willing to expose myself still further, by a declaration, that since that day in which I took my "flight on the sabbath," there has been a less powerful manifestation unto me, in his love and mercy, and all his glorious attributes have appeared less pre-eminent, since that day in which I departed from my first love; I have never heard and never witnessed a full and complete manifestation of his love. I have gone mourning over my own deviations; and perhaps, this is the cause, why I am this day separated from all that was dear and near to me in infancy; and, perhaps, for that very rebellion I am cast out as an abominable branch on this shore, where the face of none was known to me; distant from many of those who used to console me and advise me, and endeavor to keep me in the path of rectitude.

I pray for you all, that you may avoid these slips, which have produced such awful results; which have filled my bones with poverty, till I have even been obliged to cry out "the treacherous dealer, dealeth treacherously." Yea, I want you to remember, that whilst the mercy of God shines around you; whilst its voice is heard, attend to its manifestations, that you may experience the power of its preservation instead of going a mourning wanderer, occasionally calling others to repentance, when he has been with you; and craving that your minds may be preserved in calmness and love, that you may continue to enjoy all the social affections, from which I am cut off. O, my young friends, my soul has often yearned over you with feelings of affection! I well remember when I was a youth, and surrounded by my brethren and sisters, and with one of these I could ask counsel and experience comfort—with one of these I could interchange sentiments—I could reap instruction. But these privileges are lost to me forever. Now, I want you from all these circumstances, and your own experience of the knowledge of God, and the operation of his spirit upon your own minds, to avoid these slips. I want you to be willing to enter in at the strait gate. "For wide is the gate, and broad is the way that leadeth to destruction, and many there be that go in thereat: Because, strait is the gate, and narrow is the way which leadeth unto life, and few there be that find it." "And verily I say unto you, many shall strive to enter in, and shall not be able" And wherefore? because they are striving to enter in at the strait gate, and to take with them all their lusts, passions, and unsubdued affections. O, vain attempt! O hopeless enterprise! If ever you enter in at the strait gate, you must give up all these—you must be stripped naked and become destitute. We must know the leaven of regeneration of the Holy Ghost to purify our souls and rectify every affection, and crucify every passion, and subdue every lust: and then we can enter in at the strait gate. But every ravenous disposition must be excluded—every imaginary power must be withdrawn, and we must walk in the light of the law. "In a path which no fowl knoweth, and which the vulture's eye hath not seen: The lion's whelps have not trodden it, nor the fierce lion passed by it: For the Lord shall dwell there—the redeemed of the Lord shall walk there." The language of invitation is "Come with me from Lebanon, my spouse, with me from Lebanon; look from the top of Abana; from the top of Shenir and Hermon; from the Lions' dens; from the mountains of the leopards—from all the pinnacles of pride; from all the high and lofty places; from all those places which are above the natural level of that divine principle which is designed to cover the mind. Come with me from Lebanon, my spouse, look from the top of Shenir, and from the lions' dens, and from the mountains of the leopards, and from all ravenous dispositions—from all those lion-like dispositions, into that daily watchfulness, which I have recommended ; and where alone we can walk in the light of the Lord, and know him to be our counsellor. Thus shall we be preserved in every affliction ; and our wisdom being from God, we shall partake of the divine nature, we shall be endued with that wisdom, which is first pure, then peaceable, gentle, easy to be entreated, full of mercy and good fruits, without partiality and without hypocracy.'' This will enable us, not only to calm those passions, which disgrace human nature ; but it will enable us to fulfill every civil, every social, every virtuous, and every religious duty.

O my beloved friends, how precious is this privilege, these fruits how amiable, when they become inhabitants of the mind, and when compared with those of an opposite, or evil tendency. And I want it to be renewedly impressed on your minds, that there is no other medium than by that light given unto all, and which is a portion of the same light, the same power, whereby the worlds were made ; and which, to the Israelites, was a pillar of cloud by day, and a pillar of fire by night. We may rest assured, having this guide, that every propensity of our corrupt nature, must bow to its power.

I want to direct you to this living and eternal principle, which will enable you to overcome every enemy, which you may be called to encounter. It will enable you to come from Lebanon ; come with me from Lebanon my spouse, with me from Lebanon ; look from the top of Abana ; from the top of Shenir and Hermon, from the mountains of the Leopards, and from the Lions' dens.

SERMON V.

DELIVERED BY THOMAS WETHERALD AT THE "SAILORS' BETHEL," BALTI-
MORE, FIRST MONTH 4, 1826.*

Though Paul declared, that he was not behind the chiefest
of the apostles, yet he complained that when he would do
good, evil was present with him, because he found a law in
his members warring with the law of his mind, and bringing him into subjection to the law of sin and death. The
same dispositions and passions actuate us in the present day;
for the same power has possessed each of our minds; but
Paul knew another law, for, says he, I was alive without
the law once, but when the law came, sin revived, and I
died. Now, these three different laws under which the
apostle was placed, are, the being alive to the law of his
members, the law of sin and death, the law of the natural
affections, which govern the whole body, soul and spirit.
Another law in which he was alive once, was the legal dispensation which came by Moses, and in which, says he, I
profited above many of my equals, for he was trained up at
the feet of Gamaliel. He knew all the wisdom of the law
in which he profited, as became his strict profession, yet
when the law came, sin revived, and he died. Now, under
the legal dispensation, Paul rejoiced in his own righteousness, and became for God, a persecutor of the followers of
Christ; but after a peculiar manifestation of divine love and
wisdom, had called him out of the level of his own righteousness into a more spiritual dispensation, he became es-

---

* This discourse was not reported by Mr. Gould, but by one of his pupils, who
attended the meeting in Mr. G.'s absence.

6

tranged from the mind which had formerly governed him ; and now, under a sense of the feelings of compunction, he cried out, O wretched man that I am, who shall deliver me from the body of this death. It was under the power of this deliverance, that he knew all the powers of the law, and the wisdom of the law to be vain ; even that law, which was of divine origin, which came through Moses from the immediate face of God upon mount Sinai. But though the law was of divine origin, it could not remove the body of death, which can only be removed by the grace of God, through Jesus Christ. It is by the power of this deliverance from sin, that we can bear this beautiful testimony : I knew a man in Christ, fourteen years ago, caught up into the third heaven, where he heard things not lawful to be uttered. And what is heaven ? It is not merely a place, it is a state ; and verily, if our affections are placed on things above, great and unspeakable will be our pleasure and our rest. And we come to this state of enjoyment : "I knew a man in Christ, above fourteen years ago, whether in the body, I cannot tell, or whether out of the body, I cannot tell, God knoweth ; such an one caught up into the third heaven, where he heard things not lawful to be uttered." Whilst Paul continued in his corrupt affections, he was in the first and lowest heaven, grovelling in those animal propensities and those passions which are a disgrace to human nature. No doubt, Paul's rigid education brought him into a kind of systematic morality, consisting of external observances, outward principles, and doctrines in which he profited above many of his equals, and in which he was alive once : I was alive once without the law, but when the law came, sin revived, and I died. Thousands are in this situation, making a profession of external rites, according to the systematic morality of the world, and thus are brought into the second heaven. Their peace and enjoyment is placed in this : I am a good neighbor, an honest tradesman ; I am a member of the church ; I have a well grounded hope of heaven ; this is the second heaven. The mind continues cold ; the evil is not taken away ; our affections are unchanged ;

our passions are unsubdued; our lusts unsubjected. But
when we come under the influence of the law of the spirit
of life in Christ Jesus, which sets us free from the law of
sin and death, we are enabled to say, O wretched man that
I am—who shall deliver me from the body of this death?
Here is a state attainable by every individual of this assembly; yea, every individual of the whole human family
can attain unto this third heaven, and hear things not lawful to be uttered; and thus we shall experience the mysteries of the kingdom to be opened to our view, and we shall
find matter of thankfulness, according to the declaration of
Christ, I thank thee, Father, Lord of heaven and earth, because thou hast hid these things from the wise and the prudent, and hast revealed them unto babes: even so Father,
for so it seemed good in thy sight. And thus we come unto
the law of the spirit of Christ, and by its influence and operations, it opens the blind eyes, unstops the deaf ears, and
heals every malady, even unto leprosy, raised from the dead.
It brings us into a state in which we can say a mighty angel
stood, having one foot upon the sea, and one foot upon the
earth, and lifted up his right hand unto heaven, and sware
by him that liveth for ever and ever, that there should be
time no longer. Our minds will be raised by these consid-
erations, and time will be lost in hope and faith. We shall
be led into the practice of every religious, every social, and
every manly virtue. These operations will bring us into an
immortal state, a state in which we shall become kings and
priests unto God. We shall reign upon the earth, and our
dominion will be over all those discordant passions, over
discord which opens the way to all those overbearing lusts,
which drown us in perdition. All these glorious effects will
be produced, and we shall be brought into the third heaven,
and comprehend the mysteries thereof. We shall know these
things; and in our meetings, we shall be prepared by the
immediate operation of the spirit, for the preaching of the
gospel, and we shall know an angel to fly through the midst
of heaven, having the everlasting gospel to preach: and
what is the gospel? It is not contained in the systems of

men : it does not consist in a belief in notions, in doctrines, and in dogmas, which we can neither understand nor comprehend ; this is not the gospel. This is not the gospel which was preached by the angel who cried, fear God and give glory unto him, for the hour of his judgment is come, and worship him that made heaven and earth, the seas and fountains of water. And where is his judgment, and when shall the hour of judgment come ? Are we to look for it at a great distance and beyond the grave ? Are we to look for them in terror, or dread, or despair, the usual concomitants of hell ? No, verily ; my beloved fellow professors of this name, this holy name by which we are called ; even in the present day, at the present moment, the judgments are set and the books are opened. In the present moment, the inmost recesses of our hearts (for the kingdom of heaven is within) are opened before God. There is not an individual present, who cannot testify, that he has experienced often times, the spirit of judgment and of burning to rest upon him.

John said, I indeed baptise you with water unto repentance, but he that cometh after me is mightier than I, the latchet of whose shoes I am not worthy to stoop down and unloose ; he shall baptise you with the Holy Ghost and with fire. The baptism of the gospel dispensation is a baptism which is thus represented : Whose fan is in his hand, and he will thoroughly purge his floor, and gather his wheat into his garner, but he will burn up the chaff with unquenchable fire. These are the operations of this baptism which operates on our individual natures. Each soul may be saved : to each soul are the means of salvation brought ; for I believe that we are all equally the objects of the divine regard. Baptism is essential to salvation. Not indeed the going through the water, which is an emblem of the cleansing operation of the spirit. Baptism was a rite of the Jewish law. But all the waters of the sea will not purge us from one single, solitary lust or passion, but the baptism of Jesus Christ is essential, cleansing, operative and saving. There is no other baptism ; for it is declared there is one

Lord, one faith, and one baptism; one God and Father of all, who is over all, and through all, and in you all.

Thus, by its divine influence on our minds, we are instructed in wisdom; by the baptism of the Holy Ghost, we are purified from all unholiness, and unrighteousness of men, our affections are crucified by the reproofs for sin, and by degrees, we become willing to bow before its influence, and by its purifying operations, it burns up all evil within us. But when we feel those operations, instead of waiting patiently to come under their influence, we go from them into company, and by reading books in themselves not valuable and foolish, we endeavor to divert our minds from these feelings, which would have brought us into judgment. If we attend to its manifestations, it grows stronger and stronger, and works repentance, not to be repented of. My beloved, this is the gospel, this is the gospel preached in every creature. As we attend unto this gospel, to the immediate manifestations of its power, though they may appear small often times, they will grow and overtop, and overcome every evil disposition, every natural passion and propensity; and we shall experience the declaration fulfilled, the law of the spirit of life in Christ Jesus, has set us free from the law of sin and death. These effects may be produced without the necessity of administering the outward elements; without the necessity of going back again to a decreased dispensation, which was only a preparatory dispensation; for John testified, he must increase, and I must decrease. I feel little hesitation in saying, that by believing in the baptism of water, we are really and virtually denying the coming of Christ in his internal manifestation: this outward baptism, hath neither the power nor the efficacy attributed to it; according to the declaration of the prophet Isaias, Prepare ye the way of the Lord, make straight his paths. Every valley shall be exalted, and every mountain and hill shall be made low, and the crooked shall be made straight, and the rough places plain, and the glory of the Lord shall cover the earth, as the waters cover the sea, and all flesh shall see it. Now I apprehend that this is a direct allusion to the different dispositions of men. Some are rash and lofty ; some are fierce and cruel ; these are the mountains which shall be brought into subjection by the spirit. Sorrow and trouble shall fall upon them because they indulge in these dispositions ; for my friends, guilt alone can bring these feelings on the mind ; whilst our hearts are conscious of innocency, we cannot experience these feelings.

If we are under the influence of these dispositions, let our name be what it may, we shall necessarily be subject to despair and trouble ; and this state will continue until we shall be washed and purged from sin. I know of no other power or influence which is able to produce these effects ; but the purifying baptism, which I have endeavored to bring a little before your view.

The blood of Christ is his life ; not merely that blood which was shed without the gates of Jerusalem ; we must place our dependence on nothing outward. The blood of bulls, and the ashes of goats, will never take away sin ; neither do I believe that the outward blood will ever cleanse my soul from my guilt, or from the guilt of Adam. I have considered this a strong figure. It was the fulfillment of the law ; neither do I believe that that act of malignity in the Jews, in crucifying the righteous Jesus, will ever enable us to work the righteousness of God. I want it to be impressed on our minds, that this last act was yet under the Jewish dispensation, which was a figurative dispensation ; but as the consummation of all figures, the contract, if I may use the expression, was broken. But the blood is the life ; it is the circulating medium, which gives vitality to the whole system. We are thus brought into its own divine nature and holiness, and into obedience to the manifestations of God, into the life of Christ, who will not be ashamed to call us his brethren. Then we shall be begotten into the same light, and walk by the same rule, and mind the same thing ; we shall become perfect in him ; branches of the true and living vine. We shall experience the enjoyments of heaven, for the kingdom of heaven is within.

Others again are ready to despond, and to adopt the language, Has the Lord forgotten to be gracious? Is his mercy clean gone over me for ever? I apprehend that these, instead of condemnation and reproof, receive the consolations of the Lord's table, and are comforted by his spirit.

Whoever endures these operations, will come into the true faith, and know that this is a vital and an operative principle; that it overcomes the world; it does not consist in a nominal belief in opinions and dogmas, or in the authenticity of the scriptures.

Faith works by love, and we must become subject to the obedience of Christ; for faith is an essential result of this obedience to the manifestations of the spirit of God. Thus we will be increasing and growing in knowledge and religious experience; and opinions and sentiments would be indelibly scaled in the line of our experience. By these internal operations, we should be brought into the third heaven, and hear things not lawful to be uttered. I want it to be understood, that when we come to feel and to experience these things, we come to be partakers also of their divine and blessed effects. This kind of religion brings us into an experimental knowledge of the life of Christ, who will govern and rule in his kingdom, according to the declaration already quoted—the kingdom of heaven is within. I want this kind of vital and practical religion to spread and increase, and thus we shall not see those divisions which exist among professing christians, whether Papists, or Episcopalians, or Presbyterians, or Methodists, or Swedenborgians, or Quakers. The numerous divisions which arise, are not necessarily the result of the gospel. They arise from the setting up of systems and beliefs, which bring us into Babylonish darkness, and a confusion of languages. It is thus that we are brought into divisions, strife, and dissentions, and come into a state in which we say one unto another: stand by thyself, come not near unto me, for I am holier than thou.

. We must be brought down to the same level; we must be brought into a state of humiliation. Then we shall know the glory of the Lord to cover the earth as the waters cover the sea. This is the millenial state, which is not attached to times ; but when we come into this state, we shall know that a mighty angel stood with one foot upon the sea, and one foot upon the earth ; upon our affections, our corrupt passions and lusts ; and lifted up his right hand unto heaven, and sware by him that liveth forever and ever, that there should be time no longer. Our affections will be removed from sublunary things ; days, months, years, names, and all external things will sink into their native insignificancy : all that is combustible in us, will be burnt up by the spirit of judgment and of burning. When we come into this pure and holy state, we shall stand, having harps of God in our hands, and sing the song of Moses, the servant of God, and the song of the Lamb, saying, Great and marvelous are all thy works, Lord God Almighty ; just and true are all thy ways, thou king of saints.

Assuredly the design of the Gospel is, to bring us into a heavenly state, to purify us by the operation of the spirit of God ; and thus it brings us to know that there was war in heaven ; Michael and his angels fought, the dragon also and his angels, and prevailed not ; neither was there place found any more in heaven. And what are angels ? They are the ministers of God for good : He maketh his angels spirits, and his ministers a flame of fire. These angels are not what they are generally considered ; our views of angels and of heaven are taken from education and tradition ; we do not rest our belief on our own experimental knowledge of the truth, nor even on the accounts of the Scriptures themselves ; they are derived from fabulous stories ; from Homer and from Milton. But that heaven is within, according to the saying of Christ himself, in whom I believe most assuredly as the Redeemer, the Saviour, and the Mediator, not merely in his outward manifestation of flesh, but in his internal manifestation in the heart. The angel of love will cast out the demon of hatred ; the angel of hope will cast out the demon of despair ; the angel of temperance will cast out the demon of intemperance.

It was written under the Jewish dispensation, "Thou shalt

love the Lord thy God, with all thy heart, and with all thy soul, and with all thy mind, and with all thy strength," which is the first and greatest commandment. And the second is like unto it ; "thou shalt love thy neighbor as thyself ;" on these two hang all the law and the prophets. On these hangs also the fulfilment of the Gospel dispensation : wherever we fulfil this, all wars and dissensions, all squabblings are banished to the regions of eternal darkness. When we come under this divine dispensation, it leads us out of the indulgence of our natural affections and propensities. The Lord hath overcome the world ; and the divine word begets us into its own divine nature ; it regards not the changes of time ; it overcomes every evil passion : and then the angel of love casts out the demon of hatred ; the angel of mercy casts out the demon of cruelty ; the angel of temperance casts out the demon of intemperance ; the angel of hope casts out the devil of despair ; the angel of a living faith casts out the demon of infidelity ; and every ministering angel casts out its opposite, its adversary, and its enemy. And thus our minds become pure, and we can bear this testimony ; there was war in heaven, Michael and his angels fought ; the dragon also and his angels, and prevailed not, neither was there place found any more in heaven. Now, here is a state clearly attainable by all ; the means afforded are fully adequate ; they do not consist in a belief in dogmas, and sentiments, and opinions, and doctrines, so called, which are imbibed by tradition and education, but in the baptising operation of the Holy Ghost, bringing us into an obedience to the word of God, the rule of faith and practice. This name has been attributed to the Scriptures, but no name is worthy of this, but the name of Christ alone, who is the power of God. I apprehend that by this, we make the bible, which was intended to be one of the choicest blessings of heaven, into a grievous curse. If we make the Scriptures the word of God, and only rule of faith and practice, and endeavor to shape our opinions wholly by its precepts, we shall become Bible Christians ; and there is a great difference between Bible Christians, and Spiritual Christians. Bible

Christians are contending for precepts and doctrines, while yet under the influence of their carnal propensities; but Spiritual Christians by daily attending to the Spirit or Word of God, come to worship the Father in spirit and in truth. And as the spirit, or grace of God, or word, or wisdom of God, call it by what name you may, is an operative principle, it has the chief agency in all religious instruction.

Then we experience the fulfillment of those mighty miracles, which are recorded, and which remain to be operated even at the present day. When by its operative power on our minds, we receive the Gospel dispensation, and we attend thereto, it opens the blind eyes of the understanding, unstops the deaf ears, and heals every malady, even unto leprosy; it raises the dead, and casts out devils, even though we were possessed of a legion.

My beloved friends, our religion may not only direct us in youth, and in the strength of manhood; it will also be a support to us in prosperity and in adversity, in sorrow and in sickness. Then we shall be enabled to adopt the language O death, where is thy sting, O grave, where is thy victory. The sting of death is sin. We shall know that the law of the spirit of life, in Christ Jesus, has set us free from the law of sin and death. Every sting will be removed, and we shall come into that holy confidence which casts out all dread and sorrow. We shall have that evidence which cannot be removed, having the light of God to direct us day by day, and thus we shall come to know that the little stone was cut of the mountain without hands, without the aid of human learning, or of literary education, but only by an obedience to the grace of God; we know that the little stone overcome the mighty image which Nebuchadnezzar saw, and smote the image whose feet and toes were made partly of iron, and partly of potter's clay, those strong materials partially built on the truth, and partially on the clay of human invention; the little stone smote upon the feet and the toes, and break them in pieces.

When we come into this state, the scriptures will be opened to our understanding, and we shall know, and be able to acknowledge, the experience of the same spirit which dictated them to the holy men, and shall be able to declare his arm is not shortened, that he cannot save; neither is his ear grown heavy, that he cannot hear. But our iniquities and our sins have withheld these good things from us. The indulgence of our sinful natures raises an insuperable barrier to the salvation of our souls, and brings us into darkness and confusion, yea, darkness that can be felt, and for these punishments, we need not look at a great distance, and beyond the grave. Many there are, who experience the torments of hell, and the righteous experience the joys of heaven even in this life, and feel the joys and blessings of his salvation. And if we experience these things whilst clothed with mortality, whilst we receive them through this veil of flesh, what shall we not receive when we appear before him as spirits.

If, on the contrary, we are separated from this body, whilst we are in a state of alienation from him, whilst we are obstructing his divine power, we shall continue in the darkness which we have chosen. There is no repentance in the grave; as the tree falleth, so it lieth: the dead cannot praise the Lord, neither can they that are buried celebrate his name. The truth of many of these things, is considered as nothing in the morality of the world, and there are few of the greatest evils, that do not abound in an eminent degree. I am not accusing you of these evils; I wish to caution you against them; there may be some present, who are converting the choicest blessings of heaven into a grievous curse. The grain and the fruits of the earth, are transformed into a liquor, which is a very poison. Perhaps, there is in this assembly, some widowed mother, or a son weeping over the untimely end of a father, lost to the feelings of virtue, who has shortened the days which were allotted to him, and rushed uncalled into the presence of his Judge. Now let us look at the condition of the drunkard, his hungry and almost naked children, his desponding wife, whom he had vowed to love and cherish, and he himself a most disconsolate object, with a bloated countenance, and haggard mien, his ideas confused, either full of cursing or full of folly and nonsense, full of every thing that is evil, every thing that can break the heart, the desponding heart of his once beloved companion. And thus he leaves his destitute widow, in the very depths of poverty, with a helpless family of children ; totally neglecting the indispensible duty of parents to provide for their children, food and raiment, a good and suitable education ; and he leaves the forlorn mother charged with care for them, and unable to provide them bread, and they are brought to tread in the steps of their father. And thus they are not only literally pests to society ; but these are they that fill our penitentiaries, and who are in this manner brought to an untimely end. I have often considered what an awful thing it would be for me, if the blood of my children should rise up in judgment against me, and condemn me with an overwhelming condemnation.

This is a sin of a deeper die than common, and which deserves the punishment of righteous judgment ; but we have learned to look upon it as nothing, or something common which we overlook ; our minds are hardend, our affections grown callous. We have nothing to do but to retrace our steps and to return to the power of divine love, which is able to remove mountains. But if we come not under the influence of living faith by giving way to the manifestations of God, we shall be given over to a state of reprobation ; but the doctrine of unconditional election and reprobation is inconsistent with all the attributes of the divinity, and I believe it to be little better than blasphemy. We must come unto the power, and attend to the manifestations of divine light, of that light which was in the beginning with God, and was God ; we must know him to govern, and to wield his righteous sceptre in our hearts ; and then we shall know him to sit upon the throne of David, and over his kingdom to order it, and establish it with judgment and with justice, for ever and ever ; and we shall be elected heirs of God, and joint heirs with Christ, in his kingdom. But if we say, we will not have this man to rule over us ; and if we follow our own ways, and our own judgments, and rebel against the light, and attend not to the manifestations of the gospel, in faith and verity, which came by Jesus Christ, the minister of the sanctuary, and of the true tabernacle which God hath pitched, and not man, they will gradually be withdrawn, and become weaker and weaker, and we shall lose the state we once had, for ever.

These views are not the sickly dreams of an enthusiast : I had nothing prepared when I came here ; but according as I have known the terrors of judgment for sin, therefore I have endeavored to persuade men to be reconciled to God : for I have known what it was to mourn, and to be afflicted for my transgressions : I have known what it was to separate myself from the source of purity ; I have known what it was to grovel under the influence of perverted affections and propensities. But until we come under the influence of heavenly dispositions, we can never worship in spirit and in truth. Then it is, that we can come into the true Sabbath: And what is the Sabbath ? Is it one day set apart in seven ? No, verily ; it is the rest prepared for the righteous. When our affections and our minds are purified, we are brought into a state of internal worship : and then we can worship the Father in spirit and in truth. Then every day will be a Sabbath ; we shall know our works to be finished ; then we can proclaim a fast, and call a solemn assembly. Thus we shall come into the Sabbath of everlasting duration, and be enabled to pray, and not to faint ; and be able to fulfil the declaration of the Apostle : pray without ceasing, not merely by a form of words, and bowing the head as a bulrush, and raising the voice as a trumpet. I appeal to some of you : have you not felt condemnation, sorrow, and dread, in the very act of this prayer, which cannot be acceptable ? But when we come under the influence of the spirit of prayer, every aspiration of the soul, though, perhaps, not clothed in language, is acceptable as the evening sacrifice. Our minds will be stayed on him ; as it is written, thou wilt keep him in perfect peace, whose mind is stayed on thee. Then we shall receive from him that wisdom which is essential to salvation. What a difference is there between this spiritual and mental prayer, and those outward forms of prayer which are even an abomination in the sight of heaven, even that prayer which Christ taught his disciples—Our Father, who art in heaven. Now, are there not some of us, who, on our bended knees, call him father, who are not begotten in purity and holiness: but like begets its like, and God begets his like, into a state of purity. But we attend not, and consider not, how deep is the language, Our father, who art in heaven, hallowed be thy name. Are there not some who are swearing by his name, on the most common occasions, contrary to the express command of Christ and his Apostles, Swear not at all, neither by heaven, for it is God's throne; nor by the earth, for it is his footstool: neither by Jerusalem, for it is the city of the great king; neither shalt thou swear by thy head, for thou canst not make one hair white or black; but let your communication be, yea, yea; nay, nay: that is, speak the truth in all things. Our father, who art in heaven, hallowed be thy name; thy kingdom come, thy will be done: we pray for his kingdom to come, without remembering that the kingdom of heaven is within, and that we cannot pray for the coming of his kingdom, until we know him to rule in us; until we come into the obedience of the law of his spirit, and obtain the victory over our natural propensities; and, therefore, we cannot pray, thy will be done on earth as it is in heaven, whilst our affections are not purified; whilst we are under the influence of the religion which we have derived from men and books. Neither can we sing praises to his name, until we have experienced deliverance from our souls' enemies. We cannot adopt singing and prayers to God, until our minds are purified; until our affections are regulated, and we are brought into a willingness to obey the divine law; then, and not till then, shall we be able to sing with the spirit, and with the understanding also. And I am not ashamed to acknowledge, that there have been raised secret aspirations to God in my soul; and I have been led at times to pour forth thanks to God, to take courage, and to ascribe praises to his holy name.

This religion enables us to perform and to fulfil all those duties which we owe to our great Maker, and all the duties which we owe to each other. It will enable husbands to love their wives, and wives to be obedient to their husbands. This will lead them into a fulfilment of those duties which they owe to their offspring. Thus they will be enabled to keep the minds of their children tender, prepared to receive the manifestations of God, the good shepherd and husbandman, who sows the seed of the kingdom in their hearts. And so also they will bring forth fruit, some thirty, some sixty, some an hundred fold, to the praise and honor of God.

And now, under those feelings which induced me to request your company, I may say I have found it to be a relief to my mind ; and by whatever name to religion you may be called, (for God is no respecter of persons, but in every nation he that feareth him and worketh righteousness is accepted of him,) under those feelings of universal affection, I once more salute you, and bid you all farewell. And may the blessing of our Lord and Saviour Jesus Christ rest upon you all.

SERMON VI.

DELIVERED BY THOMAS WETHERALD, AT FRIENDS' MEETING, WASHINGTON CITY, THIRD MONTH 20, 1825.

I have never yet learned to spend six days in worse than idleness in order that I might have something prepared on the seventh, to feed the vain minds of the people, and fill their itching ears with words which are only a secondary medium whereby knowledge is obtained.

I am aware, that in the present age of degeneracy, there are thousands of highly professing Christians who deny the operation of the spirit of God upon the spirit of man; and who do not admit any other medium, but verbal communication, whereby they may be instructed: And as these depend on an improper medium, the doctrines, principles and opinions imbibed, are of the same nature, impure; as no stream can rise higher than the fountain. From this very cause it is, that in the world there is so much religion and so little righteousness. Instead of these terms being synonymous, as they ought to be, there are no two terms more directly opposite, in the universe. A man at the present day may become very religious, very zealous, in the cause of religion, and do much for its support; and yet indulge in all the propensities of his carnal mind. And if his misconduct goes not so far, that he receives the lash of the civil power, he passes on very well.

But is this the kind of religion that will enable us to meet God with acceptance?

No. It is not the religion of experience, or of revelation; it is not the religion of our own reflection. It is that religion which is the result of education, prejudice and habit;

and therefore it must follow, that while under the influence of these causes, proceeding from this corrupt source, we must be split and divided. And here we see, *"Mystery Babylon, the great, the mother of harlots, and abominations of the earth."* That which is out of the truth, stands not in the power of God, which is in this day as fully revealed as ever it was of old.

Whilst we stand not in this power, we stand in a power of our own creation, which power is not of God.

Since we have been sitting together, my mind has been led to look at a very ancient record, by which we are informed that in the works of creation, God placed in this firmament two lights; the greater to rule the day, and the lesser to rule the night. And he made the stars also. Now we believe this record; we believe that the sun was placed in the firmament, and that it gives light. But why do we believe it? Because we feel its vivifying influence; the evidence is indubitable, and this affords a beautiful type of that medium, through which we receive a knowledge of God. "For this is life eternal, to know thee, the only true God, and Jesus Christ whom thou hast sent." He has given us a light, which is the life of men. This light operates upon every mind; there is not an individual who has arrived to the years of manhood, without feeling its influence, however he may be bound, under the dogmas of those preceptors, unto human nature, who never received this command from God. "Go ye, therefore, and teach all nations, baptising them into the name of the Father, and of the Son, and of the Holy Ghost."

But what will that religion do for us, in that day, when this mortal must put on immortality, and this corruptible must put on incorruption?

Is there an individual who has not experienced the operation of the spirit in his own mind, and who has not, at times, felt a concern for his everlasting welfare? Are there any who cannot testify that they have, when on their pillows, had serious reflections; and in their solitary hours been led or induced to aspire unto the God and Father of our Lord Jesus Christ, for knowledge and wisdom?

Is this the result of education? No. It is the operative power of God upon our spirits, that medium through which knowledge is as certainly received as light from the sun.

This is the first moving of that embryo which is begotten in us, and as it is written, "shall rule the nations with a rod of iron."

I remember the record of the beloved apostle, who was commanded to take the little book out of the angel's hand, who stood upon the earth and the sea, having the dominion over the earthly or animal propensities, and the fluctuating imaginations of the mind, and eat it up: "And it shall be in thy mouth sweet as honey, but it shall make thy belly bitter."

I have been instructed by these words; they are analogous to this expression. "I will allure her, and bring her into the wilderness, and speak comfortably unto her." The little book, which is in the mouth sweet as honey, is a beautiful type, through which I have been led often to look at the beauty and excellence of holiness, of which we all have similar prospects, altho' we may attain not the possession thereof.

Are there any who have not experienced these feelings? No. For God remains from everlasting to everlasting, as a light unto the good and the evil; in himself unchangeable, he sends his rain on the just and the unjust; and therefore, while in this probationary state, this medium will be continued to us. We shall see the beauty of holiness, and desire to draw nigh to God, as a being pure, holy, harmless, undefiled and separate from sin. When we come to walk under the influence of this divine light, that law of the spirit of life, which operates upon the man of sin, then it becomes bitter—when thousands who have experienced the first movings of the embryo, have strangled it in its birth; here they have lost the benefit of its existence. That light, which is the life of men, becomes dim and cloudy, and they are enveloped in darkness; their sun goes down at noon.

But we can become religious without the aid of this light, this judge of quick and dead, who reproves every one of sin and transgression; we can fulfil all the rituals of the outward law of that society, of which we are members, under the influence of those early imbibed prejudices which fill the mind. We can condemn a portion of our fellow creatures to everlasting perdition;—we can profess to believe that a part will be doomed to everlasting happiness, and the rest to misery;—we can form systems for ourselves, and even give laws to God. We can become righteous in our own eyes, as did the Jews, when deeply degenerated, saying, "Come not near me, stand by thyself, for I am holier than thou."

This religion will do for us, when we have slain the witness for God in our souls; but it will not do to die by. If we attend to the monitions of this divine birth, in its first appearances—if we submit to its influence, whether it is sweet or bitter, the knowledge of God increases. We may remember the declaration of the Apostle: "When I was a child, I spake as a child, I understood as a child, I thought as a child; but when I became a man, I put away childish things." So certain as is this progress, in the opening of the rational powers of man, so certain is the progress, in spiritual discernment; and a growth in grace and a knowledge of the truth. If we begin not at the beginning, and submit not unto that teacher which never was removed into a corner, we never can receive subsequent lessons, to fit us for an habitation in that city whose walls are salvation, and whose gates are praise.

We may boast of our reason, and of being the noble work of God; but if we disobey him, we become most ignoble, and by separating ourselves from him, we become aliens from the commonwealth of Israel, enemies to the covenant of promise, having no hope, and are without God in the world. This is beautifully exemplified in the declaration of an eminent Prophet, when he compared man to the helpless infant, cast out in the open field, in its blood—It was neither salted at all, nor swaddled at all; neither was it washed in water, to supple it: yet in this situation, passing by us, he hath said unto us, live ye. He hath said unto us, when we were in our blood, live; and he hath waited for us, according to this beautiful symbol, "until thy breasts are fashioned, and thine hair is grown, whereas thou was naked and bare. Then I saw thy time was the time of love, and I spread my skirt over thee—I made a covenant with thee, and clothed thee also with broidered work, and shod thee with Badger's skins. I adorned thee also with gold and with jewels, and thou becamest mine." Has he not made this covenant with us? Has he not borne with our infirmities, cast his skirt over us, and said unto us, when in our blood, live? And as we have attended to his admonitions, he has clothed us with broidered work, and shod us with Badger's skins, and adorned us with his gold and his jewels, whereas we were naked and bare. But we have broken our covenant upon every high mountain; we have wandered from him, choosing other lovers. In this we have dealt treacherously with him, not because there was not a sufficiency of his excellency to make us superlatively comely; but because we have indulged our vain propensities, and hence separated ourselves from him, and wasted his gold and jewels on others. We have become religious without righteousness, placing opinions for religion, and declamations for gospel; but opinions are not religion, nor declamation gospel, for these stand in the reasoning powers of man. But man, by the aid of reason, the arts, sciences, and philosophy, can never come to a knowledge of God.

What is man? He is a compound being; he has an animal body, and animal or instinctive faculties, by the aid of which he can perform all the animal functions. The race of mankind are propagated as other animals are, and we die as they die. We are sensible of heat and cold, hunger and thirst, and every other feeling to which the lowest animal is liable: But there is also in man something of the nature of Deity, a spirit, which is an emanation from God. It is this alone that can comprehend God. It is by the combination of these faculties that reason is produced, by the exercise of which, man receives the power of speech, and is enabled to compare ideas, to dive into arts, sciences, and philosophy; to fulfil the social, civil, and relative duties which we owe to each other;—in short, to do all that is temporally required of us, if we pervert not this reason, and make it not subservient to our animal passions. But this compound, which we call reason, can never give a knowledge of God, because he is a spirit.

These views are confirmed by the apostolic declaration, "the things of a man are known only by the spirit of a man, which is in him; but the things of God knoweth no man but by the Spirit of God."

How necessary it is, then, that we learn to distinguish between the light of the Spirit of God, manifesting spiritual truths, and this light of reason, which is nothing more than the light of the spirit of God shining upon the instinctive faculties. These may be compared to a body which is, in itself, opaque, and without light. But when that light which proceeds from Heaven shines upon it, the reflected rays may be compared to the light of the moon, which is a borrowed light; but this is not the light whereby we feel that invigorating influence, which is produced by the rays of the sun shining immediately on ourselves, and which cause vegetation and warmth. It is of an inferior nature; but when abstracted from these animal propensities, when the soul soars into the arms of Divinity, it is lost to all lower enjoyments; the spirit is united to him in the bonds of peace, purity and perfection; and herein is the declaration of the Lord Jesus fulfilled. "The kingdom of Heaven is within you." For whatever our situation on earth may be—whether in sickness or in health, in riches or poverty, in prosperity or adversity, or upon the bed of death—if the mind is fixed in heaven, it will be to the soul an anchor, sure and steadfast, over all the powers of death, hell, and the grave.

And yet we are commuting all this, for what? For the indulgence of our passions, propensities and feelings, which are natural, and which will stand only for a limited period, perhaps but for a moment.

We indulge them at the expense of our present enjoyment, and future prospect of heaven, when we shall be unclothed of mortality. How blind must we be, to hate a religion which will support the mind under every affliction, which regulates every inordinate passion and propensity, which would again make our wilderness an Eden, our desert like the garden of the Lord. Joy and gladness should be laid therein ; thanksgiving and the voice of melody : not of that tumultuous joy, nor the delights of music, proceeding from the sons and daughters of the children of men.

When the mind is prepared for the reception of this holy principle, there is a calm, a quiet, which many of you have felt, but which can never be described by words.

Have not many of the sons and daughters of men been partakers of these joys?

When our hands have been engaged in our labors, when walking by the way, when we lie down or when we rise up, have we not been ready to adopt the language of the apostle? "It is good for us to be here ; and let us make three tabernacles : one for Thee, and one for Moses, and one for Elias." But alas! have we brought these feelings practically into our daily walk in life? I fear we have not. And hence it is, that we have been turned back again, into a state of suffering and deep affliction.

Many are willing to follow Christ to the mount of transfiguration, but few are willing to follow him to the mount of crucifixion. But we never can become partakers of his life, till we have experienced that declaration of the apostle fulfilled : "I am crucified with Christ, nevertheless I live, yet not I but Christ liveth in me ; and the life that I now live, in the flesh, is by the faith of the Son of God, who loved me and gave himself for me."

But there is a vain and fruitless hope, and a nominal belief entertained, that something was done for us centuries before we had an existence, which will wipe away our transgressions. But can a spiritual effect be produced, by an outward cause? This sacrifice was a beautiful type and consummation of all which had gone before ; and in this type was fulfilled all obedience to the *outward* and *legal* dispensations, and another more glorious opened ; which was not to depend on any of these things, but upon our willingness to be crucified with Christ, and to know our natural passions and propensities, brought into subjection and obedience.

Thus an important lesson was designed to be inculcated, by this act of malevolence in the Jews : and convinced I am, that that sacrifice, without the gates of Jerusalem, will never have the effect that many are ascribing to it. For if through his sufferings, in his outward manifestation, the work is done; and if, through his act merely, he became the propitiatory sacrifice for the sins of the whole world, why are we yet partaking of bread and wine? Why are we in subjection to another *lex scriptum* (or written law) which preachers and teachers have imposed upon us? Why then this great variety and multifarious round of ceremony, if the work is done?

But the work is yet to do, and that individually, until we experience an overcoming of evil propensities, and give up our natural lives upon the cross. Until we are crucified with Christ, we can never be made partakers of his resurrection. For until we have experienced this, we have not a victory over him, who hath the power of death, that is the devil.

Here it is that men run into errors, by building their hope of salvation on an act performed by another, and their hope of happiness beyond the grave. They have placed hell and the devil there also. But if we ever enter heaven, we must experience the fulfilment of that declaration, "the kingdom of heaven is within you." We must know this truth, on this side the grave. We must know its power to command every fluctuating imagination, and bring them into a state of stillness and quiet: For a state of happiness is a state of quietude, "Jerusalem remains to be a quiet habitation ;—not one of the stakes thereof, can be removed, neither shall any of the cords thereof be broken. There the glorious Lord shall be unto us, a place of broad rivers and streams, wherein shall go, no galley with oars, none of the superb inventions of men, neither shall gallant ships pass thereby ; because the Lord is our Judge and our Lawgiver, and not these ordinances which men have chosen. He is our King and will save us.'' Here the tacklings, with which we have been bound, are loosed ;—"here they could not strengthen their masts and spread their sails,'' and build up systems, in which they have sought something for themselves. "Then is the prey of the great spoil divided, the lame take the prey.'' But many then are ready to cry out, I have no doubt at times, in the anguish of their souls, when they feel the crucifying operation of this spirit. "Who among us, shall dwell with the devouring fire? Who shall dwell with everlasting burnings?''

Here, my friends, there is encouragement in words like these: "He that walketh righteously, and speaketh uprightly, he that despiseth the gain of oppression, that shutteth his hand from holding bribes, that stoppeth his ear from hearing of blood, and shutteth his eyes from seeing evil; he shall dwell on high: His place of defence shall be the munitions of rocks: Bread shall be given him, his waters shall be sure. Thine eye shall see the king in his beauty. They shall behold the land that is very far off.''

Here is a kind of religion, which brings the mind into a state of purity, a state of holiness and harmlessness; a state of undefiledness, and consequent communion with God, in which we experience another declaration, of Jesus fulfilled, when he was supplicating for his followers: "I in them, and thou in me, that they also may become one in us,'' wherefore, he is not ashamed to call us brethren.

These brethren have, as he did, overcome the world: Their minds are not depending on the dogmas of men ;—their hope is in him ; they feel his supporting power, and experience him to be, to them, wisdom, righteousness, sanctification and redemption. And how plain it is, how simple is true religion, and undefiled, before God the Father. It needs not much illustration by words. All may know it. The lot of every man is cast on the plain simple path ; but we never can experience this power, till we know the ministration of condemnation ; till we are willing to have reproved every thought, word and action ; till we are willing to be, to do, or to suffer what is required at our hands.

It is, therefore, an individual work. As the sun shines on the just and unjust, the thankful and the evil ; so the ministration of condemnation must be experienced by all.

If we attend to it, it will prove a savor of life unto life :— If we neglect it, a savor of death unto death. What are all these vain substitutes and subterfuges? They are what man has chosen, they are natural, they are outward. Let us look to the sacrament, so called, and when we have used it, can it nourish the soul? It may nourish the body, but the soul is spiritual, it cannot be nourished thereby. It may be used as a type or symbol ; but are we yet under the legal dispensation? No. We are not under types, or legal shadows and ceremonies. The substance is come ; the power of God is experimentally known, even that power, which is the resurrection and the life.

To eat the bread and drink the wine, to say the least of it, is a work of supererogation, and those who practise it, bring themselves under the reproof of the prophet, "who hath required this at your hands?" Neither can all the waters of the sea cleanse the soul from one solitary sin or lust. But when we come under the influence of the baptism of the Holy Ghost ; when knowing what it is, to lie under the judgments of God, which are revealed from heaven against sin and disobedience, then shall we be cleansed. And there are none, who have not experienced something of these judgments. Have we not been brought into the depths of hell? Are there not seasons, when we have been ready to cry out in the anguish of our soul, a Saviour or I die ; a Redeemer, or I perish for ever : Are there not seasons when all are sensible, that they have been doing wrong, and when sorrow fills their hearts?

Here is the ministration of condemnation, which is glorious in its season ; and if we are willing to abide under its influence, it will make way for the ministration of life. As we attend daily to what passes in our minds, we may experience many things made known to us as evils, which we have been led to undervalue, because they accord with the maxims and customs of the day, and with the fashionable religion of the world : For religion, and pride, and vanity are now connected together ; but when we come under the influence of these divine feelings, the latter will be banished from our souls for ever, and that spirit which condemns for every evil, will also speak peace to the soul for every act of obedience. Then we shall know what is meant by the declaration of the forerunner of Jesus : "But he that cometh after me is mightier than I, whose shoes latchet I am not worthy to unloose : He shall baptise you with the Holy Ghost, and with fire. This is the grace of God, wherein ye ought to stand : For the grace of God that bringeth salvation, hath appeared to all men, teaching us, that, denying ungodliness and worldly lusts, we should live soberly, righteously, and godly, in this present world ; looking for that blessed hope and the glorious appearing of the great God and our Saviour Jesus Christ."

And where are we to look for this glorious appearing, if not in ourselves ?

It is written, "Behold he cometh in the clouds ; and every eye shall see him, and they also that pierced him. And how black are the clouds in which he appears, to those who have pierced him by their transgressions, and neglected him in his manifestations. But as we attend to this baptism of the Holy Ghost ; it has an effect to cast out devils ; to remove the propensities, which have brought these dark clouds over us.

What are these devils ? Are they not those propensities in which we indulge ; and which separate us from God, the source of all purity ? There is a warfare between the angels of life in us, and the dragon and his angels ; and when we come to know them set in array, in our minds, then we experience their power. When we see the angel of love, opposed to the devil of hatred ; the angel of mercy to the devil of cruelty ; every heavenly disposition opposing its opposite, or adversary ; then we shall come to know that declaration fulfilled : "And there was war in heaven ; Michael and his angels fought against the dragon; and the dragon fought and his angels, and prevailed not; neither was there place found any more in heaven: And the great dragon was cast out."

Herein is fulfilled that declaration:—"Stronger is he that is in you, than he that is in the world; and the weapons of this warfare are not carnal, nor mortal, they are spiritual; mighty through God even to the pulling down of strong holds; casting down imaginations and every high thing that opposeth itself to the knowledge of the truth. And they will put to flight the armies of the aliens, having our feet shod with the preparation of the gospel of peace; our loins girded about with truth, the helmet of salvation upon our head. Take also the shield of faith, whereby to quench all the fiery darts of the wicked; and above all things, take the sword of the spirit, which is the word of God.

As this armor is all of a heavenly nature, so nothing earthly or corruptible can ever affect it. But what is this faith? Is it a mere nominal belief? No, verily: But when we have experienced the terrors of the Lord, in baptism, for sin and disobedience, and have also felt, that in the midst of judgment, God has also remembered mercy, and spoke peace to the soul, season after season, there is begotten in us a living faith and holy confidence, which stands not in a knowledge of the Scriptures or of systematic religion. It results from our own experience of the operative power of God. This is that faith once delivered to the saints, that living faith, which supports all those who become partakers of the joys of heaven, and is the life of all them which are sanctified. Faith stands not in opinions;—it is not bounded by time or outward circumstances, but it stands in the power of God. It unites the true believers to him; and in this, is that declaration fulfilled: "I in them, and thou in me, that they also may become one in us; and these he is not ashamed to call brethren."

This is a shield which will quench all the fiery darts from the enemy of souls. This is that sword of the spirit which is the word of God. It is the same whereby the worlds were spoken into existence, which "took flesh and dwelt among us, and we behold his glory, the glory as of the only begotten of the Father, full of grace and truth." It is he who was in the church in the wilderness; who did mighty miracles in Egypt, and wonders in the field of Zoar; who divided the Red Sea and brought Israel forth like a flock. And in this exercise of his power, he commanded them not, concerning burnt offerings and sacrifices; but this thing he commanded them, saying, "Obey my voice."

This is the end of all righteousness; the design of all true, of all pure and undefiled religion; and as we come to this, we learn to handle the weapons of our warfare, until every enemy is cast out, and every adversary brought into subjection to the angel of God: And Michael, the prince of angels will rule, and the power of God reign predominant. But if our own will governs and rules any part, and not the power of God, he will not have dominion over us; for he will not dwell in a moted temple. It is essential, therefore, that we serve him in the beauty of holiness and in newness of life. When we come to attend to his spiritual admonitions, then we shall know another declaration fulfilled: "Unto us a child is born; unto us a son is given, and his name shall be called Wonderful, Counsellor, the mighty God, the everlasting Father, the Prince of Peace."

While clothed with this armor, there will be no end to the increase of his righteousness and peace, upon the throne of David, the throne of the Lord's elect and chosen, to order it and to establish it, throughout all generations. This operative power of God is what I want us all to come to. As to the baptism with water, it is obviously inefficient: it never cleansed the soul of man from sin. If we look to the situation of Simon Magus, we find it recorded, that through the instrumentality of Philip, the Samaritan, he believed on Christ with one accord, and when baptised he was baptised also, but continued a sorcerer. He offered money, the love of which is the root of all evil; and which is the root of a great part of the religion of the present day. For, convinced I am, that these self-styled ministers, if they had no pay, would do but little preaching.

Here is an example of Simon Magus' religion. He went with the apostles, and when he saw that the Holy Ghost was received, by the laying on of hands, his natural thirst for gain was excited, and he offered them money, desiring that they would give him this power; that on whom he should lay his hands, they should receive the Holy Ghost. But "Peter said unto him, thy money perish with thee, because thou hast thought that the gift of God may be purchased with money; thou hast neither part nor lot in this matter, for thy heart is not right in the sight of God." And the bread and wine, that relic of the old Jewish passover, has no effect to nourish the soul up to everlasting life. This is proved by the account recorded of Judas, who was a partaker of the last passover, which was shortly before the crucifixion, and yet it did not preserve him. But the record says, that with the sop satan entered into him. I do not wish to undervalue any thing that is called religion, or support any thing ceremonious, or which is made the object of interest more than the object of righteousness.

Simon was baptised, but remained a sorcerer: Judas partook of the last supper, even in the presence of his divine Master; and yet Judas was a devil.

But when we come to be partakers of that heavenly gift, and live under the influence of the divine requirements, it strikes at the root of every evil and brings the mind into harmony, unity and love. It unites us to God, erects in us a new heart, and begets a right spirit; and we can thankfully acknowledge that the Lord is our righteousness.

Has it been from an attendance to this divine gift, that there are so many sects and parties now in christendom? No. It has been from a neglect of it. And do we not find those who not only neglect, but who deny the existence of revelation to man in the present day?

They say that all revelation is contained in the Scriptures of truth; when it requires a revelation immediately from heaven to give us an understanding of the Scriptures. We shall never be benefitted by them, except they are opened to us, by the same divine spirit which first dictated them: They are not the word of God, nor the only rule of faith and practice. Parts of them, no doubt, are the words of holy men, who were influenced by the Holy Ghost. They testify of that which is justly entitled to the word of life: And when we are brought to the same state, and are influenced by the same feelings which they experienced, these scriptures will be precious to us: They will be corroborative testimony ; they will answer, as face answers face in a glass ; they will come home into our souls and govern our minds. All this governing principle is love. It is not found in splendid churches, so called. It will not be found in pompous ceremonies and declamations. It operates in our own minds, where it will regulate the springs and motives of our conduct, and cast out the enemies by which it is assailed ; and thus bring the mind under the influence of that heavenly virtue, in which we can testify: "He maketh his angels spirits, and his ministers a flame of fire." And they are all ministering spirits sent forth to minister to them that shall be heirs of salvation.

Thus it will be brought into our minds, into our conversation, into our houses and families ; and as we dwell under its influence, it will shine through our conduct, and we shall become preachers of the everlasting gospel in the world and governed by the angels of God. This is loud preaching, compared with the preaching of those who preach for hire and divine for money. For here we declare what our eyes have seen, our ears heard, and our hands handled, of the good word of life, and of the powers of the world to come.

Therefore I have desired, for our own souls' sakes, that we turn into that volume of the book, and read and search our own hearts, and ascertain from what motives we act— from what kind of spirits, whether from evil angels, or the angels of the dragon, or Michael's angels, which are the power of God. Therefore, unto this light, which is the life of men, which maketh manifest all things, whether right or wrong ; to this new covenant placed in your hearts and mouths, that you may hear it and do it; unto this divine and living principle, I desire to recommend you individually: For if attended to, it will make you wiser than all your teachers. It will teach your hands to war, and your fingers to fight against your souls' enemies; and it will sustain your spirits under every trial and affliction. And when time here shall be no more, I am not afraid to leave it with you as my testimony, it will prepare for each of you: whether in the opinions of men, you may be partakers of heavenly joy or eternal reprobation; it will prepare, for all, in every situation, Scythian or barbarian, bond or free, an habitation in that city, whose walls are salvation, and whose gates are praise, and where "none of the inhabitants can say, I am sick."

SERMON VII.

DELIVERED BY THOMAS WETHERALD, AT FRIENDS' MEETING, WASHINGTON
CITY, THIRD MONTH 27, 1825.

"For to him that is joined to all the living there is hope :
for a living dog is better than a dead lion. For the living
know that they shall die ; but the dead know not any thing,
neither have they any more a reward ; for the memory of
them is forgotten." For the living, there is cause of hope
and fear ; and however the dead may have an appearance of
strength, yet they are inanimate, and hastening to corruption ; but the dog, though despised when living, is able to
perform all the duties of which he is capable ; and hence,
the only natural division, whether in man or in the inferior
part of creation, is between the living and the dead. For
"a living dog is better than a dead lion."

I have never yet learned to discover the difference, or to
make a distinction, except between righteousness and unrighteousness, godliness and ungodliness, and acts of wickedness amongst the various sects of professing christians. I
have never learned to distinguish between Catholics, Presbyterians, Episcopalians, Baptists, Methodists, or Quakers.
In all these societies I have no doubt there are living members of the Church of Christ, and in all these societies there
are probably dead members, or members of the Church of
Antichrist. And also am I convinced, that the dead members are as much more conspicuous among men, as the dead
lion is in appearance over the dog. They are often in their
societies the most active members, and often received into
them from motives impure and unholy ; and often introduced into the most solemn station into which man can be

called, the ministry of the gospel, so called. And notwithstanding their formidable appearance, they are nothing better, if wanting life, than the dead lion.

Let us look a little into the fruits produced by this death,
or by the performance of these dead members of the nominal church.

There are but two Churches in the world, the Church of
Christ and the Church of Antichrist; however, they may be
separated into divisions and sub-divisions: and if we are
not of Christ, assured I am, that Antichrist is among us.
For God is one, and his name one, and he has all power in
Heaven and Earth; as the earth is his and its fullness.

So the Church is his own, also, united to him in holy fellowship and spiritual union; but instead of having this
holy, united, indivisible appearance, at the present day,
what does it look like? What are the views of men respecting religion? Nothing better than the impressed views of
Job's miserable comforter. "Then a spirit passed before my
face; the hair of my flesh stood up. It stood still, but I
could not discern the form thereof: An image was before
mine eyes; there was silence, and I heard a voice, saying,
shall mortal man be more just than God? Shall man be
more pure than his Maker? Behold he put no trust in his
servants, and his angels he charged with folly. But this
was seen by Eliphaz, one of Job's friends, and they were
reproved, and he justified; and they were required to bring
offerings unto Job, the offer for them, before they could be
accepted, because they had not spoken right as he did."

The religion of the present day is formidable in appearance, like the spirit which Eliphaz saw, but it is not understood among the various societies of professing christians,
and they are too much afraid to investigate the subject; and
hence the maxim, that mysteries which we cannot comprehend we must believe, even things which we cannot understand. Is it possible, is it not contrary to every thing that
we can have an idea of—is it not contrary to human reason,
that a man must believe that which he cannot comprehend
or understand? It is an absurdity; it had its origin in the

8

night season, when darkness covered the mind. Many have had visions, which they could not comprehend, like Eliphaz: he imagined something, and the hair of his head stood up; and, under this excitement, he heard a voice saying, Shall mortal man be more just than God? And from a view thus imperfect, many have concluded we must continue in sin all the days of our lives. Are we then to continue in sin that grace may abound? God forbid. Neither was it designed that we should inculcate any thing, or believe any thing, which is not manifested, which our own eyes have not seen, our ears heard, or our hands handled, of the good word of life, and the powers of the world to come. It never was designed that man, as a rational being, partaking of the divine nature, should be subject to the dogmas of man; that the mind should be under the control of ministers and preceptors, who profess to lead us in the way of truth and righteousness, when they, themselves, notwithstanding all their learning, all their knowledge and wisdom, have, many of them, yet to learn which are the first principles of the oracles of God.

Here we see that divided state, which is typified by the beast of many heads and many horns, which smite one against another. Here we see Lucifer, the son of the morning, that aerial spirit, with his many spangled head. True, there is another source of confusion, and of the corruption which rules in our land: Here we see something over which our souls have long mourned. We see an abundance of rites, ceremonies, carnal ordinances, pompous parade, and self-righteousness, among the various professors of christianity; but in whom does that spirit abound, rule, reign, and predominate, which produces love, joy, and peace on earth? By whom are all the heavenly dispositions cultivated? Alas! man does not partake of the divine fellowship. Every power is not subject to God, in the human mind; and yet he makes a profession of religion. It is that mysterious religion, which cannot be defined nor understood, neither can it be practised. It is a burthen which, said the Apostles, neither we, nor our fathers, could bear. Not many practical virtues, proceed therefrom, but these are the fruits: Bible societies and missionary societies, (I can almost remember their origin in the reformed churches, so called) and many other benevolent societies, temporal and spiritual. Have not all societies, almost, except the one of which I am a member, united in these bible societies and missionary societies? These bibles are printed under their authority, and sent forth to the world, without note or comment. They boast of not endeavoring to build up one sect or another. But who has the distribution of these works? By whom are they sent abroad? They are sent abroad by another branch of the same family of horse-leeches, whose cry is give! give!! Better would it be, to print these scriptures with notes and comments, than to put them into the hands of those, who will comment in their own interested zeal and spirit, of sectarian principles. And as to their enlightening the heathen, they will increase the darkness, which we have reason to believe pervades the remotest parts of the earth. What is the religion that is inculcated along with these Scriptures of truth? The Scriptures are declared to be the word of God, and the rule of faith and practice; but they are not the word of God, nor are they the rule of faith and practice. They are the testimony of holy men, of old, who were inspired by the Holy Ghost; but they are like the dead lion, if we do not come under the vivifying influence of the spirit of God. These Scriptures have never been able, of themselves, to make wise unto salvation. They are declared to contain all the revelation which we are to look for in this dispensation; and that which is to be known of God, is revealed in them. This is contrary to the most solemn declaration of these Scriptures themselves. It is written and comes from high authority that what is to be known of God, is to be made manifest in man.

Now by whom is this manifestation to be made in man? Not by man himself, nor by man's wisdom; or the utmost stretch of a knowledge of the arts, sciences, and philosophy. Who are these man-made ministers, who pride themselves in being instructors? It is impossible for them to know the inmost recesses of the soul, and to know every working of the heart, and every moving of the imagination, of their fellow-man. Every preceptor must be superior to his pupil, in order to bring him to a knowledge of the subject which he teaches; therefore, man, being in spirit, part of the divinity, it must require for a teacher, him in whom dwells all the fullness of the god-head. To teach man one solitary truth, it requires a power superior to the spirit of man. Our comprehension is limited; we are bounded; but in him there are no bounds. To his wisdom and power, there are no limits: And therefore, it is, that he alone is capable to be, the preceptor of man. For man, bounded as he is spiritually and intellectually, is not so, in the choice of the dispositions wherewith he is endowed.

But man is a free agent, and blessed be the name of Israel's God, that the power of choice is with him. We may choose evil and refuse good; we may choose good and refuse evil. This is proved by the recommendation of the prophet, to Israel formerly: "Choose life and live, for wherefore will ye die, O house of Israel!" But principles, opinions and dogmas, have no connexion with the spirit of God, nor that pure state in man, in which these truths are experienced and understood. They can rise no higher than their natural power, and this being of an inferior nature, it can never arrive at a knowledge of God. Here is a distinction, my friends and fellow professors, of this holy name. We have been endeavoring to comprehend God by the aid of these rational powers; these powers which depend upon the arts and sciences, and the learning and wisdom of man for their expansion; hence it is, that our minds become darkened; hence religion becomes mysterious; we are split and divided by opinions of God, which are not founded on the immutable rock of ages and foundation of many generations, against which, all the united powers of death, hell and the grave, can never prevail.

Can a child in the first rudiments of education, understand the nature of that science, which is the object of his study? No. Neither can man who is thus limited in his conceptions, determine the extent of divine truths. But when the unlimited power of God operates upon the spirits of men, then they know what truth is, in their own experience. This is a teacher which cannot be removed into a corner, according to the declaration of a prophet. Yet surely that teacher shall not be removed any more. "And though the Lord give you the bread of adversity, and the water of affliction, yet shall not thy teacher be removed into a corner any more; but thine eyes shall see thy teachers; and thine ears shall hear a voice behind thee, saying, this is the way, walk ye in it."

Now let us look a little at the effects of that man-made, and man-taught religion, which is extant in the earth, whether among Catholics, Episcopalians, Presbyterians, Baptists, Methodists, Unitarians, or Quakers; or by whatever name they may be called. Let us look at its effects upon our own minds. Has it not introduced almost every thing, which is evil in itself? Do we not see "pride, fullness of bread, and abundance of idleness, abounding?" These were Sodom's sins. In her and in her daughters, neither did she strengthen the hands of the poor and needy, therefore I took them away, as I saw good. And is it not obvious to every one of us, that this pride, and every abomination which the Lord hates, abounds in the world? "These six things doth the Lord hate; yea, seven are an abomination unto him: A proud look, a lying tongue, and hands that shed innocent blood, an heart that deviseth wicked imaginations, feet that be swift in running to mischief, a false witness that speaketh lies, and him that soweth discord among brethren."

Is it not evident, that a proud look is the predominant look, of both ministers and people? Is there not a spirit, in which our various societies consider themselves holier than others? How often do we hear also, amongst professors, a lying tongue. Now this is of great extent. For it is in every species of deception, which is designed to impose on another, or to impose a kind of righteousness upon God, which is not of his own begetting in the soul. Every thing having this appearance proceeds from this lying tongue. And are there not thousands within our recollection whose blood has been shed, I had almost said in innocency? Armies have been led forth, have fought and fallen in foreign lands, not because any hatred or enmity had ever passed in the minds of the multitude; but merely to serve the interests of the one, two, or the three. Even in this land of boasted liberty, which has been so wonderfully and mercifully favored of heaven, you have seen a little of these evils. The hands that have shed innocent blood have visited these shores. These were men professing religion, and perhaps belonging to bible and missionary societies. Upon what was all this founded? It was the love of money, the root of all evil, joined to ambition, pride and avarice; and these are the grounds of a great part of the religion of the present day.

Of whom are the members of these popular societies composed? Are they made up of the virtuous of the several societies of professing christians; or are they not rather composed of all classes, the good and evil, the righteous and the wicked, the blood thirsty warrior, the cruel slave-holding oppressor, the whoremonger, the liar, the thief, and deceiver? These, I have no doubt, are many of them engaged, in the promotion of the work of righteousness, and religion in the earth. These all give their money and it is received, I have no doubt: For I have never heard of any money being refused, by those who have the government of these societies, because of the unworthiness of the individuals who may offer it. I verily believe, the hire of a harlot, or the price of a dog, both of which are an abomination in the sight of heaven, and were never to be brought to the Lord's treasury, would never be refused, by these "daughters of the horse-leech, who are crying give, give."

"They are like the three things that are never satisfied, yea, four things say not it is enough: The grave; and the barren womb; the earth that is not filled with water; and the fire that saith not, it is enough."

Now here is something so corrupt in its origin, its foundation is so impure, that the superstructure can never become solid and durable.

Can any thing on such a foundation bring glory to God;

or unite man in the bonds of peace, love and joy in the holy Spirit? No. Sooner should wickedness produce righteousness, and darkness produce light. Sooner can we, ourselves, control the will of God, by the work of our own hands.

I want these things to be indelibly impressed upon our minds. We have been deceiving ourselves with appearances long enough; with these perplexing visions, which cause our hair to stand up, and our bones to shake. We have been long enough believing these lying divinations, and neglecting the angels of God.

And yet it is declared in the name of truth, that they are all ministering spirits sent forth to minister to them that shall be heirs of salvation. And can we believe that any other effect will be produced, by this deeply rooted corruption, than "lying tongues, and hands that shed innocent blood; an heart that deviseth evil imaginations, and feet, swift in running to mischief; a false witness that speaketh lies, and he that soweth discord among brethren?" A belief in this spurious religion and gospel, stands not in the wisdom of God, but in the wisdom of man. The greatest part of the wars and fightings, and every evil which exists in the world, has its origin in these perverted, leading principles, in man's mind. The religion that is not founded in truth, how far it leads us off from the path of rectitude. But if we founded our religion on that rock which is immovable we should be all united, and be enabled to withstand the powers of death, hell and the grave; and how it would lead the mind into purity, holiness and love; and into the possession and practice of every social, every civil, every relative and every manly virtue.

How is it then, my friends, that we have been so long building upon this impure foundation? Let us look a little and see the fruits brought forth, by dispositions and conduct, opposed to this; and when every principle, in the mind, is founded in experience and the operative power of God. Where we are instructed immediately by and from God, we learn, that that which can be known of God, is to be made manifest in man. And what is it that maketh it manifest?

It is that grace of God which appeareth unto all men. Not those, alone, who are educated to be ministers of the gospel. Not only to two or three in the community; "but the grace of God, which bringeth salvation, hath appeared unto all men." Herein is fulfilled that declaration: "Behold the day cometh, saith the Lord, that I will make a new covenant, with the house of Israel, and with the house of Judah: Not according to the covenant that I made with their fathers in the day that I took them by the hand, to bring them out of the land of Egypt: But this shall be the covenant, that I will make with the house of Israel; I will put my law in their inward parts, and write it in their hearts; and they shall teach no more every man his neighbor, and every man his brother, saying, know the Lord, for they shall all know me, from the least of them unto the greatest." There is another testimony respecting preaching of the gospel. "After these days, saith the Lord, I will pour out my spirit upon all flesh, and your sons and your daughters shall prophecy, your old men shall dream dreams, your young men shall see visions, and also upon the servants and upon the hand maidens I will pour forth my spirit, and they shall prophecy." Now what is prophecy? Is it merely to declare things which are to come? No. There is another definition of it. The testimony of Jesus is the spirit of prophecy. It is also called the grace of God, and if attended to it will guide us into all truth: as it guided all the Patriarchs and Apostles in every age of the world. It was that which gave Abraham an evidence, that in his seed all the children of the earth should be blessed. This was confirmed to Isaac and Jacob repeatedly. By this, Jacob saw far into futurity and worshipped, leaning upon the top of his staff. By this, he pronounced appropriate blessings to his children which were eminently fulfilled. It was this divine power which led Moses to the deliverance of Israel, and caused him to bring them forth as a flock. The same spirit enabled him to declare: "The Lord thy God will raise up unto thee, a prophet from the midst of thee; a prophet from the midst of thy brethren, like unto me; unto him ye shall hearken in all things."

It was the same divine spirit, the same spirit of prophecy, the operative power of God, which moved Noah, and commanded him to build an ark of salvation for himself and family; from that flood which destroyed the wicked. It is the same which enabled another prophet, to testify concerning the coming of our Saviour, the Lord Jesus Christ, in that prepared body. Not that he then first became a Saviour of mankind, for he was from everlasting to everlasting, and we who are descendants of the Gentiles, never were under any other dispensation; never being under the law given by Moses. Why then is it, that we introduce Jewish ceremonies, and engraft them upon the stalk of the Christian religion? It was this same spirit which enabled the prophet to declare, when speaking of things yet to come, as if they were present. "Unto us a child is born, unto us a son is given, and his name shall be called Wonderful, Counsellor, the mighty God, the everlasting Father, and the Prince of Peace. Of the increase of his government, and peace, there shall be no end; upon the throne of David, to order it and establish it with justice and judgment for ever."

Here is a great mass of Scripture testimony, which must be an evidence of that manifestation which proceeded from the power of God. And how precious is the view of these records; not because they are written, or because the prophets declared them; but they only become precious to us, when we have seen the effects of the revealed will of God, making manifest the things belonging to our peace. Here is the patience and faith of the saints. Here it is that we may experience all that is necessary for instruction; and to support us in our pilgrimage. Here we can testify, that this spirit of prophecy is the testimony of Jesus, given unto all; and whether it enables to discover things to come, or gives a knowledge of the dispositions of our own minds, making us acquainted with the motives from which we act, and with the secret springs of the soul, it is the same spirit and power of God unto salvation; to every one who believes, whether

Jew or Gentile, male or female, bond or free, in Jesus Christ. For there is no distinction in the truth, and as we dwell in truth, it will make us free. This is real freedom ; not that freedom of which man can boast ; but it is that freedom from bondage which introduces us into the glorious liberty of the sons of God.

"For ye have not received the spirit of bondage again to fear, but ye have received the spirit of adoption, whereby ye cry, Abba, Father." There the communion is through God, by the power of his Son ; he is what he declard himself to be, a Saviour and a Redeemer. And we, as well as all others have need of this Saviour and Redeemer. Can we not all cry out a Saviour, or I die ; a Redeemer, or I perish for ever ?

But, my friends, where are we to look for this Redeemer, this salvation, if we look not in our own minds ? It is there we must know him, to regulate our views, and bring every thought, word and action into subjection to himself. For there is in man, something of the nature of Deity, a spirit of inspiration from the Almighty, which gives him understanding. If this is kept holy, and preserved from the contaminating influence of the spirit, and the corrupt maxims of the world, it will enable us to dwell in him, and see him, not only at a great distance, and beyond the grave, but even whilst clothed with mortality, we shall experience him to be a stay and a support, a teacher and instructor in Godliness.

And what are the fruits which will be brought forth ? Not those things which are an abomination unto God ; "neither a proud look, a lying tongue, or hands that shed innocent blood ; a heart that deviseth wicked imaginations, feet that be swift in running to mischief, a false witness, that speaketh lies, and him that soweth discord among brethren." None of these will be admitted under the influence of this principle ; for these are the fruits of the flesh, and irregular passions and propensities, which man partakes of while in a state of death and darkness, and while he knows not God. When we come to know him, then he brings forth the fruits of the spirit. Then it is, that we know what it is to "add to your faith virtue; and to virtue knowledge; and to knowledge temperance; and to temperance patience; and to patience godliness; and to godliness brotherly kindness; and to brotherly kindness charity. For if these things be in you, and abound, they make you that ye shall neither be barren nor unfruitful, in the knowledge of our Lord Jesus Christ." In whom, as a society, we most assuredly believe; but dare not depend on that act of wickedness in the Jews, by which he was crucified; but by a revelation of his will and power in our own hearts, bringing us into the enjoyment of his kingdom of heaven, through grace, according to his own declaration: "The kingdom of heaven is in you."

This is the root and ground of all true religion, even the bright and morning star. This is the root and offspring of David, which opens the mysteries of heaven, according to a declaration of the Apostle, comparing them to a "book with seven seals, and no man in heaven, nor in earth, neither under the earth, was able to open the book, neither to look thereon. And one of the elders saith unto to me, weep not: "Behold, the lion of the tribe of Juda, the root of David, hath prevailed to open the book and to look thereon." There still remains the same power, which opens the seals and enables us to look upon the mysteries contained in this volume, if properly complied with; and which enables us to extract that which is capable of producing peace to our souls, and happiness here and hereafter; and also to refuse the bitter works of darkness, which lead to confusion, horror, fear, dismay, and every feeling in which there is torment.

Now let us look a little at the effects produced by the adoption of these principles—this operative power of truth, spirit of Christ, grace of God, or baptism of the Holy Ghost; which separates between the joints and the marrow, the soul and spirit, and separates a man from his lusts. This principle would destroy the works of darkness; and for this cause came Jesus Christ into the world, to destroy the works of the devil. And how is this accomplished? It is by the casting out of devils, which cometh not but by prayer and fasting, from the indulgence of every evil disposition ; controlling the proud heart, the lying tongue, and hands that shed innocent blood : for these cannot bear its influence. It is the vivifying power of the love of God, operating upon the souls of men ; a teacher which can never be removed into a corner. Now look at the effects which must be produced when the mind is under the influence and government of this divine love, which is the badge of our discipleship, and the bond of our union. Where is there room for warfare ? Was there ever war begun and carried on under the influence of this divine principle, which is of God ? Never. For "God is love ; and he that dwelleth in love, dwelleth in God, and God in him." Now if we are under the influence of this principle, where is there room for wars and fightings ? They must all be banished from our minds and imaginations. We never commit violence through love, but through hatred, pride, ambition·and all those devils which are tormentors of the human soul. But when we are brought under the influence of this love, it will produce humility, meekness, mercy, and every heavenly disposition. Because these have no affinity with the works of darkness. It is designed to become a predominating principle which unites us to God. And when we come under its influence, temperance will cast out intemperance, humility will cast out pride, every virtuous, every heavenly disposition taking possession of the mind, will cast out its opposite, its adversary and enemy ; and thus the mind will become pure.

Good and evil cannot dwell together any more than humility and pride. One of them must be cast out ; and if the love of God operating upon the soul, cast out all evil propensities, where will there be room, for the lying tongue, and the hands that shed innocent blood ? Where will there be room in the mind for wicked imaginations ? Of the evil heart or feet that are swift in running to mischief, or the tongue that speaks lies, or he that sows discord among brethren.

My friends look to these things. Is it not in the minds of.men alone that these good or evil dispositions are produced? What effect would it produce in the moral world if mankind would generally refuse the evil, and choose the good? Would it not deliver the land from murder, adultery, fornication, lying, theft, and all which is the cause of staining our civil tribunals with blood, and which brings this mass of misery upon mankind? Every evil, whether civil or social, would be removed by this divine principle, which has its origin in heaven, and which operates upon every soul. Here the wilderness caused by evil would become an Eden, the desert, like the garden of the Lord. For wherever the mind is brought under the influence of this divine feeling, there is Eden; there is Paradise; there is Heaven; for there is God. And this is by the operation of preaching; of preaching the gospel. For the gospel is preached in every creature. And I apprehend, that is not preaching alone which stands in declamation. For societies to meet together and appoint one to talk to them, as it is under the present system of religion, is more likely to lead to error than truth. And wherefore? Because the very existence of this operative power of God is denied; and what is the right motive for preaching the gospel? The Apostle tells us, "A necessity is laid upon me; and woe is me if I preach not the gospel." But a society who have a head over them, who preaches for hire and divines for money; and they that put not into their mouths, they are ready even to prepare war against them, whose god is their belly, whose glory is their shame, who mind earthly things. These pervert the gifts of heaven and make God an idol. They worship neither in purity, nor in the beauty of holiness. They clothe him with their own particular principles; they declare this is truth and that is error. They bind men by creeds, systems and articles of belief. The rules of their society are laws; and by these, they give law to God. Is this to be brought into the liberty of the sons and daughters of God? No. It is to be brought into bondage, which neither we nor our fathers, or the prophets could bear; but it is a state in which we can indulge our propensities and live in the spirit of the world; and in this we delight. My beloved young friends, whether members of any of these societies or not, whose minds are yet tender and the bud is green, my mind is concerned for you. I have no doubt the world at this time appears in all its beauty, the fashions and manners thereof are lovely in your view ; but it is deceptive ; it is tinsel and not gold. You know. not much of its arts, or of its influence ; you are ready to believe that all is gold which glitters. But experience will, to your sorrow, teach you otherwise. I would to God, for your sakes that your souls might be brought into the very depths of affliction ; that you might see the bent of your minds ;—that you may experience the renovating influence of the power of God, and be fitted for an habitation in the kingdom of heaven. For it is only in the depths of judgment, I am convinced, that we can learn that which is to be known of God. It is not to be learned in the letter.

The disposition of our mind is not to be learned, while in the indulgence of these passions and propensities. I am willing to tell you a little if it may be instructive to you, to learn the narrow path, in which my soul was led. I remember the time when I walked these slippery paths. I remember when I was gay, giddy, and young ;—my mind was volatile as the air ; when I took pleasure in everything around me, whether right or wrong. My blood was brisk ; my spirits lively. I took delight in those outward things which circumstances brought around me ; but, alas ! I knew not, that a life of folly, of passion, and of pleasure, was so so severely reproveable ! But blessed be the name of Israel's God ! There was a time when he met me in a narrow place ; at a time when sickness had nearly sunk me to the grave ; when I had every prospect that this mortal must soon put on immortality ! Then was my soul visited with the depths of judgment ; my sins were set in order before me ! My mind was filled with horror ; fear and confusion were upon me, and the hairs of my flesh stood up. In this awful situation, I was continued day after day, and month after month ; like a crane or a swallow did I chatter, I did mourn as a dove. Often did I wander ; when your eyes were sealed in sleep, when no one could see me, and where no ear could hear me pour forth my complaints, to him in whom I believed; but whose comforts were withdrawn, and as I said, I was brought to the brink of. the grave; and in one of those solitary moments, when' I was willing to be, to do, or to suffer any thing which should be required at my hands—It was in one of these walks, that my soul was bowed, and when my afflictions were as great as human nature could bear; I cried out in the anguish soul, what shall I do! And after this, suddenly, the waves which almost overwhelmed me, were calmed into stillness. In remembering this time. of affliction and misery, the wormwood and the gall, my soul hath them still in remembrance; and is humbled within me.

In this calm there was a language uttered in the secret of my soul. (Now my friends, this is not the language of enthusiasm; it is the language of experimental truth:) what wilt thou do, I have the words of eternal life? I know it was impossible for me to bring these feelings upon my own mind; the certainly it must be the operation of another power. I remembered it was the language of the Apostle, and it was an evidence sealed upon my mind—that it was an impression from above; and as I attended to its manifestations, this quiet state continued for a season and I rejoiced therein.

But, alas! I forgot to rejoice with fear, and to serve the Lord with trembling. I was lifted up again. I slew the pure witness, which thus reproved me for evil; and sat my sins in order before me. I flew into the world and into its maxims; I was again brought to the depths of affliction; for this is a power which will never look on evil with acceptance or allowance.

I have no doubt it was the baptism of the Holy Ghost, which reproved me for my rebellion; for it operates as fire upon every soul which lives in this state of ungodliness, pride and impiety. And while in this state, we cannot enjoy that peace. which is the result of obedience, and which proceeds from heaven. Neither can we serve two masters, God and mammon. And after I had gone back, into this state, I had to mourn for my backsliding, season after season. But when I sincerely repented and forsook the evil way:

then, in the midst of judgment, he remembered mercy, and spake peace to my soul.

It is this experience of his operations upon the soul, that begets a living faith, and holy confidence, and unshaken love. And here is understood, that which is written, concerning that faith, which works by love, and purifies the soul. It is not that which is received by education; but by the operative power of God, upon each individual, who submits to its influence.

Here it is, in this faith that we come to be oftentimes favored, to know, that instruction is sealed upon the mind. It is the preaching of the gospel in faith and verity. It is the gospel that the Lord Jesus himself preached, baptisingly, into the name of the Father, and of the Son, and of the Holy Ghost. And this is knowledge, which can never be shaken; and there is no other name which can seal these divine or spiritual truths upon the mind; according to our several states and conditions. Where is the necessity then, for adapting systems or creeds, or articles of belief, and baptising with water? They are all human contrivances; but this bears a testimony immediately against all unrighteousness and ungodliness of men, who hold the truth in unrighteousness. It never reproves any thing but evil; it never speaks peace for good. It is a power, which may be depended on, in every situation.

Some may conclude or rather query; is there any difference between this and the imagination? Yes. The difference is as great as that between light and darkness, or heaven and earth. What does the imagination seek? It seeks the gratification of the natural mind; and will be under the influence of imaginary power, as many of you have experienced. This also, perhaps, was my most easily besetting sin. Under this, I could build castles in the air; lead conquering armies; and fill every station with dignity and applause. The vagaries of the imagination, lead us to seek something for our emolument. We are personating virtue, and pleasing ourselves with the pictures we have drawn. Yet the whole design and end is, our own honor; and this is the end of all its works. For the imagination seeks not the glory of God, but will lead us through all states and conditions, among objects created and uncreated; and give them all the glory, and place in them all our hopes of happiness; but it is all tinsel and not gold. It is the baseless fabric of a vision. It leaves a visionary kind of enjoyment. to the mind, instead of that solid comfort, which these have left, for their indulgencies. The imagination which forms these baseless fabrics, is unstable; it reproves not for evil: it leads us to imagine many things in nature, and out of nature, and always indulges in every vice, passion and lust.

But this power, which is of God, which is the revelation of God to man, the gospel preached in every creature, reproves us for every wicked thought that passes in the mind: and if suffered to grow, it will assuredly operate upon the thoughts and the imagination, until we shall know that Scripture testimony fulfilled: "Behold the axe is laid unto the root of the tree;' and every tree which brings not forth good fruit, shall be hewn down and cast into the fire." And when the axe is laid to the root of evil in our mind, and we attend to it, it will cast out as a consequence, all that does not produce good fruit. The leaves will wither, and the branches fail when we become separated therefrom: and the mind becomes an habitation of God, the temple of holiness: and herein is that declaration fulfilled, "ye are the temple of the living God. If any man defile the temple of God, him shall God destroy. For the temple of God is holy. which temple ye are."

This baptising power which preaches the gospel, is Christ in you, the hope of glory; he is begotten in us, brought forth in us; and thus is fulfilled his declaration, when his mother and brethren, without, desired to speak with him. He said unto them, "whoso believeth on me or keepeth my commandments, the same is my mother, my sister and brother." And wherefore? Because he is begotten in each of us, and though he is brought forth in weakness, in sorrow, trouble and affliction; yet if we are careful not to strangle this embryo in its birth, it will be raised in power until it will grow and increase, and overcome the vagaries of the imagination;

9

the fashions, habitual propensities, and traditional views of religion and righteousness. It will overcome these systematic forms taught by the circumstances around us in educa-. tion. It will bring the mind, the thoughts, the imaginations, and our whole conduct into a state of purity and perfection. We shall become united unto God, the Father, and to his son Jesus Christ; in whom we shall become partakers of the same nature begotten into the same life. Therefore, he will not be ashamed to call us brethren. And therefore, I desire to leave these things with you, for your serious consideration, continuing in this power. It is this which reproves for every evil desire, with which we may be assailed—and it is this which enables us to pass through this life, this vale of tears, not merely as mourners all the day long; but it will be a stay and a staff, a support and comfort in every affliction. It will open the Scriptures to our view. It will be to us the same revelation of Jesus Christ, which led the prophets and patriarchs in all ages. It is the same spirit, which appeared to them, that will give us a view of these scriptures, which are written for our instruction, edification, reproof and comfort in righteousness; that we, through faith, and comfort of the Scriptures—might have hope. It clouds not the divine truths in a mystery. The veil or outward curtain is rent in twain, by the operative power of the crucifixion of our natural passions, enabling us to enter into the holiest of all ; and whether ye will hear or whether ye will forbear. I am renewedly convinced, that, however men may teach and we receive, these doctrines which are taught by the commandment of men, will never bring us into a state of union and communion with God, nor prepare us an habitation in the kingdom of Heaven, here or in eternity. Therefore how desirable it is, that each of us should do that part of the work, which is allotted to us ; and know that divine love brought into our daily walk in life, which overcomes every thing of an opposite nature; that we may know the enjoyment of heaven here, experience a well grounded hope of everlasting happiness ; and know this truth fulfilled, that in whatever situation we may be placed—"a living dog is better than a dead lion."

SERMON VIII.

DELIVERED BY THOMAS WETHERALD AT PINE STREET MEETING, PHILADEL
PHIA, MAY 21st, 1820.

"Whereunto shall I liken the men of this generation?
and to what are they like? They are like children sitting
in the market-place and calling one to another, and saying,
We have piped unto you and ye have not danced, we have
mourned unto you and ye have not wept." Now whilst we
are under the influence of these feelings of crimination and
recrimination, it is impossible that we should "bear one another's burthens, and thus fulfil the law of Christ." It is
impossible that when any one member suffers, the others can
suffer therewith; and, on the contrary, it is equally impossible that when any thing is "piped or harped," and one
member rejoices, all the other members will be able to rejoice
with it, and to dance at the sound thereof. Whilst we are
under the influence of these childish feelings we never can
drink at the same fountain, because we are not governed by
that unerring spirit which leads into unity and not into dissension, but under the influence of those exciting feelings
which are natural to the perverted dispositions of men. Under the influence of these they become zealous, but with a
kind of zeal which the people of Israel were represented to
have possessed. They were represented by Paul as zealous,
but not according to knowledge. Hence, under the influence of these feelings, many systems have been formed, and
the duties thus enjoined may have been performed, for there
is an abundance of religion in the present day. There are a
great many high professions, and from whence does all this
spring? It originates in the ingenuity and invention of

man, whose works tend to corruption ; for "God hath made man upright, but they have sought out many inventions." And all the inventions of man, notwithstanding the beauty and excellency of their first appearance, can do nothing more than "lead to bewilder, and dazzle to blind."

I can believe in the principles and doctrines of almost all the various societies with which I am acquainted. I can believe with the Catholics, that there is no salvation without the pale of the holy, catholic, and apostolic church. With the Episcopalians, in God, the Father Almighty, maker of heaven and earth, and in Jesus Christ, his only son, our Lord, who was conceived of the Holy Ghost, born of the virgin Mary, suffered under Pontius Pilate, was crucified, dead, and buried. But that he descended into hell I dare not believe, because he declared unto the thief on the cross, this day wilt thou be with me in Paradise. I can believe with the Calvinists, that the elect only will be saved. With the Baptists, that baptism is essential to salvation. I can believe with a variety of other societies : with the Universalists, that all men may be saved. With the Unitarians, that there is "one God and Father of all, who is above all, and through all, and in you all." And I can believe with the Quakers, that "the grace of God that bringeth salvation hath appeared unto all men, teaching us that, denying ungodliness and worldly lusts, we should live soberly, righteously, and godly in this present world, looking for that blessed hope, and the glorious appearing of the great God and our Saviour Jesus Christ."

And where are we to look for this glorious appearance? Are we to look to external circumstances? No. "For God hath said, I will dwell in them and walk in them, and I will be their God and they shall be my people." Now, my friends, let us look over the whole of these systems, and the effects which they have produced on mankind. Their promoters have been very active in their operations and exertions, for, within my recollection, there has been a very great increase, and strenuous efforts have been made to cause a greater increase ; but it is all a spurious growth ; for, with the increase of religious profession, it is evident that wickedness has increased in our land, very much in the same ratio. Hence, there is something in this kind of religion, which, though it does not produce the effects proposed, is calculated to please man. Its origin is in human invention; it is planned by human wisdom. But this can never lead to any other results, than to make its followers "like children sitting in the markets and calling unto their fellows, and saying, we have piped unto you and ye have not danced, we have mourned unto you and ye have not wept."

And with respect to principles, doctrines, and matters of opinion, there is no salvation to be experienced from them. What is the salvation that we want, as men and creatures? even that salvation which was promised. "Behold, a virgin shall conceive and bear a son, and shall call his name Immanuel, which is, being interpreted, God with us:" and, in another place, it is declared, that he shall be called "Jesus," that is, a saviour, "for he shall save his people from their sins;" and this is the salvation that we want. We do not want to be saved, or to experience salvation from any thing of an external nature, or any particular kind of principles, names, doctrines, or opinions; but we want to be saved from the perversion of our natural affections, dispositions, and lusts, which separate us from God, the author of our existence, and the power whom we profess to worship. But is it not obvious, that the religion in our land has not had this tendency; that it has not brought us nigh unto God; and that, therefore, it has wanted application to the minds of individuals. And now, my friends and fellow professors, for this application. This is wanting among us; we want to have the great truths of the scriptures brought immediately home, and applied to our own minds by the illuminating influence of that divine and living principle which operates in each and every one, leading us out of sin and corruption into the glorious liberty of the sons and daughters of God—where all these discords cease and all divisions have an end, and where we shall be no longer as children sitting in the market-places. I want us all to consider what is the governing principle of the gospel: it is love, for love is the fulfilling of the law, and if our minds are under this divine influence, if they are united to God, our understandings will come to be opened, and we shall be enabled to see those things which are hid from the wise and the prudent. with all their inventions and imaginations, and revealed unto babes. Now this was a cause of thankfulness, even unto Jesus Christ, when he came to do his father's will. He said, "I thank thee, O Father, Lord of heaven and earth, because thou hast hid these things from the wise and the prudent, and hast revealed them unto babes. Even so, Father, for so it seemed good in thy sight."

And I apprehend there is no other medium whereby we can become members of the church of Christ but by baptism. But it is not a baptism with water, nor with any outward element, that can purge us from our spiritual lusts. No; all the waters of the sea combined can never cleanse the soul of one single solitary sin or lust. We may wash from youth to old age,—we may take snow water and wash ourselves never so clean, yet without this baptising influence they will only plunge us into the ditch, till our own clothes shall abhor us. I want us to look a little at that baptism which was prophesied of, and which John declared would come. What was the baptism which John alluded to? That spoken of in the prophecy of Isaiah, "The voice of one crying in the wilderness, prepare ye the way of the Lord, make his paths straight." And what is the consequence, and what must remain the consequence of this preparation? Why, "every valley shall be exalted, and every mountain and hill shall be made low, and the crooked shall be made straight, and the rough places plain." These are the effects produced by that baptism which John declared was of fire. "I, indeed, baptize you with water unto repentance, but he that cometh after me is mightier than I, whose shoes I am not worthy to bear, he shall baptize you with the Holy Ghost and with fire." Now, what are we to understand by these valleys being exalted and the mountains and hills being brought low? It has no allusion or application to the undulations of the outward surface of this earth, but it comes nearer to ourselves. There are many of us whose spirits have been rash, fierce, headstrong, proud, and cruel. These are mountains which have lifted up themselves in opposition to the divine will, and, consequently, above that divine harmony in which the pipe can sound and we can dance; in which we can rejoice with those that rejoice, or mourn with those that weep. But if we come under the influence of the Holy Ghost, it operates as fire upon these mountains until they are brought to a proper level. And rest assured, this fire will never consume any thing but that which is calculated to destroy our peace and happiness. It will only destroy the dross, tin, and reprobate silver, so that the pure gold may shine with the greater lustre. And what are these valleys that are to be exalted? Are there not among the members of the human family, those who are desponding, those who are despairing, those who are weeping, and those who are ready to adopt the language, a saviour or I die, a redeemer or I perish forever. There are those whose cup has been mingled with affliction, and what if I should say, with gall and wormwood: unto these, consolation is often opened, their minds are comforted, their spirits raised into confidence. Thus, by this operation, those that are rash, fierce, head-strong, proud, and cruel, are reduced to meekness, and those who are desponding and despairing are raised into firmness; the crooked and perverse dispositions are made straight and the rough places plain. Here is a state in which the glory of the Lord can cover every earthly propensity, "as the waters cover the sea," and give us complete dominion over the whole. Hence, we see an effect produced by this operation, which was described by the evangelical prophet, when he declared, "The wolf also shall dwell with the lamb, and the leopard shall lie down with the kid; and the calf, and the young lion, and the fatling together, and a little child shall lead them." Every opposite and perverse disposition shall be brought to the same state of innocency, and under the influence of the same divine purity, and be governed by the same illimitable principle of love. "And the cow and the bear shall feed ; their young ones shall lie down together, and the lion shall eat straw like the ox, and the sucking child shall play on the hole of the asp, and the weaned child shall put his hand on the cockatrice's den. They shall not hurt nor destroy in all my holy mountain, saith the Lord of hosts, for the earth shall be full of the knowledge of the glory of the Lord, as the waters cover the sea." It is by and through this medium, and this alone, that this wilderness can become an Eden, and this dessert like the garden of the Lord ; "joy and gladness shall be found therein, thanksgiving and the voice of melody."

Now my friends, what are the operations of this baptism, and how are they to be experienced ? Are there not many of us who commit acts under the influence of pride, ambition, wrath, cruelty, and other evil passions, which may be the cause of injuring our neighbors, and wounding our own souls ? And can any of us commit actions of this description with impunity ? Is there not something which reproves us, when our heads are laid on the pillow ? And what is this ? It is the same principle which met Adam in the cool of the day, when he had transgressed against the power of the living and omnipresent God. "And the Lord God called unto Adam, and said unto him, where art thou ?" Are not the same effects produced by evil at the present day ? And do we not hide ourselves—does not guilt make us afraid, and do we not attempt to hide ourselves from this divine power, which reproves us for every evil ? And do we not lose the benefits of these reproofs, by hiding ourselves, and by endeavoring to avoid the scrutiny of that power, which never looks on evil with acceptance or allowance ? And does not this remain with us, in the matchless mercy of a gracious God ? It is the same unto us, from infancy to old age, when hoar hairs have covered us.

Now my friends, this principle which reproves for evil actions, brings sorrow, trouble and confusion, and is the source from which spring dread and despair in the guilty mind ; yea, it leads to every feeling in which there is torment.—

in every creature, to open the eyes of our minds, to unstop the deaf ears of our understandings ; and he will continue to cast out every evil, till we gain a complete victory over all our perverse dispositions and wicked propensities. He will heal every malady of the soul, quiet every passion, and raise from a death of sin into the life of Christ, in which we experience the harmonizing power of God, which casts out devils, and brings body, soul, and spirit into the divine harmony.

Now is there any thing in a baptism with water, which can produce these effects? No. But as it was in another case so it was in this. When we eat the flesh and drink the blood of Christ, it nourisheth the soul as the baptism of his spirit cleanseth it. For it is declared, "except ye eat the flesh of the son of man, and drink his blood, ye have no life in you. Whoso eateth my flesh and drinketh my blood, hath eternal life." But we cannot become partakers unless it is by baptism in his name, and his name is his power.— But when we are thus baptized into his power, then we come to know his flesh to be meat indeed, and his blood drink indeed. And what is this blood? It is the life. It is the circulating medium which gives vitality to the whole system, and circulates through the whole system, as the outward blood circulates through the whole outward body. So the spirit of Christ circulating through the spirit of man, will bring about a conformity of thought, word, and action to its own nature ; and here we become partakers of the life of Christ, and receive benefit from his blood ; but not through that act of unparalleled malevolence in the Jews, whereby they crucified the Son of God.

When this blood, this divine life, this emanation from God comes to circulate through the whole soul, then we come to be wholly partakers of the divine nature ; then we become the sons of God. And here is fulfilled another declaration, which has been long contested. It is a doctrine of the scriptures, that those who are elected together with Christ are "heirs of God, and joint heirs with Jesus Christ ;" because they become partakers with him of the divine nature. And

Here is a truth applicable unto all, for all have experienced it. And herein is fulfilled another declaration of scripture—"And they shall teach no more, every man his neighbor, and every man his brother, saying, know the Lord; for they shall all know me from the least of them, unto the greatest of them, saith the Lord." And here is a medium opened whereby we may come to an experimental knowledge which can alone lead to life eternal. Whilst there is evil in the mind, this fire will still continue to burn until it has consumed every thing of a nature calculated to separate us from the source of purity. This is a baptism of the Holy Ghost, which operates as fire, on all the unrighteousness and ungodliness of men. And if we will submit to its operations, and turn at its reproofs, it will not only become a reprover, but a purifyer of the soul. But have we not, on the contrary, experienced the fluctuations of all those lofty imaginations of the mind, brought down into a state of stillness, when we have felt a dependence on the divine author of our existence, and have willingly waited on him. It has been something like what was experienced by its followers formerly. And it is this principle which continues to the present day, that effected all those mighty miracles which were performed among the Jews, in the outward advent of the Messiah. We remember that he opened the blind eyes. unstopped the deaf ears, and healed the maladies of their outward bodies, cleansed the leprosy, raised the dead, and cast out devils. And have these operations ceased? Were they merely limited to a few years, and to a peculiar people? No, verily. From the foundation of the world, it has not only been a medium whereby man could have access to the Father, but by which we become united to him: for it is an emanation of his own eternal and undivided power and spirit; and it has from the foundation of the world, opened the blind eyes, unstopped the deaf years, and healed all the maladies of the soul, raised the dead, and cast out devils. And even at the present day, these operations continue to produce their effects in those, and only in those who come to him.— He continues by the power of this gospel, which is preached as these continue in that election, their understandings will be more and more fully opened to many divine truths, which are hid from the wise and the prudent of this world. But by a daily abuse of our heavenly Father's will, the reverse will be the consequence, and we may become to every good thought, word, and work, reprobates.

"If any man love me let him keep my commandments." Now these commandments are not statutory, but they are prescriptive. They are not given to this, that, or any other community, but they are engraven on the soul of every individual by the finger of God, and thus they are applied to every individual. And thus does the Almighty, who governs the universe, who fills all place and all space, daily manifest himself to each individual as if he were occupied with one sole object. But is it not derogatory to man, and to the honor of his Creator, to believe that the noblest of God's creation should be left to a dependence on external circumstances, and to work out their salvation by such mean? I have no such belief at all. My faith is not founded upon such grounds as these. I never received any religion from my ancestors. I was not a prophet, neither a prophet's son ; neither was I trained up in the schools of literature, to make merchandise, more effectually, of the souls of people. I was trained up to labor, and in the school of deep affliction I learned where peace was to be found. And I am willing to tell my fellow members where it can be found. It is not to be found in systems,—it is not to be found in opinions, or principles, or sentiments, but in the operation of the spirit of God, producing principles which lead to a practical belief.

For instance, can any man become honest, except by a principle of honesty within him? Can he become merciful, except he be under the direction of the principle of mercy in himself? Can he love God the Father, and his neighbor as himself, except he be under the Government of the principle of love?

And as these fruits grow, religion becomes an individual work, and is the immediate operation of the spirit of Christ upon our spirits, performing those miracles, giving those precepts, and preaching the gospel unto those that are poor in spirit. Thus we become members of that living body of which Christ is the head, and we know him to be all and in all.

And the manifestation of Christ was not limited merely to that outward body amongst the Jews. This power operated long before that season, for it is recorded of Israel, that "they did all eat the same spiritual meat, and did all drink the same spiritual drink; for they drank of that spiritual rock that followed them, and that rock was Christ." And let us remember that *Jesus* is a saviour; and that *Immanuel* is God with us: and we need not look for this divine power at a great distance, and beyond the grave; for "the word is nigh thee, even in thy mouth and in thy heart; that is the word of faith which we preach unto you." It is in us a teacher; it is known unto all. We must, therefore, come to the conclusion, when we follow the example of Christ by a daily and hourly obedience to the operation of the spirit, that God is not found merely at a great distance and beyond the grave, for he is manifest in our flesh.

What is God? It is that divine power which first created and which yet sustains the universe. It is the divine principle which

> " Warms in the sun, refreshes in the breeze,
> Glows in the stars, and blossoms in the trees;
> Lives through all life, extends through all extent,
> Spreads undivided, operates unspent;
> Breathes in our soul, informs our mortal part,
> As full, as perfect, in a hair as heart;
> As full, as perfect, in vile man that mourns,
> As the rapt seraph that adores and burns."

It is here that we must become acquainted with that principle, omnipotent, omnipresent, and omniscient. We must know him from the operation of his power in our own minds. We must know him to open our blind eyes, to unstop our deaf ears, and heal the maladies of the soul, raise the dead, and cast out devils. And we shall then be enabled to see him throughout all his works. But I do not, and I cannot, lead you to any external object, my friends, as a primary medium of instruction. But if our minds are under the divine influence, we are prepared to receive lessons of instruction from the workmanship of his hands; for there is not a blade of grass that grows, not a leaf that flutters in the wind, nor the meanest insect that we tread upon, but declares the workmanship of a God. Here are lessons of instruction deeply and indelibly engraven upon our minds, as nothing short of infinite wisdom could have formed them, nor can now sustain them for a moment. And his care extends to all, however minute, and let their number be what it may; for he fills all space. There are none too high to be controled by him, nor too low to feel his supporting power. One of the divine penmen must have been aware of this, when he says, "Whither shall I go from this spirit? If I ascend up into heaven thou art there; if I make my bed in hell behold thou art there. If I take the wings of the morning, and dwell in the uttermost parts of the sea, even there shall thy hand lead me, and thy right hand shall hold me." And now coming to be baptized into Christ's death, we shall experience a victory over all those principles which disobedience has brought over our minds, and which have produced death. And having received the election, even the adoption of sons, and having become partakers of the divine harmony, and experienced the knowledge of God, we shall not go back to the weak and beggarly elements which produce no peace, but which will lead into bondage. But I hope better things for you, and things that accompany salvation. And when this is produced in our minds, we shall experience an holy sabbath or state of rest—a holy day. It is then, and not till then, that we can sanctify a fast. That we can "blow the trumpet in Zion, sanctify a fast, call a solemn assembly, gather the people, sanctify the congregation, assemble the elders, gather the children. Let the bridegroom go forth of his chamber and the bride out of her closet. Let the priests and the ministers of the Lord weep between the porch and the altar; and let them say, spare thy people, O Lord, and give not thy heritage to reproach, that the heathen should rule over them. Wherefore should they say, among the people, where is their God"

Whatever our avocations in life may be, our minds may be brought into obedience to the same baptizing power, and hence all these effects will be produced. And what are the priests and ministers, who are to stand between the porch and the altar, and thus pray for the people—"O Lord, give not thine heritage to reproach?" Are they individuals appointed and supported by man? No, verily. Who are these ministers of God, whom he maketh as a flame of fire? They are all ministering spirits, sent forth to minister to them that shall be "heirs of salvation." They are those ministers who are employed in casting out devils. They are those who are employed in nourishing up the soul unto ever-lasting life. And when we come to experience this fulfilled in us, then we shall know another declaration fulfilled, to our souls comfort—that "there was war in heaven : Michael and his angels fought against the dragon ; and the dragon fought and his angels, and prevailed not, neither was their place found any more in heaven." Now shall we look at a great distance and beyond the grave, for this heaven? No. Rather let us remember the declaration—"the kingdom of heaven is within you." There we are to look for the appear-ing of this kingdom, and there we are to experience his governing power—there we are to know his laws to have dominion over every other name, power, and principle in us, and know that he "rules as with a rod of iron" against all unrighteousnes and ungodliness of men, and we shall know that the sceptre of righteousness is the sceptre of his king-dom. And under the influence of this governing principle, we shall know that these angels are the ministers of God to man, for good ; and that the lion of the tribe of Juda con-tinues to open the book of the mysteries of heaven, and enables to look thereon. And remember that the seals were opened in order, and not in confusion, but one after another. These seals were opened through the mighty operation of the power of God, opening the various seals adapted to the state and condition, and to the various advancement of individuals in the christian course. What is the opening of these seals? Is it not the opening of the understanding that we may comprehend divine truths? We cannot become religious all at once—from a state of wickedness and profanity, to a state of strict adherence to the law of God. It is a cause of thankfulness in my soul that I can acknowledge at the present day, that he has been merciful in that which he required at my hands, that when my feet were first turned towards the city of Zion, had I seen all that would have been required of me, its effects would have been overwhelming. But in the mercy of God those things were opened which I was able to comprehend, and which were immediately essential. And as my understanding became opened, I saw farther. As a child in the rudiments of education can see but little; but as we advance, and add experience, our minds are enlarged, our understanding increases, till we become perfect in the art or science, which has been the object of our study. So it is in a spiritual relation. This the apostle had in view; for he says, " When I was a child, I spake as a child; I understood as a child, I thought as a child : but when I became a man, I put away childish things." Now, would to God that we may experience this growth in grace and become men, and put away childish things, and perverse dispositions which cannot unite together ; because it is an infallible and self-evident truth, that while we are under the government of these dispositions we cannot advance into that divine harmony, because of sin and transgression. We cannot become afflicted in the afflictions of our brethren, because, to do this, we must become partakers of the nature of Christ. For in all the afflictions of the Jews, " he was afflicted, and the angel of his presence saved them." " He led them about, he instructed them, he kept them as the apple of his eye."

But to return—" There was war in heaven : Michael and his angels fought against the dragon ; and the dragon fought and his angels, and prevailed not, neither was their place found any more in heaven." And what are these angels? And what are these devils? Are we to look for them in the

Paradise of Milton, or in the disordered imaginations of any of the poets? Are we to look upon angels, as women with wings, carrying the divine commands to and fro in the earth? Are we to look upon devils, as local self-existent beings, calculated to torment the human soul in lakes of fire and brimstone? Now, I have had a different view of these things; and as far as it respects myself, I see no good reason to change that view. Not that I want to impose it upon any of you—but my view is, that these angels are the heavenly and virtuous dispositions; and that the devils are evil dispositions, which, if indulged by man, and that indulgence continued, will become the tormentors of the human family. But when we come to know the angel of love, to cast out the devil of hatred; the angel of mercy, to cast out the devil of cruelty; the angel of temperance, to cast out the devil of intemperance; the angel of hope, to cast out the devil of despair—and when we know every ministering angel of God, (and they are an host) and every heavenly disposition to take possession of the mind, they must necessarily cast out the opposite dispositions, adversaries, and enemies, and what if I say devils—they will thus become the governing principle of the mind. And while we are under the influence of him who is the head of all this multitude of ministering spirits, the enemy can never be reinstated. Then we shall know the declaration fulfilled that there was war in heaven; and this being continued in our minds till judgment is brought forth unto truth, we shall come into that state in which we can see a mighty angel stand with one foot upon the sea and the other upon the earth, as we may remember the angel stood, and was raised above all the fluctuating imaginations, which are typified by the sea, and he was raised above all earthly propensities. This analogy is beautiful, and deeply instructive. In this state he "lifted up his hand to heaven and sware by him who liveth forever and ever, that there should be time no longer." Here, my friends, we are not under the influence of feelings circumscribed by days or by times, by months or years; but we are centred in that divine light in which we can say, come life or death, riches or poverty, sickness or health—Yea, all matters of a sublunary nature—all earthly things become matters of indifference to us. And wherefore? Because we shall see "another mighty angel fly in the midst of heaven, having the everlasting gospel to preach." And what is this preaching? It is what every man and woman must experience themselves—"Fear God and give glory to him, for the hour of his judgment is come; and worship him that made heaven, and earth, and the sea, and the fountains of waters." And what is worship? Does it consist in bowing down the head like a bull-rush; or in lifting up the voice like a trumpet? Does it consist in performing and fulfilling the rituals of some outward system—such as preaching, praying, and singing? Does it consist in the performance of family duties, and the adoption of a system? No. This is the fast that the Lord hath chosen—"To loose the bands of wickedness, to undo the heavy burdens, and to let the oppressed go free, and that ye break every yoke—to deal thy bread to the hungry, and that thou bring the poor that are cast out to thy house—when thou seest the naked that thou cover him; and that thou hide not thyself from thine own flesh." These are duties in the performance of which God is acceptably worshipped. He looks not to the position of the body, or to any particular form of words. He trieth the hearts and searcheth the reins of all men, and he knoweth all our thoughts, ere they are brought forth. Neither is worship restricted to any particular time or place—or to those only who are thus assembled. For we may preach, pray, and sing, and perform a great variety of outward rituals, and yet stand in infidelity. What then is worship? It consists in obedience to the operation of that divine illimitable principle, which is designed to guide out of every evil and into all truth. This is the kind of spiritual religion which is enjoined on every one of us, and is to be performed by actions, and reduced to daily practice, whether we sit in the house or walk by the way. And this law which is given should be placed as a frontlet between the eyes. "And these words, which I command thee this day, shall be in

10

thine heart; and thou shalt teach them diligently unto thy children, and shalt talk of them when thou sittest in thine house, and when thou walkest by the way, and when thou liest down, and when thou risest up. And thou shalt bind them for a sign upon thine hand, and they shall be as frontlets between thine eyes.'' But let us remember my friends, that it is not only when we are thus assembled that we ought to labor to come to this continued sabbath, in which we are brought to a state of willingness to do every thing for the glory of God, and in which we can testify with Christ himself, '' my meat and my drink is to do the will of him that sent me, and to finish his work.''

Now let us look a little at the effects which would be produced in the human family, by an universal extension of these principles of religion, and a belief in them and their effects. It is the opening of these things upon our minds, that will bring us out of that which is evil, and into that which is good. If any of us have been intemperate, we shall come under the influence of that principle which produces temperance. There is a principle in our minds, by which, if we have been cruel, we shall be brought under the influence of mercy. And this is an operative principle; it does not depend on the opinions of others—of our forefathers, the scriptures of truth, or any other external cause. There is no principle prepared by others, which can ever nourish up the soul to eternal life. Not all the costly food that can be eaten by others, will ever nourish our bodies; we must be partakers ourselves. We cannot see with another's eyes, or hear with another's ears; neither can we understand with the heart of another. If we ever come to see, hear, or understand, and to be converted, it must be with our own faculties, and not with those of another. If we are ever converted, we must experience the dealings of God with us. Here is a religion which is immediately adapted to each individual. This is a religion which can banish from the earth all evil that comes from sin; it can bruise the head of every serpentine disposition which separates us from God.

Now let us look a little at the effects which would be thus

produced in the world. Where would there be room for wars, if the angel of love should cast out the devil of hatred and envy? Where would be found quarrels in families, squabbles in neighborhoods, or war among nations? All these must die away and perish, because they stand not in love, in humility, and forgiveness, but in a perversion of those leading principles of the human mind. While pride and ambition continue, wars and dissensions will abound. If we are under the influence of temperance, where will there be room for intemperance? And here we come to see the declaration fulfilled, that, "the axe is laid unto the root of the tree: therefore every tree which bringeth not forth good fruit is hewn down and cast into the fire." And what are we to understand by this? Why, when this is the case we shall see that not merely the branches are lopped off, or the extremities destroyed, for this would only cause the tree to put forth more luxuriantly, but the axe is laid to the root of the tree. And where is this root? It is in the mind—it is in the soul. For the gospel dispensation takes not cognizance of the outward actions, or outward words, but it lays the axe to the root of the tree, or of these imaginations of the heart, from whence all the outward evil actions proceed. This must have been the design in that declaration of Christ himself, in his inimitable sermon on the mount. That sermon bears a testimony worthy to be engraven on the tablets of every heart, and bound round the horns of every altar, for it is necessary, if we would come under the government of that principle which would lead us out of every thing that is evil, and every thing which has a tendency to separate us from the source of purity, and the author of our existence. "Ye have heard that it hath been said, thou shalt love thy neighbor and hate thine enemy; but I say unto you, love your enemies: bless them that curse you, do good to them that hate you, and pray for them that despitefully use you and persecute you." Here is a precept which must put an end to all wars and fightings, yea to dissensions of every kind, among all those who come under its influence. There are a variety of other precepts, with which you are as well acquainted as I am. It was written—and perhaps it is one of the most conclusive declarations of any to be found in the sacred writings—"Ye have heard that it was said, by them of old time, thou shalt not commit adultery ; but I say unto you, that whosoever looketh on a woman to lust after her, hath committed adultery with her already in his heart." Where, then, is the evil laid? Is it upon the act? No. Rather upon the thoughts or imaginations from which the actions proceed. Seeing, therefore, that these things have been established, not only on scripture testimony, but in the line of each of our experience, I have desired that we may cease from a dependence on the works of man, whose breath is in his nostrils : and rest assured, that the enemies of man are they of his own household. They consist in those perverted dispositions, which have produced all the evil that there is in the world, which lead into all this variety of sentiments and opinions. I am not about to say that we should see all things in the same point of view, for this is an impossibility in the nature of things. This baptism, whereby we are initiated into the church of Christ, operates according to the diversities of our dispositions, many of which are rash, headstrong, fierce, proud, and cruel. All these must be brought into the depths of hell, and experience the depths of judgment. They will have to bear the furnace of affliction, when it is heated seven times hotter than it is wont to be heated. These dispositions want to be brought under the curb and reign of gospel discipline. These will view the Most High as a God of judgment. They must be led in low paths, lest they take their flight on the sabbath day. I can bear this testimony to the praise and glory of God, because herein is our safety, and we are not permitted to enjoy so much of that sabbath as others who are differently constituted. But, my friends, wherever these dispositions abound, wherever the dispositions and passions are strong, there is a proportionable revelation and manifestation of the divine power, which lifts up a standard against them. Thus, according to our various circumstances and dispositions, the more we have need of the armor of strength to overcome every enemy, every adversary, and every devil, and to cast them out. But these will look on the Most High as a God of judgment. Their minds will be kept low in the depths of humility. I am persuaded of this, my young friends, for there was a time when I was young, as you are now, and when my mind was in a state of innocency ; and when I was brought under the influence of this principle, I could testify of his mercy, and the joy and consolation that I experienced was great ; and it enabled me to keep a reign over all my actions. But, notwithstanding this, I took my flight upon the sabbath day, after which I took full swing in acts of madness and of folly ; and I can bear this testimony of laughter, that it is mad, and of mirth, what doeth it ? I was separated far and wide from the paths of rectitude. I took the broad way that leadeth to everlasting destruction. But blessed be the name of Israel's God forever, for he plucked me as a brand from the burning. He met me in a narrow way, where I had no way for escape ; and this at a time when the grave was yawning before me, and when my soul was even expecting that it would soon be closed upon me. Now were my sins set in order before me. They appeared as mountains between me and my God. Like a crane or a swallow, so did I chatter. I did mourn as a dove. Days, weeks, and months have I wandered by the way and in solitary places, in the depths of mourning. And thus it was, in one of those seasons when my soul was overwhelmed in the depths of affliction, that this language came to me : what ever shall I do? I saw no way ; affliction was before me and behind me. I was surrounded on every side with the depths of trouble, when this language was begotten in me, and I believe it was a divine intimation : "What wilt thou do ?—I have the words of eternal life." With this came a quietude, which I had not experienced for a long season. In this state of quietude there was a language spoken in my soul ! And may my soul never forget the day in which I experienced this language : "What wilt thou do ? I have the words of eternal life." But even until now I have not so fully been made a partaker of the joys of that rejoicing, in which I took my flight upon the sabbath day. And thus an evidence was sealed upon my mind, that I should not be able to become a partaker of those sublime visions, because they are something in which these high and lofty dispositions fly away unto vain imaginations. Therefore I can bear this testimony; if you are thus proud, lofty, fierce, and ungovernable, you must be kept poor. But others who are low, desponding, and despairing,—these will have different views of the Most High, and of his dealings. They will be brought under the government of a different principle. A cup of consolation will be handed to these; they will receive of the divine nourishment; they will experience the power of the divine light, which will raise them up till the glory of the Lord shall cover all their soul, as the waters cover the sea. Here all crooked and perverse dispositions shall be made straight, and the rough places plain.

Now, my friends, seeing that we are differently constituted, and that the operation of this baptism differs, according to the object which it is to effect, we cannot, nor is it essential that we should, see through the same medium to view the same objects. And thus is fulfilled the declaration of an inspired penman: Now there are diversities of gifts, but the same spirit, and there are differences of administratious, but the same Lord. And there are diversities of operations, but it is the same God which worketh all in all. But the manifestation of the spirit is given to every man to profit withal." I crave it of you, and I trust in that love in which there is no distinction, that you will not be as those "sitting in the market-places and calling one to another, and saying, We have piped unto you and ye have not danced, we have mourned unto you and ye have not wept."

SERMON IX.

DELIVERED BY THOMAS WETHERALD, AT ARCH STREET MEETING, PHILADEL-
PHIA, MAY 21st, 1820, IN THE AFTERNOON.

"I am not ashamed of the gospel of Christ; for it is the power of God unto salvation to every one that believeth." And in this there is no distinction between Jew and Greek, Barbarian or Scythian, bond or free. It extends to all—all are within its reach. And the gospel of Christ, which is the power of God unto salvation, is purely of a spiritual nature. It stands not in words: it is not bounded by opinions; for it remains to be a truth, that opinions are not religion, neither is declamation gospel. And I have no doubt that Jesus had in view the superiority of this gospel when he said unto his followers, "It is expedient for you, that I go away; for if I go not away, the Comforter will not come unto you; but if I depart, I will send him unto you."

And what was this going away? It was the going away, I apprehend we shall all unite in believing, of his outward body—that body which appeared among the Jews for a short time, and for a particular purpose. For according to the declaration of the great apostle of the Gentiles, Jesus was born of a woman—born under the law, in order that he might redeem them from under the law, that they might receive the adoption of sons. And when this great work was effected for the Jews, he told them it was expedient for them, that he should go away. "For if I go not away, the Comforter will not come unto you; but if I depart I will pray the Father, and he will send him unto you; and when he is come, he will reprove the world of sin, and of righteousness, and of judgment—and when the spirit of truth is come he will guide you into all truth.'' Here now is a plain, full, and positive declaration of the design and end of this coming, and of the operations which were to be performed by this spirit which was no less than the guidance of mankind. And on another occasion he said to his followers, ''But the Comforter, which is the Holy Ghost, whom the Father will send in my name, he shall teach you all things, and bring all things to your remembrance, whatsoever I have said unto you.'' And here is a view in which we may see not only the usefulness, but the actual necessity of this principle, which was designed to be a teacher, to bring all things to our remembrance. And he declared, that which he would give was his life, and which, said he, I will give for the life of the world. Now are we to look at this as having an allusion to the death of the body? No, my friends. It had allusion to giving that divine life which is of God, and hid with Christ in God, on condition that we will give up the life of the world—our carnal, evil dispositions, which have a tendency to separate us from the source of purity. And when we come to give up that life, which is impure and unholy, the divine life will not only be begotten, but will be brought forth in us. And this is the witness, which was borne concerning the life which was given for the life of the world and its corrupt propensities. That there is no occasion for this proverb : ''The fathers have eaten sour grapes, and the childrens teeth are set on edge. As I live, saith the Lord God, ye shall not have occasion any more to use this proverb in Israel.'' Surely, my friends, we need not this proverb ; for though our fathers have eaten sour grapes, their teeth and theirs only were set on edge. If we do that which is evil, we shall reap the reward of our wickedness ; for wickedness always brings its own reward. So again if we do that which is lawful and right, we shall reap the reward of our doings also : and this can be confirmed by another scripture testimony. ''Say ye to the righteous, that it shall be well with him ; for they shall eat the fruit of their doings. Woe unto the wicked ! It shall be ill with him ; for the reward of his works shall be given him." And now, my friends and fellow-professors of this holy name, the name of Christ, the way is so plain, until it becomes darkened by the sophistry of man, that the wayfaring man, though a fool, can not err therein.

Some may conclude that our consciences may become seared as with a hot iron, so that we cannot discern the monitions of this preceptor. But I have never known a burn—and it is a powerful allusion—indeed I know not of any animal body, in which it does not produce pain. And although we may strive to turn away from that reproof and instruction, which leads to the way of life ; and from the monitions of this living principle, still we can never remove ourselves beyond the feeling of its effects. Whenever the conscience is seared, the feeling it occasions is painful. Our punishment is as certain as wickedness is the immediate cause thereof: for as certainly as murder, theft, drunkenness, lying, swearing, backbiting, and every other evil produce in the mind disquietude, distress, trouble, sorrow, and affliction, so certainly will love, meekness, charity, and the cultivation of every heavenly virtue produce the opposite effects of joy, peace, and consolation, in every holy spirit.

Well now, my friends, how are we to attain to these ends? How are we to attain to the feeling of these joys? It is not by remaining in the first or second heavens. "I knew a man in Christ above fourteen years ago," said the Apostle, "(whether in the body I cannot tell, or whether out of the body I cannot tell ; God knoweth ;) such an one caught up to the third heaven, where he heard unspeakable words, which it is not lawful for a man to utter."

Now, I apprehend there may be many of us grovelling in the first or lowest heaven, under the government of our natural and animal propensities, which is a government but little better than that of the beasts which perish. These operate in inferior beings, and are called instinct, and are bestowed on them for their guidance. And if we pervert our rational powers, instead of being the most noble of God's creatures, we become the most ignoble ; and thus stamp upon our own selves, most indelibly, the seeds of sorrow, pain, and distress; and crucify the Son of God anew, in his spiritual appearing, and put him to an open shame. And while we are taking delight in those things which are of a carnal and a sensual nature, we are in the first or lowest heaven. For what is heaven? It is a state in which we delight to dwell, and in which our hopes of happiness are fixed.

. .I have no doubt many are ready to conclude, that they are no longer grovelling in this first or lowest heaven, but that they have ascended above it. But if they are stopping in the second heaven, they are in a still more dangerous situation. Many have taken up a profession of religion, and have adopted systems and creeds, and have subscribed to the various formularies adopted by men of corrupt minds, and reprobates concerning the true faith, to bind the conscience with. In the performance of these formularies they are endeavoring to find peace from a troubled conscience, and to get from under the feelings of that hot iron which becomes painful unto them. And here is the second heaven. These can bear an excellent character among men, of good husbands, good citizens, good neighbors, good friends; and thousands there are who have covered themselves under this plausible appearance, to their present and everlasting loss. And what do they learn by all these external performances? They learn to perform a round of ceremonies; they learn to hide this fault or that weakness, and to appear righteous in the opinion of others; but they do not learn to attend to the spirit, which Christ said would lead into all truth. These have come to the conclusion, "We will not have this man to rule over us." We will continue in the systems which we have adopted—declamation shall be our gospel, and we will have our dependence on these external things. All such are in the second heaven, because they are acting under the influence of feelings, opinions, and systems which they have chosen, and are pleasing themselves with the idol pictures which they have drawn.

But, my friends, the mysteries of the kingdom of heaven

are not here opened unto us. Nor can any rise to a higher state thereby, than that to which the Jews attained, which is only a legal dispensation, and genders to bondage. But when we come under the governing influence of that principle which opens the blind eyes, unstops the deaf ears, heals all the maladies of the soul, and raises from a depth of sin and corruption, into the light and life of Christ; then we come to experience something which is not lawful to be uttered. We come to know the operation of the spirit of God upon our spirits, and to know what it is to be reproved for every evil thought, word, and action; and so we shall know what it is to become partakers of the joys of his consolation. In this consolation, and under the influence of these feelings, we are kept from evil, and come to know what it is to labor for the bread of life, which cometh down from God out of heaven. We shall be careful, I apprehend, not to waste it in boasting. We shall be careful not to adopt any system which would have a tendency to obstruct or dissipate those feelings which are the ground of our life, and which are given "for a crown of glory, and for a diadem of beauty unto the residue of his people." But wherever the works of man, and the imaginations of man, are mixed with the creative power of God, they always produce a monstrous birth, or something which can never be the inhabitant of heaven. The faculties by which we come to the knowledge of God, are not instinctive; they are not rational, but spiritual. These spiritual faculties are placed in us as governors, to operate upon the rational understanding; and when the mind and body are brought under the same governing influence, all will become pure, and all our enjoyments will be centred in the third heaven. We shall not be anxious to have a great name and high honors among men. We shall not be anxious to become rich, or great, or wise, or good in the sight of men: but we shall become anxious in all things, "to have a conscience void of offence toward God and toward man,"

None of these will be sought from among men, for there is very little necessity for their applause, so long as we have peace in our own souls. As said the Apostle, "If our heart condemn us not, then have we confidence toward God."— And if God be for us, it is of no consequence who shall be against us. And if we abide under this divine government daily, all obstructions will be removed, and we shall be enabled more and more fully to discover those things which were before mysterious in our view. It is not essential—and I feel no hesitation in declaring it—it is not essential for us to believe a great deal, which we can neither comprehend nor understand; for where is the necessity of this?—Is the Lord's arm shortened that he cannot save? Or is his ear heavy that he cannot hear? No, verily; for it remains to be a truth, that the spirit which is come, if attended to, will guide us into all truth, and consequently out of all error; for these cannot dwell together; we cannot serve God and mammon. "No servant can serve two masters; for either he will hate the one and love the other, or else he will hold to the one and despise the other. Ye cannot serve God and mammon." And Christ also declared, when in that prepared body in which he came to do his heavenly Father's will, "And I, if I be lifted up from the earth, will draw all men unto me." Has this any allusion—or are we to be taught to believe that it alludes to his being lifted up upon the tree, that act of unparalleled malevolence in the Jews in his crucifixion, that he would draw all men immediately unto him? No, but he is in all those who are lifted above every evil propensity, and he draws them to him, and thus the declaration is fulfilled: "I in them and thou in me, that they may be one in us." These he is not ashamed to call his brethren. And wherefore? Because they are begotten by the same power, and brought forth in the same life; and here is unity and union between them, though they have still a being here on earth. Thus the sting of death is removed. The grave is deprived of its victory. Their hope of happiness is not on external and outward things, but on internal and spiritual things. And the evidences which they feel, and which are sealed upon their minds, are not those of doubt, not those of speculation; they are not evidences which they have derived from theological theories and the language of scripture, or from any outward objects; but they are produced by the immediate operation of the spirit of God upon their minds. Here, now, is a religion worthy of man and worthy of a Creator. For it leads man from the bondage of sin and corruption into the beauty of holiness and newness of life. And here may be known another declaration to be fulfilled: "Except a man be born again, he can in no wise enter into the kingdom of heaven."

And what is heaven? Is it a place at a great distance and beyond the grave, where there are all kinds of sensual rewards reserved for the sensual minds of all those who have preserved a fair character among men? No. It is a state in which we can enjoy communion with God, and in which we can know the bread of life to nourish up our souls. We may come to the enjoyment of it here; and if we come not to the enjoyment of it here, our hope of its enjoyment hereafter is unfounded: for, according to another declaration, the kingdom of heaven is within you. I have desired, therefore, that we may see this building begun from a foundation which never can be moved, and by materials which will last forever.

Remember the works and effects produced by a building which was begun formerly and never finished. And the nature of the case was this. The children of Noah increased and spread abroad upon the face of the earth, "and they said, go to, let us build us a city, and a tower whose top may reach unto heaven; and let us make us a name, less we be scattered abroad upon the face of the whole earth."—"And they said one to another, let us make brick and burn them thoroughly. And they had brick for stone, and slime had they for mortar." These materials were wholly the result of human invention. They went on with their work, depending on their own inventions, and took not stone, but brick had they for stone, and slime they had for mortar: and thus they continued till confusion came upon them, and their language was confounded.

It is no part of our duty now, nor will it yield instruction to enter into a disquisition, of what this confusion was; but I apprehend it was very much like that diversity of views and opinions, which have split and divided christendom for ages. They could not see with the same eyes—they could not have the same views of the same objects; and therefore dissensions ensued, and the very thing they dreaded came upon them. They were scattered and divided upon the face of the earth. And how eminently has this been the case with professors of the christian name, because they have endeavored to build according to systems which their own imaginations had formed; and to use the materials and works of their own creation. They have endeavored to build up a city whose tower and top should reach to heaven, to preserve them from the power of evil. And is it not obvious that all their works are vain? For with the increase of religion and religious opinions in the earth, wickedness has also increased in nearly the same ratio: and notwithstanding the abundance of religion in our land, perhaps there was never a day when Sodom's sins were more predominant. "As I live, saith the Lord God, Sodom, thy sister, hath not done, she nor her daughters, as thou hast done, thou and thy daughters. Behold, this was the iniquity of thy sister Sodom, pride, fulness of bread, and abundance of idleness was in her and her daughters; neither did she strengthen the hand of the poor and the needy. And they were haughty, and committed abominations before me; therefore I took them away as I saw good."

This is a subject which requires the serious and careful investigation of every individual of us; for there never can be an effect produced without an operative cause. And the operative cause which has produced these painful and destructive effects, stands not in the power of religion, nor in the wisdom of God, but stands in the dereliction of these. We have substituted a great deal of that which is of our own creation, that we might have a tower of our own building. We have substituted this for the immediate manifestations of that principle which continues to open the blind eyes, to unstop the deaf ears, and to heal every malady of the soul, even to the cleansing of leprosy, casting out devils, and raising from a depth of sin, to the life of God in the soul.

There has been a great deal of preaching, praying and singing; and strenuous efforts have been made to support with gold, the gospel and the Bible; and I know not what beside. But let us look at the foundation upon which they have been building. It is worse than that of Babel; for do we not see, that in all these benevolent societies, so called, money, money is the object, the love of which is the root of all evil. And from whom are these donations and subscriptions solicited? Are they solicited from the pious, the righteous, and virtuous in society, and from those who are worthy to support the cause of the divine kingdom? No, verily. They are received from the blood thirsty warrior, the cruel slave holding oppressor, from those who are turning the choicest temporal gifts of heaven into the most grievous of curses. They are received from the drunkard and the gambler—from those who have ruined themselves by extravagance, and have drawn others into the same condemnation: and what if I should say, that I verily believe, the hire of an harlot, and the price of a dog, both of which are an abomination in the sight of heaven, and ought not to come into the Lord's treasury, would not be refused. Is this, then, the foundation on which the church of God is to be built? Can any thing which is thus corrupt, ever support the superstructure? No, verily; for the vessels of the Lord's house are holy. It is evident, therefore, that self interest is the main spring of action, and not religion.

Now let us look a little at this evil. Can the warrior under the influence of a thirst after blood, support the kingdom of Christ on earth? No, my brethren, never—he never can support the cause of peace on earth and good will to men. Can he who is an oppressor of his brethren, declare that he would do unto all men as he would that they should do unto him?

Now let us turn our attention a little to a deadly evil in this boasted land of liberty. We see the choicest blessings of heaven transformed into the most grievous curse ; so that, what was designed for the support of man, is made to produce his destruction. We see the most wholesome food transformed into a fiery liquid poison. Perhaps within the recollection of each of us, we have known many, who have been bereaved of some branch of their family, and felt the desolating effects of this mournful evil. The thoughtless multitude will despise the poor drunkard ; and among these are to be found those who have ruined the constitutions, destroyed the bodies and intellects, and what if I should say, the souls of men by this perversion of the bounties of heaven. But let them beware, that they are not in the second heaven, taking a false rest, and that they do not find their state worse than that of the drunkard. I apprehend that the drunkard is not the worst of the family. The distiller and the retailer—these are the elder brethren in iniquity. These are the vultures, that are preying upon the very vitals of their weaker brethren—and interest, sordid interest is the moving cause, I therefore want us all, again to take it into serious consideration—especially if we are looking for happiness in an existence beyond the grave. See what feelings this will produce in our minds. Now if it brings peace into well regulated minds here, it will bring peace hereafter ; and if trouble, sorrow, confusion, horror, dread, and despair, it will produce the same effects in time to come. For as God is God, and changes not, so evil never changes its consequences, nor ceases to produce its effects, and its effects are misery.

Now let us turn again to the gospel, which is preached in every creature. And what is the gospel? It is that of which we need not be ashamed—it is declared to be the power of God unto salvation to all them that believe. But there is a gospel of which I may acknowledge I am ashamed. It stands in the wisdom of man—it is supported by his eloquence, and ambition for worldly honor ; and I apprehend there is very little difference in the motives of the warrior, who strives to gain a name by his valor in the field of battle, the lawyer at the bar, or the priest in the pulpit. They are

all prompted by different modifications of the same spirit—
they are all seeking for honor from man, and verily, they
have their reward. They are seeking honor which depends
upon their own works, and the works of man can never
work the righteousness of God. I want you to know your
interest better. If you will make a profession of religion,
let it be a religion which will not only do to live by in youth,
in health, and in prosperity, but in adversity and distress :
a religion which will rob death of its sting, and the grave of
its victory—a religion which will open unto us the new and
living way, which leads into that which is within the vail,
the holiest of all ; where nothing will be hid from the view,
and where we shall be able to behold the mysteries of the
kingdom of heaven opened unto us.

But the preaching, which commonly goes by the name of
preaching—what is it? It is a mere form of words, and
those who utter them are mere linguists and not preachers.
It is often prepared beforehand. And what is that preparation? Is it to cry aloud and spare not? Do these lift up
their voice like a trumpet, and cry aloud to show Israel their
transgressions, and Jacob their sins? Is it not all to build
up systems which they have adopted, by daubing together
bricks with slime, and not with mortar, till it has become
confusion worse confounded?

I want not to see these effects among mankind. I want
us to come under the influence of that gospel which is preached, where it ought to be preached, and where it was declared
that it should be preached, " in every creature under heaven."
And when we come to experience this preached baptizingly
in ourselves, we shall know that the command was not given
to preach and baptize merely : but we shall know it preached
baptizingly to ourselves. And that living principle which
preaches this gospel, is the same which baptizes with the
Holy Ghost. "I indeed baptize you with water unto repentance : but he that cometh after me, is mightier than I, whose
shoes I am not worthy to bear ; he shall baptize you with the
Holy Ghost and with fire : whose fan is in his hand, and he
will thoroughly purge his floor and gather his wheat into

11

the garner, but he will burn up the chaff with unquenchable fire.''

And what is this chaff which will be burnt? Is it not our light, airy, and trifling dispositions which we indulge to our hurt, and which separate us from everything of a heavenly nature, which is compared to wheat? This baptism of the Holy Ghost operates upon these passions and dispositions, as fire does upon chaff, and it is experienced, in a degree, by every one of us. And if so, why need we say, ''Who shall ascend into heaven and bring Christ down from above, or who shall descend into the deep to bring him up from thence;'' for what saith the spirit: ''the word is nigh thee, in heart and in thy mouth, that thou mayst hear it and do it.'' And this is the word which is preached unto you by the gospel. And now this is a matter which can be brought to each of our views, and we need no reasoning in circles; we need no eloquent declamation, to enable us to understand the truths which it communicates. It is something which brings sorrow, trouble, and confusion over the mind for that which is wrong; and as we attend to its manifestations, it speaks peace for obedience. This is the operation of the Holy Ghost, which is a fire that destroys the chaff. This is a baptism of the Holy Ghost, which operates as fire against all unrighteousness and ungodliness of men, and has been compared to something very small. Let us remember the declaration of Christ himself: ''The kingdom of heaven is like a grain of mustard seed, which a man took and sowed in his field, which indeed is the least of all seeds, but when it is grown it is the greatest among herbs, so that the birds of the air come and lodge in the branches thereof.''

Thus, this principle which reproves for evil, though small in its first appearance, if obeyed, will increase and grow, until it will overcome every vain imagination of the mind, which may be compared to the fowls, or inhabitants of the air. These birds of the air are those things which are of a light and chaffy nature. It will bring all these under its branches. It has also been likened to a little '' leaven which a woman took and hid in three measures of meal, until the whole was leavened." We all know the nature of leaven and of meal, and we know that there is in the meal no power of opposition, but it remains quiet to be operated upon. Here is the state I want us all to come into ; and then this little leaven, which is hid in each, and all of us, will begin to perform its operation on us ; thus bringing us, body, soul, and spirit, into its own likeness.

Now, my fellow professors of this holy name, when we attend to this kind of baptism, which is the gospel preached in every creature, we shall become more and more fully acquainted with its operations ; and we shall be more fully sensible of the effects which it is calculated to produce upon our minds : and we shall be able to add our testimony to the declaration, that "the work of righteousness is peace, and the effect of righteousness is quietness and assurance forever." And I want us all to become willing to come under the influence of this reprover ; for if we crucify, and will not let this divine principle reign over us, we shall become seared, as with a red hot iron. Our minds must feel distress, pain, and trouble. But if we are willing to come under the influence of this principle, that wounds to heal—and it is the very same principle—having burnt up the chaff, dross, tin, and reprobate silver, our minds will be prepared to receive that instruction which opens the understanding, and enables us to see the mysteries of the kingdom of heaven unfolded. Peace will then become an inhabitant of the mind, for no fire can burn longer than it has combustible matter to act on. And when all this is consumed, the operation will not be found painful, but pleasing. There will be a quiet—a calm, produced in the mind. But it is not that calm which we can bring upon ourselves. It is not the calm of self-righteousness, which we may be desiring to indulge, but it is an evidence unequivocal ; it is an evidence derived immediately from the fountain of light and life. Here we can wait patiently, and here we can come to an understanding of the divine nature.

Now some may be ready to query, what makes this so

small, and evil so predominant in our nature? This is another grand delusion of the arch enemy of mankind, who deceived our first parents. It is the work of a twisting, twining, and serpentine imagination, by which he has always endeavored to make truth look like error, and falsehood like truth. But, my friends, this principle, in infancy, though pure, is weak, and that which leads to evil is not stronger. Yea, it is weaker than that which leads to goodness. But we are willing, because of present enjoyment, to indulge our natural affections. We are not willing to take up our daily cross and follow him, and be governed by the higher and nobler powers. Hence these propensities grow with our growth, and strengthen with our strength. And if that which is good were equally indulged, it would grow also, and perhaps more powerfully than those evil propensities, which would necessarily decrease and become weaker. I believe, that by a daily obedience to this living principle, there is a state attainable like unto that which our Saviour experienced, when he was tempted by that same tempter which tempts us. But he overcame the tempter because there was nothing indulged in his mind, for these evil propensities to work upon. And when the tempter said unto him, "If thou be the Son of God command that these stones be made bread," he answered and said, "It is written man shall not live by bread alone, but by every word that proceedeth out of the mouth of God." The bread which we eat for the support of these bodies, and for the indulgence of our natural appetites, ought not to have the pre-eminence over that evidence which proceeds from the power of God; and when this governing principle has the dominion in our souls, it will lead us out of every thing of an inferior nature. This is the principle which has been described, as a little "leaven which was laid in three measures of meal until the whole was leavened." And as it produces these effects upon us, it administers every cup of consolation which we need for our nourishment. But we find no room to seek nourishment from any other source, because this divine principle of God governs every other spirit, and reduces it to subjection.

Again "tne devil taketh him up into the holy city, and
sitteth him on a pinacle of the temple, and saith unto him,
if thou be the Son of God, cast thyself down ; for it is written, he shall give his angels charge concerning thee, and in
their hands they shall bear thee up, lest at any time thou
dash thy foot against a stone. Jesus saith unto him, it is
written again, " thou shalt not tempt the Lord thy God."
He had not received a manifestation from the Father to do this
act. He was not about to do anything of this kind on his
own responsibility. Thus we ought not to indulge our natural feelings which would lead us to desire distinction, and to
gain a name among men. Now here is a lesson which may
be instructive ; for here we see that he withstood the craft of
the enemy, who was endeavoring to beget in him those dispositions which if indulged, must necessarily produce the
most ruinous effects. Thus the enemy of man insinuated
that he had commissioned his angels to take charge of him ;
and in their hands to bear him up, lest at any time he should
dash his foot against a stone. And I want us all to remember that it is necessary for us, not to tempt the Lord our
God. Again, " the devil taketh him up into an exceeding
high mountain, and showeth him all the kingdoms of the
world, and the glory of them ; and saith unto him, all these
things will I give thee, if thou wilt fall down and worship
me. Then saith Jesus unto him, get thee hence satan ; for
it is written, thou shalt worship the Lord thy God, and him
only shalt thou serve." Here it is, that this tempter which
appeared unto Christ appears unto us also ; and be not only
pretends to preach, but he quotes scripture. But blessed be
the name of Israel's God, that gospel which is essential to
salvation, can never be preached by men nor devils—It is
internal, and the medium through which it can be conveyed,
is no secondary medium. For it proceeds immediately from
God, and is communicated immediately to each of our spirits ;
and therefore, it is called " the power of God unto salvation,
to every one who believes," whether Jew or Gentile. And
those who believe that God has changed these privileges,
deprive themselves of this inestimable blessing—the enjoy-

ment of the third heaven, where there are things heard which are not lawful to be uttered. But while we are pursuing the gratification of the external senses in the performance of outward rituals of preaching, praying, and singing, we are not in the enjoyment of that which is given us from God, but that which our own imaginations have formed. The evil is one of immense magnitude, and I want us to take pattern after him, in whom there was no sin, in order that we may come into the same state of righteousness, into the same divine and living unity, union, and communion with the God and Father of our Lord Jesus Christ. Then shall we not only be raised above everything of human contrivance, but we shall feel no disposition to feed on these things. We shall then have no wish to appear glorious among men, neither shall we seek to have dominion over others; and according to the declaration of Christ, we shall be enabled to adopt the language which he did—"It is written, thou shalt worship the Lord thy God, and him only shalt thou serve;" and also to take the language which he afterwards added, "get thee behind me satan, for it is written, thou shalt worship the Lord thy God, and him only shalt thou serve." He was not desirous to set up himself—he was not desirous to have a name among men—he was not seeking for earthly power and dominion, but he was desirous to do the will of him that sent him: and hence it was, that he was anointed with the oil of gladness, above his fellows; and hence it was that the declaration was made, "Him hath God the Father sealed." Now my friends, and fellow professors of this holy name, I want you to attend to the preaching of devils, although they quote scripture—and although they may appear to your vain imaginations, to be superlatively seeking the glory of God, if they bear not the stamp of the divinity, if they are not the workmanship of the finger of God, they will produce evil, pain, sorrow, trouble, and affliction. And as certainly, as the Mosaic law was written on tables of stone, and as certainly as that writing was the writing of God himself, so are the laws, by which we are to be governed, if rightly governed, written upon the fleshly

tables of the heart, by the same divine illimitable power.
To which I desire to recommend you, and not to man, nor to
any of his works; but "I commend you to God, and to the
word of his grace, which is able to save your souls, and to
give you an inheritance among all those who are sanctified."

And, my friends, with respect to preaching, when we are
thus met together for the solemn purpose of divine worship;
I want us all to attend individually, to what is passing in
our own minds, and endeavor to receive instruction from the
fountain of all good, unperverted by men or devils; for it
will nourish up the soul, and enable us to distinguish between good and evil. It will prevent us from calling good
evil, and evil good; and we shall no longer take light for
darkness, and darkness for light, bitter for sweet, and sweet
for bitter. And here shall we be enabled to offer ourselves
up a living sacrifice, holy and acceptable unto God by Jesus
Christ.

And who, or what is Christ? We have been induced by
perversion of the scriptures, by prejudice, education, and the
tradition of men, to ascribe the whole of this to an human
being; and, not looking through the humanity to the
divinity, we have been ascribing the whole divinity to the
man Christ Jesus. Here is another evil that has led to great
confusion; and it will always lead to confusion, because, it
has not its origin in God; but it has its origin in human
invention. It had its origin in the darkness of that night
of apostacy which for ages overspread professing christendom. A great deal has been said about divisions and sub-
divisions, about a Triune God, distinct persons, and I know
not what.

But is Christ divided? Or is God divided? No, verily.
But as God is one, and his name one, so also, I apprehend,
that all those who come under the influence of his spirit,
will be partakers of his nature. For the scriptures declare,
"I am God, and there is none else; beside me there is no
Saviour." And do we not believe, that this divine essence,
whom we call God, fills all place and all space? One of
the inspired penmen confirms this belief when he says,

" Whither shall I go from thy spirit? Or whither shall I
flee from thy presence? If I ascend up into heaven, thou
art there; if I make my bed in hell, behold, thou art there.
If I take the wings of the morning, and dwell in the uttermost parts of the sea, even there shall thy hand lead me,
and thy right hand shall hold me." Now that which does
not admit of locality, can never admit of a division. Do we
not see the whole creation was formed by his power, and is
supported by his wisdom? Certainly, nothing short of infinite wisdom could have created the least of these things, nor
can sustain them for a moment. Under this view of the
subject—and I believe it is a correct one—we know him to be
omnipotent, omniscient, and omnipresent, and I want us all
to come immediately to him, and not view him as being at a
great distance and beyond the grave. Let us draw nigh
unto him with full purpose of heart, full of assurance, and
faith, that we may be instructed of him. And we shall then
know our hearts to be enlarged, and our understandings
opened to receive divine mysteries, and we shall be nourished
thereby unto eternal life.

And in order to have those evil spirits, with which many
are possessed, cast out, and these vain imaginations brought
low, it is essential that we come under the influence of a
spirit of prayer. But what is prayer? It is no more a
form of words than preaching is. If we come under the influence of that principle, in which we can call God, Father, our
supplications will be acceptable to him, under the influence
of the same principle which causes all our prayers to centre
in this: "Thy will, and not mine, be done."

Let us look a little, for instance, at that which is termed
the Lord's prayer. How many thousands have bowed down
their heads like a bullrush, and lifted up their voice like a
trumpet, and repeated these words. And can any who have
not partaken of the divine life, call God, Father, and not
bring condemnation upon themselves? Can any of us say,
while our minds are impure, " Our Father which art in
heaven, hallowed be thy name," while, at the same time,
many of us took his name in vain? Yea, and even swear

by his name! If ever we come to the spirituality of this dispensation, we shall no longer swear by his name, but we shall be brought under the government of the spirit of truth, in which there will be no deception and no lying. It is as disgraceful for Christians to swear as to lie, for it proves that they are not worthy to be believed; it proves that the principles of which we are making a profession, have not a tendency to lead us into perfection. In vain, then, is this language uttered: "Our Father which art in heaven, hallowed be thy name, thy kingdom come, thy will be done in earth as it is in heaven." How can we pray for the coming of his kingdom, when we will not admit the kingdom of heaven into our hearts? "Thy will be done;" when, at the same time, we are setting up our own wills in opposition to the divine will. Is not this mockery of God? "Give us this day our daily bread, and forgive us our trespasses, as we forgive them that trespass against us." Can we pray God to forgive us our trespasses, as we forgive those who trespass against us, and ask for our daily bread, when we are in no degree dependent on him, having chosen a system for ourselves, adopted opinions, and perform rituals, and call it worship? It is vain for us to crave daily bread from our heavenly Father, while we stand independent of his power, wisdom and mercy; neither while we are soaring above his dominion, can we ascribe it to him or say, "for thine is the kingdom, and the power, and the glory, for ever. Amen."

When thus assembled, it is better for each of us, unless immediately required to give a word of counsel or caution, or unless there be immediately given, from the divine fountain of knowledge, a spirit of supplication, we had better sit down and wait patiently upon God, that we may experience what the divine penman did. "I waited patiently for the Lord, and he inclined unto me and heard my cry. He brought me up also out of an horrible pit, out of the miry clay, and set my foot upon a rock, and established my goings. And he hath put a new song in my mouth, even praise unto our God." These are the effects of that pure and spiritual righteousness which proceeds from God, and which we can only attain unto through the intervention of his divine power. It comes not from man—it is not at our command ; and blessed be the name of Israel's God forever, it is neither confined to time, place, or circumstance. For, "if I ascend up into heaven, thou art there ; if I make my bed in hell, behold, thou art there." And if we should take the wings of the morning, and dwell in the uttermost parts of the sea, even there would his hand lead us, and his right hand would hold us.

Neither is it necessary, when we are thus assembled, that we should sing, as it is practised, and even required, as a necessary part of worship in these assemblies—(not the assemblies of this people, but of the generality of Christian professors)—saying, let us sing to the praise and glory of God, in some psalm or hymn suited to the occasion. But how can we sing, while our minds are under the bondage of sin, and our souls under the government of transgression? I apprehend there are very few, in an assembly like this, or in any other assembly of an equal number, who can unite in any one psalm or hymn that is commonly sung. Can we say, "Rivers of tears run down mine eyes, because they keep not thy law," when many of us have not known what it was to attend to these feelings of compunction? Can we say, "As the heart panteth after the water brooks, so panteth my soul after thee, O God," when we have not sufficiently come to that state of hungering and thirsting after righteousness, in which we can know what we say to be fulfilled." These performances will not do for us, notwithstanding they are the principal dependence of many. How vain is it to partake of a little bread and wine, when the true communion is come—the divine power is made manifest in each of us, even that divine power which is the resurrection and the life, unto all them that are sanctified. It is vain also to be dipped in water ; it is vain to be sprinkled ; it is vain to fulfil these rituals, which can reach only to the outward man. For although these outward elements may cleanse the filth of the flesh, they can never cleanse us from one solitary sin or lust.

It may be said that these are used only as types and figures by which they acknowledge the coming of Christ. But in this do they not rather deny than acknowledge his coming? For these things were only to continue till the opening of the new dispensation unto the Jews, when all that was figurative in the old dispensation was to fall and give way to that which is pure and spiritual. Now, the law by which we are governed is in accordance with the nature of the divine kingdom, which is spiritual, and it acts upon our spirits; and there is union, for spirit communes with spirit, as bodies commune with bodies. We have animal bodies, and, consequently, we have instinctive faculties, which are inseparable from the body. We have also a spirit, which is an emanation from the divinity, and, consequently, we have spiritual faculties, and these are inseparable from the spirit. It is by a combination of these faculties that we are enabled to compare ideas. And this confers on us the powers of speech, and enables us to go to great lengths in the arts, sciences, philosophy, and a great variety of other subjects which concern us as men and creatures. But the possession of all these rational faculties can never bring us to a knowledge of God, because God is a spirit. But when we learn to have our minds abstracted from all these lower faculties, when our spirits can wait patiently on God, we shall discover him by his own light. And then, and not till then, can we worship in spirit and in truth; then, and not till then, can we sing praises to the honor and glory of God. Remember—and I have remembered instructively—how it was with Israel of old, when they were encamped before Pi-hahiroth, between Migdol and the sea, with Pharaoh and the Egyptians behind them, and the Red sea before them. There was no time then for rejoicing; it was a time of affliction. And what was the command that was given? It was, "Stand still and see the salvation of the Lord." While we feel ourselves in the land of bondage, under the dominion of Pharaoh and the Egyptian task masters, we cannot sing the song of the Lord. They could not sing in a strange land, before there was a way made through the

Red sea ; but because of their obedience, they could rejoice on the banks of deliverance. Then they could sing, not merely as a form, but because they had experienced the power of God to deliver them from their enemies. After this, and a variety of other miracles, they could testify—"The sea saw it and fled ; Jordan was driven back. The mountains skipped like rams, and the little hills like lambs." And they could ask the question—"What ailed thee, O thou sea, that thou fledest? Thou Jordan, that thou wast driven back ? Ye mountains that ye skipped like rams, and ye little hills like lambs ?" And in grateful commemoration of the Lord's dealings with them they could exclaim—"Tremble, thou earth, at the presence of the Lord, at the presence of the God of Jacob ; which turned the rock into a standing water, the flint into a fountain of waters." We never can sing in a strange land, as said one of the inspired penmen—"By the rivers of Babylon, there we sat down ; yea, we wept when we remembered Zion. We hanged our harps upon the willows in the midst thereof. For they that carried us away captive, required of us a song ; and they that wasted us required of us mirth, saying, sing us one of the songs of Zion. How shall we sing the Lord's song in a strange land. If I forget thee, O Jerusalem, let my right hand forget her cunning. If I do not remember thee, let my tongue cleave to the roof of my mouth, if I prefer not Jerusalem above my chief joy."

When our minds are brought into that divine harmony in which we can make melody unto God, we shall experience these feelings, not only when we are thus assembled together, but when we sit in the house, when we walk by the way, when we lie down, and when we rise up.

O my friends, all that is capable of feeling in me this day, is aroused—seeing myself among a people who are strangers to me. We are all heirs of the same immortality, and fast hastening to that bourne from whence no traveller returns. But blessed be God, we have an advocate with the Father, even Jesus Christ, the righteous, the Messiah, the Son and sent of the Father, the light and life of God, which was in the beginning with God. "In the beginning was the word, and the word was with God, and the word was God. The same was in the beginning with God." And he is exercising his mediatorial office, not at a distance from us, but in every soul, in order to reconcile us to God.

I desire once more, my friends, to recommend you—let your name to religion be what it may—to this divine word. And remember that we can neither see with other men's eyes, hear with other men's ears, nor understand with other men's hearts ; for none can eat for us, nor drink for us. We must, therefore, each one of us, attend to the manifestations of this living principle, which will make us wise unto salvation, (otherwise we shall remain outward as they did among the Jews,) and spiritually open the blind eyes, unstop the deaf ears, heal all the maladies of the soul, and raise us from the death of sin, to the life of Christ. And in whatsoever situation we may be placed, his mighty arm will be underneath to support us. This will disarm death of its sting, and the grave of its victory. It will open unto us when time here shall be no more, a mansion of rest, in "that city which hath foundations, whose builder and maker is God." And finally, brethren and sisters, farewell. "Be perfect. Be of good comfort. Be of one mind ; live in peace : and the God of mercy, and of peace, be with you all. Amen."

SERMON X.

DELIVERED BY THOMAS WETHERALD AT ROSE STREET MEETING, NEW YORK,
SUNDAY MORNING, MAY 28TH, 1826.

Abstract propositions are to the truth, what clothing is to the human body. They are not its life. It is not dependent upon them for its existence: for they form no part of its essence, and it is not a partaker of their nature. They are a mere covering which the ingenuity of man has invented. But truth itself is a living power of divine authority. It is an operative principle—it is God in man. And it is under the influence of this divine, this living, this operative principle, if we ever experience worship performed, that we must know it—and this we must know, if ever we become the sons and daughters of God. Abstract propositions respecting truth, can never be applied to individuals. They may be applied by societies, who desire to have dominion over their members; and systems may be formed, creeds may be introduced, and confessions of faith may be forced upon the consciences of the people; but all these united, cannot form this divine, this living principle. For what authority have they? They are a mere covering. Now truth needs no covering—it always appears best in its own native and naked loveliness. There is nothing of which it is ashamed—nothing of which it is afraid; for it is guilt and sin which produce fear, horror, dread, despair, and every feeling in which there is torment.

Under this view of the subject, my fellow professors of the christian name, I am induced to believe, that there are among the professors of christianity generally, many things which have a tendency to cover and envelop the truth in mists of darkness and garbs of human invention ; which prevent from coming into that simplicity, and experiencing the effects of that power which stands not in the wisdom of man. Is it not obvious to every individual of discretion, who has arrived at the years of experience, that literary attainments, be they ever so high, if they are only of general observations—if they be not directed to practical subjects, have only a tendency to render their possessors learned fools. But to have experience on any particular subject, will make a fool into a wise man. Here, then, is the difference between abstract propositions, which cannot be applied to any useful object, and that experimental knowledge, evinced by revelation and reason. I cannot, therefore, direct my fellow men and fellow heirs of salvation to these external things. Look at the various systems with which we are surrounded, and all derived from what is called, the ancient principles of these societies. Are they not most deeply marked with superstition and idolatry? And shall we find any difference in these? Do we not observe, that through the various creeds of these societies, and the different systems which exist, the same professions of belief in abstract propositions, has led mankind into the adverse of all those feelings which were, in their native state, designed to lead them into happiness? Do we not see that in the performance of all the rituals of these societies, though morning, evening, and noon, they may pray—though they may be dipped in water, and thus experience all the baptismal influence which that external element can give—though they may become partakers of the bread and wine, as emblematic of the coming of the Lord Jesus Christ—though they may preach and pray from youth to old age ; yet all these things united, can never give a victory over one single, solitary sin or lust. But according to the declaration of Jesus Christ himself, the design of the gospel dispensation is, to lay the axe to the root of the tree—to lay the axe to the root of those dispositions, affections, and passions, which separate us from God, the source of purity ; and from which, evil words and actions proceed. And as "the axe is laid to the root of the tree, every tree, therefore, which bringeth not forth good fruit, is hewn down and cast into the fire."

I have been instructed in looking over the account left in Revelations respecting the frogs. "And I saw," said the divinely eagle-eyed Apostle, "three unclean spirits like frogs come out of the mouth of the dragon, and out of the mouth of the beast, and out of the mouth of the false prophet : for they are the spirits of devils working miracles, which go forth unto the kings of the earth, and of the whole world, to gather them to the battle of the great day of God Almighty." Whether we are under the influence of these misguided and perverted passions, which have produced wars, divisions, fightings, wranglings, and every evil among mankind ; or whether under the influence of beastly passions and propensities ; or whether under the influence of the false prophet, making a high and empty profession of the christian name, it is all one. Notwithstanding the difference of their appearance, the effects are the same ; they are all frogs—all the spirits of devils, they are all workers of miracles, they can all transform themselves. The first are those who have perverted the passions and the propensities of nature to the disgrace of humanity, such as the warrior who thirsts after blood, and to be covered with glory, by the destruction of his fellow man. The second are those who are sunk into the gratification of the bestial appetites ; and the third are those who are covering themselves with their own deceivings as with a garment. Under the influence of this spirit of the "false prophet," they can perform many religious works. But these are in a still more dangerous situation, inasmuch as they make a profession of religion. But, instead of coming to the truth, they are covering it with objects of their own creation, and abstract propositions ; and are covering themselves with a false view of their own righteousness.

Here are the transformations of that unwearied enemy, who has been in operation, since the days of our first parents—that twisting, twining, circumventing disposition of man, which leads into professions of a fair and righteous principle. It is of an external nature, and stands in a dereliction of our duties to God ; and it leads to a dereliction of our duties to one another, and hence it is, that many of us are grovelling in the very lowest heaven. For, according to the declaration of the apostle, there are various states attainable. "I knew a man in Christ above fourteen years ago, (whether in the body, I cannot tell ; or, whether out of the body, I cannot tell : God knoweth,) such an one caught up to the third heaven, and heard unspeakable words, which it is not lawful for a man to utter." And what is heaven ? It is a state of enjoyment, a state in which our hopes of happiness are fixed. If we are under the influence of any of these debasing passions—if we place our enjoyments in them, here we are in the first and lowest heaven ; and thousands there are in this situation. And it is also cause of sorrow. Thus many who have gone beyond these grovelling passions, and who may be good fathers, good husbands, good citizens, and honorable men, may be influenced by those abstract propositions, with which they have clothed their own minds. These have come into the second heaven—their enjoyment is in external things : they are in the second heaven—they have not yet attained unto the third heaven, where the apostle was admitted, and where he saw things not lawful to be uttered. But when we come to be governed by this divine illimitable principle, this power of truth operating on our own spirits, then, and not till then, we are admitted to a view of those subjects, which no man could reach by the strength of all his reasoning faculties, because they are above the power of human reason, and can never be thus attained or comprehended. No stream can ever rise higher than its fountain. But when we come under the governing influence of this baptizing spirit, we shall come into communion with God— we shall know him to open the blind eyes of our minds, to unstop the deaf ears of our understandings, and heal every malady of the soul, even to leprosy, and to raise us from a death of sin, to a life of God. These operations are of a spiritual nature—they are not dependent on times and seasons, nor on any outward circumstances ; but on an obedi-

12

ence to these manifestations. And it was in this spirit and dominion, that Adam in his creation had authority over the beasts of the field, over the fishes of the sea, and over the fowls of the air, over the cattle, and over every creeping thing that creepeth upon the earth. And while he continued under the influence of this principle, and obeyed the voice of God's law within himself, he continued to have dominion. All these dispositions were subject unto him : but in the hour when he chose his own feelings, and to pervert those propensities which were given unto him, that dominion ceased. All have had the same dominion, even every individual of the human family ; but they have disobeyed the divine command, from that time forth. And we are subject to be governed by the same passions as the beasts of the field ; and by our vain imaginations, which may be compared to the fowls of the air. We are grovelling like insects that crawl on the ground, like fishes that swim in the sea.

But, my fellow professors of this holy name, it is only in the dereliction of our duty to God, that we ever can come to this deplorable state. I never have viewed it, that we suffer any thing from the fall of Adam, for sin is original in every soul that sins. There is no use for this proverb : "The fathers have eaten sour grapes, and the children's teeth are set on edge." And there is another text, which is analogous to this. "I have set before thee this day life and good, death and evil. I call heaven and earth to record this day against you, that I have set before you life and death, blessing and cursing. Therefore choose life that both thou and thy seed may live." Who is it, then, that would be attending merely to the outside, to the clothing, by which they may have covered an image made to represent the truth, instead of coming to this principle which is internal, operative, and divine.

What is man? Is he a mere animal body brought into existence to eat, drink, sleep, and pass away like the dream of a night vision? No. Men are compound beings, having animal bodies, and in accordance with them, instinctive faculties ; but there is also in man, something of the nature of the divinity, something which is capable of discerning and comprehending spiritual truths. As there is something of the nature of spirit, there are spiritual faculties also, and by the operation of these spiritual faculties upon those which are instinctive, reason is produced. And it is this combination that confers on us the powers of speech and enables us to compare ideas, to search and dive far into the arts, sciences, and philosophy. It enables us to judge of many abstruse principles relative to abstract propositions and natural things, but it can never give us a knowledge of God, because God is a spirit. It is by endeavoring to search and find out God, that man has fallen below the brute creation. But when he comes under the influence of this uncombined and living principle, which is God in man, or "Christ in you the hope of glory," it enlarges his understanding.— And as surely as Jesus performed mighty miracles on the bodies of certain individuals, so also will this perform miracles upon the souls of mankind. It will open the eyes of the mind, unstop the deaf ears of the understanding, and heal every malady and disease of the soul—even to leprosy : it will cast out devils and raise from the dead. All these miracles are performed by the preaching of the gospel in every creature, according to the declaration of Jesus : "The gospel shall be preached in every creature." He declared, "It is expedient for you that I go away, for if I go not away, the Comforter will not come unto you ; but if I depart, I will send him unto you, and he shall guide you into all truth, and remind you of all that I have told you." Here, then, is a plain scripture testimony in support of this position. · Job declared, "There is a spirit in man, and the inspiration of the Almighty giveth them understanding."— And, said the Apostle, "We know that the Son of God is come, and has given us an understanding, that we may know him that is true ; and we are in him that is true, even in his son Jesus Christ. This is the true God and eternal life. Little children keep yourselves from idols." I apprehend that we shall all be willing to admit, that through baptism we are admitted into Christ, but not through a watery dispensation, not by a watery element. For all the waters of the sea applied to the human body, could never cleanse the soul of one sin. We are trained up in these abstract propositions, which have only a tendency to cover the truth from our view. But when we come to the age of man and womanhood, and have experienced all the vain and impetuous passions of youth; when every thing has been sacrificed to the pleasures of sense, then only our eyes begin to open; when old age is about to close voluptuous life, and when we have no other sensations than those of regret and pain for our profane and dissolute lives. It is in this interval of the passions, and prelude to the horrors of the grave, that the mind and conscience become greatly alarmed, and thus poison the last period of our existence. Happy if our feeble organs do not reduce our faculties to mere animal instinct, nor leave us one vestige of a thinking being. How often are these results produced? How often do we see an individual, who has spent the impetuous whirlwind of youth in the indulgence of his passions, which are constitutionally predominant in that period, spend an old age of useless care. Look to the works of the outward day. Can we believe that an individual, who has spent the morning of his days in rioting and idle voluptuousness, can make up his day's work in the evening? This is a moral impossibility. And if any of us are putting off the day in which we ought to become candidates to work out our salvation, it is impossible for any of these rightly to run the race set before them, or overtake their work.

I remember the day when I was going on in the broad way that leads to everlasting destruction. I was young in years, my passion violent, my will strong, and I rejoiced in my own way. I trusted in the declaration of the preacher: "Rejoice, O young man, in thy youth, and let thy heart cheer thee in the days of thy youth, and walk in the ways of thy heart, and in the sight of thine eyes; but know thou, that for all these things God will bring thee into judgment." I attended to the first part of the declaration, and, even at this day, consider it one of the matchless mercies of a gracious God that he met with me in judgment, that he plucked me as a brand from the burning, and that I am yet left, and have something of the vigor of youth, strength, and manhood. And I am fully convinced, that if I had put off these impressions till my passions had subsided, as many have done, I should have been a cast-away. Their subsiding has not been a victory their possessors have gained over them, but the want of ability to gratify them longer, that they have become separated from their darling lusts, which they have indulged to their present and eternal loss.

Let us now return again to that gospel which is preached baptizingly in every creature. It is not all the waters of the sea that can cleanse the soul of one single sin or lust.—It is not the partaking of bread and wine that can nourish up the soul to eternal life. It is not performing a round of ceremonies that can be called worship. For words are not worship, opinions are not religion, and declamation is not gospel. For words may be used which convey plain truth, but if not applied, and practically applied, it is stealing the words of holy men of old who have gone before us, or like making images of our own. I want you to seek that baptism which is more essential and effectual. And as this subject opens upon my mind, I have been renewedly instructed by the allusion which John made to an ancient prophet, when the priest and Levites were sent to inquire "who art thou?" Here the Baptist, after they had enumerated a number of queries, answered them, "I am the voice of one crying in the wilderness, make straight the way of the Lord, as said the prophet Esaias."

"Every valley shall be exalted, and every mountain and hill shall be made low, and the crooked shall be made straight, and the rough places plain and the glory of the Lord shall cover the earth, as the waters cover the sea."—Now unto what is that allusion to be applied? Not to the undulations of this outward globe; but to the dispositions of the human mind. Many among us are proud, haughty, headstrong, fierce, and cruel: and the design of this baptism is, to bring these mountains in our minds, down to

meekness. There may be many among us who are desponding and despairing, and who are ready to adopt the language, "Hath God forgotten to be gracious? Is his mercy
clean gone forever, doth his promise fail forever more."—
These he supports. The administration of this baptism has
a tendency to raise us up into a state of firmness; and when
this is the case, our crooked and perverse dispositions will
be made straight, and the rough places plain. When these
effects are produced in the mind, the glory and the knowledge of the Lord will cover and overcome every earthly
propensity, as the waters cover the sea.

These are the effects produced by the christian religion,
or the dispensation of the gospel; and it operates immediately on each individual; not in this, that, or the other society, through systematic organization, or through any medium, but through the revelation of God, unto the souls of
men. Therefore, it is essential for each of us to come to this
principle. And what is this baptism? And what is its operation upon our minds? It is plain and easily understood,
as many who have arrived at the years of maturity may testify with me, and who have experienced sorrow, trouble,
confusion, dread, and dismay, on the commission of evil
thoughts, words, and actions. Is there an individual among
us, who can do that which is wrong, wilfully, and not feel
compunctions of soul? No, verily. For we may, by sin-
ning day after day, and week after week, have our consciences seared as with a red hot iron, yet we all know this painful feeling of the fire. We may become seared with a hot
iron, so that the part which has been touched may lose its
vitality, yet underneath there must be life, and there must
be a feeling of deep distress. So it is, and so it will remain,
with all those who are disobedient to this heavenly vision,
and whose consciences have been seared as with a red hot
iron. And it is one of the matchless mercies of God, that
he does not cast off his people forever, neither does he design to "be always wroth, lest the spirits should fail before
him, and the souls which he has made."

When we come under the influence of these feelings, we

shall be made to cry out in agony, "Who among us shall dwell with the devouring fire? Who among us shall dwell with everlasting burnings?" My friends, no fire can continue to burn longer than the combustibles which give it nourishment shall endure. When we have experienced judgment, and the baptism of the Holy Ghost, which operates as fire upon all unrighteousness; and when it has performed its operation, it ceases to act as fire—it then assumes another operation. "Who among us shall dwell with the devouring fire; who among us shall dwell with everlasting burnings?" We are informed in the following text—"He that walketh righteously, and speaketh uprightly; he that despiseth the gain of oppressions, that shaketh his hands from holding of bribes, that stoppeth his ears from hearing of blood, and shutteth his eyes from seeing evil: He shall dwell on high: his place of defence shall be the munitions of rocks." The revelation of God shall not be affected by any of these combustible materials which keep the fire in existence. "His place of defence shall be the munitions of rocks: bread shall be given him; his waters shall be sure. Thine eyes shall see the king; they shall behold the land that is very far off." Here is a beautiful description of the effects produced by a submission to that fiery baptism which operates on every soul, and whether he will hear, or forbear, he cannot escape its operation. Whether then, is it better, to continue under the feelings described by this exclamation "who shall dwell with everlasting burnings?" or to come forth and dwell on high, and to have a place of defence, which shall be the munitions of rocks, and to experience the blessing of having bread given us, and to have our waters sure, and to see the king in his beauty, and in the excellency of holiness, and behold the land that is very far off? Now as we attend to those feelings, painful as they are when they have been produced by a forgetfulness of God, have they not been succeeded by a calm? Have we not been favored with a calm, and enabled to "look upon Zion, the city of thy solemnities, thine eyes shall see Jerusalem a quiet habitation; a tabernacle that shall not be taken down; not one of the stakes thereof shall ever be removed, neither shall any of the cords thereof be broken."

When we sit in our houses, when we walk by the way, when we lie down, or when we rise up, have we not had introduced into our minds quiet and consolation? We have all experienced this at one time or another. And what produced these feelings? Was it the natural conscience, education, habit, tradition, or speculation? No verily; these are feelings which do not apply unto our own minds. As to conscience, it is the effect of education and the power of habit; but this divine principle which is preached in the soul, the impress of the finger of God, is of another nature. But under the influence of conscience, which is the result of education, there is something very different. As some of us can look upon one day in seven as a sabbath in which we ought not to labor :—but there is another sabbath. And there are those who see every day alike. There are those who, under the influence of these systematic notions of religion, believe that all men *can* be saved, others that they *will* be saved, and others that none but the elect will be saved. It is this external and conscientious religion which is the result of education and tradition, that is the means of introducing all the absurdities and discordancy of opinions among mankind. But if we ever come to be followers of Christ in the regeneration, we must walk as he walked, we must mind the same thing, we must follow the same living and eternal principle that he followed, when in that prepared body in which he came to do his Father's will. Here I want us all to come—to this baptism of the Holy Ghost which reproves for evil. It is that which not only brings peace of mind, but in these the power of understanding is even opened for the reception of divine truths. Even through the medium of this cometh this quiet, this peaceful habitation. And here the scriptures appear in a precious point of view to us, containing practical truths illustrated in our own experience. And this bears testimony against all that is wicked and all that is unrighteous. But it takes no cognizance of these abstract propositions,—no cognizance of external actions, as such. "Ye have heard that it hath been said by them of old time, thou shalt love thy neighbor and hate thine enemy. But I say unto you love your enemies, bless them that curse you, do good to them that hate you, and pray for them that despitefully use you and persecute you." "Ye have heard it said, thou shalt not kill; and whosoever shall kill, shall die the death." There were other offences committed, which were amenable to the law. But in the precepts of Jesus none of these laws are recognized, because the dispositions which produce evil actions are to be rooted out.

There is one passage of scripture which I have often looked upon as more pointed than any other, and more deeply instructive. "Ye have heard that it was said by them of old time, thou shalt not commit adultery; and any man that committeth adultery let him die the death." Here is an offence, and a punishment adequate to the offence. But what said Jesus? "But I say unto you, that whosoever looketh on a woman to lust after her, hath committed adultery with her already in his heart." Here is a law which strikes at the root of the inclinations, dispositions, and passions, from whence the effects proceed. And when we can remove the cause, the effects will cease; and so it is with every other evil disposition of the human mind.

It is not mere abstract propositions that can do any thing for individuals or nations. It is the duty of each one to come under the influence of that gospel which is preached in every creature. There is not any thing performed for us by any external act or evidence. It is not by that act of unparalleled malignity in the Jews, by which they crucified a righteous person, that we are ever to experience salvation. I have no hope of salvation by the death of Jesus Christ, or by the blood shed without the gates of Jerusalem. I have hope and faith in the blood of Jesus Christ. But what is Christ's blood? It is his life. "Behold, a virgin shall conceive and shall bring forth a son, and they shall call his name Emmanuel, which being interpreted, is God with us." Now, if we ever experience salvation by Christ, it will not be by his death, but by his life, and by the power of that resurrection which nourisheth up the soul unto eternal life. Neither we go to bread and wine for this nourishment; but when we come under the baptismal influence of that holy spirit which teaches us baptizingly, the gospel which is preached in every creature, then we shall come to know what is meant by that declaration, that we shall be saved by his blood. For what is blood? It is the life, (and we have scripture testimony for the assertion,) the circulating medium which gives vitality to the whole system, as it flows and circulates through every part of the human body; so the life of Christ, operating on the whole mental and spiritual system, we become partakers of the same nature and the same life. And here is fulfilled a saying of Jesus, in a supplication for his followers: "That they all may be one, as thou, Father, art in me, and I in thee, that they also may be one in us." These he is not ashamed to call his brethren, because they are begotten by the same power, nourished up by the same light, and have the same life circulating through the whole soul. And hence our thoughts, words, and actions, are in accordance therewith. And thus we experience, that our souls have heard "another mighty angel fly through the midst of heaven, having the everlasting gospel to preach to them that dwell on the earth, and to every nation, and kindred, and tongue, and people,—saying, with a loud voice, fear God and give glory to him, for the hour of his judgment is come. And worship him that made heaven, and earth, and the sea, and the fountains of waters." Now, my friends, where are the abstract propositions? They are not of this building. They tend to the ruin and destruction of mankind. They cannot bring under the influence of this preaching, for such propositions have no part in the operations of the spirit of truth, in which we can alone hear the angel, "saying, with a loud voice, fear God and give glory to him, for the hour of his judgment is come. And worship him that made heaven, and earth, and the sea, and the fountains of waters." These are come into the third heaven, where they hear things not lawful to be uttered, and hold communion with God the Father, through the spirit of his

Son, and have all things made manifest in their view. They shall know the seals to be opened of that book which is sealed with seven seals: as many have known what it was to weep much, because no man was found worthy to open and to read the book, neither to look thereon. But by attending to these manifestations of the divine power, they will experience the seals to be broken open in proper order; and as they are prepared for the reception of divine truths, they will be manifested unto them. "For the lion of the tribe of Juda, the root of David, the bright and morning star, hath prevailed to open the book, and to loose the seven seals thereof." And thus we come to the fulfilment of the prophecies respecting him. And thus we shall know the declaration fulfilled, as declared by Moses: "A prophet will the Lord thy God raise up unto thee, from the midst of thy brethren, like unto me; unto him he shall hearken." And it was declared, that "whoso will not hear that prophet shall be cut off from among his people." And, notwithstanding he was greater than Moses, and greater than the people, he was obedient unto this law. And unto this law we must come, if we would ever be partakers of of that kingdom which Christ has declared is within you. It is there we must look for its influence. It is there that we are to know him to rule as with a rod of iron. And there we are to know fulfilled the declaration: "Thy throne, O God, is forever and ever; a sceptre of righteousness is the sceptre of thy kingdom."

It is in vain for us to be contending about doctrines and principles—about uniting or dividing the divinity. This can never bring us to dwell in the third heaven; and many numerical errors cannot constitute a theological truth; but error is still error. The God whom we worship is not local. He is not to be divided, for he fills all place and all space. And one of the inspired penmen was sensible of this, when he cried out "Whither shall I go from thy spirit? Or whither shall I flee from thy presence? If I ascend up into heaven, thou art there. If I make my bed in hell, behold, thou art there. If I take the wings of the morning, and dwell in the uttermost parts of the sea, even there shall thy hand lead me, and thy right hand shall hold me." Neither need we look for heaven at a great distance and beyond the grave : we must look for the coming of the kingdom in ourselves ; for it dwelleth with you and shall be in you. And as his own kingdom comes to be governed by his own laws, we shall come into the divine compact and harmony : we shall come to be his children. Then we shall be no longer under the spirit of bondage, because our guilt being removed, we shall receive the spirit of adoption, whereby we can cry Abba, Father. And we shall not be so much concerned to bow down the head like a bullrush, or lift up the voice like a trumpet, and call it prayer ; but we can accord with the prayer of Jesus Christ—we can call God Father, because we are begotten into his life. Therefore, we can say, without robbery or mockery, "Our Father, which art in heaven ;" and because we shall be endeavoring to do his will—"hallowed be thy name, thy kingdom come, thy will be done in earth, as it is done in heaven. Give us this day our daily bread." We can adopt this language, because we shall not be depending on abstract propositions ; we shall not be indulging in any of these things ; but we shall be nourished by a daily dependence on the will of God. We can say, "Forgive us our trespasses as we forgive those who trespass against us ;" because wherever the spirit of God is, there is love and good will to men ; and no contentions shall divide the hearts of these. Therefore, we shall be able to love our enemies, to pray for them that despitefully use us, and persecute us. Here we can ascribe "glory and honor, forever. Amen." When we come into the spirit of prayer, and not into the literal meaning of words, we shall know him, who is the resurrection and the life, to govern all our spirits and minds. And therefore the whole line of our conduct will be in accordance with this language, whether we express it or not. Here we shall not be depending upon the observance of days and times, any more than on external performances. Here we shall come into a state in which we can declare, that we saw an angel standing, as John said, with one foot upon the earth—that is, above every earthly propensity—and another upon the sea ; for we shall be placed above all the fluctuating opinions comparable to that unstable element. And he "saw a mighty angel stand with one foot upon the sea, and the other upon the earth, and he lifted up his hand to heaven, and sware by him that liveth forever and ever, that there should be time no longer." When we come under the influence of this principle, we shall see this angel and hear his voice. We shall be brought into that state, in which life or death, riches or poverty, sickness or health, will all be matters of indifference to us, and very small things in our view. Our whole hopes of happiness will centre in him who is the life of the righteous ; and we can say, "thy will, and not mine be done." There will be no contention, no speculation, no doubting, but his law will be written in our souls, and enable us to fulfil every divine requisition. This is the new covenant spoken of. "And after those days, I will make a new covenant with the house of Israel, and with the house of Judah. Not according to the covenant that I made with their fathers, in the day that I took them by the hand, to bring them out of the land of Egypt ; which my covenant they brake, although I was an husband unto them, saith the Lord. But this shall be the covenant that I will make with the house of Israel ; After those days, saith the Lord, I will put my law in their inward parts, and write it in their hearts ; and I will be their God, and they shall be my people." It is only to that people this covenant was new : for the Gentiles, of which race we are, have known no other covenant.

Look at the excellency of this dispensation. When we draw nigh to God, there is union and communion ; there is none to divide in Jacob, or to scatter in Israel. When our minds come into this state, and even while progressing thereto, our minds will not be left without an internal evidence—the scriptures will afford corroborative evidence ; and then we shall be able to look upon these, not merely as books created for our use. We shall see the writing of God in every thing that surrounds us. Not a leaf that falls to the ground, nor the vilest insect that we tread upon, but would convey a lesson of instruction ; and these lessons of instruction would not become perverted, or raised above their proper value. The scriptures would be considered, as they ought to be, the testimony of holy men of old. And when we come under the same divine influence which dictated to them, they would become unto us "profitable for doctrine, for reproof, for correction, for instruction in righteousness, that we through patience and comfort of the scriptures might have hope." And not only so, but in every other external object, we should see daily cause to glorify God, because of the multitude of his mercies. "Day unto day uttereth speech, and night unto night showeth knowledge. There is no nation, nor language, where their voice is not heard."

SERMON XI.

DELIVERED BY THOMAS WETHERALD, AT HESTER STREET MEETING, NEW YORK, SUNDAY AFTERNOON. MAY 28TH, 1826.

An investigation of what is truth, leads to a detection and exposition of error. But in order to produce these effects, it is necessary that the investigation be conducted on principles in accordance with the nature of the subject to be investigated. Mechanical truths must be investigated and proved upon mechanical principles; mathematical truths must be proved according to mathematical principles; and spiritual truths must be spiritually proved.

Now it is not in the nature of any thing, which stands not immediately in the revelation of God, manifested unto man, to enable us to pursue this investigation, so as to produce these results; for this revelation is the alone medium whereby we can come to a comprehension of God and of spiritual truths. As to matters of opinion, belief, and systems of religion, they are the works of man; and if necessary to appeal unto these, I apprehend that I could unite in belief with almost all the members of the various religious societies. I could believe that there is no salvation out of the Holy. Catholic, and Apostolic Church. I could, with the Episcopalian, "believe in God, the Father Almighty, Maker of heaven and earth; and in Jesus Christ his only Son, our Lord, who was conceived by the Holy Ghost, born of the virgin Mary, suffered under Pontius Pilate, was crucified, dead, and buried;" but that he descended into hell, I dare not believe, because he declared to the thief on the cross, "To day shalt thou be with me in paradise." I can, with those who adopt the Calvinistic platform, believe that only the elect are saved. I can believe, with some of the Baptists, that baptism is essential to salvation. With Arminius, that all men may be saved. And I can believe, with the Quakers, that "the grace of God, which bringeth salvation, hath appeared unto all men, teaching us that, denying ungodliness and worldly lusts, we should live soberly, righteously, and godly in this present world, looking for that blessed hope, and the glorious appearing of the great God and our Saviour Jesus Christ."

And where are we to look for this appearing? Are we to go back to John's time, and to view the outward advent? or are we to take a view of him through the medium of the scriptures? No, verily; for these are irrelevant unto us: we cannot apply these things which are recorded as facts, either as societies or individuals. But there is a declaration, that what is to be known of God is manifested in man; and the reasons for this is obvious, for God hath shown it unto him. Here, then, is a medium for the investigation of spiritual truths. And now with respect to the holy, catholic, and apostolic church. I apprehend that this title can be attributed to no sect or party of Christians, but to those who are guided by a holy, catholic, and apostolic spirit which influenced the immediate followers of Jesus Christ; a spirit of obedience unto every manifestation of our heavenly Father's will. These only can be saved. It is in this view of the subject that I can unite in the belief. And I can believe with the Episcopaleans in God, the Father Almighty, Maker of heaven and earth, because I never doubted his creative wisdom, nor his governing mercy. I never doubted his omniscience, his omnipotence, nor his omnipresence.— And I can believe in Jesus Christ our Lord; but this belief is not merely confined to his outward advent, for I believe in the scripture declaration, that he was from everlasting to everlasting. There was a time when, on account of the hardness of the hearts of his people, God gave them statutes that were not good, and judgments whereby they should not live; but these were designed as a schoolmaster to bring them unto Christ. "Moses was faithful in all his house as a servant, but Jesus Christ as a son over his own house, whose house are we, if we hold fast the confidence and the rejoicing of the hope firm unto the end." And as we come into this state of sonship, we become the sons of God. "For ye have not received the spirit of bondage again to fear, but ye have received the spirit of adoption, whereby we cry, Abba Father." And in furtherance of this belief, I also believe in the scripture record concerning Jesus Christ; that he was conceived by the Holy Ghost, that he was born of the virgin Mary, that he suffered under Pontius Pilate, was crucified, dead, and buried. In this, I have no doubt, I shall be considered sound by the generality of professing Christians.

Now, my fellow professors of this Christian name, what will all this heterogeneous mass of opinions avail me, if they cannot be applied to my mind for any practical purpose, or give me a victory over one solitary sin or lust? They cannot remove one obstruction which may be placed between me and my God by disobedience to his laws. Besides this, I may be baptized in the outward element of water, I may wash in snow water and make me never so clean; yet, if I am not under the influence of that living principle, by which spiritual truths are understood, it will only plunge me still deeper into the ditch, till mine own clothes shall abhor me.

With respect to the baptism which is essential to salvation—it does not consist in the application of water, nor any other outward element. And with respect to the bread and wine—it is no part of that dispensation which came by Jesus Christ, and which was from the foundation of the world to the present day. We were never under any other dispensation than that of the gospel of Jesus Christ. The law of Moses was never applicable unto us, who are of the Gentile race. We have always been under the immediate guidance of our heavenly Father, if we were only willing to submit to his manifestations. I have no idea that he has designed to cast off one part of his creation; for all are equally the workmanship of his hands : because this would make God unjust.

It may be said that this is grievous presumption ; that it is a mystery which we cannot understand ;—and it *is* too mysterious to be rationally or spiritually comprehended.— For it had its origin in that night of apostacy, which over-shadowed christendom, when "mystery Babylon, the Great, the mother of harlots, and abominations of the earth," reigned triumphant. And she is yet presenting to us the cup of her fornications, which we, alas! delight in. We are partaking of her pleasures, and if we continue, we must also become partakers of her plagues ; and we shall be thrown into a bed with her, and be tormented because of our wick-edness.

It is not opinions, or beliefs, or sentiments, that can pre-vent these effects, or preserve us from them. It must be something of a more internal, spiritual, and operative na-ture. It must be something which will remove the blind-ness from our eyes, and give us to understand the mysteries of heaven, so that they may be applied immediately to our own understandings as practical and operative truths.

And with respect to bread and wine. It was declared, "Whoso eateth my flesh, and drinketh my blood, hath eter-nal life ; and I will raise him up at the last day." But re-member the last sentence. "It is the spirit that quickeneth ; the flesh profiteth nothing ; the words that I speak unto you, they are spirit, and they are life."

Now let us look a little into these things, and see if there is any thing which will suit us. Let us look into the causes, which have produced such mournful effects ; which have caused this miserable declension from that state of pure and undefiled religion before God the Father. For, "Pure reli-gion and undefiled, before God and the Father is this, to visit the widows and fatherless in their afflictions, and to keep ourselves unspotted from sin." Those who are of the holy catholic and apostolic church, are influenced by that which is holy and apostolical. Now the followers of Jesus Christ sold their possessions and goods, and parted them to all men, as every man had need : "and the Lord added to the church daily such as should be saved." And while they remained under the influence of this holy principle, there was an accession to the church. But after a season—after a couple of centuries, there arose among them men of learning, and men of science, falsely so called. These men introduced theological propositions and questions, which tended to gender strife. They introduced into the church spurious doctrines respecting the nature and attributes of God ; and, as one false step leads to another, these have gradually led us farther from the source of light and purity.

And 'where had all this its origin? It was introduced from Alexandria in Egypt, the land where Israel was held in bondage. And how striking is the analogy! These corruptions came from Egypt into the church of Christ. They were brought by the bishop of Alexandria, who was succeeded by bishops, and pastors, and teachers ; and they grew and increased, and their authors became more anxious to subserve their own ends, than that of truth. This gave occasion for one who was eminent in his day for divine illumination, mournfully to declare, "in days that had passed, they had wooden chalices and golden priests, but now," said he, "we have golden chalices, and wooden priests."

They had sunk into the splendor of outward things—the spirit of religion was lost. Darkness had surrounded them, and the brilliancy of the first appearing of the opening of this dispensation among the Jews, became clouded ; and from step to step they grew and increased in superstition, till that dark night of apostacy came over our Israel, and involved them in that deplorable situation, of which history gives us an account. It was from a small beginning that it had its origin ; but it soon increased, so that pardons for sins were sold, and also indulgencies to commit them ; together with other absurdities, which are a disgrace to the rational faculties of man, and much more to that gift of spiritual investigation wherewith he is endowed.

But it came to pass after a season, that there were raised up men who detested those abominations, and who, coming to investigate the truth, saw some of those evils, of which but a little was manifested at first. For they could not at once come out of that midnight darkness, into the meridian light of gospel splendor. It would have blinded their eyes, puzzled their judgments, confounded their understandings, and probably have left them in a state worse than that in which they were. Very little was seen at once ; and though the individuals who made the first reformation saw but little, yet as they attended unto this little, they were bright and shining lights, for they were obedient according to knowledge.

But, alas! instead of their followers attending to that light to which they had attended, they set down in the letter where Calvin left it ; and could not be drawn one step further than where he left them. So it was with the Lutherans—so with the followers of Wesley, so with every society with which I am acquainted ; and so it has been with the followers of Fox, Penn, and Barclay. We look to them for fundamentals, which if rightly known, are engraven by the finger of God, on the tablets of every soul. For these things we have cause of lamentation and mourning. And why ? Because assuredly, in so doing we do not go forward, but backward. If we do not increase, assuredly we shall decrease.

Have we not observed the followers of Calvin to stand in that form of which he experienced the great power and light? And the longer they continued in this form, the more dead it became, till it led these societies into persecutions, divisions, dissensions, and hatred ; and caused them to become partakers of the cup of that Babylonish whore, who shall yet be stripped naked in the eyes of the nations, that they may see her shame. But it is not the Calvinists alone, who founded their system on this unjust doctrine of election and reprobation, that have here grounded and struck upon a rock. Every other society has fallen into the same snare, which the delusions of their own perverse imaginations have laid for their feet. And it is only by taking the back track, and returning in the way in which we came, that these effects can be changed, and the operative cause be changed that may produce effects which shall be more propitious.— Now is it not the case with the Lutherans, the Wesleyans, and the Quakers? Is it not the case with every society, when they have been actuated by man's reason? "If it be not so now," as has been described, "who will make me a liar, and make my words nothing worth?"

Is the Lord's hand shortened that it cannot save? or is his ear heavy that he cannot hear? Can we, or dare we, say that the work of our salvation is referred to secondary means? Has he appointed men for our teachers and leaders? No. But under the influence of this darkened state, which comes by a perversion of the divine principles of the gospel, many other abominations sprang up. We see men professing to be ministers of the gospel, and upon what do they depend for their qualifications? Do they depend on the inspiring spirit of Christ manifested unto their own minds? Is it a duty required at their hands? Can they testify as the apostle did, " Wo is unto me, if I preach not the gospel?" No, verily. But is it not obvious to every reflecting mind, that, not only here, but in the land of my nativity, there are those who "preach for hire and divine for money, whose God is their belly, whose glory is their shame?" Look at the multitude, I had almost said innumerable multitude, who are governed by the wisdom and invention of man. They support the scriptures under a false title, considering them the word of God and the only rule of faith and practice. But they are not the word of God, nor are they the rule of faith and practice. They are the testimony of holy men of old, who were guided and influenced by the eternal word and rule of faith and practice, which was from everlasting to everlasting.

Now, with respect to these benevolent associations, what are the fruits brought forth? and what are the effects produced on the minds of men and nations? Have they produced in them, that holy anthem which was raised at the advent of the Messiah, " Glory to God in the highest, and on earth peace, good will toward men?" No, verily. They have given unto these self-styled missionaries, authority over the gospel, and which will rivet the chains upon them, which have been placed there by the cunning of these deceivers.

And how are these societies supported? Let us look a little. We most of us know that it is not by contributions from the pious of all sects and parties, but we find that *money, money,* is the main-spring of action, and if this fails the whole system falls to the ground. And is the church of Christ to be built up with money, the love of which is the root of all evil? But what said Christ unto his disciples: "Whom do men say that I the Son of Man am? And they said, some say that thou art John the Baptist, some Elias, and others Jeremias, or one of the prophets. He saith unto them, but whom say ye that I am? And Simon Peter answered and said, thou art the Christ, the son of the living God. And Jesus answered and said unto him, blessed art thou, Simon Barjona, for flesh and blood hath not revealed it unto thee, but my Father which is in heaven. And I say also unto thee, that thou art Peter, and upon this rock"— that is, revelation—"I will build my church, and the gates of hell shall not prevail against it."

Now let us look a little at this other foundation, and at the materials of which it is composed. Are these effects produced, and are these supports raised, by contributions from the pious of the various sects? Do we not see that donations are received from the blood thirsty warrior, from the cruel slave holding oppressor? And are not these individuals active in the establishment of Bible and missionary societies? And as far as the money goes, theirs is as good as that of any other persons. Do we not see contributors who are drunkards, whoremongers, gamblers, and a variety of every other name and character? And what if I say, "the hire of an harlot and the price of a dog, both of which are an abomination in the sight of the Lord," would not be refused by these ministers of another and a spurious gospel. For instead of the gospel being preached in demonstration of the spirit and of power, it stands in man's wisdom—it is not free, neither is it given freely. It is a fair characteristic of that beastly nature and false prophet, so beautifully typified by the beast with seven heads and ten horns, which were pushing against one another. These beastly dispositions are of such a nature, that they are causing discord, and pushing, and confusion.

Are not these the effects produced by an increase of religion at the present day ; and is it not obvious to every reflecting mind, that with the increase of religion, there has been an increase of wickedness also. I apprehend, that this will be denied by few, who have not placed their faith and dependence in systems established by, and which stand in the opinions of others ; and which have no operative power to give a victory over the evils of the world, and bring us into the glorious liberty of sons and daughters of God, where all these distinctions must vanish ; and where there is neither Jew nor Greek, barbarian nor Scythian, male nor female, and where we shall not have any more discord nor confusion, for Christ will be in all, and through all. This was the light which was in the church in the wilderness, and followed Israel. As it is recorded, "They all ate the same spiritual meat, and drank the same spiritual drink, for they drank of that spiritual rock which followed them ; and that rock was Christ." And he "maketh his angels spirits, and his ministers a flame of fire." For, "Are they not all ministering spirits, sent forth to minister for them who shall be heirs of salvation ?"

You need not look to any certain beings who may stand in some particular or local situation for the angels of God. For what are they ? Every manifestation of his will, is his angel ; and every manifestation of his will unto the soul of man, is one of these spirits. For "he maketh his angels spirits, and his ministers a flame of fire. And are they not all ministering spirits, sent forth to minister for them who shall be heirs of salvation." Every work of the creative wisdom of God, every monument of his creating power, is an angel of God : and when they keep their place, men continue in their first estate. But when any of us pervert the dispositions with which we are endowed, and call good evil, and evil good; when we take light for darkness, and darkness for light; sweet for bitter, and bitter for sweet, then we pervert the design of our creation. Then it is, that we fall from that estate in which we were created, and rebel against the Most High. And every spirit of rebellion which is thus indulged, constitutes a fallen angel; and every fallen angel is a devil.

Now, in order to be removed and preserved from this deplorable situation, where are we to look? Are we to look unto man, who has been instrumental in leading us into this confusion by the systems with which he has surrounded us; and by the sciences which he has assumed? Shall we look to declamation, to opinions, or to outward words? No, verily. For words are not worship, opinions are not religion, and declamation is not gospel. But if we ever come under the influence of that principle which is able to make wise unto salvation, we shall know what it is to be baptized into that faith which remains to be delivered unto the saints who are in Christ Jesus. This baptismal spirit is truly of an operative nature. It was testified of by the prophets formerly; and it was declared by John, that it should increase, although he should decrease. "I indeed baptize you with water unto repentance; but he that cometh after me is mightier than I, whose shoes I am not worthy to bear; he shall baptize you with the Holy Ghost and with fire." This is the baptism which is essential unto salvation, for all. It is not a baptism which consists in washing with an outward element: but it is within the reach of all—it is internal, it is spiritual—it strikes at the root of every evil in our minds, and begets in us a clean heart; and here it is, that we can call God, Father. And how are these effects produced? Are they not obvious? Are they above our comprehension? Are we to be saved by these things which we cannot understand or comprehend? Forbid it heaven! There is a way opened, whereby we can come to a knowledge of every truth: and this is through the operation of baptism. There is a spirit in man, which is inspired by the Almighty, and which opens our understanding. And what is this understanding? It is the faculty of determining what is evil, from the effects which it produces also. For it says unto the righteous, "Say ye it shall be well with them; for they shall eat the fruit of their doings; and unto the wicked, it shall be ill with him, for the reward of his works shall be given him." And as certainly as mercy and the love of God, and all the fruits of righteousness bring peace and joy in every holy spirit, so certainly, cruelty, pride, and a host of evil dispositions which are too much indulged, bring sorrow, trouble, and confusion upon us. And thus we shall come to know what was meant by the declaration, "There was war in heaven: Michael and his angels fought against the dragon; and the dragon fought and his angels, and prevailed not; neither was their place found any more in heaven."

And what is heaven? Is it a place at a great distance, and beyond the grave, where there are distinct beings taking cognizance of all our actions? Is this the idea which we have formed of heaven? No, my fellow professors: but even at the present moment, there is judgment set, and the books are opened. At the present moment, we may hear the voice of the Son of God, and if we are willing to obey that voice, we may live. Have we not all had an acquaintance with this principle, who have arrived at the years of maturity? And can we not testify that evil brings sorrow, trouble, and confusion over our minds? That pride, fullness of bread, and abundance of idleness, bring no peace, when we sit in our houses, when we walk by the way, when we lie down, or when we rise up? Here is a spirit of baptism, of judgment, and of burning, which operates against all unrighteousness, and ungodliness of man. And the effects which it produces, are in accordance with each of our dispositions; thus bringing down the high, lofty, and proud into meekness, raising up the weak and desponding soul into firmness; and it will make all perverse dispositions straight, and the rough places smooth. But these are not momentary operations, nor the work of a day, or a week; but they are a gradual advancement from step to step, and from strength to strength. And thus we are able to testify with the apostle. "When I was a child, I spake as a child, I understood as a child, I thought as a child; but when I became a man, I put away childish things." And the reasons which he gave for this, are good; and I would to God, that the same mind were in us, that when we are children, we might speak as children; and not be so confident in these systematic attainments, which we have received from books, and from men. But let us abide in a state of littleness, till our minds shall expand, so that we may receive those things which are essential for our further nourishment and provision, and for the enlightening of our understandings in the investigation and acknowledgment of, and obedience to divine truths.

And we are informed, that "the kingdom of heaven is within you;" and it is from testimony of the highest authority. This, then, is the place where we must look, for the manifestation of divine wisdom. It is here we must look for the display of that power; and it is here we must know him who hath power and dominion, to rule and to reign by his own laws. He hath a right also to give power that Michael and his angels shall fight against the dragon, and that his place shall be found no more in heaven. And when the angel of love shall cast out the devil of hatred, and the angel of mercy shall cast out the devil of cruelty; and the angel of temperance shall cast out the devil of intemperance; and when faith, love, and fidelity shall cast out every opposite principle of infidelity;—when all the heavenly dispositions, and the principle of truth and righteousness, shall have cast out their opposites, their adversaries and enemies, then we shall come to know where this warfare was; because we shall have experienced it with power; and we shall know that "every battle of the warrior is with confused noise, and garments rolled in blood; but this shall be with burning and fuel of fire." And assuredly it will never cease its operations till every thing contrary to itself is burnt up, consumed and destroyed: for nothing of a contrary nature can stand the force of this fiery operation; therefore it will never cease till all these are burnt up in our minds; for it is because of these that we come short of the glory of God and that we have not that peace, which passeth all understanding.

How many there are, who, from their youth, and through the various ages of man, till hoar hairs have covered them, mourn because of their short comings, unfaithfulness, and disobedience; and yet, they feel the fire of his anger burn, because there is yet combustible matter in them, which must be brought under. And while this remains, the fire will abide in them to consume it. This is one of the many matchless mercies of a gracious God—that while we are disobedient we cannot eat the good of the land; we cannot become partakers of the divine harmony, and have our understandings regularly opened for the reception of divine truths. We may become children of an hundred years old; but if we continue as children, we shall never have the faith of men, and shall never have their experience.

Now this is the baptism which operates upon the soul, and leads it out of the bondage of sin and corruption into the glorious liberty of the sons and daughters of God. And it has been beautifully alluded to in the prophecy of Isaiah; and the same was alluded to by John when the Pharisees inquired of him, "Who art thou?" He said "I am the voice of one crying in the wilderness, make straight the way of the Lord, as said the prophet Esaias." "Every valley shall be exalted, and every mountain and hill shall be brought low; the crooked shall be made straight, and the rough places smooth, and the glory of the Lord shall cover the earth, as the waters cover the sea." Here is a beautiful allusion to that great variety of operation, which is necessary to the varied dispositions and passions of those who constitute the human family. Some are headstrong and fierce, these are the mountains which must be brought down into meekness, by judgment and burning. Others are lowly and desponding—the minds of these are to be comforted by a cup of consolation handed unto them, that they may rejoice therein, when they may at times despond and say "Hath the Lord forgotten to be gracious?" Every crooked and perverse disposition shall be made straight; because this baptism will burn up its undulations, and bring it to its proper level. There is no evil, which will not alike fall under its control. Thus the crooked and perverse dispositions will be made straight, and the rough places plain ; and the glory of the Lord shall cover the earth, as the waters cover the sea.

Now where are we to look for the origin of true and living faith, if it be not in this operation ? "Faith is the gift of God." And there are a variety of faiths. There is a faith, so denominated, which stands in a belief of certain systems and opinions, and which may stand in rational ideas. It was said, "Thou believest that there is one God ; thou doest well; the devils also believe and tremble." But this belief has no tendency to change or crucify our passions or lusts, for they remain devils still. There is no virtue in opinions —that is certain ; but faith works by love to the purifying of the heart. This is another principle. It is lively and universally operative in its nature, and saving in its effects. It never stands separate from the baptism of the Holy Ghost which produces it. It is the gift of God to man, because of obedience. And when, season after season, we have come to be reproved because of transgression, and when we have repented thereof, we have consequently felt the peace and joy of his consolation, season after season ; for it is a progressive work. There is then begotten in our souls a living faith, a holy confidence, which will be strength to us in times of succeeding desertion—an holy confidence, that he who called us when far off, and who has brought us thus far on our journey, will continue to perfect the work to the praise and glory of his own name and our soul's solid peace.

Here is that faith which was not only *once* delivered to the saints, but that which is delivered to the saints in *every age* of the world. Here is a medium of communication between God and the children of men. Under the influence of these feelings they come to be partakers of the flesh and blood of Jesus Christ. "Except ye eat of the Son of Man and drink his blood, ye have no life in you." What is the blood? It is that life which circulates through the whole system.

And how beautiful is the analogy between this and spiritual things. And as assuredly as the natural outward blood is the outward life, and gives vitality to the whole animal system, so does that blood which is the life of Christ, give a life of purity, holiness, and self-denying obedience to every manifestation of the Father's will. It is the life of every Christian, which circulates through his whole soul. There is no part left dark, and no part which cannot come under the influence of this heavenly and controlling principle. Here we become partakers of the flesh and blood of Christ, and are nourished by it unto eternal life.

Shall we then turn back and become partakers of the beggarly elements of bread and wine, as typical of Christ's coming in the flesh? There is no need of this, when we are partakers of that internal light and life. We need not return to external objects, for as surely as the knowledge of the glory of God comes to cover our minds, so surely shall we become partakers of his divine nature, and experience the regenerating influence of his spirit upon our minds, which will nourish up our souls unto eternal life.

Here is a spiritual religion which is applicable unto our understandings. It is a religion which all can understand. It is this baptism of the Holy Ghost, which operates on all unrighteousness and ungodliness of men. It is a gospel preached in every creature. For Christ's disciples were not sent forth merely to preach and to baptize, but they were commanded to go forth and to preach the gospel baptizingly. Jesus declared that it should not only be preached baptizingly, but he also gave these men commission that, when they were endued with power from on high, they should bear outward testimony in Jerusalem, Judea, Samaria, and in the uttermost parts of the earth. And although this medium of communication may be good, useful, or instructive, and have a tendency to stir up the pure mind by way of remembrance, it never can supersede the necessity of that inward, spiritual gospel, preached in every creature, which is, "Christ in you, the hope of glory."

Here we come immediately to know the divinity of Christ

operating on our spirits, and we need not go back to theological discussions respecting his manhood or Godhead. All that is to be done is to come immediately under the influence of his power, and it will lead us out of the bondage of sin and corruption, into the glorious liberty of the sons and daughters of God. And as we attend to these divine operations, our faith will be strengthened, our souls will be more and more nourished, and more and more acquainted with the pointings of this divine teacher, till we shall become wise in those things which are hid from the wise and prudent, and revealed unto babes. And this was a cause of thankfulness, even unto Christ himself. "I thank thee, O Father, Lord of heaven and earth, because thou hast hid these things from the wise and prudent, and hast revealed them unto babes. Even so, Father, for so it seemed good in thy sight."

And now respecting election and reprobation. The true ground of this stands not in any fore-ordination of God before the foundation of the world, but it stands in our obedience or disobedience to the law written in the hearts of all men. But if we will attend to the baptism of the Holy Ghost, which is a reprover for evil, and which speaks peace for obedience, we shall grow stronger and stronger until we overcome every thing of an opposite nature. Here we become elected together with Christ, as he was elected, because he was obedient to his Father's spirit. Here is the true ground of election. And if, on the contrary, we deny his power and are not obedient to his manifestations, our evil propensities will grow until they predominate over the good, and thus we shall bring ourselves into the state of reprobates, and we shall feel punishment—shall feel those everlasting burnings that we can never escape from. But I apprehend there is a state attainable where God will, at all times, appear in his own native loveliness, where we shall not be afraid of the operation of his power; we shall not be afraid of its rising, because we know that it only appears in judgment against all unrighteousness and ungodliness of men.

Christ himself makes allusion to this in the parable, where

he compares this work to a "little leaven which a woman took and hid in three measures of meal till the whole was leavened." And we all know the nature of meal, that it is passive and obstructs not the operation of the leaven. It is compared also to "a grain of mustard seed, which a man took and sowed in his field; which is, indeed, the least of seeds, but, when it is grown, it is the greatest among herbs, so that the birds of the air come and lodge in the branches thereof." Now these fowls of the air are the visionary imaginations of the mind. And these things are instructive, if we are willing to apply them. And do we, by this declaration, make void the testimony as recorded? No. But we establish the law. And when we attain unto this state, we shall find beauty and excellency in the scriptures, which we can never find by perverting their name. By attending to these things our understandings will be opened, and we shall be brought into the same feelings, views, and principles, which actuated the holy men of old who wrote them. We shall not be characterizing them as the word of God and the only rule of faith and practice. It is only to that divine wisdom and power which was in the beginning, which took flesh and blood as a clothing, to whom we ought to give this name, and attribute this wisdom and power.

And the scriptures of truth thus coming to have a proper influence on our minds, they will become to us more lovely, the more we are acquainted with them. They will become more and more precious, and we shall not be ashamed to acknowledge their inestimable value and their authenticity. Yet we shall not consider them the word of God, nor the only rule of faith and practice. We shall consider them as testimony corroborative of those spiritual truths which are sealed upon our minds by the impress of the divine spirit. And it is not only the scriptures of truth, but the sun and moon in their orbits, and the stars in their courses, will all testify of the mercy, goodness, and power of God. Neither shall we be induced to worship these, notwithstanding their brilliancy. We shall neither bow our knees, nor lift up our hands to any created object, because this would be denying that God who is above all. Not only these, the most brilliant objects of his creative wisdom with which we are acquainted, but all the works of his hands proclaim themselves the workmanship of deity. There is not an insect that we tread upon, which does not receive life from him. Every blade of grass, every leaf that falls, and every wing that flits the air, all receive alike, whether animal or vegetable, his superintending care. That God whom we serve, that deity whom we worship, is omnipotent, omniscient, and omnipresent. Then, where is there room for a division of God? How can we divide and sub-divide the divinity into three persons in one God? It is an absurdity; and derogatory, if not blasphemous! It is derogatory to that power which fills all place and all space. For whatever admits of division, admits of locality; but God is found every where. To this the scriptures bear testimony throughout. "Who shall ascend into heaven to bring Christ down from above? or who shall descend into the deep to bring him up from thence? For what saith the spirit: the word"—which is the power—"is nigh thee, in thy heart and in thy mouth, that thou mayst hear it and do it." And another inspired penman cried out, "Whither shall I go from thy spirit? Or whither shall I flee from thy presence? If I ascend up into heaven, thou art there. If I make my bed in hell, behold thou art there. If I take the wings of the morning, and dwell in the uttermost parts of the sea, even there shall thy hand lead me, and thy right hand shall hold me."

Now, my beloved friends, every thing capable of feeling within me, is called into action in this meeting, and I believe the Lord God has mercifully extended his presence over this assembly. And I want us to come into an examination of ourselves, and not be content with superficial observances of things imbibed by habit, by education, and tradition. "For, what does the Lord require of thee, but to do justly, and to love mercy, and to walk humbly with thy God." The inspired penman was willing to make every sacrifice. "Wherewith shall I come before the Lord, and bow myself before the high God? Shall I come before him with burnt offerings, with calves of a year old? Will the Lord be pleased with thousands of rams, or with ten thousands of rivers of oil? Shall I give my first born for my transgression, the fruit of my body, for the sin of my soul? He hath showed thee, O man, what is good, and what doth the Lord require of thee, but to do justly, and to love mercy, and to walk humbly with thy God?" Here is the whole duty of man, to "fear God, and keep his commandments." This is a corroborative testimony, as to the whole duty of man. And "God will bring every thought into judgment, whether good or evil." Therefore, I crave it of you, that you attend individually to the manifestations of that spirit of wisdom, which reproves for every evil, and speaks peace for every act of obedience. This will enable you to enjoy that peace here, which the world can neither give nor take away. In prosperity, it will preserve you from being lifted up; in adversity, it will raise you above depression and murmuring; in health, it will preserve you from temptation, and in sickness, from despair. It will disarm death of its sting, and the grave of its victory. And when time here shall be no more, we shall attain to a mansion in that building of God, that house not made with hands, eternal in the heavens; "where neither moth nor rust doth corrupt, and where thieves do not break through nor steal."

14

SERMON XII.

DELIVERED BY THOMAS WETHERALD AT ROSE STREET MEETING, NEW YORK,
WEDNESDAY, JUNE 1st, 1826.*

I apprehend it is considered that the service of the meeting is over, and perhaps we may as well quietly retire. But
I have felt a concern on my mind for the young friends.
And whatever truths have been delivered, my dear young
friends, if they can be applied to our minds, let us take
them, and be willing to make the application; and if we
cannot apply them, let them pass for what they are worth.

I apprehend that the gospel of Christ is simple, and that

---

* As the circumstances of this meeting were peculiar, and have been variously
represented, it becomes the duty of the stenographer to give a statement of facts
as they appeared to him at the time.

At an early period of the meeting Mrs. Robson rose, and continued to speak
for more than an hour. She was very soon succeeded by Mrs. Braithwaite in a
prayer; immediately after which, Richard Jordan and Elisha Bates, who sat at
the head of the meeting, shook hands as the customary signal for a separation:
but, contrary to any thing ever before witnessed by the stenographer, or by any
other person with whom he has conversed, not a solitary individual, among
more than two thousand, was seen to move!

In the course of about a minute, there was another and a similar attempt made
to close the meeting, by R. Jordan, E. Robson, A. Braithwaite, and some persons occupying the second galleries, but it was with the same effect! A profound
silence now pervaded the whole of this large assembly, and in breathless expec-
tation, every eye seemed riveted with intense interest upon the galleries. The
whole meeting, simultaneously breaking through the rules of the society, remained fixed and immovable, as if controlled by some invisible power. Such
was the effect, that the beholder might have easily conceived himself surrounded
by a congregation of statues instead of animate beings. During this interval,
Mr. Wetherald rose and delivered the following discourse, which being succeeded
by a few remarks from Elias Hicks, a short pause ensued—when Mr. Hicks and
Mr. Wetherald shook hands, and the meeting quietly dispersed.

we need not be alarmed at any extraneous or outward circumstances. It stands not in words, but in that power which is communicated immediately from God, the Father of lights and of spirits, into each of our spirits. And I have been looking a little at a record left in the scriptures of truth respecting John. He bore a high and noble testimony respecting the Messiah, that Lamb of God who was to take away the sin of the world,—for he had a view of his outward coming, and of his mission. But remember there was a time after this, when he was imprisoned, in affliction, and distress; and this wrought so much upon his mind, that, though he had been able to bear this testimony, he had now to query doubtfully, "Art thou he that should come, or do we look for another?"

And now, my young friends, there is an evidence sealed upon each one of your minds, in a greater or less degree, of those things which are essential in the constitution of a Christian. And what are these truths? There is something in your minds which reproves for every thing that is unrighteous, and all unrighteousness in sin. Sin, by indulgence, becomes a positive principle: it is not a speculative idea—it does not derive its nature from being written, but because it it reprovable in the sight of God, and *is* reproved by him. And, therefore, I want us to attend to a Saviour which is near, "Christ in you the hope of glory," which preacheth the gospel baptizingly in every creature. For the gospel of Christ stands not in words, but in power. Though we may be like John, and be thrown into prison, and our minds become confused, at times, from various objects and circumstances; yet there is no alteration in the divine principle which has heretofore reproved us. And I want us on these occasions to be still; and if we find the messengers of Christ, so called, are endeavoring to hatch up something— some declarations, whether from the scriptures or from tradition or former experience, believe them not, for we shall receive no benefit from the works of man.

When the messengers of John went unto Christ, saying, "Art thou he that should come? Or look we for another?"

He did not say, I am he. "But in that same hour he cured many, of their infirmities and plagues, and evil spirits, and unto many that were blind he gave sight." He healed all the maladies of those who came unto him. Here was an evidence indubitable ; and if we attend unto the operations of Christ, we shall receive this indubitable evidence, when our minds are prepared for it. "Go," said he, "and tell John what things ye have seen and heard ; how that the blind see, the lame walk, the lepers are cleansed, the deaf hear, the dead are raised, to the poor the gospel is preached. And blessed is he, whosoever shall not be offended in me."

Now, my friends, and you, my young friends, especially, I want you to come unto this gospel. It stands not in words —I have a higher opinion of the coming of Christ, than any external appearing unto mankind.

It was on account of the ignorance of the Jews, that laws were given them which were not good, and statutes under which they could not live. So carnally minded were they, that it became necessary that there should be a mediator, in the outward body, who should speak things which never had been spoken, and perform miracles which never had been performed, in order to draw them to something of a higher grade, and of a more spiritual nature. And that this mission in that prepared body was confined to the Jews, is evident from an abundance of concurrent testimony. When Jesus sent forth his disciples, he said, "Go not into the way of the Gentiles, and into any city of the Samaritans enter ye not. But go rather to the lost sheep of the house of Israel." And after he was crucified and appeared again unto his disciples, he told them not to go forth, but to tarry at Jerusalem, till they were endued with power from on high. "But tarry ye in the city of Jerusalem, until ye be endued with power from on high." And after that, they could bear witness to the uttermost parts of the earth. But, my friends, those testimonies which they had to bear, were borne from the foundation of the world. This is that same seed of the woman which was testified of, and which was to bruise, and which always does bruise the serpentine dispositions of man, which constitute sin. This is he that was in the church in the wilderness, as it is written. "And they did all eat the same spiritual meat, and did all drink the same spiritual drink; for they drank of that spiritual rock that followed them, and that rock was Christ." The same living and eternal power, which is the same to-day, yesterday, and for ever. And this power was manifest, not only in the flesh born of the virgin Mary, but it is manifest in your flesh. This is a saviour and redeemer, and he is, at this day, fulfilling this mediatorial office in us.

Now look a little at the circumstances attending his appearing in that outward body among the Jews. Their minds were darkened by prejudice; and the law which came by Moses, or the cloudy dispensation, was perverted. It was intended to draw them to something of a higher nature than the mere healing of their temporal maladies. He gave them many precepts calculated to introduce them into the gospel dispensation, and these were confirmed by miracles. For his design was to lead them step by step, to bring them nearer to God's salvation, and farther from those external circumstances which had crept in through the hardness of their hearts.

Now let us look a little at the office which he is yet fulfilling among us. He remains to be "Christ in you, the hope of glory." Is it not from him that we receive every good and perfect gift? Is it not the same power which created, and which sustains the world? Is it not the same manifestation of God that was in the flesh, that remains to be a teacher of his people? And is not he who performs every miracle of a spiritual nature now, the same that was temporally manifested among the Jews? Does he not now open the blind eyes, and unstop the deaf years of our understanding? Does he not cleanse the leprosy? Does he not raise from a death of sin, to a life of God in the soul? And how is this performed? As he testified to John, it is by the gospel preached unto the poor, and that baptizingly. And what is this? It stands not in declamation. The gospel of Christ stands not in words, but in power. And the preaching of that gospel in every creature, is that feeling in which we are introduced into a sense of suffering for every thing of an evil character, or which may have a tendency to separate us from God. Are there any among us, who can wilfully declare, that which we know to be untrue, and not feel compunction and confusion for it? Are there any of us who can commit an evil act, and not feel some kind of compunction, and that in proportion to the magnitude of our offences? For this is preached in every creature; and when we turn from it, and run into evil, it brings confusion, dread, horror and despair over our minds. And is there not a peace, a quiet, a calm which is not at our command?

I dare to testify of these things, my friends, but it is not because they are recorded in the scriptures of truth, but in the depths of my own experience. I am young as well as you; and I therefore feel in a special manner for this class of my brethren and sisters of the human family. Now as we attend to what passes in our minds, whether in the calm, or in the tempest which may be brought upon our minds by our disobedience and forgetfulness of God, each of these will become a lesson of instruction; and our understanding and views will be enlarged, because there will be a continued increase in our experience of its operations, whether in reproof for sin, or whether we in like manner, come to be partakers of its consolations. Our understandings will be opened by the same power and principle. And where will this stop? I have never found a stopping place, and I don't want any of you to find a stopping place. And thus, by a daily attention to the manifestation of this power, we shall be like the unslumbering shepherd of Israel—and we shall never come to an ultimatum in religion, and say, *this* shall be *my religion*, and *these* my doctrines.

But here is the whole extent, that ever an individual can come to in religion—that is, to attend daily, to the preaching of this gospel in every creature. It will lead into that simplicity and humility, which is so much boasted of; but of which, we have very little manifestation. It will lead us into every heavenly, every manly, every social, every civil, and every relative duty; and thus we might make every wilderness an Eden, and every desert like the garden of the Lord. Joy and gladness would be found therein, thanksgiving, and the voice of melody.

Now this is a kind of doctrine that we can all understand; and not come to an ultimatum in religion, like those who commence in the spirit and end in lifeless form; or begin in the spirit and end in the flesh. It is this very circumstance, that has brought christendom into that of confusion in which it is placed. We see that a great variety of the first professors and the founders of the generality of societies with which we are surrounded, and with which we are acquainted, were spiritually minded men, who according to their measure and manifestation were faithful in their day and generation, and attended to the light within. But their successors, instead of attending to it step by step while in the world, by which they might have attained a state higher than that from which Adam fell, have just set down in the form of that of which their predecessors felt the power; and thus they all become dead, dry, and formal. They must have systems, and doctrines, and principles of religion: and their doctrines, systems, principles, and religion, altogether. are a dead form; for they stand not in the operative power of God. But it is not any set of forms that can give us admittance into that city, "whose walls are salvation and whose gates are praise."

And what is that principle of religion that can do this? It is that operative power which leads out of evil. If I am a drunkard, and come under a principle of temperance, it is a manifestation of religion which gives me to see the evil of my practice; and in that light there is that divine illimitable power which enables me to overcome every evil propensity and habit. If I am cruel, and am brought under the influence of a principle of mercy and walk in its dictates, it becomes to *me* a principle of religion; but because *I* may be thus brought under the influence of heavenly virtues, and of religion, it cannot become a principle to any of *you*, except you feel its power. And so it is, through the whole routine of christian virtues; these are the principles which constitute that innumerable company of angels which compose the host of God, of which we read in the scriptures.

Thus we come to know the angel of love, to cast out the devil of hatred; the angel of mercy, to cast out the devil of cruelty; the angel of temperance, to cast out the devil of intemperance; and every ministering angel of God; every heavenly and virtuous disposition to take possession of the mind, and each to cast out its opposite, adversary, or enemy; for love and hatred, mercy and cruelty, humility and pride, righteousness and wickedness, are opposed one to another, and cause a warfare. Now let us look a little at the consequence of this divine principle of religion which leads to the fulfilling of every law. Where would there be room for discord and dissensions between individuals, squabbles in neighborhoods, or wars in nations? "From whence come wars and fightings among you? Come they not hence, even of your lusts that war in your members? But if we are under the influence of this heavenly principle, every perverse disposition will be crucified; we come to be crucified with Christ that we may live, not that we may live in our sins; but crucified with Christ, that we may live: and when we come to take up our cross and leave all these carnal lusts, affections, and passions, we can then testify, "I am crucified with Christ: nevertheless I live, yet not I, but Christ liveth in me: and the life which I now live in the flesh I live by the faith of the Son of God, who loved me, and gave himself for me." Here then is the foundation of faith; and until we come to have this experimental knowledge of God, we shall not know what it is to be reproved for evil, and to have peace spoken to our souls for obedience, neither can we have any true faith. We may have opinions, sentiments, and beliefs, as the devils have; for it is written, that the devils believe and tremble, but they are devils still. There is no operative principle in mere belief, no renovating influence. Faith is the result of an experimental knowledge of God, operating upon our spirits, rectifying our passions, and subduing every lust.

And now, my friends, I desire to leave these few remarks with you, and I want you not to become a carnally minded set of christians, for this leads to death : but I want you to become spiritually minded, for in this is life and peace. It will not only put an end to all difficulties, squabbles, and wars, but it will bring us into that rectitude of word and action, which will make oaths useless. Here is the true foundation of these two great testimonies to which this society have been brought under the influence of the spirit of love ; for as God is love, and we are brought under the influence of God, all wars must cease. And the spirit of love is the spirit of Christ: and if the cause of wars cease the effects must cease also, and on the contrary, so truth and lies, or truth and error, never can dwell together. For if we are under the influence of one of these angels, the other must be a concomitant : thus, if we are under the influence of love and truth we never can go to war or lie, because this would derogate from the character of those principles. And it is not only these two testimonies, but our minds being under the influence of mercy, here again is the origin of our testimony against slavery, and the oppression of our fellow men. And I apprehend, that while our minds are under the influence of mercy, we shall never be guilty of an act of cruelty.

Here is also the original of another testimony, against pride and vanity, whether in dress or address. It is not the cut of a coat, nor shape of a bonnet—it is not any of these external things, which some of us have any concern about, and we have not been ashamed to confess it. But when our minds have been brought under punishment for pride, every thing to deck or adorn, to gratify the vanity of mankind, will be laid by, not merely as useless, but as meretricious ornaments, tending to increase the mountains of opposition which are raised between us and our God. Here it is, that those things which have the appearance of pride, will be dispensed with, and not because it is the mode or fashion of the societies to which these are united. And I verily believe, there is much less pride in some of those who wear fashionable apparel, than in those who have adopted a particular system of religion, and have come under the influence of systematical and Pharisaical self-righteousness. I want to explain the origin of these testimonies, which this society have to bear, not from a disposition to criminate any of you, but from a belief in their accordance with the impressions made on our minds. For, if we are pure, our conduct will be pure; if we are holy, our conduct will be holy accordingly; if we are humble, we shall appear humble, and walk with humility. And if we are under the influence of the last, which is the most dignified of the angels of God, it will show itself through all our actions.

Now, unto that God, who redeemed us by his own life, and who is desirous to become a mediator to bring mankind to glory and to virtue, to the only true God and Messiah, Jesus Christ our Lord, in whom I believe, and by whom I hope for salvation here, and in eternity, I desire to recommend you, with my own soul. And I affectionately bid you farewell. Attend daily to this principle which will bring you out of sin and corruption, into the glorious liberty of the sons and daughters of God; for where Christ is, there is liberty.

SERMON XIII.

DELIVERED BY THOMAS WETHERALD, AT ROSE STREET MEETING, NEW YORK, SUNDAY MORNING, JUNE 4TH, 1826.

"Is not the life more than meat, and the body than raiment? Behold the fowls of the air: for they sow not, neither do they reap, nor gather into barns ; yet your heavenly Father feedeth them. Are you not much better than they? Which of you, by taking thought, can add one cubit unto his stature? And why take ye thought for raiment? Consider the lilies of the field, how they grow: they toil not, neither do they spin ; and yet I say unto you, that even Solomon, in all his glory, was not arrayed like one of these. Wherefore, if God so clothe the grass of the field, which to-day is, and to-morrow is cast into the oven, shall he not much more clothe you, O ye of little faith ?"

Now where is the instruction, which is to be derived from records like this? We acknowledge the superintending providence of the Most High : yet, if we would be fed, we must labor ; we must sow, and reap, and gather into barns. If we would be clothed, we must toil and spin. And, therefore, I have concluded that these expressions are parabolical or allegorical, and that they convey lessons of deep and important instruction. The sparrows are fed by the bounty of the Most High, for they sow not, neither do they reap, nor gather into barns. The lilies are clothed, not by their own labor, but by the same God who sheds the light of his countenance on all the works of his creation : for if there was no light for the lily, its beauty would never make its appearance ; and it is the immediate gift of the Most High. But mark, there is no opposition in the lily. It is willing to appear in the beauty of nature and of nature's God. It is clothed by his hand, because it is submissive to his operative power. And so, if we come under the same state of submission, we shall, by the same operative power, be clothed and fed. But all the learning and wisdom of man cannot feed the soul, nor can all our speculative ideas, notions, and opinions of religion, bring down bread and clothing from God out of heaven.

It was a declaration of Jesus Christ, when in the prepared body in which he came to do his heavenly Father's will, that that bread, which he would give, was his life, which he would give for the life of the world. But are we again turning unto external objects? Are we turning to the act of unparalleled malignity of the Jews, which crucified him? No, verily, there is another spiritual and deeply instructive allusion—"And the bread which I will give is my flesh, which I will give for the life of the world." And this is synonymous with another declaration. "If any one will be my disciple, let him take up his daily cross and follow me." It is through the crucifying operation of his spirit, that we are made willing to give up every disposition which would separate us from the source of purity. And if we are willing to "let him that stole, steal no more," and whatever evil we have been guilty of, to give it up, and avoid it;—and if we are willing to give up our life—that in which we have delighted, and in which our perverted hopes of happiness consisted—what is the consequence of becoming thus stripped of these perverted dispositions? The consequence is, that our life comes into unison with the life of Christ, and his heavenly dispositions govern us. Thus he gives his life unto us, for the life and spirit of the world.

Here is a happy exchange within our reach, if we desire it; but it is not to be gained by toiling and spinning—by sowing and reaping. It is not to be gained by a systematic observance and adoption of creeds, systems, articles, or sentiments of religion. For these are distinct from the operative power of God. And when we come to take up our daily cross and follow him, and when we come to know him to sit in judgment against all ungodliness and unrighteousness of men, his life becomes our life and we are united to him : and these he is not ashamed to call his brethren. And wherefore? Because they are begotten by the same power, and brought forth in the same life. Here is the communion of saints—herein is the ground of their faith and patience ; because this religion is not the result of education. They know that Christ has come, whose illimitable power is the resurrection and the life. And this is proved by many other corroborative passages of scripture.

I have remembered a passage which is recorded, that when Christ's disciples were at sea, there was a great storm—the sea rose and was tempestuous against them—they toiled hard, but made no advances ; and it was not until after they were almost spent with rowing, that they became willing to give up their own labors, and to depend on, and come under, the influence of this principle. And when this was the case, they saw their divine master walking on the sea ; for he was above the influence of the contending elements. "And when they saw him walking upon the sea, they supposed it had been a spirit, and cried out, for they all saw him and were troubled." "And he rebuked the wind, and said unto the sea, Peace, be still. And the waves obeyed him : and immediately the vessel was at land." Here we ought to derive instruction from this historical account, but we may read it from youth to old age, and, if it is not with a right spirit, we shall never be instructed thereby. And are not many of the parables of Christ himself hid under these allegorical allusions? And wherefore? Because the spirit of this world can never extend to an understanding of the nature of the case ; for they can only be understood in that spirit and power which dictated them. Therefore I have desired that we may cease from doing our own labor and setting up our own opinions, and that we may become willing to be divested of all religion which is the result of education and tradition ; and no longer suffer our opinions to be bounded by prejudice, and limited by those narrow, sectarian feelings which these traditional principles will assuredly inculcate. What have we to do with these things? We cannot give to the lily that light from whence its beauty proceeds? We cannot command for ourselves, one grain of that which is the spiritual life of the children of God.—Hence the utility of that divine command, "Be still, and know that I am God."

There are a variety of opinions which have been produced among christians, and which are inconsistent with the nature of christianity. And until they are done away, we never can come coolly and quietly to consider and admire the works of Providence, and receive the instruction which may be immediately received therefrom. It was an injunction of the prophet formerly: "Fear not because of the two tails of these smoking firebrands, Rezin, with Syria and Remaliah's son." They were commanded to be quiet. "In returning and rest shall ye be saved: in quietness and confidence shall be your strength." And I am not ashamed of the gospel of Christ, which is the power of God unto salvation. I am not afraid to testify unto you, that in the stillness of all these fluctuating imaginations, he will become our guide, for it is in the depths of seclusion—when secluded from man and all his works,—that we are not to know a Redeemer, a Christ, a Messiah. And if we know him not, each for ourselves—if we do not come to know "that life is more than meat," all our performances, all our systematic arrangements, will be nothing more than "sounding brass or a tinkling cymbal." Religion stands not in the power of the imagination, nor in the exertion of the rational faculties, though it operates on them.

What is man? He is a compound being, consisting in part, of an an animal body—he has in connection with this, animal, or instinctive faculties; and by the aid of these, he can fulfil all animal, or instinctive duties. These bodies are supported by food, and, as other animal bodies, they are sensible to heat and cold, and they also die and return to, and become incorporated with, this mass of earth from whence they sprang. But man, who declares himself the noblest work of God, claims a higher destiny. And from whence does this proceed? As we have an animal body, so we have a spiritual body. The apostle says, "There is a natural body, and there is a spiritual body." And it is the spiritual life which is in man, that constitutes the nobility of his nature. It is of the nature of the divinity—it is a spirit; it is comprehensive. It can comprehend things which are of a spiritual nature. For, as the instinctive faculties lead to a fulfilment of animal duties, so do the spiritual faculties, enable us to perform every spiritual duty. It is by the aid of these spiritual faculties, that we come to a knowledge of God. According to the declaration of an eminent apostle, "For what man knoweth the things of a man, save the spirit of man which is in him? Even so the things of God knoweth no man, but the spirit of God." And it is by this combination—it is by a union of these spiritual and instinctive faculties, that reason is produced—that reason which has usurped the place of the higher faculties. By this we are endeavoring to comprehend God, and by this we are endeavoring to form schemes of happiness for ourselves. Thus it is, that like the angels, we are endeavoring to rise above our state; and as certainly as they fell, through their pride and disobedience, so certainly we must fall. And this very faculty, which was designed for an incalculable blessing, is often perverted to the worst of purposes. From this perversion, wars and fightings are introduced; pride and ambition, and every other evil which becomes a disgrace to human nature, are carried on, under a pretence and appearance of rationality, till it becomes degraded below the level of instinct. For, it is a gift which may be perverted—the dispositions may be corroded—the passions may become evil, and deserving crucifixion.

But, my friends, whilst we are under the influence of these spiritual dispositions which are only applicable to the soul of man, they are not convertable or pervertable—they are one and the same, yesterday, to-day, and for ever, equally with that divine power from which they spring.

And what is the extent of these rational powers? By them is conferred the power of speech, and the power of comparing ideas. And by these we are enabled to fulfil our social, civil, and relative duties one to another. By these we are enabled to dive far into arts, sciences, and philosophy. And in the enjoyment of these, in an unconverted state, consists. much of the happiness of man in this state of being. But all these advantages can never bring us to a knowledge of God; yet, under the influence of these rational faculties, we may pretend to worship God—we may meet together and have something to say;—and in many societies, they have it prepared beforehand;—we may preach, pray, sing, baptize with water, and partake of bread and wine, as symbolical of good things to come, but the substance, the body is of Christ. The Saviour, the Messiah, is not that Christ which Mary conceived, and who was crucified without the gates of Jerusalem: for the Messiah is, from everlasting to everlasting. His mission among men commenced with their creation, and will continue until the end of time. It is that power of God which is illimitable, which pervades the whole creation, and gives life to all his works. It operates not merely on man, but it operates on all the inferior parts of his creation—it fills all place and all space. It

"Warms in the sun, refreshes in the breeze,
Glows in the stars, and blossoms in the trees;
Lives through all life, extends through all extent,
Spreads undivided, operates unspent;
Breathes in our soul, informs our mortal part,
As full, as perfect, in a hair as heart;
As full, as perfect, in vile man that mourns,
As the rapt seraph that adores and burns."

Such is the nature, power, and efficacy of this divine principle, that it is not far off, that any should say, "Who shall go up into heaven to bring down Christ from above; or, who shall descend into the deep? to bring Christ up again from the dead: but what saith it? The word is nigh thee, even in thy mouth, and in thy heart; that is, the word of faith which we preach." David was sensible of this when he says, "Whither shall I go from thy spirit? or whither shall I flee from thy presence? If I ascend up into heaven, thou art there : if I make my bed in hell, behold, thou art there. If I take the wings of the morning, and dwell in the uttermost parts of the sea ; even there shall thy hand lead me, and thy right hand shall hold me." Micah was also sensible of the spirituality of this dispensation, and of the worship which was acceptable unto God, when he says, "Wherewith shall I come before the Lord, and bow myself before the most high God ? Shall I come before him with burnt offerings, with calves of a year old ? Will the Lord be pleased with thousands of rams, or with ten thousands of rivers of oil ? Shall I give my first born for my transgressions, the fruit of my body for the sins of my soul ?" He appears to be willing to give up all, even the life of a son ; to make every sacrifice, to submit to any privation, so that he could find acceptance and favor with God. But this was not under the power of the cloudy dispensation. And what was required of him ? There were three things required, "He hath showed thee. O man, what is good : and what doth the Lord require of thee, but to do justly, to love mercy, and to walk humbly with thy God."

Here, then, was a rule for *his* conduct, and it remains to be a rule for *our* conduct : and throughout all ages and dispensations of God to man, this rule has continued unbroken : but because of the hardness of his people's hearts he gave them a dispensation suited to the state in which they had placed themselves by disobedience. But it was not permanent ; it was not operative upon the soul : and when he brought them forth, and took them by the hand to bring them forth out of the land of Egypt, he made his power manifest. "Marvellous things did he in the sight of their fathers in the land of Egypt, in the field of Zoan." He commanded them not respecting burnt-offerings and sacrifices, "but this I commanded you, saying, Obey my voice : Hath the Lord as great delight in burnt offerings and sacrifices as in obeying the voice of the Lord ? Behold, to obey is better than sacrifice, and to hearken than the fat of rams." This declaration was made when pride, folly, and oppression had brought the nations under their full influence. And

15

there are a variety of other scripture testimonies to prove that under the cloudy dispensation, there was a higher state attainable than could be attained by the law and its observance,—when guided by the spirit itself. This spirit enabled all the prophets to testify of things yet to come: it enabled them to declare a saviour. This enabled Moses to say unto them; "A prophet shall the Lord thy God raise up unto thee, a prophet from the midst of thee, of thy brethren, like unto me, unto him ye shall hearken." It was also declared by almost every succeeding prophet, respecting the coming of the Lord Jesus Christ; and also the design of that coming. It was said unto the Jews, "Behold, the days come, saith the Lord, that I will make a new covenant with the house of Israel, and with the house of Judah, not according to the covenant that I made with their fathers." Now let us look a little at the covenant delivered on Mount Sinai, in the midst of darkness, thunderings, and tempest, and the sound of a trumpet, and the voice of words: but they desired that they should not be spoken unto them any more; but that Moses should speak, and they would hear him. But the new covenant was to be of another nature, and to have a very different effect. The old covenant came by Moses, and was written on tables of stone which Moses did hew. And when these tables of stone were incribed by the finger of God, here was the work of man and the work of God also. Here was something which formed a combination, it was not wholly spiritual. These tables of stone carried even on the face of them a declaration that there was something natural, and that all was not spiritual. But the new covenant dispensation unto the people was of a very different nature. "I will write my law in their hearts." Here it was upon the workmanship of his own hands; it was not on tables which men had hewn, nor on systems which they had built, nor creeds which they had adopted. It was not like the faiths and articles of belief which have been imposed on the community, to bring them into a miserable bondage, and out of the glorious liberty of the sons and daughters of God; but it was written and engraven on the tablet of every heart. "Behold the days come, saith the Lord, that I will make a new covenant with the house of Israel, and with the house of Judah ; not according to the covenant that I made with their fathers in the day that I took them by the hand, to bring them out of the land of Egypt ; which my covenant they brake. But this shall be the covenant that I will make with the house of Israel. After those days, saith the Lord, I will put my law in their inward parts, and write it in their hearts ; and I will be their God, and they shall be my people." These laws are merely prescriptive, they are not statutory : they are not only adapted to the whole community, but operative on every individual soul ; each being under the immediate direction of the Most High. They were not intended to apply to any class or society, as such, for this could not be done. There can be no general rules for the government of mankind, while men are as variously circumstanced as we are, and while our dispositions are as various as the faces which we wear. One law can never apply to two individuals ; one baptism never can purify two souls.

And what is the baptism under this covenant? It is something which operates on the perverse dispositions of men. Some are haughty, some lofty, some fierce, some cruel, some mild, some low, desponding, and ready to despair. Now, will the same baptism cleanse the souls of all these? No. But a different operation of the same power can be adapted to these several situations and circumstances. Therefore the design and intention is to bring these to their proper level. The prophet had allusion to this, when he said, "Every valley shall be exalted." "The voice of him that crieth in the wilderness, prepare ye the way of the Lord, make straight in the desert a highway for our God. Every valley shall be exalted, and every mountain and hill shall be made low ; and the crooked shall be made straight, and the rough places plain." And as a necessary consequence, "the glory of the Lord shall cover the earth ;" and every earthly propensity shall be brought under the influence of his power, "as the waters cover the sea."

These are the effects, the glorious effects of this dispensation of God to man. And where are these operations, and what are they? And what is the power that writes these laws upon our hearts? It is "he that formeth the mountains, and createth the winds, that declareth unto man what is his thought, that maketh the morning darkness, and treadeth upon the high places of the earth, the Lord, the God of hosts, is his name." "For God speaketh once, yea twice, yet man perceiveth it not. In a dream, in a vision of the night, when deep sleep falleth upon men, in slumberings upon the bed, then he openeth the ears of men, and sealeth their instruction." And are there any of us, who have arrived at the years of maturity, who have not experienced some of these operations? We have, I am afraid, in our experience every day enough to confirm the belief that we have been endeavoring to crucify the love of God, the principle of baptism, to our own hurt, and to put Christ to an open shame. And wherefore? Because he has no form nor comeliness, that when we see him we should desire him, but he is despised and rejected of men : and wherefore? Because our dark and carnal life prevents us from coming into the life of God, and hinders us from experiencing his operative power. And hence it is, that we feel not those effects which are designed to be produced upon us.

"He is despised and rejected of men, a man of sorrows and acquainted with grief; and we had as it were our faces from him ; he was despised and we esteemed him not." You see it was written before the days of his outward advent, that he is despised ; and it is even so, that he is at the present day despised and rejected of men. He is a man of sorrows and acquainted with grief; and we have hid, as it were, our faces from him. "He was despised, and we esteemed him not. Surely he hath borne our griefs and carried our sorrows ; yet we did esteem him stricken, smitten of God, and afflicted. But he was wounded by our transgressions, he was bruised by our iniquities ; the chastisement of our peace was upon him ; and with his stripes we are healed. All we, like sheep, have gone astray ; we have turned every one to his own way; and the Lord hath laid on him the iniquity of of us all. He was oppressed, and he was afflicted, yet he opened not his mouth: He is brought as a lamb to the slaughter; and as a sheep before her shearers is dumb, so he opened not his mouth. He was taken from prison and from judgment; and who shall declare his generation? For he was cut off out of the land of the living: for the transgressions of my people was he stricken." And while we continue in disobedience to his prescriptive law, we continue to crucify him; and this is the lamb which was slain from the foundation of the world, and from the foundation and superstructure which the spirit of the world builds in our hearts. When the perverted dispositions, and those which are carnal, have the dominion in us, he is in us a lamb slain from the foundation of the power of all these carnal things.

I want us all to come out of these things, and be separated; for it is in this corruption that we see "mystery Babylon the great, the mother of harlots and abominations of the earth." For all nations and religious communities, who adopt systems, have been partakers of the cup of her fornications: but I want us to come out of her, that we be not partakers of her sins, and that we receive not of her plagues. For "her sins have reached unto heaven, and God hath remembered her iniquities."

I have no idea at all that this name, Babylon, can be properly applied unto any religious society, but unto all those who have separated themselves from God the author of our existence. These are they who become partakers of the cup of her fornications; and I would to God, in my very soul, that she may become stripped in the view of the nations, and that they may see her shame, and that we may hear the cry, "Babylon is fallen, is fallen, and all the graven images of her gods he hath broken unto the ground." And I apprehend there are many idols among us of this character. For whatever is contrary to the nature, power, and spirit of God, is of this Babylonish character. It leads to the same confusion, and is built of the same materials that another Babel was built with.

We may remember the design of this building. "Let us build us a city, and a tower whose top may reach unto heaven," to preserve us from the power of evil. They wanted to obtain a victory over the most high God. They wanted to raise themselves above the waters of another flood, which destroyed their ancestors, instead of avoiding the causes which produced such deplorable effects. For, unto the present day, like causes will produce like effects; and. there are abundant waves rolling on in succession, one after another, and, when uniting together, they form an irresistible flood, which overwhelms and destroys the wicked. Whilst they who are obedient, and who depend on the Most High, will experience themselves to be surrounded as by an ark of safety.

And what is this flood and its component parts? They are not the floods of waters with which we are surrounded—they are not the mountains with which we are surrounded—they are the waves of pride, and passion, and folly, which abound among us. There is a mighty wave of dissension, another mighty wave of pride, another of cruelty, another of oppression, and all the innumerable host of dispositions and passions in which we indulge. These are the overwhelming waves which are combined together to destroy the wicked, and to separate them from God the source of all purity, and that being who righteously dispenses deliverance from all these floods.

And this is synonymous with another declaration of the divinely eagle-eyed apostle, when he declared that "there was war in heaven: Michael and his angels fought against the dragon, and the dragon fought, and his angels, and prevailed not; neither was their place found any more in heaven." And what are these angels? They are heavenly dispositions. For "he maketh his angels spirits, and his ministers a flame of fire." And I am not ashamed to acknowledge, that I have no belief in those angels which are represented as women with wings, bearing messages from the Most High, through the regions of air; and, what if I say hell. "And of the angels he saith, Who maketh his angels spirits, and his ministers a flame of fire? And are they not all ministering spirits, sent forth to minister for them who shall be heirs of salvation?" "And the dragon fought, and his angels." And what are these angels of the dragon? "Pride, fullness of bread, and abundance of idleness;" together with many other perverted dispositions. Surely these are the curses and the enemies of the human family; and what if I say devils; for they are tormentors of mankind. And when we come to know the angel of love to cast out the devil of hatred, and when our minds are brought under the influence of that principle which loves God above all, and the neighbor as itself, it will cast out the demon of hatred from the mind; for these cannot dwell together. And when the angel of mercy shall have cast out the devil of cruelty, and the angel of humility shall have cast out the devil of pride, the angel of temperance shall have cast out the devil of intemperance, the angel of hope shall have cast out the devil of despair, the angel of innocency shall have cast out the devil of guilt, and when every divine spirit, and every heavenly disposition, comes to govern and cast out every thing of an opposite tendency, these waves will be removed, and in the ark of safety we shall be raised above all their influence, and landed in a situation as immovable as the mountain of Ararat.

Here, my friends, is a religion which is practical in its nature, and universally saving in its effects. Why then shall we go back to that which is less than meat and raiment : yea, less than the body? Why continue to labor all the night, spending our strength to no purpose? Why continue to make brick, and take them for stones? Why depend on vain and natural works?

We read that they took brick for stones, and slime they had for mortar. While we are building like this, confusion will be the consequence. The effect has verified the declaration : for mankind have been building a structure like this—they have built upon the ingenuity of their own rational faculties, and the speculations which they have formed : and hence confusion has ensued. One declares this is truth, the other that it is error—one is for brick, and another for slime. They have neither tried stone which will bear the superstructure, nor the mortar of divine love to cement it together. And hence it is, that confusion becomes worse confounded. They are dividing languages, sentiments, and opinions; and hence it is, that their language, according to the declaration of the scripture, is confounded. They cannot understand, they cannot know each other's views—they leave their work, divide and separate themselves into various families; and here dissension is continued and increased. The divine and anointing principle of love is lost among them.

And while under the influence of all these discordant principles, men with their ingenuity will have dominion over us—they will form combinations, and overwhelm us beneath them. But when under the influence of those heavenly principles, which are as a flame of fire unto Esau, they will form an ark of safety, as certainly as ever there was an ark of gopher wood, made impenetrable to the least particle of water.

Noah was commanded to make an ark of gopher wood, and to pitch it within and without with pitch. Now here is the substance: then let us come a little to the particulars, by which we may experience them in our own minds. I can not direct you to man, nor to that act of unparalleled malignity in the Jews, wherein some do rest. For the kingdom of heaven is not built upon any act of wickedness. It is not meat nor drink, but righteousness, which produces peace and joy in the kingdom. And where is it? It is not above; neither is it below; neither is it east, west, north, nor south. But what is the declaration of Christ? "The kingdom of heaven is within you." And it is there, we are to look for its operations; there we are to experience its power: it is there we are to be governed by its laws. "The axe is laid unto the root of the trees: therefore, every tree which bringeth not forth good fruit, is hewn down, and cast into the fire." Here a blow is struck at every evil disposition; for it is not merely outward acts of wickedness of which this divine law takes cognizance. As said Jesus, it was written of old time, "thou shalt love thy neighbor, and hate thine enemy. But I say unto you, love your enemies bless them that curse you, and pray for them that despitefully use you, and persecute you."

Here, perhaps, is one of the most difficult and important commands to fulfil. And wherefore? Because we do not attend unto the principle of love, which casts our hatred; and while our minds are under the influence of that feeling, we can only love our friends, and hate our enemies; and we are no better than the Pharisees. But, "Love your enemies." And is this impossible? No, verily. It is a high attainment; but if we come under the influence of that spirit of love, which casts out the devil of hatred, there can be no enmity, nor malevolence in our minds. And thus we shall be able "to love our enemies, to bless them that curse us, and pray for them that despitefully use us, and persecute us."

But, now my friends, let us consider. It is not merely believing in these precepts, as they are recorded; but it is coming under the influence of that divine law, that new covenant written upon the tablets of the heart, yea of every heart; and it ought to be engraven upon the horns of every altar. "I will put my law in their inward parts; and write it in their hearts; and I will be their God, and they shall be my people." Now when we come under the influence of this love, we cannot hate, for hatred and love are enemies; but we can pray for them that hate us, and despitefully use us, and persecute us. It was also said, "Thou shalt not kill; thou shalt not steal; and whosoever doeth these things, shall die the death." But, here the axe is laid to the root of the tree—here the judgments of God are placed against all unrighteousness and disobedience to his divine law. And if we neglect this inward and spiritual law, it will bring us back again into those things which are external in their nature, and prevent us from becoming sanctified, cleansed, and purified by that baptism which operates as fire.

It was also written, "Thou shalt not commit adultery." But Christ said, that "whosoever looketh on a woman to lust after her, hath committed adultery with her already in his heart.''

Do not these testimonies place the subject on the affections, passions, and dispositions, whence evil actions proceed? And if these are rooted out, their effects must wither, the leaves must fade, the branches must decay : thus the glory of the Lord will cover the earth, as the water covers the sea. But, my friends, these are only the effects ; let us now come to the causes. They are known unto us, but they are small. Wherefore? Because we have neglected their operation ; therefore, we experience not their power. There is something in man, which reproves for evil. "There is a spirit in man ; and the inspiration of the Almighty, giveth them understanding.'' And by the aid of this spirit, they come to know him that is true, and to dwell in him that is true. ''And we know that the son of God is come, and hath given us an understanding, that we may know him that is true, and we are in him that is true, even in his son Jesus Christ. This is the true God, and eternal life. Little children, keep yourselves from idols.'' We must begin with attending to the voice of him that crieth in the wilderness, "prepare ye the way of the Lord, make straight in the desert, a highway for our God. Every valley shall be exalted, and every mountain and hill shall be made low ; and the crooked shall be made straight, and the rough places plain.'' This has an evident allusion to the coming of Christ, and to that which was declared, "I indeed baptize you with water unto repentance, but there standeth one among you, whom you know not ; he shall baptize you with the Holy Ghost and with fire ; whose fan is in his hand, and he will thoroughly purge his floor, and gather his wheat into his garner ; but he will burn up the chaff with unquenchable fire.''

The baptism here testified of, and which is of an inward and spiritual nature, is that feeling which brings sorrow, trouble, confusion, horror, dread and despair over our minds : and which at times, causes those who are in comparative innocency, to cry out under a feeling of their poor and weak state, a saviour, or I die ; a redeemer, or I perish forever.—

Are there not many of us, who have experienced this language in the secret of our souls, when our heads have been laid on our pillows, and when we have been ruminating on things relating to time and eternity—when we have sat in our houses, when we have walked by the way, when we have risen up?

And now, what is it that produces these feelings in the mind? What is it that brings sorrow, trouble, fear, dread, and despair over our minds? It is the judgment of the Lord for our sin and disobedience. And we need not look at a great distance and beyond the grave for judgment.— We need not look for a local God seated on his throne, and keeping an account against us for every good or evil action; but even at the present day, the judgment is set, and the books are opened. And if we continue to do evil, these must be the effects,—sorrow, trouble, dread and despair: they will assuredly curse us, and lead us into confusion and distress, in every act of our lives. But if, on the contrary, when we feel trouble for any action, we leave that action and turn away from it, not rowing against wind and tide, and contending with tumultuous billows amid the storm of conflicting elements—if, when we feel sorrow and trouble for an evil action, we avoid that action, and endeavor to be still; and in that calm approach the land, we shall find a place of stability, where we can sing praises to God upon the banks of deliverance.

Here are plain and practical truths. And as certainly as the indulgence of pride, fullness of bread, abundance of idleness, cruelty, ambition, and other evils, have a tendency to afflict mankind, and to operate as a curse upon them: so certainly, will humility, love, mercy, temperance, and patience, confer blessings on every act, and bring peace, joy, and consolation, over our spirits. And our reward is not uncertain—it is not at a great distance—it is not beyond the grave: for the kingdom of heaven is with you. And if we are disobedient unto its laws, we bring ourselves unto the gates of hell. And what are these devils, these tormentors, if they are not the sense of evils which we have committed, and which bring trouble over our minds? Therefore, I feel no hesitation in coming to the conclusion, that every individual who has fallen from the witness for God in his own mind, has crucified God afresh, and put him to an open shame; and every man who has cast out the angel of the divine presence, and cultivated an aversion for all the heavenly dispositions, such an individual constitutes a fallen angel: and every fallen angel is a devil.

Now under this view of the subject, we need not say who shall ascend into heaven to bring Christ down from above? Or, who shall descend into the deep, to bring Christ up from thence? The word is nigh thee, even in thy heart and in thy mouth, to hear it and do it. This principle which reproves for evil, is instructive, for here we come to a knowledge of that which God hath a controversy with, in each individual; and the proud will feel the effects of pride, and if cruel, he will perceive the fatal effects of cruelty, and that which brings sorrow, will create an abhorrence of it. And thus it is, that the blind eyes are opened—thus it is, that the spiritual ears are unstopped, to hear the voice of wisdom; and by the operation of the same process, every malady of the soul becomes healed, and we are raised from a death of sin, to a life of Christ. And this is by the power of the gospel, which is baptizingly preached in every creature. And thus we have a fulfilment of the whole declaration, that the gospel of Christ is the power of God unto salvation to all who believe, whether Jew or Gentile.

Now in the performance of these acts, there is a daily obedience and a daily manifestation. We find that this new law is not statutory but prescriptive, and adapted to every state and condition. And as some are lofty, proud, and fierce; these are brought under sorrow and trouble—brought under the correcting power of what is called conscience; these feel the effects of their own works, and they receive the reward of their own works. "Say ye to the righteous, that it shall be well with him; for they shall eat the fruit of their doings. Wo unto the wicked! it shall be ill with him; for the reward of his hand shall be given him." As we attend daily to these manifestations, they will bring down the mountains of pride, and all those things which are above the witness for God in our souls : and the low and despairing will at times become partakers of the cup of his consolation, and be raised into firmness, the crooked and perverse dispositions will be made straight, and the rough places plain.

Thus mankind, through very different operations of the same baptism, will be brought to that mighty level in which the glory of the Lord will cover the earth, and every earthly and evil propensity will be brought under his influence as the waters cover the sea. Here it is, that we must experience this wilderness of desolation to become an Eden, and this desert "like the garden of the Lord ; joy and gladness shall be found therein, thanksgiving and the voice of melody." And it was this view of the subject that the prophet had, when he saw that coincidence and accordance of all the various dispositions which he describes ; and where the most ravenous and vicious dispositions unite with those the most meek and harmless—"The wolf also shall dwell with the lamb, and the leopard shall lie down with the kid, and the calf, and the young lion, and the fatling, together, and a little child shall lead them. And the cow and the bear shall feed ; their young ones shall lie down together ; and the lion shall eat straw like the ox. And the sucking child shall play on the hole of the asp, and the weaned child shall put his hand on the cockatrice's den. They shall not hurt nor destroy in all my holy mountain : for the earth shall be full of the knowledge of the Lord, as the waters cover the sea."

Thus we see that every rancorous disposition will be brought to meekness, and that there will be none to destroy. These are the effects of the gospel of Christ ; and this is the nature of true christianity. And until these effects are produced, and thus experienced in our minds—though morning, neon, and evening we may pray, and lift up our voice like a trumpet, and bow down the head like a bulrush, and call it prayer, or adopt systems, and speculative theories of religion, all will be useless and unavailing : for the kingdom of God stands not in words, but in power ; not in opinions, but in obedience. It stands not in sentiments, nor in the exertion of our rational faculties in rowing all day through the tempestuous sea of speculation : but it stands in, and is supported by, an intrinsic internal power, which gives us the victory over all opposing dispositions, and in the ark of safety we are raised above all fluctuating elements. And here we come to know a mighty angel to fly through heaven, preaching the everlasting gospel ; not with the wisdom of words, but with power. "And I saw another angel fly in the midst of heaven, having the everlasting gospel to preach unto them that dwell on the earth, and to every nation, and kindred, and tongue, and people ; saying with a loud voice, Fear God, and give glory to him, for the hour of his judgment is come : and worship him that made heaven, and earth, and the sea, and the fountains of waters."

Now, my friends, I have not declared these things unto you boastingly, or as though I had already attained, either were already perfect ; but I trust I am endeavoring to follow after, if haply I may rise into that state which is designed for me, or, as said the apostle, "apprehend that for which I am apprehended of Christ Jesus." And in this I would not direct you unto him as an external offering. But I commend you to God, the author of your existence. And I again commend you unto him, and the word of his grace, which is able to save your souls, and to give you an inheritance among them that are sanctified. And you may individually attain to that state, in which you will see a mighty angel stand with one foot upon the earth, and the other upon the sea : and when every earthly propensity, and every speculative operation shall be brought under his influence, he shall lift up his right hand to heaven and swear by him that liveth forever and ever, who created heaven, and the things that therein are, and the earth and the things that therein are, and the sea and the things which are therein, that time shall be no longer.

SERMON XIV.

DELIVERED BY THOMAS WETHERALD, AT HESTER STREET MEETING, NEW YORK, SUNDAY AFTERNOON, JUNE 4TH, 1826.

"The idols of the heathen are silver and gold, the work of men's hands." They were formed of materials which were the most valuable and delightful in their view. And in all ages it has been proved, that men worship that in which they most delight. There are thousands in the present day, who have said unto gold, by the language of their conduct, thou art my god, and unto fine gold, thou art my confidence. And placing their dependence on these external things—their hopes of happiness on things that perish, they have become entangled in the heathenish nature, and have become worshippers of idols.

And what are the characteristics of these idols? "They have mouths, but they speak not; eyes have they, but they see not. They have ears, but they hear not; neither is there any breath in their mouths." They have the appearance of something which is alive, but they have not the attributes of which life is composed. They have the polish of gold and the beauty of silver, but, after all, they are nothing but dumb idols. "Eyes have they, but they see not; ears have they, but they hear not; neither have they any breath in their mouths. They that make them are like unto them: so is every one that trusteth in them." For these see not with their own eyes, hear not with their own ears, and understand not with their own hearts; but are dependent on the opinions of others. For no idol, whether silver or gold, can promulgate laws for the government of a single individual, splendid as it may appear, or superb as its workmanship may be. It is a dead idol, an inanimate god, and of a corruptible nature : and they that make them are like unto them ; having neither eyes to see, ears to hear, nor hearts to understand. They are dependent on those who made the idols for laws to govern them : they are dependent on systems, opinions, prejudices of education, and tradition, for their views. And thus all are blind together, and fulfil the declaration, "when the blind lead the blind, they both fall into the ditch," and become besmeared and entangled by their own corruptions. But they cannot rise into the beauty of that holiness, which can only be attained by an individual and perspective view of Him, who first created the world and continues to sustain it.

"The idols of the heathen are silver and gold, the work of men's hands. Eyes have they, but they see not ; ears have they, but they hear not ; neither is there any breath in their mouths ; and they that make them are like unto them ; so is every one that trusteth in them." Here are workmen and works all of one nature. And as this is true of idolatry, so, on the contrary, if we are governed by the immediate operation of the spirit of God, the workmen and their works must partake of the same nature, and be governed by the same power, and animated by the same life. The same streams of vitality are united among them, and consequently they are partakers of the same divine nature. Thus they have eyes and they see, ears and they hear, hearts and they understand ; and therefore, they can speak and testify, not what books have told them, or what they may have received from books or men, but they can testify of what their own eyes have seen, their ears heard, and their hands handled of the good word of life and power of the world to come.

Now, my friends, see the mighty distinction and difference between these. Though their idols may be formed of the most valuable materials, and may be embellished with all the splendor of human art, the workmanship complete, the finishing superb, yet they cannot see with their eyes, nor hear with their ears ; neither can they animate us, or direct us to peace and virtue, or to an experience of religion or spiritual truth. But, on the contrary, those who are begotten of God, and who have known Christ brought fourth in themselves—these can learn to see with their own eyes, hear with their own ears, understand with their own hearts, and be converted by their own experience. And here is all the difference that I know of, among the professors of religion. The distinctions are not between Papists and Episcopalians, Lutherans, Methodists, Baptists, or Quakers. No, if there is any distinction, it is between the living and the dead. "For to him that is joined to all the living, there is hope; for a living dog is better than a dead lion." And wherefore? Because a living dog can perform all the functions of which his nature is capable, but the lion, when he is dead, though he may make a formidable appearance, is still fast hastening to corruption. Though he may have the appearance of strength and vigor, still he is dead and inanimate. There is no circulating medium to give vitality to his system, or enable him to perform the functions of a living lion; and he is hastening to that mass of corruption from whence he sprang.

Now there is a query in my mind, and a query with which all are interested more or less. Are we numbered among the living or the dead? Are we animated by the immediate power and life of God? Or are we merely making a profession of his name, and living under the influence of passions and propensities which are discordant with his nature? If we are fulfilling all the rituals of the various religious societies in christendom, and our hearts are not changed, we are only adding hypocrisy to idolatry, and are lying unto God. But if, on the contrary, we are individually endeavoring to do justly, to love mercy, and to walk humbly with our God, though we may belong to no name or religion, and be distinguished by no particular appellation, yet shall these grow in that love which is the crown and diadem of all the saints' assemblies.

Now, my friends, we hear of a great variety of religious principles, opinions, and doctrines. And whence have they their origin? I have been led to look at the time in which

16

Jesus appeared in the flesh : and when his forerunner bore testimony of him, and required of the people that they should repent. And wherefore? Because, said he, "the kingdom of heaven is at hand." Now here was nearly the whole extent of the preaching of John. He baptized with an outward element, which was water, and typical of that which was to succeed it among the Jews, to regulate the passions and affections, and to crucify the lusts ; thus cleansing the heart from dead works, to serve the living God. Now here was designed to be the end of this operation ; for according to the declaration of John, "He must increase, but I must decrease." And when testifying of the coming of the Messiah, and of that baptism which should accompany his inward and spiritual appearing, he said, "I baptize with water ; but there standeth one among you, whom ye know not. He it is, who coming after me, is prefered before me ; he shall baptize you with the Holy Ghost, and with fire." And there are a variety of testimonies recorded in the New Testament, which go to prove the spirituality of this dispensation, and its effects upon the mind of each individual. And there is nothing to induce any of us to believe that this dispensation is adapted to a community of Papists ; because there is nothing which is applied unto them ; neither to Presbyterians, Episcopalians, Baptists, Unitarians, nor Universalists. It is not a religion of this kind or nature. The laws which ought to govern us, come under the influence of the spirit of Jesus Christ. They are of an individual nature, and his baptism is of an individual nature. It stands not in water, nor any outward element. All types have ceased since the coming of our Lord Jesus Christ. The substance has come, which is the resurrection and the life. And shall we go back to beggarly elements, which perish with the using? Why go back to meats and drinks, to washings and carnal ordinances, to days, and times, and months, and years ; and, what if I say with the apostle, unto "the principles of the doctrine of Christ?" But what have we to do with principles and doctrines ? There is opened unto us a new and living way, even that which is within the vail. According to the declaration of the Messiah, "I am the way, the truth. and the life:" and it is this life which produces righteousness, peace, and joy, in every holy spirit.

The baptism of John was a preparatory operation. It was only designed to open the way, according to the declaration. "I am the voice of one crying in the wilderness, prepare ye the way of the Lord, as said the prophet Esaias; make his paths straight." And when these effects are produced, and the paths made straight, what is the consequence? "Every valley shall be exalted, and every mountain and hill shall be made low, and the crooked shall be made straight, and the rough places plain." And as a necessary consequence. "the glory of the Lord shall cover the earth, as the waters cover the sea." Now the apostles were led into this baptism, for they knew its power. Jesus Christ declared unto his disciples before he drank of that deep cup of suffering, which the Jews allotted to him, that it was expedient for him to leave them. And wherefore? Because they had been placing their dependence in an external medium,— they were looking to his doctrines, precepts, and opinions. They wanted to come to an ultimatum in religion. They were not willing to be learning in a progressive manner, to be first young men, then strong men, then elders in Christ. They were willing to abide where they were; they were willing to settle down there. They did not want to try fresh ground; they were afraid of untrodden paths. But he did not want them to settle down in the baptism of John, and the precepts which he had given them. And therefore. he said, "It is expedient for you that I go away; for if I go not away, the Comforter will not come unto you, but if I depart, I will send him unto you." This is the spirit of truth, which the world never can receive, and which it never has received. Its operations can only be understood, when we come under the influence of that principle which speaks peace for every act of obedience. It is here that we come to understand this; and it is only as we come under the influence of this principle of light and life, and under the influence of the Comforter that was promised, that we come to be delivered from the power of the world, with its passions and propensities, the maxims and opinions thereof.

It is only as we come into this state, that we can be delivered from the power of idols, formed of costly materials, but which want vitality, which want that which they have not, that circulating medium which gives life to the whole system. These dumb idols "have eyes, but they see not; ears have they, but they hear not; and they that make them, are like unto them." So it is with all the systems that men have formed, their creeds, confessions of faith, and articles of belief, whatever they may be; made not to rectify the conscience, but to bring the community into bondage to them. They are all of this idolatrous nature.

But as God is one, so is his power one, and it proceeds from the same illimitable source; and therefore, my friends and fellow professors, by whatever name you may be called, for I know no distiction nor difference, I want us to come under the influence of this monitor, who is able to open the understanding: I want us to be actuated by the spirit of God, in whom there is vitality, and not by dead idols; but by one who can open the blind eyes, and unstop the deaf ears of our understanding; one who can give us the victory over every evil propensity, passion, and lust; one who can enable us to fulfil every social, civil, and relative duty; one who can be found, not only at a great distance and beyond the grave, but whose spirit is now teaching us what is to be known of God, for "that which is to be known of God, is manifest in men." And wherefore? "Because God has shown it unto them." And therefore, it was expedient for his followers, that Jesus should go away. "For if I go not away, the Comforter will not come unto you, but if I go away, I will pray the Father, and he will send him unto you; and when he is come, he will remind you of all that I have told."

Now this is conformable to another declaration—"The grace of God that bringeth salvation, hath appeared unto all men, teaching us, that, denying all ungodliness and worldly lusts, we should live soberly, righteously, and godly, in this present world: looking for that blessed hope, and the glorious appearing of the great God, and our Saviour Jesus Christ." And where are we to look for this appearance? Is he not a governor and ruler? is he not the king and wonderful counsellor? And remember "the kingdom of heaven is within you;" and it is there we must look for his appearing, and there we must experience his power. We need not go to a great distance and beyond the grave to find God; we need not descend into the depths to find a devil; for we can find one in ourselves: for every perverted disposition is a contradiction of the divine harmony, and every lust indulged, thus constitutes in us a minister of evil. They are of an antichristian nature, and they are devils.

Now I want us to come into a situation in which we need not look at a great distance, and beyond the grave, for rewards of punishment; I want us to come into that situation which was the design of Jesus, when in speaking to his apostles and followers, he told them, it was expedient that an internal comforter should come, after he should be called away by that act of malevolence and wickedness of the Jews. Here the declaration was fulfilled, that he should bear our sins. And how did he bear them? Did he bear them for you and I when he suffered the utmost stretch of human malevolence in his own body? No: it was not that our sins which we commit should be washed away thereby. But he opened a way for the Jews, who had depended on external offerings; he opened unto them a new and living way into that which is within the vail. And what was his crucifixion? As it was an act of unparalleled wickedness in itself, it could not work the righteousness of God.

I have no hope of salvation in the death of Christ; but in his life and the power of his resurrection, in that divine spirit which actuated him in all his movements, and caused him to be anointed with the oil of gladness above his fellows. And while the apostles continued in this doctrine in the breaking of bread from house to house; while they continued faithful in the performance of these spiritual duties, there were added daily to the church such as should be saved. But as those who were the immediate followers of Jesus, were taken away to receive their rewards, one by one ; there arose another company, another generation ; and these brought more of human learning, together with a little more subtlety in abstruse questions and abstract propositions ; and from hence flowed divisions of sentiment : and the further they removed from the power of God, the more powerful did these abstract propositions become, till they were wrought into a kind of philosophy, which could puzzle but not instruct the mind.

This state continued and increased, till, in two or three centuries, various churches which had been united, became divorced from each other. They soon arrived at a state in which each could assail the other through envy and jealousy : and here was an inlet to still greater evils, which grew and increased. For it is a maxim which cannot be controverted, that every step in evil opens the way for increased wickedness : and on the contrary, every step which we take in the path of obedience to the divine manifestations, has a tendency to strengthen us and prepare us to advance with more firmness in the path of righteousness, which is the path of peace.

And we may remember, that about two centuries after the propagation of this christian dispensation among the Jews, such were the doubts and divisions, that bishops, governors, and rulers, fell into dissensions with one another, and creeds and systems began to be introduced. And from whence did they come? They were produced by the theological seminaries in the land of Egypt, the house of bondage. For here it was that they began, under a perversion of this dispensation, instead of ministers preaching in the demonstration of the spirit of the gospel. And it was in Alexandria, that these differences first originated. And I want us to be careful in tracing these evils ; for they have not their origin in the christian dispensation ; they stand not in the nature of the christian religion itself, but in a perversion and declaration of its principles. It has been by substituting a religion of idols in its place, and oppositions of science, falsely so called, that they have been introduced into the christian religion. And thus darkness was increased day by day, till now instead of cultivating the mind that was in Christ, there was a disposition to show who could become the most subtle reasoners in support of this or the other party. Then councils were called to decide on what should be considered faith, and what not; this was pronounced canonical, and that heretical or heterdox. The books of the Old and New Testament came under this supervision. Some were pronounced canonical, and others heretical; while some which had been pronounced canonical were now become heretical.

Here, my friends, is the origin of this mass of confusion, this mass of false philosophy, this mass of tradition; and here is the foundation of the present systems of the Christian religion. The scriptures, which had thus undergone the revision of various councils, and which, at different times, had been pronounced spurious and canonical, became the ground of faith and practice. They were declared to be the word of God, and the rule of faith and practice. But is the word of God thus changeable, and subject to the caprice of men and the false philosophy of the times? Is it to be supported by opinions and traditions, or to be cast down by the same? No, verily. But that which is the true word of God was from everlasting to everlasting. It is immovable and immutable. It cannot be twisted and turned by the opinions of men. It cannot be shaken. It is divine. It stands in the immutable power of God.

But now the scriptures had become a test of faith and practice; and as the various councils had decided what should be canonical or heretical, so did others abide by the precepts of their leaders. There was a new power created: they had lords over the heritage—a kind of priesthood, who were regularly educated, who declared the opinions that they had imbibed from tradition and education. Here was the ground-work of darkness, and darkness was added to darkness, till mankind were brought into that dismal state of apostacy, which, for many centuries, overspread Europe. The true church fled into the wilderness, and the floods, which the dragon cast out of his mouth, were too high for her to return.

After a while there were other spirits raised up—there

were Calvin, Luther, and others. These were raised up to bear testimony against a few of the superstitions and absurdities of the age in which they lived; and some of them sealed their testimony with their blood, after having borne many persecutions for Christ's sake, and for the sake of the gospel. But their views were dim—they were like a mere twilight; but they were as much as could be borne, in that dark night of apostacy. These individuals were faithful; and, I have no doubt, they were anointed of God: they were stepping stones to the revolution and reformation which was brought about in public sentiment.

But they saw not all; and here is the misery of it, that their followers, like some of old, have wanted to come to an ultimatum in religion, and have therefore been willing to sit down with Calvin and Luther, with full assurance. Instead of attending to that divine light which led them, and instead of advancing from that ground, they settled down upon the platform that they had builded. They merely came into the form of that of which Calvin and Luther had felt the power. And, even at this day, is it not obvious that the Calvinists and Lutherans boast of their originals, but will not step one step further than where these reformers left them? And why is it, that we had rather eat the bread that others have labored for, than use our own? We are willing to become partakers in their religion, but are not willing to come into that state ourselves to which they attained—to understand with our own hearts, and to be converted by our own experience.

In process of time others were raised up, and certain individuals were enabled to make another step further forward: and again the followers of these took their stand, and have stood in the form of that of which the reformers felt the power.. There was a Wesley and a Whitfield who were brought a little on the way—another step; but their followers remain stationary. There are thousands of the followers of these bright and shining lights, who are standing in the form which has been given them; but they are nothing better than dead lions. They have the appearance

of religion, but they want the circulating medium. They
want the power of God; and as they have it not, they are
like the dead lion, formidable in appearance. They are
mighty in external performances, and for want of that humility which is the result of Christian experience, they have
been loud in praying, preaching, and singing. Hence I believe there is in this and other societies, so much of those in-
decent performances which are a disgrace to human nature,
such as dancing, falling down, shouting, and jumping : and
under this animal excitement they have continued till human nature has been wearied with exercise, and, when the
storm has left a calm, this has been called a conversion.—
But it is nothing more than animal excitement, and the calm
is nothing but the cessation of the storm, which has spent
its force.

I want not to carry charges against any society—I am not
blaming the followers of Wesley or Whitfield ; there are
those who have produced the same effects in every society.
Even the followers of Fox, Penn, and Barclay, cannot be
drawn one step further than the place where they left them.
We appeal unto them as fathers, notwithstanding we are
commanded to call no man father or master, "for one is
your master, even Christ, and all ye are brethren." While
we are looking backward, we never can see to go forward.
We know that, in our natural body, we can never move safely
forward while we are looking backward, and so it is in a
spiritual sense. But I want us to come to understand the
nature of these things—to come into the power of religion.

Now, in the dark night of apostacy, which overspread
christendom, the priesthood gained great power over the
consciences of the people : they sat in the place of God,
above all that is called God or worshipped. They assumed
the power and prerogative of pardoning sins, and granting
indulgencies to sin ; which was contrary to the nature and
power of the christian dispensation. Thus they imposed
heavy burthens on the properties and consciences of the people. They made a purgatory and undertook to deliver souls
from purgatory for money, the love of which is the root of
all evil.

Is there any religion in such things as these? Can any man rationally believe religion can consist in such notions as these? No: but it is the result of tradition, education, and credulity. Men may attempt to believe it, but never can believe it, except they have the minds of children; for if we believe this, it is without evidence. It is a faith, but it is not a saving operative faith; it is not powerful in itself; it is not that faith which works by love, and which is saving in its effects.

But when the reformation came, so great was the love of money, and so deeply rooted were the priesthood, that it has never been expelled from any of these reformed systems; and even at the present day are not teachers preaching for hire and divining for money? And even in this boasted land of liberty, they are ready to declare war against all who do not put into their mouths. I have said it, and I am not afraid to say it again, that I have never seen an account of any nation where the inhabitants were in more absolute ecclesiastical bondage than in this boasted land of liberty. They appoint teachers, believe their declarations, and under the influence of these false opinions they indulge a spurious and interested ministry, a ministry which stands not in the power of God, but in the wisdom of man.

And have not their opinions and creeds, sentiments and practices, subverted the Christian church? Yet how zealously have mankind engaged in support of theological seminaries; and for the support of gospel ministers, so called? But it is an absurdity! It is an impossibility, it is out of the power of man, and of the arts, sciences, and philosophy, to constitute one single solitary minister of the gospel. I know of no medium by which a minister of the gospel can come rightly to stand in that station, except he be called of God, as Aaron was called. He cannot be qualified to preach the gospel, except in the school of Christ. And what is it to be learned there? I apprehend, the principal part of the learning necessary, nay, all, may be acquired in the school of Christ. It teaches us to regulate every affection, to crucify every passion, to subdue and overcome every lust, and every propensity which separates from the source of purity. And it is not till these effects are produced, that we can ever come rightly to be ministers of the gospel of our Lord and Saviour Jesus Christ. We may be ministers of idols, which can neither see nor speak, and in which there is not the breath of life: but we cannot be ministers of the living God unless we are governed and actuated by his power and spirit, and receive immediately of his divine inspiration. Here we came into obedience to the word of God, and this becomes our rule of faith and practice.

And is it not obvious, that when men with interested minds undertake to preach the gospel of Christ, they will preach conformably to their own views? Is it possible that men, receiving one, two, three, or four thousand dollars a year, can faithfully testify their sense of the slips and wickedness of those who employ them? No; this fault must be covered, and that weakness overlooked, because they preach for hire, and divine for money, "whose God is their belly, and whose glory is in their shame, who mind earthly things." It is the blind leading the blind, and both must fall into the ditch. And have they not formed an abundance of societies, which bear the name of benevolent societies, missionary societies, bible societies, mite societies, cent societies, and an abundance of others: and what is the mainspring of all these? It is money,—it is not any particular virtue, or any requisition of the divine power upon their own minds; but money, money, is the mainspring of action. And do we not hear daily complaints, that when this is withdrawn they must fall to the ground?

Is then the church of God going to be built up with money, the love of which is the root of evil? No, verily : if ever the foundation is rightly laid, it must be laid where it was declared that it must be laid : "For other foundation can no man lay, than that is laid, which is Jesus Christ. Now, if any man build upon this foundation, gold, silver, precious stones, wood, hay, stubble; every man's work shall be made manifest: for the day shall declare it, because it shall be revealed by fire; and the fire shall try every man's work of what sort it is. If any man's work abide, which he hath built thereupon, he shall receive a reward."— Though he may build of these materials, he can only receive the reward of his own works; but this will not bring peace from God, and advance him in the way of the kingdom of heaven. "If any man's work shall be burnt, he shall suffer loss: but he himself shall be saved; yet so as by fire." Because having submitted to the fire, its operation is to rectify every passion, lust, and perversion of the mind; and this is the baptism of the Holy Ghost, which is represented as operating like fire against all unrighteousness and ungodliness of men.

How vain and how futile is the idea that men whom men have chosen, called, and appointed to explain abstract, abstruse, metaphysical speculations upon christianity, can ever become rightly qualified for the ministry of Christ? They may be able to administer the ordinances of the church—to wash us in water and call it baptism—to administer bread and wine and call it communion; but all the waters of the sea can never cleanse a soul of one sin or lust. And all the bread and wine, among all the nations of the earth, can never nourish up the soul unto everlasting life.

They may say that all these are typical of good things yet to come—that they are figurative and symbolical. But, my fellow professors, are we yet as children under the schoolmasters of types, figures, and symbols, when the law is fulfilled, and when the power is come—that power which is the resurrection and the life? If ever we are baptized into the nature of Christ, it must be into the nature of Christ's death, —we must be crucified with him. It was his human nature that was crucified, and it must be our natural affections and corrupt views. This the apostle had a view of, when he declared, "I am crucified with Christ: nevertheless I live; yet not I, but Christ liveth in me; and the life which I now live in the flesh, I live by the faith of the Son of God, who loved me and gave himself for me."

Now that baptism which is of water, it is obvious, can never cleanse the soul of one single sin, and neither can bread and wine nourish up a single soul to eternal life. But if we come under the baptism of the holy Ghost, which operates as fire upon all unrighteousness and ungodliness of men, we shall not come under the influence of a teacher whom men can pay, whose god is his belly, whose glory is his shame, who minds earthly things. The sublime truths of this dispensation need not to be brought under the power of any teacher, but the "minister of the sanctuary, and of the true tabernacle, which God has pitched, and not man ;" and this teacher is "Christ in you, the hope of glory." And as we come under the influence of that baptism which is spiritual, we shall find that it will bring sorrow and trouble over our minds for every thing which is evil.

Is there an individual among us who can say that which is not true, and feel no sorrow for it? We can hide this before our fellow men, but there is a witness for God in our own souls, which will bring confusion, horror, and dread, for every act of evil. And have we not all experienced conviction for these evils, in such a way as to convince us that it is not the result of education, tradition, or any system which we have adopted? No. It is God in man. It is "Christ in you, the hope of glory." It is Christ manifest in your flesh, come to rule in his own kingdom, and to govern by his own laws. And "a sceptre of righteousness is the sceptre of his kingdom." And it is this that rules with a rod of iron over all unrighteousness and ungodliness of men. And we can none of us commit an evil act with impunity.

I know it is written, that the conscience may become seared as with a red hot iron. Well, my friends, agreed that it may become seared, so that there is no feeling in the part which is burned, still there may be feeling under it ; and the feeling produced by a burn is painful. It is not the dead flesh, but the living flesh which will continue to feel as long as life continues in us. And none will believe that spirit can be annihilated, of course it will continue to burn and not be quenched. For I have no idea that we can sin till we shall not feel the wound, for God is just ; and as certainly as we transgress against that law which is written in every heart, so certainly shall we be delivered over to the tormenters ; so long shall we find sorrow, trouble, confusion, horror, dread, and despair. Have not many of you heard the drunkard lament over his fallen state ? Have not many of us heard those addicted to vices, desiring to be delivered from such evils,—very much like the apostle formerly : "Who shall deliver me from the body of this death ?" But afterwards he could thank God, through Jesus Christ, whose power operated to his deliverance from every perverse disposition.

As we attend to this power, which is the baptism of the Holy Ghost, it will beget an abhorrence in our minds, so that when we come to feel this, we shall be ready to start back and say, "Who among us shall dwell with the devouring fire ?" Here we dread its operation—"Who among us shall dwell with everlasting burnings ?" O, my friends, this speaks what we want to experience, and what we want a knowledge of. For its operations are what we want, to remove the dross, tin, and reprobate silver—those deceptions which exist in the mind that has never been reduced to give up every thing contrary to the divine will, and without any partiality. And when the effects which are required, are produced by this baptism, the mind purified, every affection regulated, and drawn into the divine influence, our passions crucified and slain, every lust subdued, body, soul, and spirit brought under the influence of the gospel of the Lord Jesus Christ, it ceases its fiery operations, and then we can dwell with God, because all combustible matter is consumed, the wood, hay, and stubble are burnt up. We are not now afraid of this burning, for these can become partakers of divine consolations. For they know, that "he who walketh righteously, and speaketh uprightly ; he that despiseth the gain of oppressions, that shaketh his hands from holding bribes, that stoppeth his ears from hearing of blood, and shutteth his eyes from seeing evil : he shall dwell on high : his place of defence shall be the munitions of rocks ; bread shall be given him ; his waters shall be sure. Thine eyes shall see the king in his beauty, they shall behold the land that is very far off."

Where now are the wise men ? "Where is the Scribe ?

Where is he that counted the towers?" Is the mind dependent on their wisdom? No: it is useless to those who come under this divine influence for themselves. For they can testify that which their own eyes have seen, and that which their own ears have heard, of the good word of life, and the powers of the world to come. These are not scared; they are healed. And I want it to be understood as my view, that we can never, while under the influence of any carnal passions, feelings, affections, or lusts, become partakers of this divine harmony, and know our habitation fixed upon that immutable rock, where all the powers of death, hell and the grave, cannot prevail against us. Neither can we as societies, regulated and systematized under the influence of creeds, systems, articles of belief, or confessions of faith, as regularly organized bodies, ever be admitted into the kingdom of heaven; because the power of the gospel operates upon each individual. All the passions must be regulated, all the affections crucified, and all the lusts subdued: and then we come individually into the third heaven, where we may hear things which are not lawful to be uttered. As said the apostle, "I knew a man in Christ about fourteen years ago, whether in the body I cannot tell, or whether out of the body I cannot tell; God knoweth: such an one caught up to the third heaven, where he heard unspeakable words, which it is not lawful for a man to utter."

And there are many heavens. There are many of us placing our hopes of happiness on external objects, and who are indulging the propensities of a corrupt nature. And wherever our hope of happiness is fixed, there is our state of enjoyment—there is our heaven; for heaven is not a mere place, it is a state. And while we are grovelling under the influence of animal, or instinctive faculties and feelings— while we are regulated by these, and our passions are without a governor, we cannot advance farther than the lower heaven. There are many who come farther than this, and take a stand in the second heaven. There are many who are making a profession of religion, and join themselves to this, or that society, in which they become zealous in the performance of external rituals, and thus many of them bear the character of good moralists, good husbands, good fathers, good friends, and honorable tradesmen. These often take delight in their name, and assume a kind of pharisaical self-righteousness. Here they take their lodgings in the second heaven. But the mysteries of the kingdom of heaven are not opened: they are above their view. They cannot give an account of the light in themselves, by its operations. They believe,—but wherefore? Because they have been taught. But who taught them? Their ministers and parents, or those who had gone before them. It was not the result of their own experience, but it was the result of superstition and tradition. It was not the work of God, but the work of man: and it stands not in the power of God. These, therefore, cannot advance further than the second heaven, where, though they may be less exposed to the censure of men in their situation, still it is equally dangerous with that of those who are influenced by the indulgence of animal or instinctive propensities.

But when they leave these things, and come under the regulating influence of the divine power, they know that there is a principle which reproves us for every evil thought, word, and action, thus bringing sorrow, trouble, and confusion over our minds. Here is communion with God. And as we attend to these feelings, and as the dispositions which produced them have been purged out ; and when they have disappeared, then we adopt the language,—thy will, O God, be done. We can adopt the language of Christ, "Thy will be done on earth, as it is done in heaven." Then we shall be prepared for the joys of divine consolation ; then it is, that the spirit of judgment and burning loses its awful character, and appears as a spirit of judgment to them that sit in judgment, and for strength to them that turn the battle to the gates.

It was this that taught the hands of David to war and his fingers to fight against his soul's enemies. It was this which enabled those who were faithful to it, to subdue kingdoms, work righteousness, obtain promises, stop the mouths of lions, quench the violence of fire, escape the edge of the sword, out of weakness to be made strong, to wax valiant in fight, and turn to flight the armies of the aliens. And thus has been produced in all ages, great effects, which can not be attributed to any other power,—introducing into that which is good, that which is holy, that which is heavenly. Here they are in the third heaven, where they hear things not lawful to be uttered, and which never can be understood by man till he comes to hold communion with God the Father, through the spirit of his Son ; and know him to be what he called himself, the Saviour, the Christ. And wherefore? Because we shall know him to be unto us wisdom, righteousness, sanctification, and redemption, if we have not formed systems of our own, but minded the same divine rule, and walked in the same things ; experiencing him to draw us step by step along. For the axe is laid unto the root of the tree of corruption in the mind. He has placed the axe unto the root of the tree, and every tree that brings not forth good fruit, every disposition in the human mind, which has a tendency to separate us from God, the source of purity, must be cut down, the branches wither, the leaves fade, and the fruit be destroyed, by this cutting down.

But, my friends, we must come to see the necessity of coming unto God, the Judge of all. We are not called to Mount Sinai, where the law was given in the midst of darkness, and thunderings, and lightnings, the sound of a trumpet, and the voice of words ; but we are called to Mount Zion, and unto the city of the living God, the heavenly Jerusalem, where are the spirits of the just made perfect ; where there is a holy harmony—where there is heavenly union—where we can sing everlasting praises to his name. And not because we have been taught these things by men, but because we know what it is to be brought out of the bondage of sin, to stand as on a sea of glass mingled with fire ; for all the corrupt materials of wood, hay, and stubble, have been removed from our minds. And when we stand on this sea of glass, the fire can never make any impression on us ; therefore when we stand on this sea we can sing "the song of Moses the servant of God, and the song of the lamb, saying, great and marvellous are thy works, Lord God Almighty; just and true are thy ways, thou King of saints. Who shall not fear thee, O Lord, and glorify thy name? for thou only art holy; for all nations shall come and worship before thee; for thy judgments are made manifest.''

Some may be ready to conclude, that this system will strike at the root of religion: and it is at the root of all false religion that I would strike. If we only cut off the branches, the corrupt tree may afterwards recover; but I want to see every beastly disposition slain. I want us to come into that divine harmony in which we can sing praises to the living God, and worship him in the beauty of holiness, and in newness of spirit and of life. And when we come into this state we shall know an end to all divisions and dissensions—we shall know an end to every thing which has brought all these many miseries upon mankind. For wherever the spirit of God is, there is love; "for God is love; and he that dwelleth in love, dwelleth in God, and God in him." Where love is the governing principle it will cast out hatred; and where humility governs the mind it will cast out its oppo-site, pride; and where temperance governs the mind, it will cast out intemperance. And every heavenly disposition, when coming to operate in the heart, will cast out its oppo-site, for they cannot dwell together. And if we are under the influence of these heavenly dispositions we shall experi-ence all our enemies cast out; and this must bring an end to all wars and fighting among nations, squabbles in neigh-borhoods, and contentions among individuals.

This will enable us to be good husbands, to love our wives and not to be bitter against them. It will regulate every affection, disposition, and passion: and it is this and this alone that can enable wives to be "obedient to their own husbands." And what is this obedience? It is an obedi-ence to that divine love which ought to be the governing principle of every husband's heart. This will lead to a clo-ser union, closer than natural affection; the man governing the woman, love governing each. Here will be divine harmony, which conflicting sentiments can never break. Because it stands not in the wisdom of man, but in the operative power of God. And do we not know, that it was in this view, the apostle spoke. He had no illusion to the inferiority of women; but man represents the understanding, and he was representing woman as the affections and feelings: and when these become united they are helpmetes. The feelings will take the edge from the asperity of the rougher nature, while the strength of the judgment will guide and govern the feelings. Here is that holy communion which constitutes marriage. Many are united together in what have been called the bands of matrimony, who never were married. And what is marriage? It is not merely an external ceremony; but when minds are brought under the regulating influence of that love in which the feelings submit to the judgment, those who are united in those bands are married in an holy harmony, and the natural affections are sanctified by divine love. These are enabled to fulfil their duties one to another, and to those over whom they have charge. Thus they are enabled to fill the station of fathers and mothers.

But, my friends, how are we to be prepared to fill these stations, while acting under the influence of violent passions, and feelings of anger and hatred, or any of those things which can alienate the affections from one another—while acting under the influence of dispositions in which the feelings, judgments, or imaginations, are formed on the platform of corruption? This is a situation in which we can become helpmetes one to another only in temporal and eternal ruin!— not helpmetes in our advancement to that city whose walls are salvation and whose gates are praise.

I want us, therefore, individually to come under the influence of that which operates upon the understanding, feelings, judgment, and affections, and which will not only lead us into every duty required of us by God, but will enable us to filfil our duties one to another. Here, also, our heads will not be so full of religion, as that we shall not be anxious respecting external performances. But all our actions will be so regulated, as to bring glory to God in our whole conduct.

Here Christ being begotten and brought forth, we are enabled to sing the heavenly anthem which always has accompanied the advent of the Saviour: "Glory to God in the highest, peace on earth, good will to men." And this will be found, not merely a vocal acclamation, but will rise from a heart replete with love to God; and, influenced by divine wisdom and the feelings excited by divine love, we shall be enabled to fill all the avocations of time. And when we come under the influence of these harmonizing feelings, if difficulties occur,—if we are brought into sickness, or tried with adversity,—when our head is on a rolling pillow, and when death itself shall approach our dwelling, this principle, which has been our morning portion, will be the staff of our old age, and our evening song.

How much better is it to dwell in these heavenly dispositions, under the influence of this regulating principle, than to indulge all the feelings and passions of our perverted nature—such as "pride, fullness of bread, and abundance of idleness." While these are indulged, we may pray once, twice, or thrice a day, bow down the head like a bulrush, or lift up the voice like a trumpet; we may perform family worship, so called, by calling our families around us, and by reading or repeating to them, in a dead, dry, and formal manner, a form of words; but this is only adding hypocrisy to sin, for we worship only dumb idols, formed or created by ourselves. And there is too much of this worship—too much preaching, praying, and singing, in public and in private. I don't want to discourage any right exercise. I only want that there should be less religion, and more righteousness in the land. I want us to come nearer the great pattern set us. I know not of any New Testament account of Psalms being sung, but once; and that was when Jesus and his disciples went forth into the garden in the cool of the day. But I never heard that they sung any Psalms in the assemblies of the people. Neither do I believe that we can find one Psalm, in the whole collection usually employed in churches, which would be adapted to an assembly like this.

Can we now begin and sing: "Rivers of tears run down mine eyes, because they keep not thy laws:" when, perhaps, many of us have never known what it was to have our hearts converted, and brought into judgment because of our own sin? Or can we say, "As the heart panteth after the water brooks, so panteth my soul after thee, O God," when we have never known what it was to give up to that feeling which would draw us nigh to him, but have been living under the influence of our natural feelings and passions? And I believe, if we ever come rightly to sing unto God, it must be when we are delivered from these things. It has instructed me, to look at Israel while in the land of Egypt and surrounded by Pharoah and his host. It was a time of deep humiliation—it was no time for singing. But when a way had been made through the deep; when the sea had been commanded and it obeyed, and stood in an heap on either side till they had passed through in safety, and their enemies had been drowned ; when they had seen his salvation—then could they rejoice and sing upon the banks of deliverance. "I will sing unto the Lord, for he hath triumphed gloriously. The horse and his rider hath he thrown into the sea. The Lord is my strength and song, and he is become my salvation. He is my God, and I will prepare him an habitation ; my father's God, and I will exalt him."

Here was a song adapted to the occasion: It was not the experience of David, set to the music of Handel. It was not the music of one, and the style of another—nor was it any set form of words ; but the feeling of the whole nation, for all had triumphed. Pharaoh's chariots and his hosts had he cast into the sea—his chosen captains were also drowned in the Red Sea, with the horse and his rider.

Now when we have experienced the same deliverance, and overcoming of our souls' enemies, we shall have each a word of consolation in our own hearts, and we can make melody unto God—we can sing with the spirit, and with the understanding also. For our understandings will know the operation of the spirit—it will be sealed upon our own minds. Thus we shall be enabled to sing unto the most high God, with the spirit and the judgment, and to make sweet melody unto him in our hearts.

We have also oftentimes seen and heard long prayers, both extempore and written. I have seen prayers written and printed—prayers to be used at all times and all seasons, of all lengths and dimensions, and adapted to every purpose, before meat and after meat. And these have been used by individuals whose almost every act was in direct contradiction to the purity and holiness, and that divine love which are the characteristics of every follower of Christ. Now if we come to pray aright, we must pray with the spirit and the understanding also.

And what is prayer? Is it a form of words? Is it bowing down the head like a bulrush, and lifting up the voice like a trumpet? Will you call this prayer, or an acceptable offering unto God? When there was a fast called, a solemn assembly sanctified, what was to sanctify the fast? "Sanctify a fast, call a solemn assembly, gather the people, sactify the congregation, assemble the elders, gather the children, and those that suck the breast. Let the bridegroom go forth of his chamber, and the bride out of her closet. Let the priests, the ministers of the Lord, weep between the · porch and the altar, and let them say, spare thy people, O Lord, and give not thy heritage to reproach, that the heathen should rule them. Wherefore should they say among the people, where is their God?" Let all situations be brought forth, and come under the divine influence of the spirit of God. Let the priests and ministers, or all the heavenly dispositions, stand as between the porch and the altar—let them pray unto the Lord, "Give not thine heritage to reproach, that the heathen should rule over them. Wherefore should say among the people, where is thy God?"

Now when we come thus to pray, we shall do it with the spirit and the understanding. We shall not pray statedly, once, twice, or three times a day, but in every act of our lives we shall know worship; when we are at our labor, when we walk by the way, when we lie down, and when we rise up. Then will our services be acceptable unto God, "as in the days of old, and as in former years." This is the fast which the Lord hath chosen : "to loose the bands of wickedness, to undo the heavy burdens, and to let the oppressed go free, and that ye break every yoke. Is it not to deal thy bread to the hungry, and that thou bring the poor that are cast out to thy house? When thou seest the naked, that thou cover him ; and that thou hide not thyself from thine own flesh?" Here now is a fast acceptable unto God, and one that will bring peace to our own minds.

Let us look a little at that prayer which was taught by Jesus Christ to his disciples. "Our Father which art in heaven." Now we can never know him to be our Father, till we are created into the same power, and brought forth in the same life ; and not till then, can we properly say, "Our Father which art in heaven." And when we are living in obedience to that which is manifest in all hearts, then we can pray, "Hallowed be thy name, thy kingdom come, thy will be done ;" because if we are keeping his statutes and laws, his spirit will govern us, and then we can pray, "Give us this day our daily bread." And wherefore? Because we have formed no system for our government : we are not looking to the carnal systems and opinions of men ; we are not looking to performances which other men can do for us. And therefore, we can adopt the language of Christ, "Give us this day our daily bread, and forgive us our trespasses, as we forgive those who trespass against us." And under the influence of this principle, we shall feel a being delivered from evil. "Deliver us from evil, for thine is the kingdom, and the power, and the glory." We can ascribe this, because every one of us may thus experience the power of supplication to rest upon us. And it is here, that we can come to feel, that these supplications are precious in the sight of God, as the evening and morning sacrifice, or as incense offered up.

And these prayers, these spiritual oblations, can be offered in our daily avocations—when we sit in our houses, when we walk by the way, when we lie down, and when we rise up. And when we come to know this, the voice of the true shepherd, then we shall know the gospel preached baptizingly in every creature. It is the same spirit which opens the understanding, which outwardly unstopped the deaf ears, opened the blind eyes, and healed the maladies of their bodies; among the Jews; and which raised them from the dead. It is the same principle which yet operates spiritually; which unstops the deaf ears of our understanding, heals the maladies of the soul, even unto leprosy: which raises from a depth of sin, into the life of Christ. And thus we become united together with God; and as many as are led by the spirit of God, they are the sons of God. "For ye have not received the spirit of bondage again to fear: but ye have received the spirit of adoption, whereby we cry, Abba, Father." The spirit itself beareth witness with our spirit, that we are the children of God. And if children, then heirs; heirs of God, and joint heirs with Christ. If so be that we suffer with him, that we may be also glorified together.

These he is not ashamed to call his brethren. Here is divine harmony, in which all dissension will come to an end, and in which wars and fightings will be known no more. "And they shall beat their swords into ploughshares, and their spears into pruning hooks. Nation shall not lift up sword against nation, neither shall they learn war any more." Because all evil dispositions will be rooted out. And the ardent desire of my soul is, that we may be delivered from that religion which stands not in righteousness, and from the power thereof. And that we may come immediately into the spirituality of that gospel which is our pride and our boast, and cease from our present grievous misconduct, and disobedience to its precepts, and know every ministering angel of God to rule in our souls, and every adverse spirit to be weakened thereby and cast out. Then we can sing unto the Lord, and rejoice in his salvation; and can testify from whence this salvation proceeds, because we shall have to know every operation in our own experience.

It is written, "Except a man be born again, he cannot see the kingdom of God." And can a man be born of the spirit of God, without his own knowledge? There never was a natural birth without trouble and sorrow. So here, our passions, affections, and lusts, are so dear to us, that it is painful for us to feel them eradicated and slain by the revelation of divine power ; but the operation must be borne, if ever we become to be inhabitants of that city whose walls are salvation, and whose gates are praise. And the inhabitants of that city never did and never can become a people dwelling in iniquity ; but every high and lofty disposition will be brought down, and every low and desponding disposition will be encouraged, and every rough and crooked disposition made straight, and every rough place plain.

And now, my friends, "come with me from Lebanon. Look from the top of Amana, from the top of Shenir and Hermon, from the mountains of the leopards, from the lions' dens ;" from all these high and lofty dispositions ; all these beastly natures in which many of us have too much indulged. Let us come into the nature and meekness of the lamb—into that lamb-like nature which Christ was, and we shall experience the same peace, the same joy, the same consolation, which the righteous in all ages have experienced, and which is the effect of communion with God, through the spirit of our Lord Jesus Christ, which is the Word of God, and which was in the beginning with God, and which was God. And this was not the scriptures, but the Word of God which created and sustains the world. And this power is unlimited in its operations, and saving in its effects. And as we come under the influence of this principle, it will harmonize every feeling of the mind, give us to see the beauties of nature, and of the author of nature's works. We shall not be looking at the blaze of beauty which may burst around us from the works of his animal or vegetable creation merely, but we shall look through all, up to nature's

God. There will be a hymn of gratitude raised in our souls, and we can unite with the poet:—

> "These are thy glorious works, parent of good,
> Almighty! thine this universal frame,
> Thus wond'rous fair; thyself how woud'rous then!
> Unspeakable, who sit's above these heavens,
> To us invisible, or dimly seen
> In these thy lower works; yet these declare
> Thy goodness beyond thought, and pow'r divine.
> Speak, ye who best can tell, ye sons of light,
> Angels; for ye behold him, and with songs
> And choral symphonies, day without night,
> Circle his throne rejoicing; ye, in heaven,
> On earth, join all ye creatures to extol
> Him first, him last, him midst, and without end."

Thus we shall receive instruction immediately from the operation of Christ's spirit, which will show us every evil. Our understandings will be opened for the reception of every truth essential to our salvation. And all the circumstances with which we are surrounded will be lessons of instruction; and we shall be enabled to look through nature, up to nature's God.

That this may become the experience of each of us, is the earnest desire of my heart. And now, in conclusion, I finally bid you farewell in the Lord, and in the power of his love, desiring that he will cause our deliverance, so that we may praise his mercy upon the banks of deliverance, who remaineth to be glorious in holiness.

SERMON XV.

DELIVERED BY THOMAS WETHERALD, AT FRIENDS' MEETING, WILMINGTON, DELAWARE, JUNE, 8TH, 1826.

It is a truth "that God hath made man upright ; but they have sought out many inventions." And in nothing, I apprehended, has the invention of man had so great a tendency to frustrate the designs of omnipotence, as in those subjects connected with religion.

What is religion in itself? It is an operative principle. It is God in each of our souls, reproving condemning, and bringing into sorrow, trouble, and condemnation, for every offence which we commit against the divinity. And as we submit unto this, we shall also experience joy, peace, and consolation, for every act of obedience unto this same divinity.

Here is the sum total of religion. And it is as we attend unto these individual manifestations, that we come to experience a growth in grace, and in the knowledge of the truth. And there needs none of the inventions of man ; but if we attend immediately unto the manifestations of the principle, we shall advance from a state of negative purity, into a state of positive virtue ; and into communion with God, the Father of spirits. And we shall know his life to be our life, and his spirit to nourish up our souls into this life, which is life everlasting.

But let us look a little at the systems which the ingenuity of man has invented, by which they impose on us a variety of circumstances which are totally unconnected with our natures, and which cannot be applied to us as individuals ; which are applicable to us only as a community. And they so evidently betray their origin, that it has often been a matter of surprise to me, that mankind will be so hood-winked, while they are bound under systems so full fraught with absurdity. These impose on us a certain routine of belief. And from whence is this belief drawn? In some cases from the views of the ancient heathens—in others they have been devised by the ingenuity of man in later ages—and some, perhaps, have been formed of the two combined, thus producing a heterogeneous mixture which passes for faith, and by many is looked upon as such. But it conveys no knowledge of God, for there is no knowledge of God contained in it; and none of us can convey that which we have not in our possession. Therefore these systems being built upon a sandy foundation, the superstructure must fall.

These systems impose a routine of rites, ceremonies, and ordinances; and these are called worship. But their effect is only upon our imagination and external senses; it has no tendency to bring us to the footstool of God, or to bring us into that spirit in which we can alone adopt the language, Abba, Father: nor to reduce the spirit of our minds to that state in which perfect love will cast out all fear. Were our minds brought under the influence of the divine spirit, which is of a universal nature, the language of every soul, brought under this operation, would assuredly be, Abba, Father. And the anthem, which has always been sung on the advent of the Messiah, would be found on our tongues:—"Glory to God in the highest, and on earth peace, good will toward men."

Now that which has been dignified with the name of religion, bears ample testimony of its origin, for it leads into strife and enmity. And is this a characteristic of the divinity of the gospel of Jesus Christ? No. It is not obvious that the features of these systems bear evident marks of their founders? Some have approached much nearer the truth than others; and others again have been much more remote. But in one thing they have all agreed in a very remarkable manner, and that is a full and convincing proof of the corruptibility of their origin:—they have evidently imposed,

not only systems of belief, which pass for faith, and ceremonies, which pass for worship, but, under the influence of interested motives, they have imposed their avaricious feelings
upon the community, and under their constitutions have applied to the benefit of the few, what they have taken from
the many. The multitude are made to serve the interest of
a few individuals—men of interested minds, and, what if I
say, reprobates concerning the true faith.

The whole of this system is corrupt and without foundation. And notwithstanding all the preaching, praying,
singing, and baptizing with water ; notwithstanding all the
principles and doctrines which the invention of man has so
beautifully systematized ; yet all these cannot produce the
desired effect. Because they can not remove one single
stumbling stone, which separates us from the divinity. The
whole of this systematized religion, which has been adapted
to communities, has not that individual nature which will
regulate one inordinate passion. It can never crucify one
solitary lust. Hence it is, that the Christian world, as it
consists at the present day, and all the individual members
of the Christian church, who are built up in the inventions
of man, form a component part of "mystery Babylon the
great, the mother of harlots and abominations of the earth."
And it must be obvious to every reflecting mind, that religion has wonderfully increased in our land. And as religion
has increased, very much in the same ratio rites and ceremonies have increased ; and as they have increased, genuine
christianity has gradually declined.

Under this view of the subject, these systems must necessarily be judged rotten to the very core. And where is there
a remedy for a disease, so rotten, so unsound and alarming?
It never can correct itself—there must be a counteracting
power ; and this is not to be found in opinions and sentiments, or in what are called principles and doctrines of religion, but in our own hearts, and there only. And when we
are willing to come under the influence of that principle
which is God in man, or Christ manifest in your flesh—

"Christ in you the hope of glory"—then we shall believe, and the foundation of this belief is the knowledge of God.

The systems which the ingenuity of man has invented, lead directly into a kind of polytheism, in accordance with the views of the heathen. They have already three Gods in one person. But this is wholly contrary to our views of the attributes of God, and contrary to the scripture testimony, which declares that God is one, and his name one. "Is there a God besides me? Yea, there is no God; I know not any." "I, even, I, am the Lord, and besides me there is no saviour."

What is God? Is he a mere isolated being, placed in a heaven at a great distance, sitting upon a throne, and taking notes of all our conduct, and placing them before him, to be brought forth at a day yet to come? Is this the idea which we entertain of the Deity? To be sure it is in accordance with the systems which the ingenuity of man has invented; but it is not in accordance with the nature of the divinity, nor with our own experience, in relation to his attributes. Even at the present day, hour, and moment, we are brought to judgment—the judgment is set, and the books are opened: because God is not only omnipotent and omniscent, but he is omnipresent—he fills all place, and all space. We need not look up to heaven, and say, who shall bring him down from above, nor into the depths, to call him up from thence. For what saith the spirit? "The word is very nigh unto thee, in thy mouth, and in thy heart, that thou mayest do it." "In the beginning was the word, and the word was with God, and the word was God: the same was in the beginning with God: all things were made by him," and without his immediate operation, was nothing made that was made. "In him was life, and the life was the light of men." This word was life and light, and it is unto this divine light, this operative power of God in the soul of each of us, that I want to direct all our attention; and not to any of the systems which the ingenuity of man has invented. And when we come under the operation of that divine illimitable principle we obtain a knowledge of God, through the operation of his spirit. Hence our faith is firm, because it is not built on another's experience, or the ingenuity of another's invention. Thus we can testify, what our eyes have seen, our ears heard, and our hands have handled, of the word of life, and of the powers of the world to come.

Another inspired penman, testifies of the universality of the divinity, in this manner, "It is high as heaven, what canst thou do? Deeper than hell, what canst thou know?" And there are a variety of scripture testimonies to this effect. But is there not a testimony superior to all others, engraven indelibly on our souls? Are there not testimonies linked one with another, as closely woven as a garment? And yet each thread, if sound and true, will assuredly bear its share of the burthen, because they are not become rotten. But they which are woven by the inventions of man, cannot bear the burthen; and though man may attempt to cover himself with a garment of this corruptible texture—"the bed is shorter than that a man can stretch himself upon it: and the covering narrower, than that he can wrap himself in it."

I have been instructed in this meeting, by an account which the apostle gives of the righteousness of the saints, which is compared to fine linen, clean and white. Now, my friends, what is this linen composed of? It is composed of many very fine threads, so nicely woven together, as to give beauty and strength to the whole. These threads being combined, receive strength from one another; and so it is with christians, if they are daily under the influence of this divine principle,—every act of their lives, and every thought will form a fibre like unto the threads of the linen. And as they become united together, our whole lives will become a tissue of regularity, union, and cementing strength, beautifully compared to a garment. And I am also convinced, that it is only by this uniformity of thought, word and action, produced by the power of God in the soul, that we ever can experience that peace which passeth all understanding; or ever come to know the only true God, and Jesus Christ whom he hath sent. And on the contrary, if we neglect this operation, he will "laugh at our calamity, and

mock when our fear cometh." We shall become linked together, united, and woven, and covered with a garment of
our own corruptions.

· Now let us look at this picture a little, and see if it is not
in accordance with what we have witnessed of this principle:
and see if we have not found our actions, though we may
have been at a great distance from each other, varied in consequence of a connection, and which connection has had an
influence over our lives. Every act of obedience to a good
principle, gives strength to the mind, and weaves into the
garment, something of a heavenly nature, which may be
compared unto fine linen. Thus every act of obedience produces strength; and every act of disobedience, and forgetfulness of God, produces weakness, and gives a predominancy
to those dispositions which lead into sorrow, confusion, destruction, and death. There are many different views taken
of this subject in the scriptures, but they all lead to one
point. In the old covenant, under the laws of Moses, the
people were led into the use of meats, drinks, and washings,
as typical of the cleansing operation of the spirit, and that
nourishment whereby the soul is supported and nourished
unto eternal life; and there are many beautiful allusions
made to this. There was a priesthood instituted by divine
appointment from amongst men. But wherefore? Because
the people had sought out so many inventions, that their
hearts had become hardened; and therefore, he gave them
statutes which were not good, and judgments by which they
could not live. Therefore, this law was written upon tables
of stone: the writing was by the finger of God, but the workmanship of the tables was the labor of man. Moses was
commanded to hew them, after those were broken which God
had given him of the same likeness. And he hewed them,
and God wrote thereon this imperfect law, which was at that
time as high as their weak state could bear. It was intended as a schoolmaster or teacher, to lead them up to God. It
was typical; and we need not go back to washings, to the
blood of goats and bulls, or to the ashes of an heifer; be-

cause we may realize this cleansing spirit, and know the blood of Christ to cleanse us from every sin.

Now I don't want to direct your attention to any thing which is external. I don't want to turn your attention to that unparalleled act of atrocity, which crucified one of the most righteous of beings. No, surely; for we can never be saved by any act of wickedness. The crucifixion of Christ was a piece of unparalleled wickedness, in which they said, "his blood be upon us and our children." And it was eminently upon them, and it has been upon their children, and upon their offspring—upon all those who have continued in the same state of hardness and unbelief. And wherever we continue in this state of hardness and unbelief, we as assuredly shed the blood of Christ as it was shed without the gates of Jerusalem. And what is the blood of Christ? Has it relation merely to the outward animal body? No: for it is a truth, that the blood is the life; and unto this very circumstance all the bloody offerings under the law had evident allusion. The blood is the life—the circulating medium which gives vitality to the whole system. It is only the life of Christ—a life of purity, of holiness; a life which was produced by a daily obedience to his Father's spirit—which can enable us to worship him acceptably, or to adopt the language, Abba, Father.

And what are the operations of this spirit, and how are they to be felt in the mind? We may be querying after this manner, not knowing where to look, and ready to say, "Who shall ascend into heaven to bring Christ down from above? or who shall descend into the deep to bring him up from the dead?" But what saith the spirit? "The word is nigh thee, even in thy mouth, and in thy heart; that is the word of faith which we preach." But, alas! we have often fulfilled the prophecy of Isaiah. We have despised and rejected him in his spiritual appearance. "He is despised and rejected of men; a man of sorrows and acquainted with grief; and we hid, as it were, our faces from him: he was despised, and we esteemed him not." And wherefore? Because we want something of a more splendid nature. We want something better adapted to our own wills and inclinations. We want a saviour by whom we can be indulged in the gratification of our animal passions and propensities, and in the fulfilling of those principles which lead us to follow our senses. Here we have formed our ideas of Christ, and given him those miserable transformations by our own more miserable inventions; which, instead of bringing us to a knowledge of God, have enveloped us in darkness till confusion is worse confounded.

And many are ready to deny the operation of this divine principle, which speaks in every soul. Many say that revelation has ceased, and that all the revelation which we are now to look for, is contained in the scriptures of truth. But the scriptures speak of a priest—an high priest. And he is not called our king, priest, and prophet? Our king to govern us, our priest to instruct us in our duty to God, and our prophet to open divine mysteries to us. And of what order is he? He is not after the order of Aaron, but after the order of Melchisedec—after the order of an everlasting and unchangeable priesthood. "Without father, without mother, without descent, having neither beginning of days, nor end of life, but made like unto the Son of God, abideth a priest continually." And he is, thus are all his followers, partakers of the same nature, not founded on systems formed by prejudice and tradition, but begotten of God, and him alone, into the same divine life, and brought forth in the same divine power. And here it is, that unity is maintained and experienced, because, being partakers of the same faith, we are governed by the same spirit, and every opposing disposition, every evil spirit, is cast out.

However diverse our opinions may be upon religious subjects, if we are under the influence of this divine and governing principle, and life of Christ, this circulating medium which gives vitality to the whole system, we shall be gradually knit together—our spirits will mingle, and we shall travail for one another's welfare in love, and we shall be enabled to bid each other God speed. But this depends on a daily attention to this principle; and one of the apostles laid this injunction: "Therefore leaving the principles of the doctrine of Christ, let us go on unto perfection, not laying again the foundation of repentance from dead works, and of faith towards God." Leaving the principles and doctrines of Christ, and not depending verbally on the precepts which he gave: leaving them—there was another resting place in view—"Let us go on unto perfection, not laying again the foundation of repentance from dead works, and of faith towards God, of the doctrine of baptisms, and of laying on of hands, and of resurrection of the dead, and of eternal judgment. And this will we do if God permit." Now if this is our individual care and concern—if our minds are above all things, endeavoring to come under the influence of this principle, which rectifies every act and subjects all our affections, we shall be led into the situation of babes in Christ, then young men, then strong men. Our experimental knowledge will increase. And although children are as perfect as those of mature age, and the work of the same great Creator, and under his immediate care and providence, yet their minds are not developed. And while we are children, though we are not able to distinguish our right hand from our left, yet if we are preserved in innocency and in fear, light will be given us; and if we are obedient to the discoveries of truth, we shall thereby experience a growth in strength and wisdom, by which we shall experience peace equally with those who have attained to greater experience. And as every act of obedience gives experience, our minds will grow from that of babes unto that of young men, and our increase of experience will make us strong in love and in the power of God, in which we can testify of his mercy and of his judgments. This will produce that wisdom which stands not in length of years, neither is governed by number of months; but "wisdom is gray hairs unto man, and an unspotted life, old age."

These views will bring religion into a different form. It has been external, but it will become internal. It has been natural but it will become spiritual. It has taken cognizance of the outward acts of wickedness, such as adultery, lying, swearing, and stealing. The laws of the Jews, were only different modifications of the same principle. But this is no part of the gospel dispensation : it takes no cognizance of these thinks ; but it lays the axe unto the root of the tree— to the imaginations from whence the words and actions proceed. And as we attend unto this gospel power, it will bring everything which has a nature different and contrary to itself into subjection. The tree which grows from the root of corruption will wither ; its branches will wither, its leaves fade, and the roots decay. So also when the mind becomes pure, like the tree which is good, so the fruit will be also. But if the tree be impure, the fruit will be also impure. Here is a criterion by which we may judge : "For men do not gather grapes of thorns nor figs of thistles"—"neither doth a spring send forth salt water and fresh." This is a medium we may judge ourselves by, if we are willing to come to judgment. This law operates on our spirits ; and by a daily attention to this divine principle, there will be a daily increase of our experience, and we shall find that its power will increase, till every thought, every imagination, and consequently every word and action, will be brought into obedience to the gospel of Christ.

And when we come to experience these things, we shall know what the divinely eagle-eyed apostle meant by the declaration, that there was war in heaven ; and which is one of the most beautiful illustrative passages left on record. "There was war in heaven : Michael and his angels fought against the dragon ; and the dragon fought and his angels." And what are the angels ? Every work of the creation is an angel of God ; but these in a peculiar manner have allusion to the dispositions of the human mind. These constitute the angels that engage in this combat. They are the angels of love, joy, peace, temperance, patience, brotherly kindness, charity, and a host of other heavenly virtues : and the angels of darkness, hatred, cruelty, intemperance, lust, idolatry, murder, lying, stealing, and a host of evils which compose that dragon which is spoken of.

Now when we come to know the angel of love ; when we

can feel that we love God, and that supremely, and our neighbor as ourselves, then that divine feeling will cast out its opposite, its adversary : it will cast out hatred. The angel of mercy will cast out the devil of cruelty ; the angel of temperance, the devil of intemperance. And every heavenly and divine disposition of the mind, will become predominant, and then we shall be enabled to testify of that state which the Lord declared of, when he said, "the kingdom of heaven is within you." It is there we must look for his appearing, and there we must experience his power, and know him to rule as with a rod of iron, over all unrighteousness and ungodliness of men. It is there we must look for his appearing, and there we must experience his power, and know him to rule as with a rod of iron, over all unrighteousness and ungodliness of men. It is there we must know that a sceptre of righteousness, is the sceptre of his kingdom ; and that what is to be known of God, is made manifest in man. And wherefore? The answer is plain : "for God hath shown it unto him." And if we come not to know an admittance into the kingdom of heaven, while we are clothed in mortality, and to know a victory over our lusts and evil dispositions, our hope is not well founded ; we have not an anchor sure and steadfast, through all the vicisitudes of life. We have not that which will disarm death of its sting, and the grave of its victory. And we shall be enabled to bear this testimony, which is immutable in its character, "we know that it has passed from death unto life, because we love the brethren."

Now if we attend to this principle, we shall not be at a loss for systems in and by which to worship the Father of our Lord Jesus Christ. And what is worship? Is it merely to preach, pray, and sing? No, verily. There is no worship in these things ; unless, they be in obedience to the immediate requirements of the divinity. I know of no man, nor body of men, whether synod, presbytery, or convention, that are able, or who have power to ordain one single solitary minister of the gospel of Christ. And those who receive such appointments, and emoluments from men, are not preaching the gospel of Christ, but it is another gospel. It stands in an outward observance of rituals and performances, which have no power in regulating the passions, or crucifying the lusts ; but which indulge pride, ambition, and a variety of other feelings, in which we can never work the righteousness of God. And what does this preaching teach? Merely to support the systems which individuals have adopted ; and not to direct the people to the "ministry of the sanctuary, and of the true tabernacle which God has pitched, and not man," but to these regulated ordinances, rituals, systems, and ministers, which give not acceptance in the sight of God. They are seeking the honor of men, and they have their reward.

But when we are brought under this divine and regulating influence, every act will be an act of worship, because it will be calculated to bring "glory to God in the highest, and on earth peace, good will toward men." Here we shall learn to fulfil the injunction of Christ, "What I say unto you, I say unto all, watch." This divine love in which he lived, and in which all his miracles were performed, operating in us, in the most trying circumstances we can adopt the language, "thy will, and not mine be done." And whenever a disposition is raised in us, to crave of our heavenly Father, "if it be thy will, remove this cup from me," it will centre in this, "not as I will, but as thou wilt." Here is another victory gained over the power of evil and recrimination,— that spirit which repels force by force, and attacks enemies with their own weapons. Here the glorious gospel is found triumphant; and though our bodies have been slain by the hands of men, as the body of Jesus was, yet assuredly being under this influence, we shall rise superior to all the powers of corruption, as he rose again the third day, and which is beautifully typical of the resurrection which we may experience, when we have fallen by the power of evil.

And as we attend to this spirit, we shall be enabled to offer up worship, holy and acceptable to God, through the operation of the same divine power and principle, which is a manifestation of God in your flesh. And all our performances being under the influence of the divine spirit, it would cause unrighteousness to vanish from the earth, wars would cease, every evil would be overcome of good—the angels of God casting out all our enemies. Thus, "the wilderness would become an Eden, and our desert like the garden of the Lord ; joy and gladness would be heard therein, thanksgiving and the voice of melody."

All the systematized works of man, never can advance this work one step. If we ever have pure religion, and undefiled before God, it must be by attending to the operation of his power in our own spirits, thus enabling us to overcome every thing of a corruptible nature, and to know a passing from death unto life, because we have loved the brethren.

Now with respect to watery baptism, it has passed away, together with all the relics of the former dispensation, forever. They are not at all adapted unto this, which is wholly spiritual. The baptism of the Holy Ghost has most assuredly superseded the necessity of baptism with water. For if the inside of the cup and platter, or of the principles, affections, and dispositions, from which our actions proceed, become cleansed, the outside will necessarily become clean. For throughout the creation, like produces like. And if our dispositions are of a heavenly character, they will produce actions of the same character. And I apprehend, if we place our dependence in outward ordinances, we deny the coming of Christ in the flesh, and bring ourselves under the baptism of John ; and we are returning to types and figures, rites and ceremonies.

Neither need we go to bread and wine, as typical of that nourishment which we receive through the body and blood of Christ ; because the substance itself is come, and its power is experimentally known, even that power which is the resurrection and the life. And when we know the life of Christ, this operative principle, which is a governing principle—and when life of Christ is predominant in our souls, when this circulating medium is spread over the whole system, it gives life, power, and vitality to the whole soul ; and here we are nourished and raised up to magnify the name of God. And from this operation, faith itself proceeds. "By grace are ye saved through faith; and that not of yourselves; it is the gift of God." Faith, and mere belief, are essentially different and distinct. We may believe many things which are not essential to constitute us christians; for the devils believe and tremble, but they remain devils still. There is no regenerating influence in this belief; but when we come daily to attend to the principle which reproves for evil—and not what man may have constituted a reproof for evil—when we attend to these admonitions, we shall in due time become partakers of a cup of consolation, which the divine power gives us; and we shall increase our experience, and as we increase, our faith becomes more sound. And there can be no faith without works—there can be no living faith without works, I want us all, therefore to come to an examination, whether our faith is a mere belief imbibed by education, forged and fostered by prejudice, which have led to the adoption of these systems; or whether it has been produced by the immediate operation of God upon our spirits.

And it is our obedience or disobedience which constitutes the true ground of election and reprobation. It is absurd, and, I had almost said, blasphemous, to suppose that God has fore-ordained any of the workmanship of his hands to eternal misery, when he declared in the beginning, and which remains to be a truth, that all his workmanship was good. But there are many who are disposed to find no difference between prescience and fore-ordination; but it does not necessarily follow that because God knoweth all things from all eternity, he has fore-ordained them. There is a spirit in each of us, and if we attend to it, it will lead to God; but if we neglect it, we fall into darkness. And what is darkness? It is the absence of light—it is not a positive power; and when light is introduced, it is necessarily lost and disappears. And thus it is with evil: and we don't need to go to a separate and distinct evil spirit, in order to find a tormenter, for every act of wickedness brings with it its own torment. And if we are attentive to that principle which brings peace, it will grow and increase; and we shall

more and more fully witness its power, till every thing of
an opposite nature is wholly subdued. And when evil is
presented to our mind, there will be no temptation left for
us to join in, or unite with it; and thus we shall become
elected together with Christ, even as he was, through obedience, elected. And we shall become heirs of God, and joint
heirs with him; and as we must learn, so he also learnt
obedience by the things which he suffered.

But if, on the contrary, we will not come under the influence of the Holy Ghost, that divine principle, that holy
spirit, our progress will be retarded—we shall be confounded,
and our minds will be more and more hardened, till we may
be left to obey every evil thought, word and action. But if,
through obedience, when good be present and nigh, we join
in with it, it will increase and cast out the evil. This is the
consequence of its holy operation, notwithstanding it may
be different in all those who experience its power. The
proud and lofty it will bring down into meekness, and those
who are weak and desponding it will raise into firmness,
and thus exemplify the declaration of one of the prophets:
"Every valley shall be exalted, and every mountain and
hill shall be made low, and the crooked shall be made
straight, and the rough places plain." And then the glory
of the Lord can and will cover the earth, as the waters cover
the deep.

My mind has desired for you, and for mine own soul also,
that we may be willing to try these things for ourselves. I
desire to direct you not to man, nor to the teachings of men,
for it is only as we come to have our understandings opened,
that we know the testimony of Jesus to be the spirit of
prophecy. And whether it shows us our own state and condition, or the situation of those around us, or things yet to
come, it is the same spirit which inspired the holy men,
patriarchs, and prophets, in all ages. "The testimony of
Jesus is the spirit of prophecy;" and how directly is this
in opposition to that abominable doctrine, that revelation
has ceased. And on what is the church of Christ built? Is
it not built upon the revealed will of God? What said

Christ? "Whom do men say that I, the son of man, am? And they said, some say that thou art John the Baptist, some Elias, and some Jeremias, or one of the prophets. He said unto them, but whom say ye that I am? And Simon Peter answered and said, thou art the Christ, the son of the living God. And Jesus answered and said unto him, blessed art thou, Simon Barjona, for flesh and blood hath not revealed it unto thee, but my Father which is in heaven. And I say unto thee, that thou art Peter; and upon this rock I will build my church, and the gates of hell shall not prevail against it." Now the church is not built on Peter, but on that power which revealed unto Peter that he was Christ. And it is this power which must give us an understanding of things which are true, and which must enable us to dwell in those things which are true, even in Jesus Christ; this is the true God and eternal life: "I in them and thou in me, that they also may be one in us."

Now when we come to experience these effects produced in us by the operation of this holy principle, then the scriptures will be valuable to us as corroborative testimony; for then shall we have pourtrayed before us the experience of men in former ages—those who have trodden the same path of self-denial and obedience. They will be unto us a comfort;—they will be profitable for doctrine, for reproof, for correction, for instruction in righteousness; and we through faith, and comfort of the scriptures, shall have our hope increased. Then, not only the scriptures themselves, but every other external evidence, yea all the workmanship of the hand of God, will be corroborative testimony. And every action of our minds will form an instructive lesson unto us. Even our slips, misses, and short comings in the path of righteousness; these will be warnings to us for the time to come.

Now this, my friends, is loud preaching. It is the gospel of Christ preached in every creature. It is the Comforter which was testified of by Christ—"It is expedient for you, that I go away: for if I go not away, the Comforter will not come unto you; but if I depart, I will send him unto you. And when he is come, he will reprove the world of sin, and of righteousness, and of judgment;" and he shall "bring all things to your remembrance, whatsoever I have said unto you." And in attending to this divine principle, it would make us wiser than all our teachers; we should be enabled to see our own state and condition, and our understandings would be opened to those things which yet appear mysterious: for there is nothing mysterious in religion. It is so plain, that no one can err therein. It is "the way of holiness; the unclean shall not pass over it; but it shall be for those; the wayfaring men, though fools, shall not err therein. No lion shall be there, nor any ravenous beast shall go up thereon, it shall not be found there; but the redeemed shall walk there: and the ransomed of the Lord shall return and come to Zion, with songs of everlasting joy upon their heads: they shall obtain joy and gladness, and sorrow and sighing shall flee away."

Religion never was mysterious, till it was clothed in abstract propositions, and false science. Abstract propositions are to the truth, as covering is to the human body. They form no part of its essence. They have a tendency to cover it, and hide it from the view of the mind; and thus much of its benefit is lost, for truth needs no covering; it never appears in so great purity, as in its own naked loveliness. Therefore, to this principle, which is the life of God in the soul, I desire to recommend you; for it will lead you, and guide you into all truth. It will lead you out of the bondage of sin and corruption, into the glorious liberty of the sons and daughters of God. It will lead you into the spirit of adoption, whereby you can cry, Abba, Father. It will thus enable you to "love your enemies; to bless them that curse you, do good to them that hate you, and pray for them which despitefully use you and persecute you." It is this divine principle which will support you in adversity, preserve you in prosperity, and be with you in all the trying circumstances of life. It will disarm death of its sting and the grave of its victory. And it will open a new and a living way, even unto that which is within the vail, the holiest of all;—where all the ingenuity of human invention can never come;—where every disposition being in accordance with the divine purity, we shall bow before the divine foot-stool, and in the language of the scriptures, and of our own experience, we shall find indubitable evidence, which will enable us to adopt the language of Abba, Father. Because we shall be begotten into the one life, by the one spirit, and thus we shall experience that hope which will be an anchor unto our souls, sure and steadfast, and which will never be separated from us. And we shall have an evidence, that when we have done with time here, there will be prepared for us "a building of God, an house not made with hands, eternal in the heavens; where moth and rust corrupteth not and where thieves do not break through and steal."

www.ingramcontent.com/pod-product-compliance
Lightning Source LLC
Chambersburg PA
CBHW021047030726
47496CB00006B/1719